Midnight Come

Midnight Come

Michael David Anthony

FELONY & MAYHEM PRESS • NEW YORK

MIDNIGHT COME

A Felony & Mayhem mystery

PRINTING HISTORY
First UK edition (HarperCollins): 1998
First U.S. Edition (St. Martin's): 1999
Felony & Mayhem edition: 2008

ISBN: 978-1-934609-26-2

Manufactured in the United States of America

Library of Congress Cataloging-in-Publication Data

Anthony, Michael David
   Midnight Come / Michael David Anthony.--Felony & Mayhem ed.
      p. cm.
   "A Felony & Mayhem mystery"--T.p. verso.
   ISBN-13: 978-1-934609-26-2 (pbk.)
   ISBN-10: 1-934609-26-9 (pbk.)
   1. Church of England--Government--Fiction. 2. Parsonages--England--
   Fiction. 3. Parricide--England--Fiction. 4. Canterbury (England)--Fiction.
   I. Title.
   PR6051.N77M5 2008
   823'.914--dc22

                                          2008034536

In memory of James Kane of Corston
'Meus primus amicus a puero'

ACKNOWLEDGEMENTS

For their painstaking reading of the manuscript and their detailed suggestions and advice, I am indebted once again to my friends, Clare Harkness, Tim Dowley and Clifford Forde. Also I would wish to acknowledge the kindness of Francis Pettitt, whose patience and expertise kept the somewhat elderly 'writing engines' turning over.

The icon above says you're holding a book in the Felony &
Mayhem "British" category. These books are set in or around the
UK, and feature the highly literate, often witty prose that fans of
British mystery demand.

———◆•◆•◆———

For more information about British titles, or to learn more about
Felony & Mayhem Press, please visit us online at

www.FelonyAndMayhem.com

Or write to us at:

Felony and Mayhem Press
156 Waverly Place
New York, NY 10014

Other "British" titles from

FELONY&MAYHEM

MICHAEL DAVID ANTHONY
The Beckett Factor

ROBERT BARNARD
Death on the High C's
Out of the Blackout
Death and the Chaste Apprentice
Skeleton in the Grass
Corpse in a Gilded Cage

PETER DICKINSON
King and Joker
The Old English Peep Show
Skin Deep

CAROLINE GRAHAM
The Killings at Badger's Drift
Death of a Hollow Man
Death in Disguise
Written in Blood
Murder at Madingley Grange

REGINALD HILL
A Clubbable Woman
An Advancement of Learning
Ruling Passion
Death of a Dormouse

ELIZABETH IRONSIDE
Death in the Garden
The Accomplice
A Very Private Enterprise

JOHN MALCOLM
A Back Room in Somers Town

JANET NEEL
Death's Bright Angel

SHEILA RADLEY
Death in the Morning
The Chief Inspector's Daughter
A Talent for Destruction

Midnight Come

Apart from the historical characters and incidents referred to, the events of this book are completely fictitious, and the city and diocese of Canterbury depicted, along with all their various inhabitants, are, once again, but 'the baseless fabric of a dream'.

'Ah, Faustus,
Now hast thou but one bare hour to live,
And then thou must be damn'd perpetually. Stand still, you
ever-moving spheres of Heaven, That time may cease, and midnight never come.'

—*Doctor Faustus* by Christopher Marlowe

PART ONE

CHAPTER ONE

'*V*eni, veni, Mephistophile!'

Through the silent precincts rang the loud summons, the words booming and resonating along the paved passageway below the window. At the sound, the grey-haired figure at the desk raised his eyes from the papers lying under the beam of the anglepoise lamp and frowned across the otherwise darkened room. He listened a moment, then, removing his reading glasses, rose stiffly and, crossing to the window, peered down through the grimy cluster of diamond panes.

All day the fog had lain across Canterbury, obscuring the sun and giving a more than usually dank and melancholy feel to the autumn streets. Along the oozy, winding banks of the twin-channelled Stour, the mist had steadily wafted up and thickened as the short day waned, curling up under the overhanging gables and around the weed-draped and lichened piles of the medieval pilgrims' hostel known as the Weavers (now an almshouse for the elderly) spanning the sluggish stream. Smothering in turn the venerable remnants of Greyfriars, Blackfriars and the ruined Dominican Priory, it had spread like some foul exhalation or conjured ectoplasm out from the river into the surrounding streets. Blending with the steaming exhausts of the city traffic, it proceeded to creep its way through a host of ancient backways and lanes, finally reaching out across the greasy, worn cobbles of the Buttermarket through the ancient Christ Church Gatehouse and on into the grounds of the cathedral itself. With night now fallen, it clung as an oily miasma about the single lamp outside the outer door of the offices of the Diocesan Dilapidations Board, giving a sickly, yellowish glow to the light, in whose dim beams, as the onlooker peered down, the mouth of the low-roofed cloistral passage of Dark Entry opposite smoked like the mouth of Hell— either that, or else a tunnel from which a steam-train had recently burst.

'*Veni, veni, Mephistophile!*'

The cry rang out again. Almost simultaneously, a phantom shape materialized at the passage entry, a gowned, hooded figure, stepping out from impenetrable blackness into misty lamplight. Thinking whoever it was must be one of the cathedral clergy, and curious to know which of them had chosen to wander the precincts on such an evening in full regalia, Harrison leaned further forward, shielding his eyes against the glass. As he did so, the figure below raised its head, and Harrison, with an involuntary gasp, found himself looking down upon a mouthless, chalk-white face, blank and devoid of all human feature save for a huge pair of eyes as unnaturally large and lifeless as the sockets of a skull.

Stretching out its wide-sleeved arms, the apparition took a step forward, then suddenly, with a giggle of laughter, it tugged back the scarlet hood to expose a thick shock of shoulder-length auburn hair. Completing the transformation, the wearer then lifted and slid back the hideous plastic mask to reveal the face of a smiling teenage girl. The same moment, out from the passage behind her poured forth half a dozen smaller figures, dressed in tunic and hose, each with a set of horns on its hooded head and dragging behind a long forked tail, all of whom immediately began dancing wildly about the girl—one of them, wielding a massive toasting-fork, the spectator above recognized as the long-time favourite of his wife, the irrepressible young probationary chorister, Simon Barnes.

Suddenly understanding, Harrison burst out laughing. At the instigation of the dean, and much against the wishes of the more staid of Chapter, Christopher Marlowe's *Doctor Faustus* was soon to be performed in the cathedral nave by the pupils of the King's School (aided by some of the younger children from the choir school) in honour of the four hundredth anniversary of its author's death. Clearly the first dress rehearsal had recently ended, and these prancing young imps and devils below were, like the girl herself, merely some of the juvenile actors making a boisterous return to the playwright's ancient *alma mater* in the northwest corner of the precincts to partake of the customary pre-bedtime sandwiches and cocoa.

As Harrison watched, the portly form of a man emerged from the shadows to join the players. Obviously, having spotted the approaching costumed figures, he'd been the one who'd instigated the youngsters' impromptu performance with his loud, summoning cry. Now, stepping forward, his bald pate gleamed in the lamplight, allowing the onlooker to recognize him as his near neighbour, Alan Tubman, who recently, after a lifetime's service as classics teacher and, more latterly, senior housemaster at the King's School, had moved his meagre bachelor traps, along with an extensive collection of books, into the quiet backwater enclave of Bread Yard to enjoy a well-earned retirement.

Invisible above, the watcher remained looking down as the podgy, avuncular Tubman stood laughing and talking among the youngsters. Eventually the group moved away out of sight in the direction of Green Close, their voices fading abruptly as they passed beneath the Selling Archway.

Returning to his desk, Harrison drew the anglepoise down, and, bending low, resumed squinting at the document lying in the bright pool of light. Brows knitted in concentration, he read on through the tortuous legal phrasing, until finally, reaching the end, he drew out and unscrewed a fountain pen, and on the dotted line at the bottom of the final page, above the printed words, *Colonel R. D. Harrison, Hon Sec, Diocesan Dilapidations Board, for and on behalf of the See and Diocese of Canterbury*, signed his name with a flourish.

Having done so, he picked up the paper and briefly blew upon it to dry the ink, smiling once more at the memory of the extraordinary little scene he'd recently witnessed. Seeing in his mind's eye young Barnes capering about the ominously blank-faced, hooded figure of Satan's gloomy emissary, waving that absurdly large toasting-fork, he again burst out laughing, and, giving the ink a final puff, declaimed aloud Tubman's Faustian summons: *'Veni, veni, Mephistophile!'*

Hardly had the words left his lips, however, before his smile faded, and he turned, peering across the darkened room with a look of indignant surprise. Someone had begun beating loudly and insistently at the outer door below.

Certain that one of the cathedral staff on their nightly rounds had noticed a gleam of light from the window and was now officiously checking up on him, Harrison wearily rose to his feet as the urgent knocking was repeated. Determined to give the intruder short shrift for this unnecessary interruption, he passed through the outer office and descended the short flight of stairs to the vestibule entrance. There he unbolted the outer door and opened it, only to find himself staring out into foggy emptiness.

Annoyance increasing by the moment, he peered out, looking around until he spotted the indistinct form of his caller standing craning up at the reflected light on the panes overhead. Taking the short, heavily muffled figure as that of the chief verger (or vesturer, as that official is traditionally known at Canterbury), he called out irritably, 'Yes, confound you. What the devil do you want?'

'Richard?' came the somewhat startled reply. 'Is that you?'

Taken aback, Harrison remained in the doorway as the unmistakable shape of Dean Ingrams materialized from the misty darkness.

'I'm so sorry, Dean,' he said, moving aside for the cleric to enter. 'I mistook you for somebody else.'

'Evidently, my dear chap!' With a wry smile, his visitor stepped over the threshold, overcoat and muffler gleaming with droplets of moisture. 'Look, I'm sorry to intrude like this, Richard,' he said, brushing the damp from his shoulders and sleeves, 'but remembering that you mentioned doing some overtime here in the office while Winifred's out teaching her evening class, I thought I'd call by on my way back from looking in at our young friends' dress rehearsal. I hope you don't mind.'

'Not at all—absolutely delighted,' answered Harrison with rather forced enthusiasm. 'Do come upstairs. We can perhaps raid Miss Simpson's desk for the means of making ourselves a pot of tea.'

'How kind.'

Leading the way, Harrison remounted the stairs to the outer office. There, as the kettle gradually stirred into life, he knelt, rummaging through the bottom drawer of his secretary's desk, drawing out tea bags, a jar of dried milk, sugar lumps and a half-consumed packet of Garibaldi biscuits.

'Well, I must say, this is pleasant!' exclaimed Ingrams, rubbing his hands appreciatively and looking about with evident approval at the ranks of faded marbled ledgers and file-boxes lining the walls all the way up from uneven floor to slightly bulging ceiling. 'You know, Richard,' he continued with a certain wistfulness in his tone, 'I often envy you, quietly working away up here, secure from the more immediate perplexities of a troubled and transitory world.'

Harrison looked up at his old friend with a sympathetic smile. 'It sounds, Dean,' he said, closing the drawer and then struggling upright, 'as if you've just had another brush with our vesturer. Winnie mentioned that Simcocks is somewhat opposed to the staging of *Faustus* in the nave.'

'Somewhat opposed!' Ingrams laughed good-naturedly. 'My dear fellow, you've simply no idea! The man's adamantly against it. According to Simcocks, performing the work of a blaspheming atheist on sanctified ground is sacrilege, and as good as to invite a similar violent end to that which overtook poor Faustus and his equally unfortunate creator. So there you are,' he added with a chuckle as the other switched off the now boiling kettle, 'the day I'm found torn to pieces by devils or stabbed through the eye with a twelve-penny dagger, you'll at least know the reason why—it will simply be yet another example of a "Great reckoning in a little room."'

'Great reckoning?' murmured Harrison abstractly, peering down through the steam as he concentrated on filling the teapot.

'Shakespeare's phrase from *As You Like It*. In full, the quotation goes: "It strikes a man more dead than a great reckoning in a little room." Apparently the bard had in mind the terrible occurrence in Mrs Eleanor Bull's tavern at Deptford in the early summer of 1593 when his young rival is supposed to have been stabbed to death during a dispute over the bill, or the *"recknynge"* as it was then known.' Breaking off, Ingrams gave a self-conscious laugh as his friend gave the contents of the teapot a quick stir and then began filling two mugs. 'Forgive me,' he said, 'but with these anniversary celebrations this year, as you see, I've been boning up a little on our friend Kit Marlowe's life.'

'I'm most impressed, Dean,' said Harrison, handing over one of the steaming mugs with a smile. 'Now I suggest we carry our drinks on through to my own room. It's a chilly evening, and, at the risk of incurring the archdeacon's displeasure, I have a small fan-heater running in there.'

❀ ❀ ❀

'So what is it you're beavering away on at this late hour, then?' asked Ingrams, glancing at the pile of legal papers on the desk as he took the offered chair. 'Not still busy divesting the diocese of its lands and properties, I hope?'

'I'm afraid so,' answered Harrison, going round to his seat. 'These', he said, moving the documents aside to clear a space for his mug and biscuit plate, 'are the title deeds of a few of our remaining grace-and-favour dwellings that we plan to auction off.'

Ingrams gave a slight sigh and shook his head sadly. 'One realizes, of course,' he said heavily, 'that the financial storms continue to rage upon us, and that young Michael Cawthorne has the archbishop's mandate for these sell-offs; nevertheless, so enthusiastically does our good archdeacon lighten ship, that I sometimes wonder what poor skeletal ghost of a vessel our diocese will be when it eventually makes port.'

Though Ingrams spoke his own thoughts entirely, out of loyalty to his immediate superior, Harrison made no reply. Instead, sipping his tea, he glanced across at his visitor, noticing how strained he looked, and wondering what it was that had brought him to his office on such an unpleasant night.

No explanation was immediately forthcoming. Uncharacteristically silent, Ingrams sat hunched in his chair, frowning down at the contents of his mug. After a few moments more, Harrison cleared his throat. 'Forgive me for saying so, Dean, but you look a trifle fatigued tonight.'

'Do I?' Raising his head, the cleric gave a weary smile. 'No, my dear fellow, it's nothing, I assure you, merely perhaps watching those youngsters at their rehearsal reminded me of the communiqué I received from my daughters' headmistress today. According to Miss Hawkins, it seems that fees are again to be raised. Of course,' he added hurriedly, 'it's only a day school the twins go to, but even so, as I said to Margaret over breakfast this morning, any more increases and we'll be reduced to taking in washing at the deanery!'

Although Harrison smiled politely at the typically mild little joke, he was certain that something more serious than either school bills or a slight brush with the notoriously cankerous vesturer was troubling his normally genial friend. Nibbling a biscuit, he sat back and awaited the inevitable revelations.

'Talking of Michael Cawthorne,' resumed Ingrams at last, 'he called round to see me earlier.' He paused, a flash of pain crossing his chubby face. 'He was not, I regret to say, exactly the bearer of the happiest news.'

Harrison received the final statement without the slightest surprise and said nothing: from bitter experience, he'd learnt that unexpected visits from Archdeacon Cawthorne tended not to add to anyone's peace of mind. Indeed, the notion of his immediate superior being a bringer of happiness seemed almost as unlikely as one of the four horsemen of the Apocalypse taking it into his head to ride out with a cornucopia of human blessings.

'He brought this,' continued Ingrams, drawing an envelope from an inner pocket. 'Heaven knows,' he said, passing it over, 'our archdeacon has his detractors, but in this matter at least, he has behaved with the greatest possible delicacy and tact.'

'Indeed?' murmured Harrison, endeavouring to mask his scepticism. Taking the proffered letter, he held it under the lamp. To his amazement, he found it addressed to Cawthorne by means of single letters cut from a newspaper and glued to the envelope, the first character of each complete word being a coloured capital, obviously culled from some glossy magazine or other, the whole effect creating the impression of a crude, childish parody of an illuminated manuscript.

'Read what's inside,' prompted the dean. 'It's absolutely appalling!' He got to his feet and went over to the window. 'Wrongly handled,' he added, grimacing as he peered out into the fog, 'this matter could have direst consequences for us all.'

Harrison looked up at the speaker's back with a frown. Then, putting on his reading glasses, he carefully drew the enclosed sheet from the envelope.

Many a disturbing missive had crossed Harrison's desk during his time as secretary to the Dilapidations Board: alarming reports of subsidence, cracked walls, toppled chimneys, accounts of the effects of both wet and dry rot, of the deathwatch beetle, of horrendous damage from leaking roofs and burst pipes. Never, however, in all his years at Canterbury had he been obliged to read a more bizarre message—and certainly not, even in the case of some of the younger clergy, one nearly as garbled and badly spelt as the one now in his hand.

The Rev Maurice Lambkin MA (Cantab) is a hypocrite lyre; all Wetmarsh Marden and Fordington folk well knows his carryings' on with that fowl witch Stella Gittings laid his poor wife in her grave. Let him beware the wrath to come. The wages of sin is death.

He read the short note through twice, then glanced again at the envelope to confirm that it had been posted first-class from Fordington the previous day. Doing so, he noticed that the envelope flap had never been gummed down, and that the missive had been dispatched with it merely folded inside.

'Well, Richard? What do you think?'

Aware how upsetting the note must be to his friend, Harrison decided to make as light of the matter as possible. He looked up and met Ingrams's troubled face with a smile. 'As you say, Dean, it's absolutely appalling!'

'Yes,' answered the cleric gloomily, slumping heavily back down into his chair, 'but the question is, how does one explain it?'

Harrison shrugged and again gave the ghost of a smile. 'Who knows?' he said. 'Rural inbreeding, perhaps—that together with the lamentable inadequacies of certain of our state schools. Reading this,' he continued, once again holding the limp sheet of paper to the lamp, 'one perfectly understands why so many, like your own good self, make such huge sacrifices to have their children privately educated.'

Obviously too upset to appreciate the other's well-meaning attempt at humour, Ingrams frowned in momentary bewilderment. 'No, no,' he cried. 'I wasn't asking your comment on the written style. It's the content I'm interested in, and what on earth I'm going to do about it.'

'Do?' repeated Harrison in some surprise. 'My dear Dean, why on earth should you do anything?'

'Because Maurice is a very old friend of mine,' burst out the cleric. 'I've known him since our time at theological college together. I'm even godfather to his unfortunate son. It's my duty to protect him as far as possible. God knows,' he concluded, shaking his head sorrowfully, 'the poor fellow has suffered enough as it is!'

Harrison, of course, knew the Reverend Lambkin quite well. He'd met him in the deanery once or twice, and over the years he'd corresponded with him in regard to the upkeep of his church and his large Edwardian rectory. In fact, only a few weeks before, he'd driven over to Fordington to discuss with him personally the matter of a trust cottage in his parish that the archdeacon was determined to sell off. Despite his rather uncharacteristic reluctance to accede to Cawthorne's wishes on that embarrassing occasion, Maurice Lambkin was a quiet, gentle, scholarly man, who, somewhat ill-advisedly for one of his temperament, had begun his ministry with a zeal to serve the deprived and the outcast, first running a Cambridge University Mission for homeless alcoholics and the like from among the capital's wretched army of derelicts, later becoming priest-in-charge of a rundown inner-city London parish whilst continuing his work among ex-prisoners and other of society's rejects. Finally, emotionally and physically exhausted by the strain, he'd moved to the Canterbury diocese, obtaining the incumbency of his present small country living on the southern bank of the Stour immediately across from the isle of Thanet. There, in rural obscurity, he'd lived for the last eighteen years or so, bringing up a young son and continuing to nurse his chronically asthmatic wife until her comparatively early death just six months before.

'I take it, Dean,' said Harrison, choosing his words carefully, 'that you don't think there's any truth in what this note alleges: that there's been some sexual impropriety between Lambkin and this woman?'

At the suggestion, Ingrams's face contorted in horror. 'Between Maurice and Mrs Gittings! Surely not! I can't believe it!' He began pacing the tiny room, rubbing up the hair on the back of his head, in his customary fashion when agitated. 'Maurice was always a devoted husband and father—and with Stella Gittings of all people! The idea doesn't bear thinking of!' Calming at last, he looked round at Harrison. 'It's clear, my dear Richard, that you have no idea who Mrs Gittings is. She's a highly respected church worker: a lady deacon no less—the very person, indeed, whom the archbishop himself appointed to help relieve Maurice of some of his duties during the final stages of his wife's illness.'

'I see.'

'No! No!' burst out the other passionately. 'Forgive me, but I really don't think you do! Apart from being married, Stella

Gittings has been accepted for ordination as priest; all being well, she'll be one of our diocese's first female ordinands, and will be priested here in the cathedral, the very home of the whole Anglican communion, and at the hands of the archbishop himself! That's why the whole matter's so particularly delicate,' he said, resuming his seat, 'and why it must be looked into. Imagine it—sexual impropriety between a clergyman and his married female assistant in the face of a dying wife, then the woman in question going on to receive ordination! If the press got hold of the story, it could trigger the mine that's threatening to rip the Church apart!'

Despite the fervour surrounding the issue of women's ordination into the priesthood (a fervour that had, if anything, only grown since Synod had finally passed the measure by a narrow vote the year before, with numbers of the Anglo-Catholic clergy and laity threatening or actually going over to the Roman Church), until now Harrison and Ingrams had carefully avoided all mention of the subject between them. Both conservative men by inclination, fearing and disliking any change in what to them seemed the natural order of things, out of simple good manners and a natural delicacy, each had shied away from airing an issue that he instinctively knew would embarrass the other. Now, seeing the sensitivity of the matter, Harrison sat frowning down at his desk, only too easily envisaging the scandal if the assertions of the anonymous note proved to be true.

'I imagine', he said at last, 'that, as a strong supporter of women's ordination, Dr Cawthorne must be very concerned. That is why, I imagine, he brought you the note: he knows that Lambkin and yourself are old college friends, and wants you to go over and discuss these absurd allegations with him.'

'That was indeed his wish.'

'Well, why don't you do just that, Dean? Simply show Lambkin the note and see how he responds?'

Ingrams shook his head. 'With almost anyone else I would,

but Maurice has always been such a sensitive soul, and, remember, the poor fellow has already been through one nervous collapse which forced him to give up his London ministry. If possible, I wish to spare him this, especially with Bridget's death still so recent, and that wretched son of his causing him so much worry. I really don't think the poor fellow can take much more.' Breaking off, Ingrams reached into his pocket and drew out pipe, tobacco and matches. 'Heaven knows,' he resumed, beginning to pack the pipe-bowl, 'I cannot believe there's the slightest grain of truth in the story. And yet, if there isn't,' he said, shaking his head sorrowfully, 'what sort of person would compose such a wickedly pernicious communiqué?'

'What sort of person indeed?' murmured Harrison, studying the note again as the dean lit his pipe. 'Clearly, as it was sent directly to Dr Cawthorne, it's from someone acquainted with the disciplinary structure of the Church—someone who knows that archdeacons are responsible to their bishops for the behaviour and morals of the junior clergy.'

Holding it under the light once more, he squinted closely at the sheet: like the envelope, its message was composed of individual words and letters cut from printed matter, this time with only the first letter of each sentence having a large coloured upper-case letter. 'You know,' he murmured thoughtfully, 'there are some curious anomalies about this thing. At first sight, it's a lamentable example of clumsy syntax and a failure of verbal agreement, with a misapplied apostrophe, various misspellings, to say nothing of the split infinitive, and yet...'

'Yes?' prompted the dean, removing his pipe and leaning forward eagerly. 'Yet what?'

'This semi-colon, for example.' Harrison pointed at the paper. 'You see it there correctly applied, linking the two closely related first sentences. In other words,' he went on with a smile, 'what we have here might be termed as brutish semi-literacy, momentarily graced with what we might call the punctuational refinement of a Virginia Woolf. Added to that,' he continued, 'is the curious business of these misspellings, some words correct, others almost perversely wrong.'

'You mean,' said Ingrams, 'this is an educated person pretending to be something else?'

'Either that, or someone trying to create just that impression. Whichever, a person with guile and wit enough to cloak their handiwork with intriguing ambiguity.'

Ingrams stared wonderingly at the speaker for a moment, then burst out laughing. 'Richard, you amaze me! I never realized before what a perfectly Byzantine mind you possess! I came here for the advice and practical help of a plain, bluff military man. What do I get instead—a mixture of detailed observation and subtle interpretation that would do credit to a Richard Hooker or any other among the greatest of our theologians!'

Harrison blushed, uncomfortably aware that he'd momentarily allowed his long-established mask of a diligently plodding ex-Royal Engineer to slip. 'No, no,' he said hurriedly, 'you flatter me, Dean. What I said was nothing, I assure you—merely a few elementary deductions.'

'My dear chap,' said Ingrams, laughing again, 'you're sounding more like Sherlock Holmes by the moment! Now I'm even more sure that, in coming here to ask you to act in this matter, I'm doing the right thing.'

'Act in this matter?' It was now Harrison's turn to look incredulously at the other.

Ingrams nodded. 'While at the deanery, the archdeacon happened to mention that one of these properties you're planning to sell off lies within Maurice's domain.'

'Hannah Bright's cottage over in Wetmarsh Marden, you mean? Yes, indeed—in fact, when you arrived, I'd only just finished checking through and signing our application to the Charity Commissioners for the winding up of that particular trust fund. But what about it?'

'Only that Michael Cawthorne says you're sending our new young lady architect over to inspect the property this week.'

'That's correct,' answered Harrison. 'Miss Middlebrook is going over tomorrow morning to make an evaluation. I have the keys ready for her here in this desk.'

'Just so—and now you know the reason for this visit. Please, Richard, as a favour to me, may I beg you to accompany her.'

'Accompany Miss Middlebrook?' Harrison stared across the desk at his friend. 'Good Lord!' he exclaimed. 'For heaven's sake, why?'

'To ask a few questions around the parish and gather as discreetly as possible what information you can about the relationship between Maurice and Mrs Gittings.'

'Spy, you mean?'

Ingrams looked distressed. 'That's an unpleasant word, but I suppose that's exactly what I'm asking.' He paused, looking earnestly at his companion. 'Much as it must pain such a straightforward, plain-dealing man as yourself, for the sake of the Church, and also for that of Mrs Gittings and Maurice, I want you to go under the cover of diocesan business to ascertain the truth of the matter.'

CHAPTER TWO

'Really, Richard! I can't think what Matthew was thinking of, asking you to become some sort of Peeping Tom!'

Harrison frowned but said nothing. In the hour or so since Ingrams had left his office, the fog had steadily thickened, and now, returning from having collected his wife twenty minutes late from a chilly annexe of the City College of Art, driving was requiring all his attention. Sitting forward, craning over the wheel of his elderly Volvo estate, he peered through the drifting wreaths of mist, out of which the dipped beams of the oncoming vehicles appeared and swam past like the twin searchlights of a succession of submersibles probing the murky depths of some blank, featureless ocean floor.

'And what about Helen Middlebrook?' the voice at his side continued remorselessly. 'What is she supposed to think, with you suddenly insisting on accompanying her on her first assignment? After your undiplomatic comments at her interview, it'll look as if you don't trust her even to inspect a small cottage on her own.'

'That can't be helped,' answered the driver unhappily. 'Whether I like it or not, I've now given Ingrams my word.'

Winnie looked round to argue, but realizing from long experience that further protest was useless, she slumped back in her seat and gazed ahead. 'Well,' she resumed after a short silence, 'all I hope then is that Maurice never gets to hear you've been round his parish, inquiring into his private life! Or Jonathan either, if comes to that. Like his father, he was always such a private, self-contained sort of person and very close to his mother: he'd hate the idea of anyone snooping around, prying into family affairs.'

Engrossed in negotiating a roundabout, Harrison didn't immediately take in the implications of what had been said. As he did so, however, he glanced round in surprise. 'Winnie, did I hear you right just then? Are you saying you actually know the Lambkin lad?'

'Of course I know him!' Scornful impatience rang in his wife's voice. 'And so do you, only you've forgotten!' Out of the fog the pale orange glow of a bicycle's rear lamp emerged like some weak, wavering will-o'-the-wisp. Winnie ceased speaking and waited until the stooped shape of the cyclist was safely behind before resuming. 'Jonathan was in his final year at the King's School when we first moved here. In fact, he was at that garden party Margaret and Matthew gave to introduce us to everybody—or have you forgotten that as well?'

Frowning, Harrison gazed ahead into the murk. Truth was, even though reminded of it, he had only the haziest memory of that now distant event. Indeed, apart from his general discomfiture at being introduced to what had seemed a bewildering succession of clergy and their wives, all he could distinctly recall was the sight of Cawthorne's predecessor, the late Dr Crocker, wandering the deanery rose-beds clad in antique clerical gaiters and frock coat, his thin, tall shape bending and sniffing among the pools of bloom like some ink black, ecclesiastical wading bird.

'Well,' resumed Winnie, 'I assure you that Jonathan was

there that day, whether you remember or not. He was with a school friend; such nice, polite young men, both of them! Jonathan had just postponed going up to Cambridge for a year; his friend, I forget his name, was about to enter one of the armed services.'

'Damn it! Yes, you're right!' burst out her husband suddenly. 'I recall now: the young fellow was going into the army, wasn't he? Same regiment as his father, I believe.' In contrast to the unremitting blanket of fog round the car, the metaphorical haze in Harrison's head had cleared, revealing a good-looking, athletic youth standing in the shade of the deanery apple trees, fair hair and freckled face dappled by the canopy of leaves, speaking with boyish enthusiasm to himself and Major Coles, the King's School bursar, of his recently awarded cadetship to the Royal Military College at Sandhurst.

'Yet you can't remember Jonathan?' asked Winnie. 'He was the quieter, more self-contained of the two—an altogether more imaginative, scholarly sort than his friend. You must recall him, surely.'

'Well, I don't,' answered Harrison impatiently, drawing the car to a stop at the intersection of Northgate and Broad Street. 'All I know of that particular young man is what Ingrams tells me,' he said, peering either side as he began cautiously edging the vehicle across the road. 'It seems that the fellow's been living off social security in some ghastly squat or other in London ever since university. On top of that, he's managed to get himself arrested by the police for disorderly behaviour during street demonstrations on a number of occasions. Apparently,' he added, accelerating on into the Borough, 'he still turns up back in his father's parish from time to time, looking like some sort of damn gipsy, with a ponytail halfway down his back and a ring in his ear!'

The tortuous semi-circumnavigation of the cathedral now almost completed, the walls of the precincts rose above the car on their left. Ahead, Mint Yard gateway glowed through the fog at the top of Palace Street, misty beams from the dormitories and upper rooms of the King's School behind bathing the narrow entrance in a hazy, faintly lutescent light.

'Poor Jonathan!' sighed Winnie, peering up at the tiers of lit windows as they swung into the precincts. 'Everyone here was so disappointed that he failed to complete his final exams at Cambridge. Alan Tubman was talking to me about it only last week—apparently, great things were expected of that boy.'

'Poor Jonathan!' snorted Harrison, driving across Mint Yard and on through the inner archway into the wide quadrangle of Green Court. 'Poor old Lambkin, I'd say! Educating that useless sprog here must have cost the poor devil an arm and a leg! God only knows how he managed it at all on a parson's stipend!'

'Well, he didn't actually,' came the emphatic answer. 'Jonathan's education was paid for by one of the pair of wealthy spinster aunts in Northern Ireland who brought Maurice up after his own parents were killed near the end of the war. According to Margaret, she set up an educational trust fund for Jonathan in her will shortly before she died.'

Although confined to a wheelchair through the effects of the polio contracted soon after their marriage, Winnie constantly managed to amaze her husband by her intimate, detailed knowledge of what was happening and being thought, not only among the cathedral community, but throughout the diocese generally. Useful as the information often was, Harrison was anxious at that moment, however, to avoid further discussion on the subject of the unfortunate Lambkin family. He therefore refrained from making any comment on the deceased woman's misguided philanthropy, and swung the car in under the Bread Yard Archway, devoutly hoping that the subject of his impending visit to Fordington might remain safely forgotten for what little remained of the evening.

❀ ❀ ❀

For the moment he had his wish. The car garaged, he unfolded Winnie's wheelchair and trundled her over the cobbles to the door of their terrace cottage. A light supper was prepared, then eaten off trays in the sitting-room. This over, husband and wife sat either side of the fireplace, enjoying their customary pre-bedtime cocoa, while the television babbled in a variety of accents about financial and political events—earnest faces and gruelling scenes of bomb outrages, mass starvation, riots and armed rob-beries flickering successively across the screen.

Neither sitter, however, paid it much attention. Having heard the news headlines, Winnie had resumed her rereading of *Middlemarch* which she'd begun the day before, and was now lost in the quieter, more predictable, scenes of mid nineteenth-century English provincial life. Equally absorbed, her husband sat completing *The Times* crossword puzzle, a placid, complacent smile hovering on his lips as he lightly pencilled in the answers. Out in the hall, the grandfather clock began chiming; then through the foggy darkness outside, Great Dunstan joined in, each dull, hollow boom of the cathedral bell serving only to emphasize the silence and peace of the precincts.

'*Pony so oddly like a dog*,' muttered Harrison to himself as the final stroke faded. He sipped from his mug, gazing down at the paper. '*Like a dog*,' he repeated, wrinkling his brow. Finally he looked across at the figure opposite. 'Can you help, dear? I need a six-letter word, an anagram of *"Pony so"*. I imagine it's either the actual name of a particular dog or perhaps one of the lesser-known canine breeds.'

'Snoopy,' murmured Winnie, turning over a page of her book.

Harrison frowned. 'What do you mean, "Snoopy"?' he said. 'Who or what the devil is that?'

'Charlie Brown's dog,' answered the other evenly, continuing her reading. 'He's a cartoon character that everyone in the world has heard of apart from you, I imagine.'

With a glance over his reading-glasses at his wife's bent head, but making no riposte, Harrison turned back to his crossword. 'S-n-o-o-p-y,' he pronounced slowly whilst filling in the six blank spaces. Having done so, he gave a derisive snort. 'Damn ridiculous sort of name!'

'Very appropriate in the circumstances, I'd have thought,' responded his wife, continuing to read.

Harrison's face darkened, but, refusing to rise to the bait, he determinedly resumed his struggle with the crossword, starting now to rack his mind for a four-letter word representing *A vexatious Greek with a soft spot for a cleaner.*

'Anyway,' resumed Winnie suddenly, 'the whole notion of a liaison between Stella Gittings and Maurice is evident nonsense! There must be twenty years between them at least.' She paused, then, laying aside her book, she looked across at the figure in the opposite chair. 'It's got to be nonsense, Richard,' she continued. 'Surely you see that. Whatever may be said about Maurice, he was always a devoted family man—the last person to be carrying on an affair at any time, let alone when poor Bridget was alive! And what about Stella Gittings herself, for that matter? She's the epitome of respectability and good sense, as well as being perfectly happily married, as far as I know.'

Harrison wearily folded his paper and sat back, not answering immediately. What had been said about Maurice Lambkin was surely true: the idea of him carrying on a secret affair with any woman, let alone a respectable, married lady deacon, seemed unlikely to say the very least. The same went for Stella Gittings; according to Ingrams, she was exactly the staid, matronly type of Winnie's description: a woman respected for her practical, no-nonsense approach to her parochial duties as well as being the archbishop's personal choice of assistant for Lambkin.

'Aren't I right?' insisted Winnie. 'You surely don't believe there can be any truth in that ridiculous note?'

'I suppose not,' answered Harrison reluctantly. 'At first sight, the idea of a sexual liaison between those two appears highly unlikely. Nevertheless, if there wasn't at least an element of truth in what it suggests, why should someone go to the bother of concocting that wretched note?'

'That, I'd have thought, is as obvious as your anagram just now,' came the immediate answer. 'Whoever did so is clearly against the idea of female priests, and is attempting to prevent Stella Gittings's ordination by slandering her name.'

'Good Lord!' exclaimed Harrison, laughing. 'How in heaven's name do you make that out?'

'Easy—just show me the note again.'

Intrigued, Harrison drew from his inner pocket the envelope Ingrams had left in his safekeeping. Extracting the folded sheet, he passed it to Winnie, who glanced through the message and then held it up for his inspection. 'There,' she said, indicating one of the gummed-on words, 'you see the term "witch" employed to describe Mrs Gittings. Wouldn't "bitch", "whore", "harlot" or something of the sort have been the more likely word for a woman who is meant to have been stealing a dying woman's husband before her very eyes? Why then use the word "witch"?' Pausing, she smiled. 'However paranoid the sender was, I doubt if he or she literally believes that Stella Gittings dances naked under the full moon, offering up the blood of the newborn of Fordington and Wetmarsh Marden to Hecate or Lucifer—nor', she added, laughing, 'conjuring spells to attract the lascivious attentions of a middle-aged country parson!'

Despite himself, Harrison joined in the laughter. 'So,' he said, becoming serious again, 'you see the term "witch" employed as an insulting epithet for a woman invested with priestly powers, and conclude that its use suggests a prejudice against female ordination.' Reaching out, he took the note back and again read it through. 'Yes,' he murmured, nodding, 'you may have put your finger on something. As you suggest, this whole thing could be nothing to do with Lambkin directly—just an unpleasant attempt to blacken Mrs Gittings's name.'

'Exactly,' said Winnie. 'So what's the point of this ridiculous expedition tomorrow? At the very least, it risks upsetting young Helen Middlebrook for no good reason.' She paused, then added earnestly, 'Darling, why don't you go and ring Matthew now, and tell him that, after further consideration, you don't think the trip would be wise, and that the best thing for all concerned would be to destroy the note and forget about it?'

Harrison shook his head. 'I can't. As I've told you already, I've given him my word.'

With an impatient sigh, Winnie turned back to her book. A minute or two later, however, she again raised her head and looked across at her husband. He, in the meantime, had returned to his crossword puzzle and was now triumphantly filling the last vacant space with the word *Ajax*. 'Richard,' she said with a troubled look, 'is there something you haven't told me?'

'About what?' murmured Harrison evasively.

'You know very well what about!' Winnie's frown darkened. 'Come on!' she demanded. 'You're hiding something. What's the real reason you accepted this ridiculous mission?'

Reluctantly, Harrison raised his eyes to meet hers, knowing exactly what he would see: the wariness, the distrust, the downright suspicion he'd sown years before in her once trusting nature. During the time he'd spent in military intelligence, Faustus-like himself, he'd been lured so far into the dangerous delights of secret knowledge and power that lies and half-truths became an almost automatic reflex; finally, only a desperate desire to save his marriage giving him the strength, he'd resigned his commission, exchanging the dark, fascinating labyrinths of deceit and trickery for the safe, dull routines of diocesan administration.

'Well?' pressed Winnie. 'What's the reason? Why are you,

who so much hates leaving your office for any reason, suddenly proposing to go off on this embarrassing wild-goose chase?'

Harrison gave a rueful smile. 'As ever, my dear, you're quite correct: apart from wishing to relieve Ingrams's mind, there is another, rather more personal reason for my wanting to go over to Fordington tomorrow. Truth is,' he continued, 'I feel that Lambkin was rather hard done by over the matter of the Bright Cottage. For some reason, he was very unhappy about having the property sold off and the trust wound up, and to tell the truth, I feel a trifle uneasy about the part I played in pressurizing him over the matter.'

'So you should,' answered Winnie severely. 'I only wish', she added, 'that you had nothing to do with all these awful rationalization schemes of Dr Cawthorne's. They're upsetting people all over the diocese.'

'I know,' answered Harrison, 'but as I've said to you before, if I didn't help implement them, he'd soon find someone who'd push them through far more thoroughly than I'm willing to do. Anyway,' he added, 'now at least you know the real reason for my agreeing to Ingrams's request: if I can go over tomorrow and quietly clear this matter up, I'll feel a little easier about the way poor old Lambkin has been treated.'

Winnie visibly relaxed. 'Well,' she said, resuming her book, 'just make sure you're discreet, that's all. For heaven's sake, don't go barging in with seven-league boots on as you're so prone to do.'

Having helped his wife to bed, Harrison went round the house to check that everything was secure. As so often, late though it was, he took the opportunity of returning to the sitting-room for a few minutes' solitary reflection. He poured himself a small whisky, then, turning off the lights, went to the window, drew back the curtains and looked out into the night.

The fog had slightly lifted. Above the still-lit windows of Alan Tubman's cottage opposite, he could now make out the dark blur of the cathedral. Sipping his drink, he gazed towards it, planning his itinerary for the next day. First he'd drop Helen Middlebrook off at the Wetmarsh Marden cottage before driving the three miles back to Fordington itself to surprise Lambkin with a courtesy call, ostensibly merely to inform him that the diocesan architect and he were in the parish, carrying out a preliminary inspection of the cottage. Whilst talking with him, he'd casually bring up Stella Gittings's name to observe the rector's response. His real intention, however, would be to contrive a meeting with either George or Mavis Frome.

According to Ingrams, it had been Mavis, then a local widow in her late thirties with a teenage daughter to bring up, who'd been originally taken on by Lambkin to help his already ailing wife with the running of the house and the care of his small son. A year or so later she'd married George Frome, whom the rector had previously employed as a part-time gardener and general handyman. Since then, for Lord knows what tiny financial reward and the use of the converted rectory stables as a home, the pair had devotedly served the Lambkin family, Mavis acting as housekeeper and cook, George as general factotum as well as church verger.

On his previous visit, Harrison had taken an immediate liking to the couple: the woman was a warm-hearted, homely soul; her husband, a stocky, broad-shouldered, rather taciturn ex-sailor, who'd been pensioned out of the Royal Navy after a shipboard injury had left him lame in one leg. If anything untoward had happened between Lambkin and his female assistant, either in the lifetime of his wife or since, these two would almost certainly know of it and just as certainly disapprove, and the mere mention of Stella Gittings' name would be bound to produce an unmistakable reaction in them. Apart from the Fromes, there were also the two churchwardens, whose names and addresses he knew from the correspondence he'd had with them as trustees of the Bright Trust. One of these was a retired airforce wing commander, who, as a fellow ex-serving officer, seemed an obvious choice as someone to consult if, after the rectory visit, he still had any worries regarding the allegations of the anonymous note.

His course of action decided, Harrison took another sip of his drink, then turned to look out across the courtyard towards the low archway entrance of Bread Yard. Its mouth was as black as Dark Entry's had been when the eerie figure of Mephistophilis had stepped forth into the misty lamplight. Even now, hours later, the image of that hooded phantom gliding out of the foggy darkness still somehow haunted his mind. Eyes on the archway, he drained his glass, then felt in his pocket again for the curious note sent to the archdeacon.

Nothing, of course, that he'd said to Winnie had been a lie; his primary reason in agreeing to Ingrams's request to investigate the allegations in the note had been the good of the Church and his friend's peace of mind. His wish to do Lambkin a good turn was also genuine for, in truth, he detested his new-found role of diocesan hatchet man, and felt distinctly uneasy about the part he'd played in pressuring the clearly unhappy widower into agreeing to the winding up of the Bright Trust. Compelling as they were, however, these reasons alone might not have prompted him to exchange the comfortable routines of his office for the potential pitfalls and embarrassments of the coming visit had not one apparently trivial detail about the envelope continued to play on his mind. Now, as he turned it over in his hand, he found himself wondering yet again why it had been posted unsealed. Unusual as this was, especially on a letter sent first class, ordinarily he might have discounted the matter as a mere quirk on the sender's part. Somehow, whether from simple fatigue or as a result of the shock he'd experienced when he'd looked down upon that chalk-white, featureless face in the lamplight, that unstuck flap had, for some reason, given him a curious sense of unease. Now, holding the envelope between his hands, he moved the loose flap with his thumbs, frowning as he thought of the possible implication of that unsealed strip and also of the ominous concluding phrase of the note itself.

Raising his head, he looked back across the cobbles to the archway, staring towards it as if expecting to see that hooded, blank-faced spectre materialize again. He remained standing there, empty glass in hand, gazing out into the misty darkness until roused from his reverie by the solemn, reverberating sound of Great Dunstan striking the midnight hour.

CHAPTER THREE

'This is, of course, no reflection on your professional competence, Miss Middlebrook.' The speaker gave what he hoped was a reassuring smile. 'As I say, it's merely that a minor administrative matter has cropped up in the locality, requiring my personal attention.'

Despite the delicacy with which he'd broached the subject, just as Winnie had warned and he had feared, Helen Middlebrook was clearly affronted by Harrison's announcement of his intention of accompanying her on her first diocesan assignment. Smartly dressed in pinstripe jacket and skirt, and carrying a brand-new attaché case, she'd arrived punctually at quarter to nine to collect the cottage keys, all breezy confidence and smiles. Now, less than five minutes later, she stood before his desk, a lanky young woman in her late twenties, running her fingers through her gingery hair and staring down at her feet with the look of a disgruntled schoolgirl.

Harrison's heart fell. In spite of her academic record and the reputedly brilliant part she'd played in helping restore the fire-damaged York Minster, he'd been against her appointment from the start, having an instinctive sense there was something brittle about the bright-eyed self-assurance she'd displayed before the appointments board. Unable, however, to put his finger on any concrete ground for his misgivings, and fearing an unconscious prejudice—for her comparative youth, her gender, or even perhaps because of her antipodean origins—he'd limited himself to a few pointed remarks on her complete lack of practical experience in the bread-and-butter work of building maintenance and general repair.

As it turned out, he might as well have saved his breath. Wooing the traditionalists with her undoubted enthusiasm for the preservation of ancient architectural gems, whilst soothing the suspicions of the archdeacon and his coterie of cost-conscious evangelicals with a panegyric on modern, multi-functional building design, the young Australian achieved the minor miracle of pleasing both opposing factions among the selectors. Amidst the general rejoicing at this unlikely accord, Harrison's tentatively voiced doubts went virtually unheard, and he ended up silently acquiescing as Cawthorne finally rose to proclaim her the unanimous choice of the board.

Now, shocked at her reaction, he was momentarily lost for words. Luckily, at that moment there came the sound of feet on the stairs and then that of the door of the outer office opening. 'Ah, good!' he exclaimed. 'It seems that my secretary has arrived. If you'd like to bring your briefcase, Miss Middlebrook, we'll go through and break the news of our little joint excursion to her.'

So saying, he led the way through to find the new arrival contemplating the evidence of the impromptu tea party of the previous evening. Disregarding Mary Simpson's initial look of reproach, and then the obvious surprise with which she received the news of his decision to accompany the new young lady architect over to Wetmarsh Marden, he requested her to cancel all his appointments for the day. This done, he hurriedly left, looking forward to the chance of repairing relations with Helen Middlebrook during a pleasant country drive together.

His hopes of doing so were soon dashed, however. In the confines of the car, the atmosphere was, if anything, even worse than it had been during the drive home with Winnie the evening before. Apart from monosyllabic responses to his various remarks, his passenger sat staring ahead, hardly saying a word as he battled through the last of the rush-hour traffic. By the time they were finally clear of the city and heading out along the main Sandwich road, his attempts at conversation had lapsed altogether.

Although the fog had lifted during the night, traces of its passing still lay in the hollows of the ground and clung as a misty veil among the branches of the trees. With the cloud rapidly thinning overhead, the Volvo and its silent occupants sped on along the A257, and by the time they had turned off shortly after passing Ash-by-Sandwich, and plunged into the maze of lanes and narrow by-roads leading northwards towards the muddy banks of the Stour estuary, the sun had finally broken through, bathing the autumnal landscape in russet, red and gold.

The loveliness of the scene was quite lost on Harrison. Like the fog, his unease about the anonymous note had all but dissolved overnight, and he'd woken that morning already regretting his decision to investigate its unlikely allegations. Now, with his fears of the previous evening seeming patently absurd, and with his taciturn companion making him feel more uncomfortable by the mile, he found himself wishing profoundly that he was back in his office, sorting through the morning mail with Mary Simpson's coffee-making machine bubbling away in the outer office.

'Do you mind if I smoke?'

Surprised at the unexpected question, he glanced round at his passenger. Normally, he'd have resented the request, as he detested the smell of cigarettes. Now, though, he felt only too relieved by her speaking at all. 'Yes, of course, by all means,' he said, leaning forward to open the ashtray, 'though I'd be grateful if you wouldn't mind opening your side window a shade.'

'Right.'

A farm tractor and trailer appeared in front. As he impatiently beeped the horn, he was conscious of his companion striking a match and lighting up. By the time the grinning wretch in the cab ahead eventually deigned to pull over to allow him past, he found that Helen had her window fully wound down and was leaning slightly out, inhaling deeply and then carefully blowing the smoke outside.

His heart warmed at the sight, realizing suddenly that he'd misjudged her. What he'd taken as sullen disgruntlement was clearly nothing more than simple nervousness—a fear, presumably, of not measuring up in his eyes (understandable, perhaps, in light of his remarks at her interview). With hopes rekindled for their future working relationship and feeling much happier, he drove on, wondering nevertheless how such a simple task as the survey and evaluation of a country cottage could give rise to such an obvious degree of apprehension.

In less than quarter of an hour they were entering the obscure domain to which Maurice Lambkin had retreated years before with his already sick wife and their young son. Not even its most devoted adherents could describe Fordington as a pretty village. Standing two or three miles back behind the scrubland and boggy fields that bordered the nearby river, it had originally consisted of little more than a straggle of cottages running along both sides of an S-bending road, with the small steepled church of St Philip's and its adjoining rectory perched on the slight eminence at the eastern end, opposite the venerable Ferryman Inn. Despite its lack of aesthetic appeal, clusters of modern private houses and bungalows had sprung up in recent years almost to double the population. As a result, a prefabricated classroom stood in the yard of the village primary school, and plans were already afoot for the repair and enlargement of the old wooden parish hall, or 'Reading Room' as it was always called, the cost to be met with a portion of the proceeds of the Bright Cottage sale.

Using the sketch-map and written instructions enclosed by the senior churchwarden with the keys, Helen Middlebrook directed them past the rectory gates, then along the narrow lane past the churchyard out of the village towards the river. Soon they were back in open countryside again, following a serpentine trail between wind-bent hedges and thistle-strewn fields towards where the waters of the sluggishly rolling Stour gleamed ahead, with the flat acres of the isle of Thanet stretching into the hazy distance beyond, only the tall radio mast at the famous old fighter station of Manston, three giant cooling chimneys and the fine Norman tower of St Mary the Virgin at Minster breaking the dreary monotony of the otherwise almost featureless landscape.

The curved iron roofs of a pair of Dutch barns and an imposing, high-chimneyed farmhouse rose into view, with the hamlet of Wetmarsh Marden visible beyond. A few minutes later the Volvo turned a tight bend past a cowyard gateway and, watched intently by a head-craning herd of inquisitive cattle, drew to a stop beside the gate of Hannah Bright's Cottage—or Bright Cottage, as it was more usually known.

Despite its name, it appeared more a house than what is normally thought of as a cottage. Apart from the unfortunate late Victorian addition of a single-storeyed extension, referred to in the appendix to the deeds as 'the mission hall', as well as a substantial nineteenth-century porch, planted around with rose bushes and surmounted with a grey slate tablet on which was inscribed in fine italicized lettering the date and details of the charity foundation, it was a perfectly proportioned example of Georgian domestic architecture in miniature. Brick-built, white-painted and elegantly high-gabled, it stood within a low-walled garden, backing on to a grassy slope leading down to the banks of the river. Separated by a good quarter of a mile from the hamlet proper, the two-hundred-year-old building and its modern, asbestos-roofed garage stood in virtual isolation, neighboured only by the large Jacobean farmhouse facing it across the lane.

Turning off the engine, driver and passenger sat for a moment in a silence broken only by the lowing of the cows. The whole scene was one of complete rural tranquillity, and looking up the short path towards the cottage front door, Harrison couldn't help wistfully thinking that this was just the sort of quiet retreat he'd like for his retirement—although the likelihood of his getting anywhere half as pleasant was, to say the least, highly improbable with the constant selling of grace-and-favour dwellings under Cawthorne's regime. Chances were, he thought to himself bitterly, that he and Winnie would end their days in shabby rented rooms or in sheltered accommodation on some sprawling council estate.

'It's rather sweet,' said Helen, breaking into his thoughts. Having arrived, she seemed in no hurry to leave the car, and turned from peering at the cottage to look across at the farmhouse. 'But what an odd place for this woman, Hannah Bright, to have built her cottage,' she went on, looking about her. 'Why choose such an isolated spot, and why, with all this space around, plant it directly in front of the farm?'

'That, I'm afraid,' answered Harrison, 'was the whole idea. I regret to inform you that the building you're about to survey is what, in this country, is known as a spite house.'

'Spite house?'

'Exactly that: one built out of pure vindictiveness, just to block somebody or other's view—a comparatively common practice apparently before these more enlightened days of planning control.'

'Is that right?' With wondering incredulity, Helen glanced again between the two facing buildings. 'God! I see what you mean! The cottage blocks the front windows of the farmhouse

completely. All the same,' she added, frowning, 'I don't understand: why go to all that trouble and expense?'

Harrison smiled. 'Because revenge is sweet, my dear Miss
Middlebrook, and those who pursue it single-mindedly will go to
almost any length to see it satisfactorily accomplished. This cottage, for example, was reputedly built by the wealthy ex-fiancée
of the farmer who lived here at Sanctuary Farm towards the latter end of the eighteenth century. Apparently, the couple had
been engaged for some sixteen years, and, understandably getting
a trifle impatient at the delay, the lady pressed her beau to name
the wedding day.'

'Sixteen years? Jeez! The pair of them must have been mad!'

'That may well have been the case,' answered Harrison,
warming to this refreshingly straight-spoken young woman.
'Anyway, I'm sorry to say that the man in question ungallantly ter-
minated the engagement on the spot, apparently on his mother's
advice. The aggrieved spinster subsequently purchased the piece
of ground opposite his house, and, having built her cottage and
spoilt his view for ever, passed the property into the care of the
local incumbent and his two churchwardens, having first established a trust fund for its maintenance, stipulating that the cottage was for the use "of any decayed clergyman of the Established
Church, his widow or any other faithful, godly servant or servants
of the same within the parish boundaries deserving of pity."' The
speaker laughed. 'An example, one might say, of good arising from
evil.'

Frowning, the other shook her head. 'I can hardly believe it,'
she said; 'such hate and desire for vengeance in such a quiet,
peaceful spot.'

'What was it the great Sherlock Holmes said?' responded
Harrison, now thoroughly relaxed and enjoying himself. '"The
lowest and vilest alleys of London do not present a more dreadful record of sin than does the smiling and beautiful countryside."' Breaking off, he laughed again, pleased that his former

misgivings about his new young colleague's suitability were proving so completely unfounded. 'Well,' he resumed, 'pleasant as this is, I'd better be pressing on, I suppose. If you like to hop out, I'll return in two hours' time, then perhaps we can go and have a spot of lunch together. The Ferryman Inn back in the village provides quite an adequate table, or so I'm informed.'

Instead of smilingly acquiescing and clambering out as expected, Helen Middlebrook merely lowered her head and began nervously running her fingers through her hair just as she had back at the office. Disconcerted, Harrison regarded her in dismay for a second or two before tentatively asking, 'Is anything wrong?'

Obtaining no reply, he glanced back towards the cowyard, then along the lane towards the hamlet, noticing that a rather elderly looking car had been left apparently abandoned on the verge. 'Look,' he said, turning back to his passenger, 'perhaps this is rather a lonely spot. If you feel at all concerned about the isolation, why not lock yourself inside the cottage?'

For some reason his words caused the other to shudder. Turning, she looked up at him, her cheeks growing red.

'Colonel,' she said, 'do you think there are many spiders inside?'

'Spiders?' Flabbergasted, Harrison stared at her.

'I'm afraid', she said, dropping her gaze, 'that I suffer a little from arachnophobia.'

Harrison was dumbfounded. The notion of a diocesan architect being afraid of spiders seemed as unlikely as an Eskimo fearing snow or a doctor the sight of blood. Then, remembering the funnel-web spider and other potentially fatal insects of her native land, it occurred to him that her phobia might explain why she had originally forsaken her native shore. True or not, he at least now understood the cause of her silence and obvious nervousness during the journey over: faced with poking about an empty country cottage, she'd clearly been bracing herself to meet all the giant, hairy-legged monsters of her nightmares.

He cleared his throat. 'Well, I don't think there can be many spiders in the place as Wing Commander Sparrow informs us in his note with the keys that, apart from the mission hall, the place was cleared out and cleaned after the last tenant, the Reverend Holloway, died two months back. Nevertheless,' he added, opening his door, 'if it's any help, I'll happily accompany you inside and wait until you've got the feel of the place.'

'What's the matter? Is the lock jammed?' The speaker peered over the architect's shoulder as she turned the key a second time and again shook the handle of the heavy oak door. 'No,' she answered, 'the key turns all right. It feels to me as if the door's bolted inside.'

'It can't be!' muttered Harrison impatiently. 'I expect it's just that the wood has swollen a little. If you'll step aside, I'll see what a bit of brute strength can achieve.' So saying, he took the other's place and, twisting the handle, rammed his weight against the door. Though it gave slightly beneath his shoulder, the door remained rock-solidly shut. Pink in the face, he tried again with exactly the same result. 'I'm afraid it's jammed tight,' he murmured, brushing down his coat sleeve. 'I suppose it gets very damp out here by the river, and I doubt if the door has been opened for weeks. We'll just have to go round to the back and let ourselves in through there.'

Jingling the bunch of large, old-fashioned keys, he led the way round the outside of the house, following the path between the overgrown front lawn and the mission hall wall. Glancing up through the metal-framed windows overhead as he passed, he noticed the faded yellow curtains inside were drawn, and that behind the small panes hung clusters of cobwebs. To prevent his companion noticing, he increased his pace, guessing already that the cottage was not exactly in the best state of repair, and therefore not likely to make anything like the profit the archdeacon hoped.

Dipping under a rusting, umbrella-shaped rotary washing-line that shared the back yard with a concrete coal-bunker, he went straight to the blue-painted back door. Selecting the most suitable looking of the keys, he inserted it to find that it turned easily enough. Depressing the thumb-latch, he confidently pushed open the door. It swung barely two inches before coming fast against a modern, fine-linked security chain. Taken aback, Harrison stared at it in consternation. 'I don't understand,' he said, looking round. 'If the house is empty, how the devil can the front door be bolted inside and back door chained?'

The girl shrugged. 'Squatters, perhaps.'

'Squatters!'

Harrison felt his blood pressure rise, and he remembered the car parked along the lane. Had the wretched young Jonathan, he wondered, informed some of his layabout London friends of this empty cottage in his father's parish? Was the diocese now going to have the trouble and expense of obtaining a court order to expel a whole parcel of impertinent ruffians?

Turning back to the door, he furiously rattled it against the chain, then, leaning forward and pressing his mouth to the gap, bellowed into the house, 'Hallo! Hallo! Is anyone in there?'

His words echoed dully in the hollow silence. Going to the nearest window, he peered in at a tiny, bleak, unmodernized kitchen, whose walls were dotted with mould, but whose bare work surfaces, to his enormous relief, showed no sign of recent use.

'I don't think there's anyone living here,' he said, turning back to the girl. 'I suppose some old tramp may have found his way in and he's sleeping off an alcoholic binge.'

'Shouldn't we go for the police?'

Harrison glanced at his watch and shook his head. 'No, there isn't time. I have far too much to do. The best thing is to look round the place to see if there's a window we can get through. If you try the house proper, I'll take a quick shufti back round the outside of the mission hall.'

'There's no way in,' said Helen Middlebrook a few minutes later as they met again at the back door. 'All the windows are tight shut with their latches fastened.'

'Yes,' said Harrison, nodding. 'I found the mission hall ones the same. From the look of them, I'd say they haven't been opened for years.'

'What shall we do? Smash a pane?'

Harrison considered. Breaking a window meant more time wasted as well as needless expense, as it would involve finding someone willing to come over and repair it later. There was obviously only one course of action to take. 'Right,' he said, making up his mind, 'stand back—I'm going to break that confounded chain.' For the third time that morning, he drove himself against a closed door, again achieving nothing beyond further bruising his shoulder. A sense of futility engulfed him: it felt as if he was going to be there all day, slamming himself against unyielding surfaces. Retreating a few yards, he fairly ran at the door, hurling his whole weight against it in pent-up frustration. With a crash, this time the woodwork flew open, and he half fell into the dingy, narrow passage beyond.

'Colonel, are you all right?'

'Yes, I think so,' muttered Harrison, wincing with pain and rubbing what he feared was a dislocated shoulder. Glancing at the door, he saw that he'd managed to rip the end of the chain completely out of the frame. Turning away, he shouted, 'Hallo! Anyone home?' Hollow silence greeted his cry. Certain now that, after all the noise, there was no one inside to hear him, he turned back to the girl who was peering anxiously in. 'Just a moment, Miss Middlebrook, while I glance round to see that all is well.' So saying, he stepped into the small scullery-cum-kitchen beside him.

Thankfully, though the room was drab and unpainted, there was not the slightest sign of any insects. Nevertheless, he went over and peered down into the shallow, old-fashioned square sink, knowing the likelihood of finding some spider trapped by the slippery porcelain. There was nothing in the sink, however, apart from one dead match, but as he bent over, he caught a faint whiff of what smelt like paraffin. He sniffed, wondering at the smell, then, turning away, went back out into the passage. 'Right then, Miss Middlebrook,' he said with a cheery smile, 'do step in. Welcome to Sleeping Beauty's castle!'

Though innocently said, it was, in the circumstances, an unfortunate remark, and Helen momentarily froze in the doorway, her face paling visibly. Cursing his thoughtlessness, and wondering wherever the phrase had sprung from, Harrison watched as she now cautiously entered, fearfully looking about for the giant, all-enveloping cobwebs of the traditional fairytale. Seeing that the passage was relatively clean, however, she brightened considerably.

'All right,' said Harrison, handing her back the keys. 'I'll follow you round while you take a quick look in the rooms. After that, I really must be on my way.'

The extent of Helen Middlebrook's phobia rapidly became clear as they began their tour of the ground floor. There was something truly pitiful about the way she tentatively opened doors and looked in, face rigid with fear, then relaxed and smiled round at him as she found each empty interior surprisingly clean and insect-free. As Harrison emerged from what was obviously the dining-room and followed her down a narrow hallway towards the front door, he couldn't help visualizing the horrors in store for her among an endless succession of ancient vicarage cellars, dusty church crypts, vestries and belfries.

Equally as apparent as his companion's phobia was the poor condition of the house. With its peeling plaster and the all-pervading smell of damp, it was obvious that, despite its charming exterior, Hannah Bright's cottage was a prime example of cheap eighteenth-century jerry-building—'Nothing but a damned whited sepulchre,' Harrison muttered aloud as he knelt and peered in at the small forest of black fungi growing at the back of the stair-cupboard.

Hardly had the words left his lips before he heard a key being turned in a lock almost directly behind him. Glancing round, he was just in time to see Helen opening what he guessed was the door of the mission hall.

'I say,' he began, rising to his feet, 'I really wouldn't...'

It was too late. His words were cut short by a piercing scream. Next second the young architect was out of the room, her face ghastly pale, eyes wide, her mouth contorting. Before Harrison had a chance to move, she'd thrown her attaché case aside and was clinging to the banisters beside him with both hands, her entire body trembling and convulsing.

Remembering that Wing Commander Sparrow had mentioned in his letter something about the room being stacked with various items left over from when it was used for the Sunday school and prayer-meetings, Harrison scrambled to his feet with a vision of piles of mouldering hymn books, kneelers and other ecclesiastical lumber, all crawling with beetles and blotchy-legged spiders.

'Don't worry, Miss Middlebrook,' he murmured soothingly as he squeezed past her. 'I'll just take a quick peep, then close the door.'

'No, Colonel! Don't look!'

Ignoring the moaned cry, Harrison went to the half-open door. As he reached it, however, he heard Helen retch loudly, and, glancing back, saw her suddenly bend double and vomit violently on to the floor. Immeasurably shocked, he stared at her, wondering how such a profoundly afflicted person was possibly going to carry out her diocesan duties, and, at the same time, feeling an inward rage as he remembered Cawthorne's complacent grin as he'd triumphantly proclaimed her appointment. Turning back to the door, he pushed it open and peered into the curtained dimness within. As he did so, all thought of the archdeacon and of his worries for the diocese vanished immediately, and, with heart and stomach seeming to convulse together, he froze on the threshold, appalled and sickened at the sight that met his eyes.

To a large degree, his imaginings on the state and contents of the mission hall had been uncannily accurate: chairs were stacked in heaps; tattered hymn books lay in untidy mounds; rolled carpets, framed religious prints and cardboard boxes were piled high, along with sections of what obviously had been an altar. What held his attention, however, and rooted him in the doorway, were the two human occupants. Virtually headless, skull an oozing, bloody mass, one hung bowed forward in a high-backed wooden armchair, wrists bound together behind the back of the seat; the other, lying a few feet in front, was sprawled across a toppled chair amid a confusion of books and boxes, head similarly blown apart by the sawn-off, rather rusty-looking shotgun that lay fallen beside the outstretched yellow-gloved hand.

Struggling to gulp down his own rising nausea at the sight and the smell, Harrison stood before that motionless butchery, dimly conscious of Helen being sick again behind him, and of the continuous buzz from the cloud of bluebottles circling over the shattered bodies and the wide pool of half-congealed blood stretching out across the dusty, uneven parquet flooring almost as far as his feet.

CHAPTER FOUR

'I trust you're beginning to feel a little more yourself, Miss Middlebrook?' Harrison anxiously studied the architect's deathly pale face as she tremblingly sipped the water he'd brought out to her from the cottage kitchen. 'I'm afraid,' he said, 'this has not been at all the sort of experience you expected on your first diocesan assignment.'

'Too bloody right!' murmured the other tonelessly, cupping the plastic beaker in her shaking hands and turning to stare glassily over the wall of the back yard across the river beyond. 'Jesus Christ!'

Obviously a highly strung young woman at the best of times, the hideous scene of mayhem and carnage she'd stumbled upon had, understandably enough, shaken her to her antipodean roots. 'Look,' said Harrison gently, 'just wait here a moment while I slip back inside to retrieve your attaché case.'

Receiving no reply, he left her standing in the sunshine, still staring into the distance, and went back inside the cottage.

Carefully stepping over the patch of vomit in the hall passage, he went first to retrieve the bag from where it had been thrown down outside the now relocked mission hall door. Straightening from picking it up, he happened to glance through the dusty glass panel of the inner porch door. Doing so, he saw that Helen had indeed been correct in her assertion that the outer door was bolted within—the lower of the pair of bolts was pulled to, though the draw-knob had not been tucked down flush but protruded at a right-angle to the woodwork behind. He then went to the foot of the narrow staircase and stood looking up at the dark little landing above. For a few seconds he remained listening intently before hurrying back to rejoin his companion outside.

Though she was now drawing hard on a cigarette, Helen had not moved, but remained gazing trance-like across the wall at the desolate acres of Thanet—ancient 'Thanatos' to the Romans, the appropriately named 'Isle of Death'. To Harrison's relief, however, he saw that the colour had begun to return to her cheeks, and that her previous continuous ague-like trembling had now subsided to the occasional convulsive shudder.

'Ah, good!' he exclaimed with as much heartiness as he, in the circumstances, was able to muster. 'You look a lot better already. Now,' he continued briskly, 'I'd like you to take your bag and go straight over to Sanctuary Farm. Ask whoever you find there to contact the police, then remain where you are. I want no one entering the cottage grounds or laying a finger on that car parked further down the lane until they arrive.'

The authority in his voice and his businesslike tone had their effect. Emerging from her reverie, the girl nodded dumbly, then, taking her case, started to walk away. After a few steps, however, she paused and looked back. 'Colonel, those two...' She swallowed and struggled on. 'Those two people inside, do you know who they are?'

Harrison shook his head. 'I've not the slightest idea. Now off you go, please, and make that phone call—the sooner the police get here, the better.'

'Right.' Taking a last suck on her cigarette and then throwing the stub aside, Helen hurried away, disappearing from sight round the end of the mission hall. The moment she'd gone, Harrison went straight over to the coal-bunker and began rooting among the rusty pieces of iron piled beside it. Although reasonably certain that there was no living person in the house, he was nevertheless determined to check and, still haunted by the grisly sight in the mission hall, he needed the comfort of a heavy weapon.

Selecting a rusty old poker, he re-entered the cottage, this time locking the back door behind him and dropping the keys in his pocket. Going straight to the stairs, he crept up to the first floor, then burst into each of the empty bedrooms in turn, throwing the door open and entering, weapon raised. There was nothing: like the downstairs rooms of the cottage proper, all three chambers were completely bare and surprisingly clean. With similar results, he checked the bathroom and lavatory. Although he had no way of reaching the overhead trapdoor to the loft, peering up, he could see that, like the windows of the mission hall, unbroken strands of tiny cobwebs guaranteed that it hadn't been opened for a considerable time. Finally satisfied that there was no living soul in the building apart from himself, he descended again to the hall.

At the foot of the stairs, he paused to check his watch, guessing that it would be another ten minutes at least before the first police patrol car arrived. He looked at the locked door in front of him, and then, laying aside the poker, he dipped into his pocket and drew out the keys.

Despite his years in intelligence work and the various scenes of carnage he'd beheld in the course of his military career, nothing had ever hardened him to the sight of the victims of cold-blooded killing. It had been horrific enough, God knows, to see the riddled bodies of those gunned down in wayside ambushes in

Cyprus, Kenya and Malaya; to have witnessed the ripped-open, dismembered torsos of adults and children blasted apart by mine or bomb in Yemen and Aden, and then finally in Northern Ireland. There had always been, however, a particular horror in encountering those who had died trussed like animals to face the slaughterer's knife. Now, after a decade spent in the quiet, ordered routines of Church administration, the urge to walk on down the passage and let himself back out into the fresh air was almost overpowering. The last thing on earth he wanted was to stir up again the barely suppressed nightmares of the past by facing what lay behind the locked door. Nevertheless, impelled by some obscure sense of duty, he turned the key and pushed back the door to confront the literal ruins of the delicate little mission so confidently entrusted him by the dean.

As the door opened, the murmur of flies arose. With the stink of blood in his nostrils, and what seemed like the same faint tang of paraffin he'd earlier smelt in the kitchen sink, Harrison stood a moment on the threshold, swallowing hard as he peered once more into the shadowy interior; then, leaning across the dark channel of semi-congealed blood, he seized the bottom edge of the nearest curtain. Yanking back the limp, sun-rotted material, he sent a shaft of brilliant light over the bowed, bound figure in the chair, causing an additional cloud of flies to rise buzzing into the air.

Able now to see that, by pushing the door fully open, he could quite easily step across to the dry passage between the end wall and the stacks of furniture and extraneous lumber, he cautiously entered, feeling unease at this unauthorized intrusion, yet at the same time trusting to his professional experience and expertise not to move or disturb anything in the slightest, or do anything indeed that might contaminate the scene of the crime.

Taking long, careful strides, endeavouring not to touch or even brush anything at all with his clothing, he made his way forward until he was able to lean across the piles of dusty boxes and tattered old hymn books to peer closely at the slumped figure bound to the chair.

Except for the lower jaw, the face had been blasted to pulp by what, he guessed, had been both barrels of the sawn-off shotgun fired directly into it at extremely close range. The front of the cranium was nothing but a bright oozing mess of brain, membrane and bone to which adhered a sodden mass of what obviously were chicken breast feathers, some of which also lay in tiny piles on the corpse's lap and scattered upon the shoulders and on the floor round the chair. Nevertheless, although the face was completely ruined, from the grey strands of hair at the back of the shattered skull, and from the celluloid, wide-banded collar that circled the neck, Harrison had not the slightest doubt that his intuition had been correct: that the slumped body in the chair was none other than that of the Reverend Maurice Lambkin, the dean's old friend from theological college days and, latterly, incumbent of the parish.

Despite what he'd said to Helen, he'd guessed the identity of this and the other body almost the moment he'd first peered into the room, but realizing the dreadful implications, he'd lied to her in an instinctive desire to postpone as long as possible the scandalous sensation that would inevitably now break upon an already grievously beleaguered national Church.

Whatever his earlier revulsion at the thought of inspecting the scene, now that he was actually in the room, Harrison found himself curiously detached. Long training and experience had taken over, and almost coldly he stood regarding the late rector's body, focusing his mind on details: the shabby, crumpled grey suit the corpse was wearing; the badly scuffed shoes on its feet; that the jacket collar was not quite turned down at the back of the neck; and that Lambkin had dressed for his last day on earth in odd socks, and even then, had somehow contrived to present himself before his Maker with one of them on inside out.

Crouching, he examined what looked like a length of brand-new washing-line binding the cleric's wrists behind the chair. A crude granny knot had been used, and he noticed that, tight though they'd been bound, one hand had torn almost free of its bonds, leaving the flesh raw and the clean white rope smeared with blood.

Not the horror of the physical details themselves, but the thought of the helpless man's struggle to wrench himself free as the gun was levelled at his face now made Harrison inwardly shudder. Straightening, his face contorting at the thought of the doomed man's final moments, he began carefully moving on again round the piled lumber until he reached a passage clear through to the second body. With the same long-strided care as before, moving from one island of dry flooring to the next, he picked his way forward until he was standing over the prone form which lay sprawled across a toppled chair, incongruously wearing a pair of oversized rubber kitchen gloves on its hands.

This body, too, was male and once again the gun had been discharged at point-blank range; again there were the clots of blood-congealed feathers embedded in the gaping wound. This time, however, it seemed that a single shot had been delivered, and not aimed directly into the face this time, but slightly upwards from beneath the right side of the jaw. Although the entire top left side of the head was missing, enough of the features remained to show that they belonged to a young, rather good-looking man in his mid or late twenties. From that and from the scruffy blue jeans, the soiled leather jacket, the long auburn hair drawn back into a ponytail and secured with an elastic band at the nape of the neck, and also from the thin gold ring in the upturned ear, Harrison was in no more doubt as to the identity of this second corpse than he'd been of the first. Just as he'd feared, the body was clearly that of the rector's son—the unfortunate Jonathan, who had apparently caused his father so much worry and heartache in recent years, and whose abysmal performance at Cambridge and wastrel, turbulent life since had so surprised and disappointed his old housemaster and the rest of the King's School staff.

Leaning down, Harrison peered at the twelve-gauge double-barrelled shotgun: it was an old-fashioned hammer-gun, sawn off close to the stock, and, although recently oiled, its slightly rust-pitted barrels and battered butt-plate indicated long, rough usage, presumably at the hands of some hard-working farmer. One hammer, he saw, was fully depressed; the other half-cocked, indicating, as he'd guessed, that only one barrel had been discharged on the second firing.

Straightening, he ran his eyes across the channel of dark blood that spread between the two corpses. Half immersed in the gory mess were a couple of spent cartridges, as well as two ripped-open cushions with piles of sodden feathers strewn about them—the cushions obviously having been used to deaden the sound of gunfire. Closer to his feet, floating in the blood beneath the base of the chair, was an empty matchbox and its scattered contents; and there among them, half wedged beneath one of the lower tilted legs, was a set of keys identical to the bunch he'd left dangling from the keyhole.

As he gazed down, he noticed that among the matches beside the key-ring was one that, though unused, had been snapped into a V-shape. Frowning, he stared at it a moment, then raised his head and looked around until his eyes fell on a brass paraffin hurricane lantern standing on an upturned box, its glass all sooty and black. Next to it stood a fuel can, presumably containing liquid for the lamp. Confused, he gazed at the old-fashioned lantern, then remembered that the electric supply to the cottage would have been disconnected after the Reverend Holloway's death. Next to the box on which the lamp and can had been placed was a large, rather scruffy holdall with its zip fully back, exposing a pile of shirts, the top one of which was clearly smeared with marks of what he guessed was gun-oil. Also in the bag were scattered a few unused twelve-bore cartridges.

Turning away, Harrison looked across at the body of Lambkin. As he did so, for the first time he noticed a crumpled ball of clean white paper lying beneath the chair to which the rector's corpse was secured. Retracing his steps, he moved back round the room until he was able to lean across and examine the half-unfolded paper ball closely. Without surprise, he saw that the paper, like the envelope in his wallet, was emblazoned with the now familiar pasted-on letters and words, and, squinting down, he was just able to make out the words: '…his carryings' on with that fowl witch Stella Gittings laid his poor…'

From the evidence, what had happened was only too apparent: clearly there had been a violent quarrel between father and son over the contents of that anonymous message; goaded by the allegations on the note, the highly strung, obviously unstable young man, in a frenzy of rage, yet at the same time with cold-blooded cunning, had returned to the parish and somehow lured his unsuspecting victim to the deserted cottage, presumably some time during the previous evening or night. There he'd bound him to a chair and then blasted him in the face at extreme close range with both barrels of the shotgun, almost decapitating him in the process. Finally, overcome either by remorse or horror at his deed, he had not made his escape as he'd obviously planned—wearing the rubber gloves to avoid leaving fingerprints—but instead, had sat down in the chair opposite his dead parent, and there, alone in the dim light of the paraffin lamp, had turned his weapon upon himself.

Across the windless autumn fields there came the faint oscillating wail of a police siren. Careful as ever, Harrison began making his way back to the mission hall door. Once outside in the passage, he relocked the door and removed the keys, then, having picked up the poker, he hurried to the back door. Letting himself out, he threw his improvised weapon among the collection of old iron before striding on round the house to arrive on the front path just as a white patrol car, blue light flashing, squealed to a stop immediately behind the parked Volvo.

In front of the farmhouse a motley collection of people had assembled. As Harrison went to the gate to greet the police, Helen Middlebrook and a burly middle-aged man, presumably the farmer, crossed the road towards the police car, followed closely by three small, grubby children and a gaunt woman wearing wellington boots. The uniformed driver immediately jumped out, raising both hands to wave the group back across the lane. His colleague, a dark-haired young man in his early twenties, went straight over to meet Harrison at the garden gate. 'What's happened, sir?' he asked. 'We've had a report of bodies found in this cottage.'

'I'm afraid that is true, Constable.' A movement at one of the first-floor windows opposite made Harrison glance up to see the wizened face of an old woman gazing down. 'I regret to report', he continued, looking back to the policeman, 'that the local rector, the Reverend Maurice Lambkin, has been bound and tragically shot dead by his unhappy son, who then appears to have turned his gun upon himself.'

'A murder and a suicide, you say?' Blanching, the young man looked past Harrison towards the house.

Again, Harrison glanced up to meet the blurred pale face at the window. 'Technically, that's correct,' he said, a deep, cold anger rising in him now for the first time as he thought back to the scene in the mission hall and of the crumpled ball of paper lying beneath the dead rector's chair, 'but from what I know of the matter and from what I've observed in the cottage, I'd choose to say that, at least in moral terms, two murders have been carried out, both of them committed by some pernicious, sick-minded person unknown!'

PART TWO

CHAPTER FIVE

Not marching now in fields of Trasymene
Where Mars did mate the warlike Carthagens;
Nor sporting in the dalliance of love,
In courts of kings where state is overturn 'd;
Nor in the pomp of proud audacious deeds,
Intends our Muse to vaunt his heavenly verse...

With an inward groan, Harrison momentarily closed his eyes as the amplified voice of the child echoed under the lofty roof. God knows, he thought bitterly to himself as the shrill, piping tones continued to ring out through the darkened spaces overhead, it had been a hard enough day as it was, without this now on top of everything else.

The morning had begun badly, with the usually sedate and decorous monthly meeting of the Dilapidations Board descending rapidly to something like the rutting of stags, with each of its stouter-hearted members locking horns in turn with Cawthorne over his plan to reduce even further the general vicarage repair fund, necessitating cutbacks that would inevitably condemn a whole swathe of diocesan clergy and their long-suffering families to yet another winter of chilblains, frozen pipes and leaking roofs. The afternoon, however, Harrison had found far more gruelling, for, just as the cathedral clock began striking two, Dr Benham, the county coroner, finally reopened the adjourned inquest into the deaths of Maurice and Jonathan Lambkin. As a result, he'd had to sit all afternoon in a crowded courtroom, listening to every last grisly detail of forensic evidence concerning the horrific find in the Wetmarsh Marden cottage. Tired out and emotionally drained by what he'd been forced to relive, and knowing he had to return next morning to give his own account of the discovery of the bodies, he now sat, on this bitterly cold November evening, wrapped in his overcoat on a hard wooden seat near the front of the cathedral nave, facing the final and most exquisite torture of the day: an almost two-hour-long juvenile performance of Christopher Marlowe's *Doctor Faustus*.

> *'Nothing so sweet as magic is to him,*
> *Which he prefers before his chiefest bliss:*
> *And this the man that in his study sits.'*

With a low bow and a sweep of his arm, the small boy playing chorus retreated from the stage that had been erected where the altar normally stood at the foot of the steps leading up to the magnificently carved choir screen. As soon as he was gone, similarly clad figures in tabard and hose were wheeling forward and arranging the fittings of a book-lined, candlelit study, finally drawing the dust cover from the bulky object that stood centre-stage, revealing a battered grey monster of a sofa. Irritated at the incongruity of such an item in an otherwise purely medieval setting, Harrison frowned disapprovingly, deigning not to respond as his wife gave his arm an encouraging squeeze.

Hardly had the stagehands retreated before their place was taken by a gangling, anaemic-looking youth wearing patched, ragged blue jeans and a baggy, oversized T-shirt, emblazoned with a garish advertisement for RADIO KENT. Imagining this was yet another, more informally dressed, member of the stage crew, Harrison watched the newcomer heap the books he was carrying in front of the sofa. However, as he proceeded to flop down on the floor beside them, there to start flipping through each volume in turn, Harrison realized with scandalized incredulity that this pale, spotty adolescent in his questionable garb was meant to represent no less than the tragic hero of the play—the world-renowned Dr John Faustus of Wittenberg.

There was a slight touch on his arm, and Winnie was smiling up again, obviously amused and delighted by the director's originality. Unable to share her pleasure, Harrison turned back stony-faced to the stage as the unlikely young player began to speak.

Surprisingly, the youth turned out to be a gifted actor. Launching into Faustus's opening speech outlining the allurements and limitations of each of the traditional medieval academic disciplines of philosophy, medicine, law and theology, and finally rejecting them all in favour of the dangerous and forbidden occult, he subtly created the impression of a character dangerously cut off from reality and hovering close on mental collapse.

Despite himself, Harrison felt his interest grow, and gazed, fascinated, at the images of incipient insanity burgeoning around the young scholar as, with almost suicidal defiance, he conjures Mephistophilis out of hell and bargains his immortal soul against twenty-four years of voluptuous life and unlimited earthly power. Good and evil angels appeared and reappeared on the steps behind, while arms, legs and grinning devilish faces protruded at intervals from the depths of the sofa as visible extensions of a tortured mind.

'Now, Faustus, what wouldst thou have me do?'

As the figure of Mephistophilis rose up on the stage through a cloud of smoke, adorned in the scarlet robe and blank mask the girl-actor had worn when she'd appeared at the mouth of Dark Entry, Harrison again felt Winnie's touch on his arm. This time he returned her anxious look with a reassuring smile, then turned back, intrigued, to watch Lucifer's melancholy ambassador played as a further projection of Faustus's sick mind.

With the scene shifting to the buffooneries of the subplot, his attention gradually began to wane, however. As it did so, his thoughts returned to what he'd heard at the inquest and to the questions that had been occupying him ever since stumbling across the two bodies nearly a month before. As he'd originally feared, with its juicy ingredients of supposed sex scandal, poison-pen letters, parricide and suicide, the story of the deaths of Lambkin and his son had given the media yet another field day at the expense of the long-suffering Church. Nevertheless, despite the interest the story had aroused and its horrendous details, it was difficult to see why the chief constable had seen fit to call in a team of metropolitan detectives for so straightforward a case. Equally surprising was that, despite all their resources and the pains they had obviously taken with the case (Helen Middlebrook and himself having being grilled separately on two occasions in the bowels of the Old Dover Road police station), it appeared that the authorities had still not discovered the identity of the sender of the anonymous notes, whose unfounded assertions had clearly precipitated the tragedy.

> 'Homo, fuge! *Whither should I fly?*
> *If unto God, he'll throw me down to hell—*
> *My senses are deceiv'd, here's nothing writ—*
> *O yes, I see it plain; even here is writ,*
> Homo fuge! *Yet shall not Faustus fly.*'

The loud-cried words drew his attention back to the play. With Mephistophilis standing with arms spread out over him like some huge scarlet butterfly, the youthful actor had fallen to his knees and was gazing aghast, trembling and maniacally gibbering at the terrible warning displayed in the flesh of his arm. Now, however, it wasn't some Dostoevskyan antihero spinning into madness that Harrison saw, nor even a medieval scholar ineffectually struggling between salvation and damnation. Instead, before him there seemed the very image of the wretchedly unhappy Jonathan: the lonely introvert, retreating from Cambridge to an idle, useless existence in a squalid London squat. There, like this same tormented character on stage, he had allowed the tendrils and weeds of depression and despair to grow up and overwhelm him, sinking, sick-souled and mentally unstable, to a point where he actually believed the ridiculous assertion that an affair between his gentle, unassuming father and a perfectly respectable female assistant had hastened his mother's death.

Now hardly hearing the play as it continued, Harrison went over the known sequence of events as they'd been outlined that afternoon at the inquest. Apparently at about quarter to ten on the night of the tragedy, George Frome and his wife had heard Lambkin start up his car in the garage next to their home. Thinking he'd been suddenly called to the bedside of a sick or dying parishioner, neither had been greatly concerned or surprised at the time, despite the thick fog and the fact that he'd not called in to inform them of his movements as he normally did. Mavis had retired to bed half an hour later while her husband sat up to await the wanderer's return. When, however, by midnight the car had still not returned, Frome had woken his wife to express his fears, and together the pair of them had sat up a further hour or so, too worried to sleep, yet too timid to contact the police.

The only other witness to the events of that fateful night had been the porter on duty at the small railway station at Minster, across the river on the isle of Thanet, some ten miles or more by road from Fordington, where Lambkin had met his son off the eleven o'clock London train. Recognizing the rector, the porter on duty had spoken to him, finding him strangely nervous and abstracted. He'd subsequently seen Jonathan disembark and meet his father, carrying the large holdall that was lying open in the mission hall the following day. After the train had left, he then overheard the two of them arguing together out in the station car park, Jonathan at one point thumping his fists on the car roof and cursing loudly about something or other. Finally, both plainly upset, father and son had clambered into the car and driven off into the fog, neither to be seen alive again.

According to medical evidence, both men died roughly an hour later, around the time when George Frome had woken his wife to inform her that their employer had still not returned. It was presumed that Jonathan had rung his father from London, requesting him to meet him off the train, and to bring with him the spare set of keys for the empty cottage as well as one of the pair of hurricane lanterns that were hung in the rectory garage. Why Lambkin should have agreed to this extraordinary request was puzzling, as was where Jonathan had obtained the sawn-off shotgun that he'd presumably been carrying in the holdall. What seemed absolutely clear, however, was that the young man had arrived at the station highly worked up, having apparently received an identical copy of the anonymous note sent to the archdeacon, and that he'd travelled down that night armed and prepared to carry out his murderous intentions.

Barely aware of the happenings on stage, Harrison's mind ran on, imagination taking over where the known facts left off. He visualized the final terrible confrontation between Lambkin and his son in the midnight cottage: the shouted accusations, the vehement denials, the wild struggle and the binding of the terrified older man to the high-backed chair—the prisoner's desperate pleadings as the shotgun was raised and levelled, the shouted words cut short by the thunderous explosion, and finally, ears ringing from the double discharge, the wretched killer staggering back to a facing chair, appalled and sickened by his deed and already fumbling to reload his still-smoking weapon.

> *'But fearful echoes thunder in my ears,*
> *"Faustus, thou art damn'd!" Then guns and knives,*
> *Swords, poison, halters, and envenom 'd steel*
> *Are laid before me to dispatch myself.'*

As the play ran its predetermined course towards the terrible reckoning, when the unhappy, tormented Faustus has to pay his side of the bargain that he, knowingly and wilfully, has sealed with the powers of darkness, Harrison remained grim-faced, the horrific images in his head prompted and spurred on by the words and actions on stage. Even through the wild antics at the Vatican and in the court of the German Emperor, as well as the ridiculous nonsense of the horsedealer and rest of the sub-plot's foolery, his expression didn't change, merely darkening as events moved to their climax, as the despairing Faustus, alone in his study at night, awaits the striking of the clock when the Devil will come, and when he must pay the inevitable price of his pact with evil.

> *'Ah, Faustus,*
> *Now hast thou but one bare hour to live,*
> *And then thou must be damn 'd perpetually.*
> *Stand still, you ever-moving spheres of Heaven,*
> *That time may cease, and midnight never come.'*

Not even the sight of young Simon Barnes and his friends wriggling out of the ingeniously contrived sofa to chase Faustus round the stage with giant toasting-forks could lift the spectator's mood. As the youngsters caught and dragged their struggling victim forward to stuff him down head-first into the ominously livid, gaping hole now opened in the sofa, Harrison saw again in his mind's eye the wildly strewn and overturned chairs in the mission hall and the lake of congealing blood stretching across the floor with the murmur of flies circling and buzzing above it.

> '...Faustus is gone: regard his hellish fall,
> Whose fiendful fortune may exhort the wise,
> Only to wonder at unlawful things,
> Whose deepness doth entice such forward wits
> To practise more than heavenly power permits.'

As the diminutive chorus bowed and withdrew, the outburst of clapping brought Harrison back to the moment. Blinking, he looked about him as the applause continued, uncertain whether it was proper to clap inside the cathedral. Happening to look to where the dean, as chairman of the school governors, sat in the place of honour in the front row with his wife and teenage daughters, and seeing him enthusiastically joining in the applause, he felt it safe to do the same as the young actors trooped back on stage to take their bow.

'Well, dear?' Winnie smiled round as the lights came on. 'And how did you enjoy it after all that fuss you made about coming?'

'I must admit', he answered guardedly, rising to his feet, 'that I found the experience a great deal more engrossing than I envisaged.'

'I told you it would be good,' said Winnie as he bent and released the brake of her wheelchair. 'A lot of people from the school told me that the new head of English is a brilliant director.' She turned and smiled up at him as he manoeuvred the chair out into the growing crush in the aisle. 'And didn't dear little Simon do well?'

'Yes, indeed,' grunted Harrison. 'The little brute looked quite at home wearing horns and a tail.' The words had hardly left his mouth when a voice called out from the melee behind: 'Richard! Winifred! May I have a very quick word?'

Turning, he found the dean pushing through the crowd to catch them up.

'A great success, don't you think? A truly remarkable performance!' Beaming, Ingrams looked from one to the other as he reached them, but even now, at this moment of triumph, Harrison could discern the underlying sadness in his face, and knew that his friend had found the afternoon at the inquest at least as much a strain as he had.

'On the spur of the moment,' continued Ingrams, 'Margaret and I have decided to throw a modest little drinks party to congratulate the director and as many of the school staff as we're able to round up. I trust you'll both be able to join us.'

'What? Now, you mean, Dean?' Harrison stared incredulously at the speaker.

'In twenty minutes or so, yes. You will come, won't you, even if you can only stay a short time?'

With his heart set on getting home, the last thing Harrison wanted was to have to attend a social gathering, but before he had chance to make his excuses, Winnie intruded. 'Oh, Matthew, that's a lovely idea! How exciting! We'd love to come, wouldn't we, darling?'

Even now, Harrison might still have resisted had he not read the look in his wife's face, alerting him to the fact that the dean needed all the support they could give him. Mustering a smile, he turned back to Ingrams. 'Yes, of course, Dean—we shall be only too delighted to attend.'

Lights glowed behind curtained windows, and across the moonlit lawn of Green Court floated the muted sounds of revelry by night. The undoubted success of the evening's performance and the enthusiasm engendered by the unusual and powerful interpretation of the play permeated the deanery drawing-room, investing the guests with unwonted zest and gaiety. Glasses clinked, laughter and voices rose and fell as the production and the individual performances of the actors were discussed and appraised, and even if Margaret Ingrams's homemade vol-au-vents and sausage rolls, and the somewhat limited choice of wines (a modest riesling and a highly economical Bulgarian red) fell somewhat short of the customary oysters and champagne, the atmosphere had more than a touch about it of the traditional first-night celebratory supper party at the Savoy Grill or Café Royale.

The women sat chatting easily in small intimate groups, while the majority of the men congregated about the bespectacled, dark-bearded figure of the director, the undoubted toast of the occasion. Appropriately adorned in bow tie and velvet waistcoat, he stood before the fireplace, flanked by the imposing figure of Canon Barton-Chadwick, the bluff, hearty King's School headmaster, and Dr Quirk, his deputy, or undermaster—both of them, in the manner of bridesmaids, basking in the reflected glory of the modestly blushing centre of attention.

Nevertheless, if the spirits of Wilde, Irving and Garrick temporarily graced the Ingrams' drawing-room, other spectres were unavoidably present also. Nowhere in the diocese had been more shaken by the dreadful occurrence at Wetmarsh Marden than the cathedral close—the majority of its inhabitants remembering Jonathan at the school—and the horrific news of the killing had stunned and saddened the little community. For the dean, the loss of both his old college friend and his godson in such circumstances had come as a doubly shocking blow. Genial and affable as ever, he now circulated among the guests, aiding his wife and daughters in replenishing plates and glasses. Nevertheless, there was an uncharacteristic strain about his smiles, and, in conversation, his attention would occasionally wander, and he'd stand a moment, bottle or tray in hand, staring past the speaker with a preoccupied expression, as if dimly hearing distant voices or seeing faces other than those physically present in the room.

As usual at such events, Harrison had soon withdrawn from the heart of the fray. Urged by Ingrams, he'd spent an uncomfortable twenty minutes as an awkward and somewhat tongue-tied member of the group clustered around the director. Gradually, he'd managed to extricate himself, covering his retreat, first by exchanging pleasantries with the school chaplain, then by engaging in a discussion on building insurance with Major Coles. Now, as the bursar wandered off to replenish his glass, he surreptitiously glanced at his watch, then looked over to where Winnie sat talking with Mrs Barton-Chadwick and the wife of one of the junior masters, wondering how long it would be before he could withdraw from the field altogether and retire home to bed.

'Do you mind if I join you a moment, Colonel?'

The voice broke through his thoughts. Turning, he found himself facing the short, rather corpulent form of Alan Tubman.

'Not at all,' he responded, forcing fresh sociability from dwindled resources as he met the retired schoolmaster's podgy-faced smile. 'A great success the play tonight—a refreshingly original treatment of an old story, I thought.'

'Original, certainly,' replied Tubman, taking a sip of his wine. 'Though, speaking personally, I must admit to preferring a slightly more traditional approach.'

'Quite,' murmured Harrison, deflated by the response. Discomfited at the thought of appearing dangerously avantgarde in the schoolmaster's eyes, he looked down at the carpet, at a loss what further to say.

'Mind you,' continued Tubman, dabbing at his lips with a handkerchief, 'I'm being perhaps a trifle unfair: the staging of such an old favourite as *Doctor Faustus* is bound to conjure up ghosts.'

'Ghosts?'

'Of pupils past, Colonel—those generations of boys I remember playing the parts.'

Pausing, Tubman meditatively swirled the wine in his glass, gazing down at the liquid with a brooding melancholy on his flabby, heavily jowled face. 'Naturally,' he resumed, at last looking up, 'after the inquest today, I have poor young Jonathan particularly in mind. I so clearly remember him acting the part of the horse-dealer when he was only in his first year and still such a small boy.' He gave a wan smile. 'As you can imagine, with his background, he was perfect for the role.'

'Indeed?' murmured Harrison, wondering what on earth the fellow meant. How growing up in a country rectory was meant to be any preparation for playing the part of a disreputable and dishonest horse-dealer, he couldn't for the life of him think; even for an eccentric old bachelor like Tubman, this view of clerical family life seemed singular, to say the least.

'Mind you,' continued the schoolmaster, 'there was another reason for the play tonight making me think of Jonathan. I don't know if you ever met him alive, Colonel, but, with that great bush of auburn hair and that heart-shaped, rather delicate face of his, there was a curious physical resemblance between him and his famous, or should I say infamous, predecessor here at the school. I refer, of course, to Marlowe himself.'

'Really?'

'Oh, yes, very much so: the similarity was striking if the unsigned portrait that was discovered in 1954 and now hangs in Corpus Christi Hall is indeed that of the young playwright, as is commonly supposed. And I would say', added Tubman, taking another sip of his drink, 'the resemblance between them went a good deal further than mere looks.'

'How very interesting,' answered Harrison politely. 'In what other ways were they similar?'

'Well, in intelligence, certainly. Despite the disappointment over his final university examinations, Jonathan was bright. Also he had that interest and ability in the thespian arts I've already referred to. At one time, in fact, I thought he might choose the stage as a career. Added to that, both he and Marlowe were from comparatively modest backgrounds—one the child of a city shoe-maker, the other a poor country parson's son; both won scholar-ships to Cambridge and went to the same college—though, admittedly, the choice of Corpus Christi was a typically roman-tic, self-conscious gesture on Jonathan's part.'

Harrison frowned but made no reply. Though no expert on the subject, he knew that Marlowe's life had been famously dis-reputable: public quarrelling and street fighting; a spell in Newgate Gaol after someone was killed in a brawl; writing pam-phlets mocking religion; and generally creating such an unwhole-some reputation that even now, four hundred years later, the cathedral vesturer described him as 'a blaspheming atheist'. He fully realized that such wild, creative, intemperate noncon-formists as Byron, Shelley, Marlowe and others of their short-lived ilk were bound to be attractive role-models to many adolescents. Nevertheless, he couldn't help the sneaking feeling that Jonathan's choosing to identify with such an apparently lax and dubious character as the notorious Kit Marlowe—even allowing a schoolboy obsession to determine his choice of uni-versity college—might well go a long way to explain his apparent failure to apply himself to his undergraduate studies.

'And then again, after Cambridge,' continued Tubman, 'the similarity continued with both of them leaving to live, shall we say, somewhat irregular lives in London.' Pausing, the speaker shook his head sadly. 'And now finally, this last terrible similarity: the two of them, the brilliant, successful, widely known Christopher Marlowe, and the unhappy, obscure Jonathan, both losing their young lives so tragically, and each in such a violent, sordid and unlikely way.'

'Unlikely?' repeated Harrison. 'I don't quite follow. Wasn't

Marlowe meant to be a braggart and brawler—just the type of fellow to end up getting knifed to death in some bar-room scuffle? As for young Lambkin,' he said, dropping his voice and glancing across the room to make sure Ingrams was safely out of earshot, 'from what I hear, he was similarly just the sort of oversensitive, unstable misfit to be goaded to madness by those absurd allegations in the anonymous note.'

Instead of answering, Tubman raised his almost empty wineglass and swept it slowly around the assembly, peering through at the blurred images of his fellow guests. 'Through a glass darkly,' he murmured, then looked back up into Harrison's face. 'Isn't that how we see reality, Colonel, and isn't it also how we see each other—through a glass darkly?'

'To some extent, yes,' replied Harrison stiffly. 'We all tend to hide a great deal of ourselves from those around us.'

'Yes, indeed,' replied Tubman, nodding. He paused, then continued with a sudden passionate earnestness. 'But not children, Colonel. Children we see directly, as it were, face to face, and they in turn perhaps see us the same way. Having had Jonathan in my house for over five years, and seen him grow from boy to young man, I believe I can say that I knew his nature as well as anyone: he was always remarkably strong-willed and self-contained, the last person to run amuck and lose control—and certainly far too intelligent to be taken in by what you yourself just termed as absurd allegations against his father.'

Embarrassed, Harrison looked down, again not knowing quite what to reply. Clearly, from Jonathan's evident failure at university and his subsequent wastrel life, time had lent a distinctly rosy hue to the schoolmaster's memory of his old pupil.

'Colonel,' continued Tubman, 'I understand you were a witness to the dreadful scene over in Wetmarsh Marden, and that you'll be giving evidence at the inquest tomorrow. That is really why I came over to speak. I want you to tell me if there is any chance that a third person was involved in the deaths of Jonathan and his father, and if you have any reason to think that what you and Miss Middlebrook found in Bright Cottage that day might have had a different explanation than the apparently obvious.'

Harrison shook his head. 'No, it's impossible,' he said. 'The cottage was secured with locks, chains and bolts from the inside, and the room where the bodies were lying had been similarly locked from within. I myself possessed one of the two sets of keys; the other was lying inside the room.'

'Couldn't someone have had them copied?'

Once more Harrison shook his head. 'They were large, old-fashioned keys which would have required time and a skilled locksmith to copy—and the Reverend Lambkin apparently kept all his keys carefully locked in the rectory safe.'

'And presumably there's no chance of anybody having got out through a window?'

'No, I looked carefully. All the windows of the mission hall were secured with latches. Apart from that, the frames were rusted and cobwebbed, and clearly hadn't been opened for years.'

Tubman stood for a moment, staring in front of him before he spoke again. 'You know,' he said, 'having the care of boys over many years teaches one to be extremely suspicious. Forgive me for saying so, but all those locks, bolts, chains and rusty window frames you mention sound almost too much of a good thing, if you know what I mean.' Pausing, he studied Harrison searchingly. 'Are you absolutely sure there was nothing there, some tiny fact that can't be easily accounted for? Something perhaps that the police might have missed?'

Feeling as if he were back in school himself, standing once more under the formidable and searching gaze of his own house-master, Harrison bowed his head, and for the umpteenth time went back over all he'd observed in the cottage. Finally, he shook his head. 'No,' he said. 'There was nothing whatever in the house or the room I can't explain. Everything points to things having happened just as they appeared.'

'I see.' Tubman gazed into his glass. 'In that case,' he added heavily, 'doubtless the inquest jury will bring in verdicts against Jonathan of unlawful killing and of subsequent suicide when of unsound mind.' He sighed, and then looked across to where Ingrams stood among the hierarchy of the school staff, cradling the family Siamese cat in his arms and absently tickling the animal under its chin as he listened to whatever the headmaster was saying to him. 'At least,' he added, 'after that, I suppose, our dear, good host over there and all the rest of us will then have only these long-delayed funerals left to endure.'

(HAPTER SIX

'Colonel and Mrs Harrison, I presume?' The speaker was a bright-eyed little man, dapper and neat, with immaculately combed greying hair and the tiniest triangle of white protruding from the breast pocket of a well-cut pinstripe suit. Emerging from the small knot of figures outside the church porch, he came forward to greet the latest of the mourners toiling up the gravel path, twirling one end of his bushy, handlebar moustache as he approached. Halting in front of Winnie's wheelchair, he consulted a clipboard and ticked off a name. 'Right,' he said, beaming at the couple with a wide toothy smile, 'all tickety-boo! I've laid on a couple of chaps to help you to your seat, Mrs Harrison. You and your husband will be sharing the second pew back from the front on the right-hand side, along with Mrs Ingrams and her daughters.'

'Thank you.'

Imperiously waving forward a pair of gawky, black-tied youths, the sprucely attired functionary stood aside and watched as the wheelchair was eased over the lip of the porch. This accomplished, he turned again to Harrison. 'The name's Sparrow, Colonel, senior churchwarden here at St Philip's. I trust you received your joining instructions safely.'

'Yes, indeed,' grunted the other, who'd barely recovered from the exertion of wheeling his wife up the gravelled incline. 'Most useful—thank you very much.'

The moment the trim, moustached figure had stepped forward, Harrison had known this could be no other than the retired wing commander who had originally forwarded him the cottage keys, and who, only four days before, had sent the details and time of the funeral service, along with a printed note pointing out the likely difficulties of parking close to the church and stressing the necessity of early arrival.

'Yes, a pity about the need of all this formality,' said Sparrow, turning to look down the slope towards the low-roofed lych gate, beneath which a woman was seated at a baize-covered card-table, checking off the names of the mourners from the list in front of her. Beside her stood a uniformed policeman, there presumably to prevent the sizeable crowd of sightseers and press cameramen from pushing past into the churchyard. 'Still,' continued the churchwarden, 'after all the unfortunate publicity there's been, it cannot be helped, I suppose. Especially,' he added, darting a significant glance at his companion, 'in light of our chief mourner's very regrettable decision.'

'Quite.'

Anxious as always to avoid becoming embroiled in local controversy, Harrison hastily excused himself and hurried on into the porch. Passing between wreaths and bouquets fragrant with blossom, he took the proffered order-of-service card at the door and entered the church with the somewhat unworthy thought that, if nothing else, death had at least released the late incumbent from the burden of the officious little bantam cock of a churchwarden he'd left strutting the gravel in the sunshine outside.

Wing Commander Sparrow's instructions had clearly had their effect, for although at least fifteen minutes remained before the start of the service, the nave was already crowded. Acutely aware of the hushed crowd on either side, and feeling oddly self-conscious, Harrison continued up the aisle to where Winnie was being helped into a pew beside Margaret Ingrams and the twins. After she was comfortably installed and the wheelchair removed, he took his place at her side and, having briefly knelt and prayed, sat back to take stock of his surroundings.

St Philip's, Fordington, was pure Victorian, a replacement for the quaint, hipped-roofed, wood-turreted church that had originally stood on the slight elevation at the eastern end of the village, and to which the black-timbered old lych gate outside had belonged. With its low pine pews, the bright colourwork on its brass commemorative tablets, the patterned floor-tiling and the pseudo-medieval, oddly androgynous, figures in the stained-glass windows, the influence of Pugin and Morris was omnipresent, giving a sense of something alien and false to this arbitrarily imposed, London-designed supplanter of what had been familiar and beloved of generations of small tenant farmers and estuary fishermen.

Mercifully unblessed with a strong aesthetic sense, Harrison felt nothing of this. For him, St Philip's was simply a practical-sized and solidly constructed edifice—in cost and upkeep, an example to the vast majority of its neighbours. Nevertheless, impervious though he was to its artistic shortcomings, he could-n't help sensing there was something uncomfortably odd about the atmosphere within the church. A sideways glance to meet Winnie's raised eyebrows confirmed his impression, and, after staring ahead for a few moments more, he cautiously turned to look at the pews behind.

As expected, there were many faces he knew; clergy and wives from the surrounding parishes, others from further away. Alan Tubman was there, sitting with Canon Barton-Chadwick and one of the matrons from the school. Directly in front of the headmaster's party, Cawthorne was seated with his pretty, if perhaps somewhat insipid, young wife. Instead of the turtleneck sweater and dark corduroy jacket he habitually wore about the precincts, he was now appropriately dressed in orthodox ecclesiastical attire, his gingery red hair and heavily freckled face looking more youthful than ever above the severe black stock and wide-banded clerical collar.

Even Helen Middlebrook was present, he noted with approval. For the rest, the congregation seemed to be made up mainly of what he imagined were some of the late rector's parishioners—a motley collection of dowdy-looking women for the most part, with a scattering of florid-faced men of middle age and upwards. Unexceptionable and predictable though the gathering appeared, there was, nevertheless, an unusual edginess about it. Although one pale-faced, dark-haired young woman was openly tearful, the majority, especially the locals, sat grim-faced and tense, with the looks of disapproval more commonly glimpsed among those awaiting the appearance of certain brides than of those expecting the imminent arrival of the dead.

After what the wing commander had said outside, it was only too easy to guess the reason why, and Harrison turned to look back towards the altar with a frown. A few moments more passed, then there was a low whispering at the church door, followed by the rustle of clothing and the tap of an approaching cane.

Feeling an almost tangible increase in the tension about him, Harrison remained staring fixedly ahead as the sounds grew nearer. Then, from the corner of his eye, he saw the frail, stooping shape of an old woman in black furs being helped past him to the foremost pew by George Frome, the dead rector's longtime verger and general factotum. He watched as the grizzled ex-sailor helped his elderly charge into the empty pew immediately in front, noticing the tattooed anchor on the back of the man's right hand as he passed her an order-of-service card. Looking up, she smiled and whispered, 'Thank you, George. Don't worry. I'll be perfectly all right now.'

'Very good, ma'am.'

Respectfully nodding, Frome withdrew, and through the hush came the intermittent drag of his left leg as he retreated. Hardly had the sound died before there began the tolling of the bell. As the mournful, slow ringing continued, Harrison stared at the withered nape of the old woman's neck. He'd instantly guessed who she was: Miss Christabel Lambkin—one of the pair of wealthy spinster aunts who had brought up the orphaned Maurice Lambkin after his parents' death, and who now, as the last living representative of the family, remained, like the ancient lych gate outside, an isolated remnant of a world passed and gone.

As suddenly as it began, the bell ceased ringing. From outside came the crunch of feet and rattle of wheels. The sound grew, then, as the cortège entered the porch, Dean Ingrams's voice rang through the church, triumphantly proclaiming the traditional opening words of the funeral service.

Harrison rose to his feet with the rest as his friend processed slowly past. Similarly robed in surplice and cassock, a second figure followed: Mrs Stella Gittings, the apparently literal, if unlikely, *femme fatale* of the anonymous notes.

Mounting the chancel step, Ingrams and his pleasant-faced, if slightly dumpy, assistant turned and waited as a pair of frock-coated attendants wheeled forward a coffin on a stainless-steel bier. Having fussed it into position, they bowed and withdrew. A short silence followed before there came the slight squeak and rumble of other wheels, and a moment later a second coffin was being trundled into position beside the first.

Although no flag covered them, and both were completely unadorned apart from a simple coronet of white carnations placed on one end of each, as so often in the past and in so many distant places and lands, Harrison found himself gazing at the coffins, wondering at the capacity of the pair of identical wedge-shaped containers, not only to shield, but to give an outward form of dignity to even the most hideously mangled of flesh. Something, however, seemed wrong about their symmetry, and it was a moment or two before he realized what it was: though the small wreaths were positioned to lie exactly parallel with each other, the two coffins lay in diametrically opposed directions, the head of the ordained priest traditionally facing the altar, while beside him, the body of the other lay head towards the brightly glowing western window—father and son lying there together as children, as it were, left to sleep at either end of one shared bed.

As the service commenced with Ingrams reciting the words of the ninetieth psalm, Harrison looked again at the bended head immediately in front of him, wondering at the extraordinary moral courage of this frail-bodied octogenarian who, according to Winnie, in defiance of doctor's orders, had made the long, mournful journey from her Northern Ireland home to this remote Kentish village twice now in six months—and who, against the express wishes of the parochial church council and in the teeth of local opinion generally, had insisted, not only on a joint funeral service, but on having both killer and victim interred together in the late Bridget Lambkin's grave.

'*The grace of our Lord Jesus Christ, and the love of God, and the fellowship of the Holy Ghost, be with us all evermore.*'

'Amen.'

The murmured response to the final blessing died on the windless air. For moments, the only sounds were the cry of gulls over the distant marshes and the constant cawing of rooks from among the rectory elms; then all at once the quiet of the churchyard was broken by a derisive trumpeting neigh—the sound emanating from one of a pair of mud-caked Shetland ponies who, in apparent accord with parish opinion, had stood observing the double interment across the fence of an adjoining paddock with much snorting and tossing of shaggy heads, and the occasional stamping of hooves.

As if woken from a trance by this uncouth interruption, the crowd at the graveside opened their eyes and looked up. For a moment no one stirred, then, leaning heavily on George Frome's arm, old Miss Lambkin moved forward to the pile of dry soil heaped before the grave. Supporting herself on her ivory-handled cane, she bent and, using the trowel provided, threw down a scoopful of earth upon the lid of the topmost coffin. This accomplished, she straightened and, assisted once more by the verger, returned to stand beside the two surpliced figures at the head of the grave, a black-dressed, little withered doll of a woman with a lean, sharp face and dark, button-like eyes.

Whether from uncertainty regarding the order of precedence or from reluctance to express any further blessing on the controversial proceedings, no one immediately stepped forward to follow the chief mourner's example. Instead there was an awkward pause, broken only by a self-conscious scuffling and clearing of throats. Harrison felt Winnie's hand grip his arm. 'Come on!' she whispered. 'Wheel me over. I wish to give the old lady my support.'

Jerked from the reverie into which he'd fallen, Harrison reluctantly did as instructed, pushing the wheelchair forward. Bending, Winnie took a handful of the soft loam and tossed it down into the grave. Harrison hesitated, then followed her example. As he straightened, he inadvertently looked across the open grave to meet Wing Commander Sparrow's expression of scandalized surprise.

Despite the evident disapproval of the senior churchwarden, the majority of the mourners now began pushing forward to fling down their own small token of earth on the topmost coffin and to heap around the grave the various wreaths and bouquets they'd carried from the church. From among them, Frome emerged, escorting Miss Lambkin away from the crush, followed closely by the robed figures of Stella Gittings and the dean.

'Well done, Winnie! And you, Richard, as well!' Out of the throng appeared Margaret Ingrams and the twins. As they congregated round the wheelchair, the former smiled down at its occupant. 'I hope, Winnie, that you've managed to persuade Richard to join us all at the rectory.'

'Yes,' answered Winnie. 'We're very much looking forward to meeting Miss Lambkin, aren't we, dear?'

'Yes, indeed,' murmured Harrison vaguely. He was gazing at the crowd round the grave, his attention centred upon Cawthorne. As he watched him and his wife make their ritual obeisances, he wondered what was going through his mind. Having hardly ever met Maurice Lambkin, and presumably never his son, he wouldn't be properly human, he thought, if at least one part of him wasn't thinking of the rambling Edwardian rectory and its two-acre garden now fallen into his hands. After all, in the present economic climate, no archdeacon in England worth his salt could fail to rejoice at the savings in maintenance costs alone the sale of the rectory would mean to the diocese, to say nothing of the handsome sum that it was likely to realize on the open market.

These somewhat cynical thoughts were interrupted by the appearance of Alan Tubman. Having bent to pay his brief tribute of dust, the old schoolmaster stood bare-headed before his ex-pupil's grave, a look of profound melancholy on his heavily jowled face. As he turned away, his place was taken by his seeming antithesis: a slim, elegantly dressed, sleek-haired man in early middle age, whose appearance and bearing, together with the virginally furled umbrella he carried, bore the unmistakable stamp of official authority.

Laying down the white-flowered wreath he carried, the mandarin figure remained a moment, head inclined, before briskly walking away. At a loss to understand what possible connection such a person could have had with either of the deceased, Harrison watched the elegant figure make his way past the church and down the path towards the churchyard entrance. There, however, his speculations were interrupted by the sight of the bulky shape of Chief Inspector Dowley, who stood talking with one of the two constables beneath the lych-gate roof.

As Harrison looked in surprise towards his old acquaintance, Dowley happened to glance up. Momentarily their eyes met, and then, with a quick word to his colleague, the chief inspector turned away and, pushing past the descending stranger, began heading up the path against the stream of departing mourners. Before he was halfway up the steep incline, he veered aside to cut across the grass towards the small group gathered round Winnie's wheelchair.

'Excuse me a moment, dear,' said Harrison, interrupting what his wife was saying about Ingrams's sermon. 'There's someone I believe wants a word with me.'

Swivelling round, Winnie observed the approaching figure with a frown. 'Richard,' she called as he began moving away, 'don't be long. Remember we're expected at the reception.'

Harrison barely heard her: he was already heading across to where the burly policeman was threading his way between the headstones towards him.

'I'm sorry, Colonel, to drag you away, but seeing you here, it occurred to me that a little chat might be useful.'

'Yes, of course.'

With one accord, Harrison and his companion turned and walked on among the grey, weather-beaten Victorian tombstones to where, matching the miscellany of small modern estates of private bungalows and houses that had sprouted around the village in recent years, the dead of the last half-century lay crammed virtually shoulder to shoulder under a hotch-potch of variously coloured granites and marbles. Pausing beside a particularly glossy black headstone whose polished surface faintly reflected the thick duvet of semi-transparent purple chippings at its base, they stood, looking across towards the now flower-lined grave from which the last of the mourners were now retreating.

'A damned ugly business!'

Harrison glanced at Dowley's beefy red face. His appearance at the funeral had come as a complete surprise, for as far as he was aware, the Canterbury-based CID officer had played no part in the extensive inquiries into the deaths of Maurice and Jonathan Lambkin, and now that the inquest jury had brought in their expected verdicts, and the team of metropolitan detectives and forensic experts had returned to the capital, he'd naturally assumed that authority had washed its hands of the bloody happenings in Hannah Bright's cottage.

'Needless to say,' began Dowley in a sour tone, 'now that the London boys have all buggered off, we country bumpkins are left with the tidying up as usual.'

'Tidying up?'

'Discovering the identity of whoever sent those anonymous notes. We still haven't a line on anyone, and that's why I wanted to talk to you, Colonel.'

'I'm sorry,' answered Harrison, shaking his head. 'I can't help. I'm a stranger here myself, and I didn't really know the Reverend Lambkin at all well.'

'That's right,' answered Dowley. 'As you say, you didn't know him at all well. And yet,' he said, turning to look at Harrison, 'you suddenly decided to cancel all your appointments for the day to go plunging across half of Kent to investigate the plainly ridiculous assertion levelled against him in the note sent to Dr Cawthorne!'

Harrison gave a slight shrug. 'As I have told your colleagues, Chief Inspector, I came over to look into the matter because I was requested to do so by the dean.'

'And just happened to stumble across a couple of corpses in an empty cottage, I suppose?' Dowley gave a sceptical laugh. 'Come on, Colonel! For old times' sake, tell me: what was it that really brought you dashing over here?'

With the westering sun already beginning to draw long shadows among the gravestones, Harrison turned from his inter-rogator's gaze and looked up at the church steeple. Just as when Winnie had similarly pressed him to explain his decision to accompany Helen Middlebrook that day, he found himself reluc-tant to disclose suspicions that, even now, he hardly dared admit to himself.

'What made you take that note so seriously?' pressed Dowley. 'What was it about that semi-literate message, with its childishly gummed-on words and its nonsensical assertion about an affair between the rector and his lady assistant that brought you here?'

Harrison sighed and, glancing over to the far corner of the churchyard, was just in time to see Margaret Ingrams wheeling his wife through the connecting gate into the rectory garden. 'There was one little thing that struck me as odd,' he murmured, watching the figures disappear. 'I found it strange that the enve-lope flap hadn't been licked down.'

'Not licked down?' Puzzlement clouded the policeman's face.

'My dear Chief Inspector,' said Harrison, turning back to him, 'since, in its wisdom, Her Majesty's Post Office saw fit to revoke its special cheap rate for unsecured mail, when did you last receive anything unsealed through the post, apart from the odd Christmas card and dental appointment reminder? And when did you ever get anything unsealed with a first-class stamp on it?'

Still uncomprehending, Dowley stared at his companion for a second or two before bursting out, 'Of course! You were thinking of genetic fingerprinting—of us being able perhaps to identify the sender from the spittle used on the gum!' Admiration briefly shone in the policeman's broad face, but then, as fast as it had come, his smile disappeared, and his countenance became broodingly thoughtful. 'But what you're really suggesting is that the whole thing was pre-planned—that the compiler of those notes knew exactly the reaction likely to be provoked in the rector's lad. And that, presumably, is what you meant when you said to the constable that there hadn't been just one murder in the cottage but two; that both of them, the Reverend Lambkin and his son, had been murdered by some person unknown.'

'In a moral sense, yes,' answered Harrison quietly. 'Anyway,' he continued, 'it merely struck me that someone would have taken such care to avoid leaving any trace of bodily fluids on the envelope only if he or she had a good idea that it was likely to be submitted to forensic inquiry. In other words,' he said, turning to walk on towards the now deserted open grave, 'that there was at least the possibility of a full-blown murder inquiry.'

Dowley followed in his wake until they were both standing before the flower-ringed lip of the grave. 'Colonel, why didn't you say a word about this theory of yours to the investigating team?' he asked as the other drew out a spectacle-case.

'Because it's just a theory, Chief Inspector.' Having put on his reading-glasses, Harrison squatted down and began peering among the wreaths.

Dowley watched curiously. 'What are you looking for?'

'Nothing much,' grunted Harrison. 'I'm just interested in the identity of someone I noticed earlier.' He turned over another of the attached cards. 'Ah, yes! This is it, I think!' he exclaimed, examining it closely. 'Now, that's very interesting. Why should a Home Office representative have attended the funeral?'

Dowley looked perplexed for a moment, then his face cleared. 'Because of all that work Reverend Lambkin did back in his London days, I suppose. Didn't he have a lot to do with the homeless and the rehabilitation of ex-prisoners and the like, and wasn't he an assistant prison chaplain for a while?'

'Yes, of course. I was forgetting.' Deflated, Harrison rose to his feet and looked about. As he did so, he glimpsed a scruffily dressed elderly man observing them from among the tombstones with an expression of what seemed like pure malevolence on his gaunt, leathery face.

'What the devil…' he began, but even as he spoke, the apparition disappeared, ducking out of sight behind one of the larger of the Victorian headstones.

Dowley laughed. 'I don't know about you, but for a moment then I thought it was Old Nick come to claim his own!'

Not a smile passed Harrison's lips: his every inclination was to go over and demand what that unpleasant-looking individual thought he was playing at, skulking near an open grave. Aware of the time, however, he turned back to Dowley. 'I'm sorry, Chief Inspector, you'll have to forgive me. I really must go and join my wife at the reception.'

'One moment, Colonel.' Dowley took his arm. 'Look, you're the only one of us two who can go through that little gate over there without questions asked.' He pointed towards the corner of the churchyard. 'You can pass through it and move among all these churchwardens, lady deacons, parish councillors and the rest without causing the faintest ripple.'

Harrison frowned. 'Exactly what are you asking me to do?'

'Just to continue doing what you always do,' answered Dowley with a smile. 'Go on swimming round in that calm little pool of yours—and while you're at it, keep your eyes and your ears open to test if your theory is correct, and that some wicked great pike is hidden deep down there somewhere in the shadows. Someone with guile and motive enough to have contrived Reverend Lambkin's death at the hands of his son.'

A look of doubt must have crossed Harrison's face, for Dowley gripped his arm tighter. 'Do it, Colonel!' he urged. 'Swim your little pond, keeping your ears and eyes open. And then, who knows, perhaps together we'll hook and draw Leviathan by the nose!'

CHAPTER SEVEN

Somewhat in the manner of an old Norman motte-and-bailey castle, Fordington church and its adjoining rectory, along with its sold-off glebeland paddocks, stood well above the surrounding houses, dominating the village and adjacent landscape. As Harrison passed through the linking gate between churchyard and garden, he glanced out towards Wetmarsh Marden, glimpsing the Stour gleaming orangey-red in the light of the declining sun. Following weed-strewn crazy paving between empty flowerbeds and a shadowy orchard dell, he emerged beside a broad lawn, beyond which stood the tall, redbrick Edwardian rectory, its east-facing wall entirely bearded over with thick-stemmed, densely woven wisteria.

Proceeding to the front of the house, Harrison paused beneath the venerable mulberry tree that stood at the corner of the lawn and looked down the drive towards the white-painted metal gates that directly faced across the road to the Ferryman Inn. To the right of the gates lay the partly concealed roof of the converted stables where George and Mavis Frome lived, and behind which the highway curved out of sight, the pavements bare now of the vehicles that had lined them earlier.

In the gathering dusk, with the funeral over and the sightseers gone, Fordington seemed to have fallen back into primordial slumber. Apart from a trickle of smoke from its chimneys, nothing in the village moved, and even the rectory rooks had at last fallen silent.

So tranquil was the scene that, standing among the lengthening shadows, Harrison was reminded of the time when he and Helen Middlebrook had sat together outside the cottage, he telling her the history of the old house, she finding it hard to reconcile the original owner's thirst for vengeance with the charm of the setting. At the time, he'd made a slight joke of the young architect's naivety. Now, looking out over the hushed scene, he himself found it hard to believe that anyone living in such a peaceful locality could have devised the malicious messages that had prompted the tragedy. What, he wondered, among the homely routines of parochial life could a harmless country parson like Lambkin have possibly said or done to provoke anyone into asserting the preposterous lie that, by flaunting an affair with his female assistant before her face, he'd driven his ailing wife to a premature grave?

Only one answer came to mind: that the anonymous letters, like the ancient spite cottage itself, must have been the bitter fruit of frustrated love; that, knowingly or unknowingly, the Reverend Lambkin, like the owner of Sanctuary Farm two hundred years before, had brought down upon his head all the proverbial fury of a woman scorned. Poison-pen letters were, after all, traditionally female weapons, and it was only too easy to imagine how the bereaved widower, receiving an abundance of tea and sympathy from numerous village ladies, had unwittingly aroused the tender longings of some lonely spinster's heart—the rector's very rectitude and diffidence serving only to promote and prolong the illusion.

The more Harrison considered, the more likely that seemed to be the explanation: innocently aroused love, either neglected or finally disabused, festering into direst hatred. And yet, if he were right, what sort of ice-hearted Jezebel must the woman have been, devising so cruel and unnatural a vengeance as to use the bond between mother and son to goad the emotionally vulnerable young man into the killing of his own father?

Such speculations on the female psyche made him suddenly think of his wife, and, remembering her appeal to him not to be long, he broke from his musings with a guilty start. Skirting the parked cars in the rectory drive, he hurried on to the porch to find that the front door had been left open, presumably in anticipation of his imminent arrival. Aware of the time he'd spent in the churchyard with Dowley, and then dawdling beneath the mulberry tree, he stood on the threshold, hearing the faint murmur of voices and tinkle of teacups from down the hall. Reluctant to venture in unannounced, he jerked the old-fashioned wire door-pull. Almost at once, the stout, dumpy form of Mavis Frome emerged at the far end of the passage, wearing a flowery pink apron over her black dress. Seeing who it was, she came bustling forwards, all fluster and smiles. 'Ah, there you are, Colonel! Do step in, sir. Your wife's been wondering where you have been.'

Despite the warmth of her greeting, Harrison couldn't help noticing that the woman's eyes were swollen and red-rimmed. Understandably, the day was obviously proving emotionally gruelling for one who, along with her husband, had served the Lambkin family with Martha-like devotion for so many years.

'Now, if you'd like to come this way, Colonel.' Having taken his coat, his conductress led him down the hall to the drawing-room. 'You just go along in and join the company inside. I'll go and make you all a nice fresh pot of tea.'

Before Harrison could protest, she was disappearing towards the kitchen, leaving him standing outside the door, behind which the voices seemed to have grown oddly quiet. For a few seconds, he waited in vain for the hum of conversation to resume before finally bracing himself and turning the door knob.

Despite Chief Inspector Dowley's touching faith in his ability to glide unnoticed and unremarked among the various parish officials and dignitaries, Harrison's entrance felt not so much like slipping into familiar waters as doing a violent belly flop into a tranquil and—to judge by the atmosphere—decidedly brackish pool. What little conversation there was died away, cups were lowered and faces turned.

For an instant, he remained in the doorway, the assembly ranged like a tableau before him, a representation of nothing so much as one of Queen Victoria's stuffier tea parties. The majority of guests stood dotted around the drawing-room in stiff, awkward groups, while, at the centre of proceedings, framed against the French windows, sat Christabel Lambkin, for all the world like the veritable Widow of Windsor herself: a withered figure in black, leaning forward, eyes fixed on him, both hands resting on her cane. Flanking her on either side sat Winnie, the dean and his family—the twins perched on high, straight-backed chairs. Completing the picture, Wing Commander Sparrow stood behind in the manner of an aide-de-camp, holding a plate of miniature sausage rolls, disapproval writ large on his face.

'Ah, Richard! There you are!' cried Ingrams with evident relief, smilingly rising to his feet. 'We were about to send out a search party.'

'I do apologize,' announced Harrison, avoiding Winnie's eyes. 'I was unavoidably detained—a somewhat pressing matter of diocesan concern.'

'Not at all,' replied Ingrams sympathetically. 'I fear all of us lay far too much upon you. But now let me introduce you to our hostess. Miss Lambkin,' he said, turning to the old woman, 'allow me to present my friend, Colonel Harrison, who as secretary of our Dilapidations Board, will be taking a large responsibility for the future of this rectory.'

'Indeed?'

Advancing, Harrison bent and gently shook an arthritically knotted hand. Doing so, he met a pair of alarmingly shrewd eyes looking appraisingly up into his own.

'And will the property now be sold off, Colonel?'

The question was disconcerting: instead of the few muttered words of condolence he'd been prepared to deliver, he found himself suddenly having to answer for Church housing policy before a roomful of strangers. Colouring, he cleared his throat. 'Yes,' he murmured, 'I believe that is the intention of our vicarage committee: a house and grounds of this size is deemed inappropriate to the modern clergyman's needs.'

'And also to the size of his stipend, I imagine?'

Again there was the same shocking directness to the old woman's words, and for the first time Harrison glimpsed the ironic humour lurking in her eyes. Shrunken and frail though she was, Christabel Lambkin was clearly a true descendant of those doughty old Presbyterians who, back in the seventeenth century, had settled the Ulster plantations with Bible and sword. Standing before her, he was able fully to appreciate the mettle of one who, in ancestral tradition, had not only ridden roughshod over local sensibilities by her insistence on the double burial, but by obliging her principal opponents to attend, was proceeding to make something of a Roman triumph of this dour little funeral feast.

'Well, Colonel,' she resumed, 'if the rectory is going to be sold, what may I ask is going to happen to the Fromes? After their years of service to my nephew and his family, I assume your Church will assume some responsibility for their welfare.'

Standing under the old woman's gaze, it felt to Harrison as if he were occupying some Victorian prime minister's place, being forced to answer for government policy before a potentially indignant queen. As for the question itself, though he hadn't considered the matter until now, he knew the answer at once: as domestic servants, the Fromes had no possible claim on the diocese, and with the monthly meeting of the vicarage committee due next day, they'd almost certainly be receiving a formal notice to quit sometime during the coming week.

'You don't intend throwing them out on the street, I presume?'

Harrison groaned inwardly; in effect, that was exactly what was intended, yet to say so was unthinkable. 'No, of course not,' he answered, forcing conviction into his voice. 'That the diocese would never allow. All, I assure you, shall be done to find them suitable alternative accommodation.'

'In the immediate locality, I hope. Mavis, I believe, has a married daughter here in the village.'

Only thankful that Cawthorne was not present to hear him, Harrison bowed his head. 'Certainly, ma'am.'

'I'm relieved to hear it,' came the stern rejoinder. 'I know that they've both been most concerned about the matter.'

Mercifully, there came a tap on the door at that moment, and the couple in question entered, Mavis bearing a loaded tray, her husband limping behind with a steaming teapot—their friendly natural manner in striking contrast to the starchy stiffness of the majority of the guests.

'George and I thought you could all do with a fresh pot of tea,' announced the housekeeper, beaming round. 'And, Colonel, I've cut some egg-and-cress sandwiches for you specially.'

Carefully avoiding Winnie's look, Harrison accepted the proffered provisions with embarrassed thanks. Deeming it prudent to make a tactical withdrawal for the moment, he moved away to join a tall, hatchet-faced woman who stood at the French windows, gazing forlornly out across the darkening lawn.

The choice of Miss Gillmore as interlocutor was not, as it turned out, the happiest he might have made. She, it appeared, was headmistress of the village school, and after the exchange of the usual meteorological pleasantries, conversation moved rapidly to the deplorable condition of the parish hall. The so-called 'reading room' was apparently utilized at times by the school as an overflow classroom. Having vainly attempted to disclaim responsibility for the leaking roof and the inadequate heating, Harrison was finally able to escape only after reassuring her that the proposed extension and repairs would be speedily effected once the delayed sale of Bright Cottage had gone through.

In the churchyard, he'd separated from Dowley, buoyed up by the notion of quietly moving among his fellow guests, effortlessly picking up a wealth of gossip concerning Lambkin's private affairs. Now, however, surveying the drawing-room from the vantage of the fireplace, it seemed that his chance of extracting any useful tittle-tattle from this constrained little gathering was virtually nil. Nor, eyeing the various females present, was he any more encouraged: they appeared an eminently respectable, sensible-looking crowd—women, like Stella Gittings herself, far more likely to be organizing a neighbourhood watch scheme or running the Mothers' Union than nursing an unrequited passion for a local cleric.

A wave of despondency passed over him: far from helping to trace the elusive poison-pen writer, all he'd so far done by attending the reception was to land himself with the additional task of rehousing the Fromes. Gloomily, he sipped his tea, then turned to place his cup and saucer on the mantelpiece. Doing so, his attention was caught by the framed photograph next to the centrally positioned clock. It was a colour snapshot of the Lambkin family sitting together on the lawn, French windows behind them, wisteria in bloom, with Jonathan as a child, perched between his parents on a garden bench.

Standing in what had been their living-room, conscious of them newly reunited in the grave, Harrison peered at each of the three figures in turn; first at the unnaturally thin, obviously sick, woman in her floral, short-sleeved dress; then at the sensitive-faced boy close at her side, one hand placed protectively on her arm, his head already crowned with that bush of auburn hair on which Tubman had remarked; finally at Lambkin himself, who sat slightly apart from mother and child, looking oddly isolated and out of place sitting there in the bright sunshine, a careworn look on his heavily lined face.

There was a poignancy about all three, but it was this last of the trio who held the onlooker's attention. Studying the cleric's familiar features, he experienced an almost physical pang of sympathy for the man who'd nursed his wife through her long decline, forced to watch her gradually dwindle and fade before him just like the dreams he must have had for his son—the two separate tragedies of his life, his wife's illness and Jonathan's failure at Cambridge and subsequent wastrel existence, culminating finally in those last unimaginable moments of horror in the dim-lit mission hall.

'Excuse me for interrupting your thoughts, Colonel—may I introduce myself and my wife?'

Jerked from his meditations, Harrison turned to find himself confronted by a well-dressed, prosperous-looking couple in their early or mid forties.

'The name's Tony Brandon,' continued the speaker. 'Gwendolen here is people's churchwarden. I, for my sins, am chairman of the parish council.'

Taken aback by the appearance of this couple, so utterly different from the one in the photograph, Harrison stumbled something out about the unseasonably good weather. Thereafter conversation glided on oiled wheels over a variety of subjects until, finally excusing herself, Gwendolen Brandon moved away, leaving the two men alone at the mantelpiece.

'I was interested, Colonel, overhearing what you were saying about the future of this house. As you say, it's far too large for the modern family, as well as very expensive to maintain.'

'Quite,' murmured Harrison, raising his head and following the other's eyes to the depressingly familiar damp-stains that ran along the top of the French windows.

'Well, if it is to be sold,' continued Brandon, dropping his voice, 'I might possibly be interested myself. Amongst other things, I dabble a little in property development.' His teeth gleamed. 'Between you and me, I've always thought this place would make an ideal private nursing-home.'

The suddenness of this move to matters of business took Harrison by surprise. His shock must have shown in his face, for Brandon quickly went on, 'But perhaps this isn't quite the occasion to speak of it. If you like, I can ring your office in the next few days, then we could perhaps discuss the matter to our mutual advantage.'

'I'll give you my card.'

Affronted though he was at the blatancy of the approach, and wondering what exactly the fellow meant by 'mutual advantage', Harrison swallowed his indignation. As somebody with his fingers on the local pulse, Brandon might possibly prove an invaluable source of information. Turning aside so that neither Winnie nor any of the group round Miss Lambkin could see, he handed over his card, acutely conscious as he did so of the little family at his elbow so trustingly smiling up at the camera on that summer afternoon long ago.

❋ ❋ ❋

Like so many of the brightest lives, the winter day was as brief as it had been dazzling. Within half an hour, the sun sank beneath the horizon, blazing fiery red to the last. To those in the drawing-room, however, the spectacular sunset went unnoticed, for through the east-facing windows, night swept down like easy death, the long shadows on the lawn merging by imperceptible degrees into the general gloom, and the light dwindling so gradually that the curtains remained undrawn long after darkness had finally fallen.

A combination of guilt at his late arrival and a desire to pick up any piece of useful information kept Harrison at the reception until the end. Forcing himself, he'd begun circulating among the other guests as soon as Brandon rejoined his wife. First he mended fences with the wing commander, complimenting him on the efficacy of the funeral arrangements and the excellent state of the church fabric. With the now-appeased churchwarden as escort, he then penetrated the groups of locals, ingratiating himself by commiserating with them over the annual amount the parish was expected to pay into central Church funds, as well as with the apparent difficulty of finding an able-bodied young man willing to take over the duties of village sexton. Unsurprisingly, from here talk moved naturally to the deficiencies of modern youth—from which, with only the faintest of promptings, Harrison was able to steer conversation round to the subject of Jonathan's relationship with his father.

Strangely enough, nobody seemed to have much definite information on the subject. Throughout his schooldays, the boy had boarded at Canterbury, and so, like many parsons' sons, hadn't been known well in the parish at all. Though obviously deeply attached to his mother, Jonathan's relationship with his father had seemed close enough during his childhood. In those days, he'd been a well-mannered, rather serious boy—though a bit of a dreamy loner even then. Since leaving university and taking up his disreputable life in London, understandably Lambkin had generally avoided the subject of his son, and though Jonathan had continued to visit him occasionally, this presumably had been, in the wing commander's words, 'merely for what further dosh he could squeeze from his old man.'

With Mrs Gittings present, naturally the anonymous notes were not alluded to—nor, unsurprisingly, was the slightest hint dropped of any questionable relationship between the late rector and any female parishioner. Finally, with the tea party beginning to break up, Harrison returned to the sanctuary of the fireplace. There he was joined by Ingrams and, with their backs to the glowing coals, they watched the guests taking their farewells of Miss Lambkin. Again it was an imperial scene: the withered little figure in black graciously shaking hands in turn with each of the head-bowed local chieftains who had recently risen up and striven against her in vain.

'Yes, indeed,' remarked Ingrams, drawing out his pipe from his cassock pocket, 'our hostess remains a formidable lioness.'

'Quite.'

'Nevertheless, my dear fellow,' continued the dean with a sympathetic smile, 'I'm sorry that you yourself should have come in for a bit of a mauling earlier. Having to answer for the Fromes' future was rather hard on you, I thought.'

'No, not at all,' answered Harrison. 'It's right and proper that she should be concerned for the wellbeing of loyal and faithful family retainers. Trouble is,' he added, gloomily, 'this policy of selling off grace-and-favour dwellings severely limits my freedom of action.'

With a troubled expression, Ingrams drew out a penknife and began scraping out the bowl of his pipe into the fire. 'Still,' he said, brightening, 'from past experience, now that you've taken the matter under your capable wing, I'm confident that a perfect solution will emerge.'

Before Harrison could reply, he heard his wife's voice, and, turning, found that she'd wheeled herself over, accompanied by Margaret and the twins. 'Richard,' she said, 'I feel it's time we were leaving. Miss Lambkin is obviously worn out.'

'And we should be doing the same, Matthew,' added Margaret Ingrams. 'Christabel has a long journey home ahead of her tomorrow.'

'Yes, of course.'

The dean led the group across to where the old woman now sat alone, head slumped, her eyes closed.

'Ah, Matthew!' She blinked up as Ingrams gently touched her arm. 'You're about to leave, are you? You, Margaret and the girls have all been such a wonderful support.' Benignly, she slowly looked from face to face until her gaze fell on Harrison. 'Oh, good, there you are, Colonel!' she exclaimed, seeming to shake off her drowsiness at once. 'I was hoping for another word. Could you and your wife possibly spare me a few moments for a private talk?'

'Certainly,' answered Harrison, considerably taken aback. 'Only too delighted.'

'Right,' intruded Ingrams, 'in that case, we will say good-night. But remember, I shall be returning, tomorrow morning to run you to the station. In the meantime,' he added smiling at Harrison, 'I leave you in the very safest of hands.'

In the lamplight, with the windows pitch-black behind her, the old woman sat, hands on lap, head slumped, while out in the hall the murmur of voices continued. Harrison, who had drawn up a chair, looked round at Winnie, and for a moment husband and wife exchanged questioning glances.

Envying the leavers and profoundly wishing that he'd slipped away earlier himself, Harrison turned back to stare at the carpet, hearing Mavis call out a final farewell from the front door. Only when the housekeeper's footsteps had died away did Miss Lambkin look up. 'I understand, Colonel,' she said, 'that you were among the first to come across the bodies.'

Harrison was momentarily lost for words. Until then he'd been certain that it was the Fromes' accommodation that was to be discussed, and he'd spent the last few minutes racking his brain for that perfect solution the dean had so confidently predicted. 'Yes,' he answered stiffly, 'unfortunately I was—I happened to be visiting the parish as part of my official duties.'

'So tell me,' continued Miss Lambkin, eyeing him narrowly, 'from what you observed, were you entirely satisfied with the outcome of the inquest?'

If the first question had shaken Harrison, the second surprised him more. Disconcerted, he stared back at the wizened, sharp features before him, seeing the same earnestness there as he'd observed in Tubman's face when the old schoolmaster had asked a similar question. His first thought was to give the same answer he'd given Tubman, but a warning look from Winnie checked him. 'I think,' he said guardedly, 'given the evidence presented, the jury had no alternative but to bring in the verdicts they did.'

It was evidently the correct answer, for the old woman smiled. 'A very diplomatic reply, Colonel. I begin to see why Matthew sets such store by your judgement.'

'Really, the dean is too kind,' he murmured, looking down.

'You both realize,' said Miss Lambkin, 'that I haven't the slightest faith in that verdict. I believe Jonathan to have been entirely innocent of his father's death. It's for that reason alone that I had him buried with his parents.'

Harrison stared at the speaker. Until that moment he'd assumed that the old woman's insistence on the double burial had been prompted solely by Christian charity—that the dual funeral service, like the symbolic throwing down of the trowelful of earth, had represented nothing beyond a commendable forgiveness for a deeply unhappy, gravely disturbed young man.

As if reading his thoughts, Miss Lambkin resumed. 'I am not a sentimental person. I don't come of sentimental stock. My forbears and I have lived by a law that says that those guilty of the shedding of blood shall not pollute hallowed ground.'

The ensuing silence was broken by Winnie. 'Miss Lambkin,' she said gently, 'what is it that makes you believe that Jonathan didn't kill his father?'

'Because he wasn't stupid,' came the blunt answer. 'The assertions in those vile notes were so patently absurd that Jonathan wouldn't have believed them for a moment.'

'I agree that Jonathan was always an exceptionally able boy,' replied Winnie gently. 'Sadly, however, he underwent some mental crisis while at university, and, by all accounts, was never the same afterwards.' She paused. 'We surely can't expect a mentally disturbed person to think logically, so perhaps we shouldn't be completely surprised, given how close he'd always been to his mother, that he reacted so terribly to those vile assertions in the notes.'

Miss Lambkin faced Winnie directly. 'I talked with Jonathan here in this very room after his mother's funeral, Mrs Harrison. I know what was said about him in the papers—that he'd been sponging off social security and been in trouble with the police—but the young man who spoke to me that day and who stood at the graveside supporting his father was neither mad nor a weakling; if anything, the contrary.' Breaking off, she turned back to Harrison. 'And so, Colonel, I ask you again: as a practical, ex-military man, is there not some method by which another hand could have killed Jonathan and his father?'

Again Harrison thought of the rusted widow frames, the

bolted front door, the chain on the back door, and the bunch of keys lying beside Jonathan's toppled chair. Finally, taking a deep breath, he said slowly, 'I do not say that it couldn't have been done; I merely say that I can't see how.' He paused, then added, 'Also, I can't see why it should have been done. What motive would there have been? I understand from the dean that, apart from a few hundred pounds to the Fromes, whatever little property your nephew was possessed of passes entirely to you.'

Miss Lambkin bit her lip and looked down. 'You're quite right, Colonel,' she said after a pause. 'I'm obviously deluding myself, partly out of guilt perhaps. Looking back now,' she added, raising her head, 'I know my sister and I should have been more generous in every way to Maurice and his wife.'

'No, no,' interposed Winnie. 'You really mustn't blame yourself.'

'Oh, but I do, Mrs Harrison! I do! And I always shall!' Anguish momentarily contorted the old woman's face. 'I never visited Maurice once in all these years until Bridget's funeral back in the spring. Now I can't rid myself of the feeling that, if only my late sister and I had shown that couple just a modicum of Christian charity, this whole thing would never have happened: that somehow, the terrible occurrence in the cottage that night had its seeds in our own bigotry and narrow-mindedness.'

Pained, Winnie looked down at her lap. Feeling equally uncomfortable, Harrison cleared his throat. 'I wonder,' he murmured, 'if there is anything practical I might do to help.'

'How kind!' Recovering her poise, Miss Lambkin smiled. 'But really, I don't think there's anything. Matthew has generously agreed to arrange everything.' She paused and shook her head. 'No, Colonel, the only thing I would request of you is to arrange alternative accommodation for the Fromes. They've been so kind to me during both my short stays here.' She paused. 'I suppose you haven't yet managed to think of anything in the locality suitable for them?'

For a moment Harrison didn't answer, but then he nodded. 'Yes,' he said, speaking slowly and with great deliberation, 'as I've been sitting here, I think I may have at last hit upon the solution to that particular problem—though,' he added with a grimace, 'it's one that will inevitably, I fear, entail a degree of fluttering within certain of our ecclesiastical dovecots.'

CHAPTER EIGHT

'Confound the archdeacon!'

The vehemence with which the phrase was uttered was reinforced by the speaker thumping his magnifying-glass down and twisting round in his seat to face his tormentor. She, however, apparently oblivious of the outburst she'd evoked, remained, head bowed, placidly reading under the light of the standard lamp.

Indignantly, Harrison glared across the sitting-room at his wife. It was typical of her, he thought, having finally goaded him to respond, now to sit and continue with her book exactly as if she hadn't said a word. For a moment, he made as if to say something, but then, changing his mind, turned back to the dusty, grey bundle of papers on the bureau before him. Taking up his magnifying-glass again, he bent forward and recommenced squinting at the faded brown ink, his brow puckering as he attempted to decipher the long-dead law-writer's spidery hand and the obscure eighteenth-century abbreviations.

'Yes, that's all very well,' intruded Winnie's voice, 'but you realize that it's not just Dr Cawthorne's feelings that are involved? What you propose runs entirely counter to diocesan policy.'

This time it was Harrison who didn't answer; glass in hand, he remained bowed over the documents he'd rushed to collect from his office the moment they'd got back from Fordington. Nevertheless, not another legal phrase or a word entered his brain as the calm, reasonable voice behind him continued remorselessly. 'Of course, I agree: renting Hannah Bright's cottage to the Fromes would seem an ideal solution. I merely point out that the application to have the trust wound up has now gone through, and that the Charity Commissioners have accepted it. Therefore I repeat what I said before, if you try to get their decision reversed at this stage, all you'll do is end up making yourself highly unpopular with a great number of people, especially the archdeacon.'

Resisting the impulse to burst out with exactly the same sentiment on that particular personage as before, and thus potentially keeping the dialogue continuing in circles indefinitely, Harrison clenched his teeth and continued staring blindly down at the papers. What Winnie was saying about making himself unpopular was true; indeed, it was so blatantly obvious that it was galling to hear it spelled out. Added to that, he found it particularly irritating to hear Winnie of all people raising objections, no matter how reasonable. She, after all, detested Cawthorne's rationalization programme, and had always made it abundantly clear that she disapproved entirely of his having any part in the selling-off of what had originally been donated in perpetuity for the relief of the poor and the needy.

'Well, darling? Aren't I right?'

Taking a deep breath, Harrison turned to face her. 'No, you are not, as it happens,' he answered coldly. 'At least, not entirely so. You forget that the Charity Commissioners' decision was only provisional. They still have to make a final ruling. If for any reason they should fail to do so, there's no possible way the cottage sale can go ahead, however distressing that personally may be to our archdeacon!'

'Yes, but that's only a formality, surely,' answered Winnie. 'The Commissioners are bound to accede to the diocese's application. After all,' she added acidly, returning to her book, 'they have the affidavit you pressurized Maurice into signing, declaring that there were no suitably qualified tenants requiring the use of the cottage.'

'That,' burst out her husband, 'as I've already said, was before we had George and Mavis Frome needing a home. Now the position is completely changed. From what I can make out from these,' he said, turning to the deeds and tapping them for emphasis, 'as "faithful, communicating members and servants of the Established Church" and as "longtime residents of the parish", the Fromes are fully qualified beneficiaries under the original terms of the trust. As such,' he continued, his voice rising, 'whatever Cawthorne and the entire bench of bishops should wish, the Fromes are legally entitled to the use of the cottage for the rest of their natural lives at the originally stipulated rent!'

After the day's exertions and the long drive back to Canterbury beside a decidedly uncommunicative husband, Winnie was feeling quite worn out. Once supper was over, she'd thankfully retreated back into *Middlemarch*. Being forced to endure a succession of sighs, grunts and groans emanating from the corner of the room as she'd tried to read, until now she'd been in a mood only to listen with half an ear to what had been said regarding the cottage, preferring the lucidly explained dilemmas and problems of the inhabitants of George Eliot's fictional town to the impatient and slightly incoherent answers to the queries she'd raised. Now, however, finally understanding the position, a smile lit her face. 'You mean the decision to wind up the trust could be legally challenged? But, Richard, that's absolutely wonderful! What a clever old stick you are!' She paused in sudden doubt. 'But, darling, do you really think it's possible to have the Commissioners' decision reversed at this stage?'

'Very possible,' grunted her husband, rising stiffly to his feet and going over to the window. 'That's if, of course,' he resumed, peering between the curtains, 'someone concerned with the sale should happen to raise an official objection.'

Something in his tone checked Winnie's joy. Confused, she swivelled the wheelchair round and looked across at his back with an expression of concern. 'You don't mean yourself, do you?' Pausing for an answer, but receiving none, she burst out in alarm, 'Richard, you're not actually saying you're prepared to go over the archdeacon's head yourself, are you?' She paused again for an answer, and again receiving none, cried out passionately, 'But, darling, you couldn't possibly! Not as a senior diocesan official! It would be the end of your Church career! Even if you succeeded in getting the Charity Commissioners to change their ruling, you'd still be forced to resign.'

'I've no choice, damn it!' came the bitter retort from the figure at the window. 'You heard me back there in the rectory: I've given Miss Lambkin my word.'

Across the yard in front of him, a single light glowed upstairs in Tubman's cottage; above and behind loomed the inky black shape of the cathedral, a dark, massive, brooding presence, rearing against the stars—in Harrison's eyes, a representation in physical form of the mighty institution he served, and against which he was now committed to pit himself as a sort of unwilling David confronting a beloved Goliath. 'Anyway,' he added without great conviction, gazing up at the huge edifice, 'it's worth it, I suppose. The Fromes are decent sort of folk, and, God knows, if anyone deserves that cottage, it's surely them.'

'I know,' cried Winnie, laying aside her book and wheeling herself forward, 'but if it means you losing your job! What will we do?'

Her husband shrugged and turned to face her. 'I've still got my army pension,' he answered. 'Doubtless we'll scrape by.'

'What, with you taking up jobbing gardening, I suppose!' Fear had brought a sharpness to Winnie's tongue, and there was a passionate intensity in her eyes as she addressed him. 'Come on, Richard! Be realistic, for goodness sake! Where would we live? This house comes with your job, and no one, I promise you, is going to find us a pretty little cottage to live in for a peppercorn rent!'

Harrison didn't answer. That very same thought had been tormenting him ever since making his rash promise to Christabel Lambkin and it had nagged at him throughout the entire journey back to Canterbury. Indeed, it had been that which had set him burrowing through the musty trust deeds in the hope that his memory of the details had been wrong, and that the Fromes had no legal claim on the cottage after all.

'Isn't there another way, darling? Couldn't someone beside you make the appeal?'

'I'm afraid not,' said Harrison, shaking his head. 'It has to be someone officially or immediately concerned. There isn't anyone else but me.'

'But there is, surely!' cried Winnie. 'What about the church-wardens, for instance? Couldn't they write to the Charity Commissioners and withdraw the affidavit, explaining that circumstances have changed since they and Maurice signed it?'

'Yes, of course. But why should they?' answered Harrison wearily. 'After two hundred years, the original trust fund doesn't go half the way towards the cost of maintaining that wretched cottage. Getting rid of it means getting rid of an endless drain on parish resources. Also, as you know, according to the agreement I made with Lambkin, a portion of the sale price will go towards the refurbishment of the village hall. Do you think either Wing Commander Sparrow or that dreadful Brandon woman would be willing to lose such a deal for the sake of a couple of old fogies like the Fromes?' Pausing, he shook his head sadly. 'No, my dear—this, I fear, is a classic case of being hoist with one's own petard.'

There was a brief moment of silence, then Winnie's eyes lit up. 'What about the Fromes themselves, then? They're directly involved! Couldn't they appeal to the Commissioners?'

Hope momentarily rose in Harrison's face, but as quickly as it had come, it vanished. 'Yes,' he said, 'but how can they? They're simple, uneducated people. They've no more knowledge of their rights under the terms of the Bright Trust than those under the Magna Carta. Anyway,' he added despondently, 'even if they did, they wouldn't have the faintest idea of how to go about trying to obtain them.'

'Yes, but couldn't you tell them? Show them how? You could do it quietly, without anyone knowing.'

Harrison's countenance darkened. 'Good God, woman! What are you saying? You mean, go behind the Church's back and start creeping round among the laity like some *agent provocateur*!'

'Yes,' answered Winnie emphatically, 'if that means you can secure the cottage for a married couple who need and deserve it, whilst at the same time remaining in a position to go on having a constraining check on Dr Cawthorne's policies—to say nothing of us being able to stay on in this house.'

'But it would mean my pretending one thing and doing another.'

Winnie looked at him steadily. 'Isn't that exactly what you've been doing most of your life? Duplicity, I thought,' she added bitterly, 'was your special area of expertise!'

Harrison winced, but made no answer. What she'd said was true: it was, God help him, exactly how he'd spent most of his adult life, and, in a sense, it described accurately what he'd been doing since the archbishop had seen fit to appoint Cawthorne archdeacon: pretending support for his cutbacks, whilst at the same time applying the brakes to their implementation and generally back-peddling as fast as he was able.

'I'm sorry, darling! Forgive me!' Wheeling forward, Winnie took his hand and looked earnestly up into his face. 'I'm just tired and a bit frightened, that's all: I don't want to lose our home and our life here.' She squeezed his hand and pressed it against her cheek. 'I know what you do is always for the best, but honestly, dear, you've got to protect yourself. And anyway,' she added, smiling up through a glaze of tears, 'what can be so wrong in simply informing people of their rights, especially if, by doing so, you can put a roof over their heads whilst keeping the one we've got above ours?'

Across the silent precincts Great Dunstan struck the hour, two dull, heavy booms of the bell reverberating and fading among the labyrinth of walls and passageways. At the first stroke, Harrison opened his eyes. At the second, with a despairing sigh, he rolled over on to his back and began scratching furiously at his left shoulder. Since the horrific discovery in the mission hall, it had been so often the same: after the long-established routines of bedtime had been religiously gone through, he'd turn off the light and slip into sleep as naturally as a child—only to wake a couple of hours later, hot, sticky with sweat and itching from head to foot, as if, instead of flannel pyjamas, he'd inadvertently slipped on the very nightshirt of Nessus.

With Winnie's even breathing at his ear, the recollections of the previous day began coming back in succession: the two coffins lying side by side before the chancel step; Sparrow's scandalized expression across the open grave; the faces turning at his late appearance in the rectory drawing-room—and then, finally, standing before the entire company, blurting out that rash and quite unnecessary promise to resettle the Fromes.

At the memory, Harrison scratched even harder at his shoulder, cursing himself again for having ventured anywhere near Fordington. What in hell's name, he wondered, had impelled him to exchange the comfortable security of his office for the dangers and uncertainties of direct diocesan involvement? Winnie could have travelled over with Ingrams and his family to represent them both at the funeral. If only she'd done so, and he'd remained at his desk, he might well have been quietly sleeping now, future secure, instead of this: lying like the doomed Faustus as he'd seen him depicted in the play, writhing in horror on that ingeniously contrived sofa as he'd waited for the midnight hour to strike.

The thought of clocks and the passing of time reminded him that the vicarage committee was meeting at nine in the morning. Among other things, the future of Fordington Rectory was due to be discussed. Therefore the subject of the Fromes' continuing occupation of the stable block was bound to arise. What was he to do? Sit calmly writing up the minutes as if the couple's future was no business of his? Or was he to make a clean breast of it: announce that he'd taken it upon himself to see the Lambkins' servants rehoused, and that, consequently, he'd be aiding and abetting them in contesting the application to the Charity Commissioners that he himself had originally signed?

Either way seemed unthinkable: silence dishonourable, a traitor's act, while confession would inevitably lead to a call for his resignation and the subsequent loss of his home. In the latter eventuality, what would then happen to Winnie and himself? His thoughts were much as they'd been when he'd sat with Helen Middlebrook outside the cottage, considering the likely possibilities of what had then seemed his still comparatively far-away retirement. They had no money to buy anywhere of their own. At best, it meant a set of shabby rented rooms, or, more likely, a council flat—though perhaps even that sanctuary might be denied if it was ruled that, by openly opposing his employer's agreed policy, he'd intentionally made himself homeless.

'Richard, whatever's the matter?' came the sleepy, irritated voice at his side. 'What are you writhing around for?'

'Sorry, just feeling a little thirsty, that's all. I think I might fetch myself a glass of water.'

Before Winnie could object, he was out of bed and groping for his dressing-gown. Pulling it on, he went out into the hall, and, having collected a tumbler from the kitchen, went into the sitting room to pour himself a large whisky. This he drained off at a gulp, shuddering and grimacing at the taste, wondering, as so often in the past, how the sweet nectar of midnight invariably transformed into the bitter vinegar of sleepless dawn. Determined, however, to numb his mind, he recharged his glass, and then, with it in one hand and the bottle in the other, went over to the still open bureau.

Bound together with what once had been bright red ribbon, but now had long since faded to a grubby pinkish brown, the ragged bundle of deeds lay folded where he'd left them, the heavily discoloured outer sheet jotted over and defaced by generations of lawyers' clerks. Whether from his dreadful associations with the building they represented or from his present dilemma, the grimy, corpse-grey heap of old parchment seemed to reek of death and decay, and as he stood gazing down at it, he was struck by the fanciful notion that something of the original trust founder's vengeful spirit somehow still lived and bred like bacteria between the musty sheets, having power even now, after two centuries, to doom and ruin the lives of all who had anything to do with that charmingly situated, exquisitely proportioned, yet essentially shoddily constructed cottage.

Slumping down on the chair before the papers, he sipped his whisky, thinking of the woman who had gone to all the trouble and expense of originally building the place. What had she been like, the long-dead Hannah Bright? Some sort of whitebonneted version of Miss Havisham, a Jane Austen run mad? He imagined her brooding and plotting the blight of her ex-fiancé's life behind drawn curtains with the help of some bewigged clever lawyer, contriving between them to cloak vengeance and hatred in the shining white robes of Christian philanthropy.

'Clever! Clever!' he murmured aloud, as if seeing before him the woman's triumphant smile. As he did so, his thoughts skipped the years, moving from the dead Hannah Bright to the still-living writer of the poison-pen notes. What similarly vindictive, sick-souled sort of person could he or she be, he wondered? Once again, he found himself straining to think of what imagined slight or insane jealousy could have prompted that equally subtly devised, but far more directly terrible, revenge. Even without Dickens's help, there were plenty of precedents for the likes of Hannah Bright; but what sort of unfathomable monster was the person who'd contrived the destruction of a harmless country parson, cutting out and pasting on those letters and words to inflame his unstable son into bringing down himself and his father in an orgy of blood and ruin?

Recharging his glass, he took another deep gulp of the whisky, then, leaning back in the chair, closed his eyes. Doing so, the photograph on the rectory mantelpiece returned to his mind: the small boy pressed against his mother's side; the earnest, weary-looking cleric seated next to them.

Whether through the effects of alcohol or general fatigue, there dawned on him the realization of what, until then, he'd only obscurely sensed: his deeply felt, continuing obligation to the man that he'd been entrusted by Ingrams to protect. It accounted for his continuing restlessness and his broken sleep-pattern since that morning when he'd stood gazing in at the two shattered bodies, knowing his mission had failed. It was also presumably why, against his better judgement, he'd felt the need to attend the funeral and the reception afterwards, and also why he'd accepted Dowley's request to help in the hunt for the anonymous letter-writer. Above all, it explained why he, normally so cautious and circumspect, should have risked his entire future and reputation by making Miss Lambkin that rash, unguarded promise to obtain the Bright Cottage for the use of the dead man's servants.

At this realization, his spirits rose. What until then he'd seen as perversity in himself, he now saw as honourable necessity. Therefore it perhaps followed that what Winnie had suggested was, after all, not only expedient, but also right: that just as it was his duty to continue moderating and delaying the worst excesses of Cawthorne's schemes by clandestine means, so equally it was secretly to help the Fromes obtain their rights. Another happy thought struck him: if he was to aid the verger and his wife, it meant that he'd have the opportunity of finding out from them any theory they had as to who had sent the notes. Obviously they'd been questioned by the police already, but with their seeing him as their benefactor, there was every chance of squeezing out of them any useful little titbit of information they'd either knowingly or unwittingly held back.

Doubly certain now as to his duty, he picked up his glass and bottle and rose rather unsteadily to his feet. Going to the window, he gazed out between the curtains. Clouds had gathered since he'd gone to bed, obscuring the stars. Above the unlit yard, the cathedral rose as dark and massive as before. No longer, however, did it seem the stern Goliath of the evening; it was now the reassuring sentinel of night, mother church of a benign and tolerant institution, sheltering every shade of opinion and belief, and generally steering a broad middle passage towards ultimate truth. Its way, Harrison determined, would be his. Both to serve the diocese, and also to fulfil his obligations to Lambkin and the dean, he would temporize, equivocate, remain silent where necessary, fudge when forced to—generally hide his light under a bushel and not allow his right hand to know what his left did.

Content, his course now clear before him, he went to pour himself a final drink. To his surprise, he found the bottle empty.

He blinked down at it for a moment then, raising his glass, swallowed the few remaining amber drops. Having done so, taking glass and bottle with him, and picking up the copy of the day's newspaper from the arm of the sofa as he passed, he went out to the kitchen to hide the evidence of his late-hour contemplations.

CHAPTER NINE

'Darling, do you really think you've got time for another cup? It's getting very late.'

Beyond a noncommittal grunt, Winnie received no reply. Frowning, she watched her husband pour the tepid remains of the coffee pot into his cup. Protracted as his breakfast had been, she'd observed it had been an almost entirely liquid affair, comprising one glass of fresh orange juice and two cups of black coffee, balanced by a single half-slice of dry toast. Having noticed a discarded screw-top left on the sitting-room table, she'd already ascertained that the whisky bottle had disappeared from the drinks cabinet during the night, and was quite certain that it now lay empty in the kitchen waste-bin, concealed beneath the suspiciously stuffed-in copy of yesterday's *Times*. She, therefore, perfectly understood the cause of his present abstinence, just as she knew both the reason for his restlessness in bed and subsequent nocturnal drinking spree. What she didn't know, however, and what she'd have dearly loved to find out, was what he'd finally decided regarding the Fromes' claim on the cottage. She nevertheless refrained from inquiring, for there was that about his face and general demeanour that morning that warned her that the bow was not only bent, but drawn almost to snapping, and that it was advisable at present to keep well clear of the shaft. Deciding to postpone any probing until lunchtime, she limited her present efforts to getting him off to his meeting on time.

'Isn't that the quarter-to bell now?'

For Harrison, breakfast had been pure torture; yet, if he could, he'd gladly have extended it indefinitely. He had an abominable headache, his throat was dry and he felt utterly exhausted. Far worse, however, was to find that all his certainty and resolve of the early hours had evaporated now that he was only minutes away from taking his place on the vicarage committee. The knowledge that he, a trusted senior official, was secretly planning to prevent the sale of a redundant and ruinously expensive trust property was bad enough, but a terrible new thought had now entered his mind: by urging the Fromes to obtain their rights by law, he would surely be encouraging others to do the same, and if every possible claimant began appealing to ancient laws and statutes for their rights, the result could be financially ruinous, not only for the diocese, but for the entire Church.

'Richard, you'll have to go! It isn't fair to keep the rest of the committee waiting.'

If Winnie had mentioned Cawthorne (which she was careful to avoid doing), he might well have sat longer, sipping the bitter dregs until the last drop. As it was, he merely nodded, rose to his feet and, bending, gave her his customary parting kiss on the cheek. A minute or two later he had left the house, umbrella in one hand, briefcase in the other, and was striding away across the Bread Yard cobbles under a sky as unmitigatedly gloomy and grey as his mood.

❊ ❊ ❊

'Good morning, Colonel. May I take your things?'

If anything, the attendant's respectful greeting served only to deepen the new arrival's sense of unease. Still panting slightly from his brisk walk round the north side of the cathedral, he slipped off his coat and passed it over. Doing so, he glanced round the hallway, the overpowering smell of fresh paint and polish reminding him unpleasantly of schooldays and his invariable feelings of dread when arriving back at the start of yet another academic year.

The venue for the meeting was new, one of the elegant terrace of large, eighteenth-century houses standing along one side of the triangular open space behind the main entrance of the precincts, having Christ Church Gatehouse at its apex and the west end of the cathedral as its base. Built, like its companions, as a home for senior residential canons, it alone had tenaciously clung to its original purpose while each of its neighbours in turn, as if contaminated by the commercial breezes wafting in from the Buttermarket, had sunk in social station, becoming either gift shops, tea-rooms or offices for various local architects, accountants and lawyers. Now, with its long-time incumbent forced by age and infirmity to move into the Weavers' Home for the Elderly, it too had finally succumbed to the spirit of the age, having been recently stripped out and refurbished as a diocesan conference centre under the name of 'Seminar House'.

'If you'd like to go upstairs, sir. Your meeting's in Room Six—just follow the red arrows along the second-floor landing.'

Beneath the benign gaze of various of the present archbishop's predecessors, Harrison ascended the highly polished stairs, following the small plastic arrows as directed. Outside the door of the designated room, he paused briefly to check his watch before entering just as the first heavy boom of the Dunstan bell echoed dully across the dew-sodden lawns outside.

'Ah, our good colonel! Exactly on time as ever!'

Young Michael Cawthorne, as the dean habitually referred to him, sat framed against the window at the further end of a long light oak table, with the committee members, clerical and lay, ranged either side before him. Dressed informally in black turtle-necked sweater, sleeves drawn back to the elbow, he leaned negligently back in his chair, one knee cupped in his hands, appearing if anything more youthful and unlike a senior Church dignitary than ever to the new arrival.

'Good morning, Archdeacon—ladies and gentlemen.'

Harrison took his customary place opposite Cawthorne at the end of the table, and, having drawn the minutes book from his briefcase, spread it open before him. Helen Middlebrook was sitting on the committee for the first time, and as their eyes met, she smiled. Since their dreadful shared experience in Wetmarsh Marden, he'd felt a comradely bond between them, and her friendly smile now came as one bright ray of sunshine piercing the gloom of the heavily overcast day.

'So,' began Cawthorne briskly, leaning forward to consult his notes, 'to begin with Chillenden Vicarage.' He looked down the table. 'Perhaps you, Helen, as our newest member, might care to kick off. Let's have your estimate of the likely cost of modernization.'

As the architect's tones filled the bare-walled chamber, Harrison's pen began busily scratching across the pages of the minutes book. From beneath the window came a gradually increasing sound of voices as the usual daily quota of visitors began flocking through the medieval gateway. Across the precincts, first the quarter then the half-hour rang out while the talk of roof-tiling, dampcourse and drainage, property prices and valuers' estimates continued as the futures of some half-dozen clerical residences were variously discussed and decided upon.

Just as informality of dress disguised his essentially authoritarian nature, so the archdeacon's cheerful, smiling demeanour hid an inflexible will, and, having obviously decided in advance exactly the time to be allocated each item, he handled the meeting with the same remorseless efficiency as he managed the diocese generally, breaking in on the most earnest of discussions to brightly announce 'Time's up', and then immediately to call for a vote. This concluded, he'd briskly move on to other business, as apparently impervious to the doubts of the waverers as the hostility of his critics.

'Right, that's agreed then: Reverend Arthur and his wife will move into the semi-detached on the Merryfield Estate, thus carrying the Church to the heart of the community while helping to husband diocesan resources.' Triumphantly, the speaker ticked off the latest item on his list, then leaned back in his chair. 'So', he said, 'we come finally to the question of Fordington Rectory.'

Harrison gripped his pen hard and stared fixedly down at the minutes book while the voice continued. 'I informed you at the last meeting, as part of our ongoing rationalization programme, St Philip's should temporarily come under the wing of one of the local clergy teams. Whether or not the parish ever gets its own incumbent again, the present rectory is obviously far too large for modern needs, and should therefore be sold off as soon as practically possible.'

There was a general murmur of assent.

'As the late rector leaves no widow, there is no difficulty about vacancy. As soon as the house is cleared, the sale can proceed.' Pausing, Cawthorne placed his fingers together and smiled round the table. 'And here, I'm afraid, we come to a slightly delicate matter. As some of you may know, Dean Ingrams was an old friend of Maurice Lambkin. As such, he is named chief executor and will be personally arranging the house clearance.' Once again a smile flitted across the cleric's wide mouth. 'Beloved and indispensable as our dear dean is, he is, shall we say, not exactly at his happiest when dealing with practical affairs. I wonder, therefore,' he continued, looking down the table at Harrison, 'if you, Richard, being a close friend, could perhaps oversee whatever arrangements he makes whilst at the same time giving him any advice he might need.'

Cold fury ran through Harrison at the patronizing reference to Ingrams, and the man's presumptuous gall in making such a request. Icily, he returned Cawthorne's gaze, hardening his heart against him and all his works, determining then and there that, whatever the cost or risk to the diocese or to himself personally, he'd see justice done for the Fromes.

'I shall, Archdeacon, always be pleased to give the dean help or advice at any time he might ask for it.'

Neither his tone nor the implied rebuke appeared to register with Cawthorne in the slightest. Smiling, he merely replied, 'Ah, good! I was certain that we could depend on you. And that only leaves us with one other small matter to settle.' Pausing, he surveyed the faces before him. 'It appears that Maurice Lambkin engaged the services of a pair of live-in servants to run the house during his late wife's long illness. They were apparently allowed the use of the converted stables as their home. I've already taken legal advice, and there is no question of their having any claim whatever on the diocese. They will, therefore, be asked to leave the property within a stipulated time.'

'What will happen to them?'

It was Helen Middlebrook who asked the question, and from the expressions of those round the table, it was plain that her concern was shared by the majority present. Cawthorne smiled at her indulgently. 'Happily,' he said, 'that appears to be no problem. I rang the dean after his return from the funeral yesterday. It seems that our own Colonel Harrison here has already stepped into that particular breach.' Beaming, he turned towards Harrison. 'Is that correct, Richard? You have personally agreed to arrange alternative accommodation for the Fromes?'

If Harrison's heart had been ice a few moments before, now it was water: the one thing he hadn't bargained for was that Ingrams might have informed Cawthorne of his publicly stated undertaking to rehouse the Fromes. Now, remembering that Ingrams had arranged to go over to Fordington that morning to take Miss Lambkin to the station, he had a sudden terrible fear that, despite her promise, the old woman might inadvertently let slip his intentions regarding Bright Cottage.

Conscious of the faces looking round, some with surprise, others, including Helen Middlebrook's, with open admiration, he cleared his throat. 'Yes, it's true that I have promised to do what I can to help them.'

'And very noble and generous of you, I'm sure.' Cawthorne's teeth flashed. 'But you understand, that is entirely a private matter between yourself and the individuals concerned. There is no question of any official diocesan involvement.'

'Of course not.'

'And though I'm sure the couple in question are, as the dean assures me, the very salt of the earth, I nevertheless feel that the interests of the diocese demand that the matter be dealt with formally. I, therefore, propose that notice to quit is served, giving them a generous two months in which to vacate the rectory grounds.'

The speaker glanced round the table, receiving somewhat reluctant nods and murmurs of assent to his proposal. 'Right,' he continued, turning again to Harrison, 'in that case, Richard, I wonder if I might prevail on you further: perhaps you'll arrange for the necessary legal instrument to be drawn up and served.' He paused and considered. 'It's Friday today, so shall we say that the process should be completed by Tuesday at the latest?'

'Certainly. I'll have the necessary documentation typed up this afternoon,' answered Harrison. He paused, then added, 'In fact, I shall make it my business to drive over to Fordington tomorrow morning and deliver the document in person.'

'Excellent! Just the little personal touch that's needed! After all,' added Cawthorne beaming, 'the last thing we want, in view of all the regrettable publicity surrounding the tragic events in that parish, is to upset the couple any more than we absolutely need to.'

The buzzer sounded on the desk. 'Yes, Mary?'

'Cave-Brown and Kent have just sent round an envelope for you, Colonel. Would you like it brought in?'

'Ah, good! I've been expecting it. Yes, bring it through at once, if you would.'

Harrison turned in his chair and looked towards the window. Bent over a series of survey reports as the short afternoon waned, he hadn't noticed until now that the rain, which had been threatening all day, had begun falling. He sat thoughtfully watching the waterdrops gathering on the panes, gleaming against the passageway lamplight as they swelled and ran like tears down the small diamond-shaped sections of glass.

Behind him, the door opened and his secretary entered, bearing a long white envelope.

'Thank you—if you wouldn't mind waiting for a moment.'

Taking the envelope, Harrison opened the unsealed flap, and, extracting the enclosed papers, began checking them through. Doing so, he was struck by the disquieting thought that, unless he was careful, a similar communiqué, couched in the same precise legal language, would soon be arriving for him, requiring Winnie and himself also to vacate their home by a certain hour of a certain day.

Separating the duplicate from the top copy, he handed the former to the waiting girl. 'Right, Mary, if you'd be good enough to file it under Fordington Rectory, please.'

'Would there be anything else this evening, Colonel?'

Harrison glanced at his watch and nodded. 'Yes, perhaps one little thing,' he said. 'You could ring and tell my wife that I'm leaving the office now, but warn her that I may be slightly delayed in getting home as there's a call I must make on my way.'

Outside, the rain was falling in a heavy drizzle. Pausing beneath the Selling Archway, Harrison opened his umbrella, then, stepping out into Green Court, he began following the gravel path round the edge of the lawn to where, through the teeming darkness, the lit windows of the deanery glowed before him.

It was Judith, the slightly taller of the twins, who answered the door with the family Siamese cat draped over one shoulder.

'Good evening, my dear. I was hoping for a short word with your father. Is he at home?'

The girl looked uncertain. 'I'm afraid Daddy's very busy, Colonel. Jane and I have been told we're not allowed to disturb him for any reason at all.'

'I see.'

Disconcerted, Harrison wondered what best to do. Normally, hearing Ingrams was at work, he would have hurriedly made his apologies and left. Now though, having rung the Fromes to inform them that he and Winnie would be visiting next morning, he needed to know what, if anything, had been said by Miss Lambkin regarding Bright Cottage. Luckily, as he stood there debating what to do, the girl's mother appeared in the hallway.

'Richard! I thought I heard your voice! Do come in out of the rain. You've come to see Matthew, I expect?'

'Yes, but I understand he's in purdah at present.'

'Don't worry,' said Margaret Ingrams, laughing. 'I think it's quite safe for you to enter. In fact,' she added, taking his umbrella, 'from the expression on his face when I popped my head round his door a few minutes ago, a visit from you is just what the poor lamb needs.'

The dean's study was everything that such a room should be: a true ecclesiastical den, complete with deep leather armchairs and a battered old horse-hair sofa. In this cluttered, musty-smelling sanctuary, Ingrams, temporarily escaping his more immediate responsibilities, could nestle down amidst a comforting welter of paper and books. With its shutters now closed and both bars of the electric fire glowing bright in the shaded lamplight, never had his old friend's retreat seemed more snug and inviting to Harrison as he peered through the smoke-layered dimness to where the dean sat, pipe in mouth, at the centrally positioned desk, a crammed wastepaper basket wedged between his knees.

'Ah, what a very pleasant surprise!' burst out the occupant at his appearance. 'Do come in, Richard, and close the door. Forgive me if I don't rise,' he said, waving his pipe over the piles of paper in front of him. 'You find me very much engaged in a cleansing of the Augean stables, I fear!'

Harrison surveyed the heaped confusion doubtfully. In many ways, Ingrams was the ideal dean: an amiable, good-natured scholar, whose gentle spirit and moderate views acted as a benediction on the lives of all within the precincts, soothing the occasional quarrel and generally quelling those outbursts of rancour and bad-feeling inevitable to any such community. In simple practical matters of administration, however, as Cawthorne had more than hinted, he was not exactly the most efficient of men. Splendid as God's coachman, sitting up on his box in his finery, encouraging his somewhat mismatched and unruly team with the maximum of diplomacy and minimum of whip; unfortunately, not nearly so impressive when down amidst the muck and straw of the stable yard.

'I take it,' said Harrison, bending to gather up the sheets that had slipped to the floor, 'that all this is to do with the Lambkin estate?'

'Exactly,' murmured Ingrams, peering at an old garage bill before crumpling it and stuffing it into his basket. 'All this was literally laid in my lap this morning. I'm now endeavouring to sort out what needs to be forwarded to Maurice's solicitors and what can be safely discarded.'

'Quite a task, I imagine.'

'Yes, indeed,' answered the dean heavily. 'As I say, positively Herculean.'

Harrison smiled sympathetically. 'I trust Miss Lambkin caught her train on time?'

'Oh yes, thank you—I saw her safely on her way.'

Relieved that no mention had been made of the cottage, Harrison felt nevertheless that he ought to probe a little further. Therefore, with studied casualness, he asked, 'And George and Mavis? How did you find them? I trust they're bearing up after the strains of yesterday.'

'The Fromes? Oh, they both seemed very well—certainly most heartened when I backed up Christabel's assurance that suitable alternative accommodation would be found for them.' Ingrams's smile broadened. 'As I told them, with you dealing with the matter personally, they're as good as home and dry already.'

'Let us hope so.' Safe in the knowledge that the old lady had kept the secret as promised, Harrison turned his attention back to the desk. 'Well,' he said, 'so what exactly is all this you're sorting through?'

'Maurice's personal papers and letters, including those that the police originally took away—and also some of poor Jonathan's.'

Harrison frowned. 'You're taking responsibility for his affairs also?'

'Someone has to,' answered Ingrams. 'He was my godson, after all, and, whatever his shortcomings, I was always very fond of the boy.' He paused, meditatively sucking his pipe, then shook his head. 'But I must say,' he added, 'I'm finding things rather different than I had envisaged.'

'Indeed?'

'Yes, surprisingly so,' murmured the dean, burrowing among the papers. 'Somewhere under here is a letter forwarded to Christabel by his solicitor as the only surviving family member.'

'Jonathan's solicitor?' said Harrison, taken aback; from everything he'd heard regarding the young man's lifestyle, it was hard to believe that he should have anything as respectable as a personal solicitor—unless, of course, it was some legal-aid lawyer who had befriended him after one of his numerous scrapes.

'It should be somewhere here,' continued Ingrams. 'Ah, yes! Here it is!' He drew a long envelope from the base of the pile, in appearance identical to the one now in Harrison's inner pocket. 'Here, take a look yourself,' he said, handing it over.

Harrison peered at it curiously, surprised to see the embossed inscription in the top left corner. Littlebone & Gibb of Gray's Inn was a small but highly respected firm of London solicitors, one that over the years had dealt with a number of delicate matters on the diocese's behalf. Putting on his spectacles, Harrison drew out the enclosure.

'Yes,' said Ingrams, catching his look of puzzlement as he read, 'it surprised me, too. As you see, there's quite a substantial sum in his bank account. I thought Jonathan was meant to be living off Social Security.'

'And this is equally unexpected,' added Harrison, glancing again at the text; 'it says here that the rent of his council flat has been paid for the next three months.' He turned to the dean. 'I'd gathered from you that he was living in some rather disreputable community of squatters.'

'Exactly,' answered his friend, nodding. 'That indeed was the impression I gained from his father.'

Harrison handed back the envelope and went over to the fireplace. He stood a few moments, apparently contemplating the array of objects on the mantelpiece, as if either the propped-up boomerang, the tubs of pencils and pipe-cleaners or the framed photograph of the twins in school uniform held the answer to the questions now rising in his mind.

'Dean,' he said, turning round, 'I take it it's true that Jonathan did fluff his exams, and that he came down from Cambridge without a degree.'

Ingrams shook his head. 'No, that isn't quite correct. He didn't fail his exams exactly: he simply never took them. Jonathan was awarded aegrotat.'

'Aegrotat?'

'A sort of honorary degree, given those who, for some good reason, usually of health, are unable to sit their final papers.'

Harrison frowned. On that foggy evening when he'd been disturbed from his work by Tubman's summoning call, he'd looked down from the window to see the ghostly figure of Mephistophilis emerge from Dark Entry—and had witnessed that figure, so eerily strange and ominous, suddenly transformed by the removal of the mask from the wearer's face. Now it was as if the letter from Littlebone & Gibb had done the same for Jonathan Lambkin: a veil had been partially lifted, and instead of the brooding, discontented failure, he'd glimpsed another Jonathan—the boy who had won both his godfather's and housemaster's affection, and the person who'd so impressed Miss Lambkin with his bearing at his mother's funeral.

'This aegrotat? Why was it awarded? Was it something to do with his mother's illness?'

'No,' said Ingrams. 'This was more than four years before Bridget died. According to his father, it was given because he was so hard hit by poor young Stephen Hardwick's tragic death.'

'Hardwick? Was that the boy who was at school with him here, the young fellow I met at your garden party—the chap who was going on to Sandhurst?'

'That's right. He and Jonathan were very close, almost like brothers. Stephen spent the majority of his holidays over in Fordington while his parents were stationed overseas.'

'And what happened to Hardwick? How did he come to die?'

'I'm not sure of the details,' Ingrams replied. 'Maurice said something about an accident during military training on Salisbury Plain. Alan Tubman would doubtless know; I seem to remember he went to the funeral and wrote an appreciative piece on him for the school magazine.'

Harrison went over to a window and, pulling back a shutter, stared out into the dark. He remained before the rain-splattered pane for a few moments before turning round. 'This is just an odd thought, Dean,' he said, 'and it may sound completely absurd, but do you think it possible that we, the police and everyone else have been wrong about those anonymous notes, and that they were never actually aimed at Lambkin himself, but were really sent to torment the boy?'

'Torment Jonathan? Good Lord! But why, for heaven's sake?'

'I don't know,' answered Harrison, 'but as nothing has been discovered indicating any close personal relationship between his father and Mrs Gittings or any other woman in the parish, there appears no reason on earth for anyone wishing to hurt or embarrass Lambkin himself. On the other hand, neither of us know what Jonathan was up to in London or where that money in his bank account came from. As it appears he'd been misleading his father and everyone else as to the sort of life he was leading, it seems more than likely that he was engaged in some nefarious business or other—possibly involving drugs.'

'Drugs?' Ingrams looked horrified. 'No! No!' he burst out, shaking his head. 'I refuse to believe it! Jonathan was an unhappy lost soul perhaps, but never a drug racketeer!'

Though hating to distress his old friend, Harrison shrugged. 'Who knows?' he said. 'Drugs could account for both his unorthodox appearance and lifestyle—and if he was involved in the criminal underworld in that or any other way, he might well have had enemies, and one of them, knowing how close he'd been to his mother, could possibly have composed those anonymous notes as a way of finally unbalancing him. In other words,' he added, 'we have to at least consider the possibility that Maurice Lambkin was never the real target at all, merely the innocent victim of a vicious plot against his unfortunate son.'

CHAPTER TEN

Splashing through puddles, the Volvo swung off the main road to halt before the white-painted metal gates. As it did so, the rain that had been falling steadily since it had left the outskirts of Canterbury suddenly redoubled its force, drumming torrentially down on the car roof. Unwilling to venture out until it eased, the driver turned off his wipers, and the two occupants sat silently looking ahead through the rapidly blearing windscreen.

Wavering and indistinct through the streaming glass, Fordington Rectory rose on the skyline before them, a shuttered dark shape at the top of the drive, its air of desolation reinforced by the bare, dripping branches of the trees that partly screened it from view. Two days before, the house had stood in bright sunshine, doors thrown open in welcome to the guests at Miss Lambkin's reception; now, with the funeral over and the old woman gone, it stood forlorn and deserted, awaiting the house-clearers' vans and an uncertain secular future.

'It'll make quite a good nursing-home, I suppose,' said

Winnie, finally. 'At least it's well off the road and away from the noise of traffic.'

Faced with the prospect of having to get out and open the gates, Harrison made no immediate reply. Though the down-pour's full fury rapidly passed, the rain continued falling heavily, and he cursed himself for having been beguiled by the spring-like sunshine over breakfast into venturing out without either mack-intosh or umbrella. 'Well,' he murmured disconsolately after a few moments more, 'it's obviously either a matter of getting soak-ing wet, or else remaining sitting here until we're both in need of residential care ourselves.'

So saying, he turned up his jacket collar and clambered out into the rain. Head bent beneath the deluge, he hurried forward and began lifting back the first heavy gate, dislodging a miniature waterfall from the ornate ironwork as he did so.

'You get back inside, Colonel! I'll let you in.'

Turning at the call, he saw George Frome hobbling round the corner of the converted stables, head and shoulders protected by a sack. With a grateful wave, he scrambled back into the car as the verger emerged through the rain to start hauling open the gates.

'Right! In you come, sir!' Improvised headgear clutched beneath his grizzled chin, Frome beckoned the Volvo through the entrance, then proceeded to limp on ahead, urging it into the sanctuary of the stable yard with continuous sweeps of his arm, for all the world like some impatient, hooded Quasimodo.

Wearing the same pink pinafore as she'd had on after the funeral, Mavis stood peering from the doorway of her home. As the Volvo drew up, she hurried forward. 'Put this over your shoul-ders, Mrs Harrison,' she said, thrusting a mackintosh in through the front passenger door. 'George will give your husband a hand in getting you inside.'

With Frome's assistance, Harrison unfolded the wheelchair and helped Winnie into the seat. This accomplished, she was trundled directly into what had obviously been the stable saddle-room, but which was now a snug little parlour with a coal fire burning brightly in the grate.

'Oh, this is lovely!' exclaimed Winnie, looking appreciatively around as she was positioned beside the hearth. There was a cheery brightness about everything in the room: copper ornaments and chinaware glinted on an old-fashioned dresser; a rose-bud-decorated oilcloth covered the central table and snow white antimacassars adorned the arms and backs of armchairs. Completing the picture of cosy domesticity, a tabby cat lay stretched out before the fender while, from its cage beside the window, a blue-breasted budgerigar chirped away merrily.

'Now, sir,' said their hostess, turning to her male visitor, 'why don't you sit yourself down with your wife beside the fire and get yourself dried through?'

'But what about you, George?' asked Harrison, addressing the obviously soaking-wet verger.

'Don't worry about me, Colonel,' he answered with a friendly grin. 'After twenty years at sea, I reckon I'm used to a fair bit of water by now. But if you'll excuse me a moment, I'll give Mavis a hand with getting the tea things in.'

'Of course—do carry on.'

Touched by the couple's hospitality, Harrison squeezed past Winnie and, stepping carefully over the sleeping cat, eased himself into the facing armchair. There, with his damp jacket and trousers beginning to steam in the heat, he looked about him with interest. On the dresser he noticed a variety of royal commemoration mugs; over the fireplace hung a reproduction of a painting of an aircraft carrier passing through the Straits of Gibraltar, flight deck crammed with aircraft of fifties' vintage. A television set dominated one corner, its casing overspread with laced cloth on which were arrayed a number of framed photographs. At the centre of these stood a studio portrait of Frome in the uniform of a naval petty officer. Next to it was another of him, this time in civilian dress and assisting Mavis with the cutting of their wedding cake. Beside these were pictures of various youngsters—obviously Mavis's grandchildren by the daughter of her previous marriage—all of them, including an infant, with the same curly hair and wide, oval faces as their grandmother.

'All right, both of you?'

Their hostess had re-entered and now stood in the doorway, steaming teapot in hand, anxiously regarding her visitors. Winnie turned and smiled up reassuringly. 'We are very comfortable, Mavis, thank you.'

'Yes, indeed,' murmured Harrison in agreement. 'Speaking for myself, I feel very much at home.'

And that's exactly what he did feel. For him, the cluttered ex-saddle-room stood in much the same relation to Fordington's little estates of modern private bungalows and houses as, back in the precincts, the dean's study did to the so-called Seminar House—both isolated outposts of a gentler, kindlier, more dependable age. Now, as he watched his hosts lay the table with a set of what was clearly their best crockery, any lingering misgivings he had regarding his present errand finally dissolved, and, stretching out his hands to the fire, he leaned contentedly back, fully determined to serve the interests of this homely, old-fashioned couple to the best of his ability.

Teapot poured and cups passed round, the four sat talking together, Frome and his wife sitting up at the table, their guests remaining comfortably ensconced beside the hearth. The funeral, the change in the weather and the state of the village hall were variously discussed, all to the pleasant background accompaniment of the now purring cat, the chirps of little 'Lord Nelson' in his cage, and the continuing drumming of rain on the weed-strewn cobbles outside.

'Well,' said Harrison, finally turning to business, 'doubtless you've both guessed the reason for this visit. As I believe Miss

Lambkin informed you, I've undertaken to do what I can to find you alternative accommodation in the locality.'

'It's very kind of you, sir, I'm sure,' answered Mavis heavily, 'but with all respect, I don't rightly see what you can do. We can't afford no private rents, and there just ain't the council houses there was. Only reason my Sal and her Bob got their place was that the cottage came with his farm job. If he ever loses that, it will be the same for them as for us—out on the pavement with nowhere to go.'

'Quite,' murmured Harrison, uncomfortably reminded of his similarly insecure position. 'So,' he continued, 'I believe it comes to this then: if you and George wish to remain in the parish, there's only one possible place for you, and that's Bright Cottage.'

At his words, a look of shocked amazement registered in both his listeners' faces. They glanced at each other, then Mavis broke out, 'I don't understand, sir. After you come over the first time, Rector called George and I into the study to tell us that the archdeacon was set on having it sold off.'

Disconcerted by the reference to his own part in pressurizing their late employer, yet at the same time wondering what on earth had possessed Lambkin to discuss delicate diocesan matters with his domestic servants, Harrison nodded. 'Quite right,' he said. 'That still is Dr Cawthorne's intention.'

'Then what's the use in talking of the cottage?' burst out his hostess, her broad face flushing. 'George and I ain't got the money to buy the blooming place!'

Somewhat taken aback by this petulant outburst, Harrison looked to Winnie for help. Before she had a chance to speak, however, Frome intervened. 'Now come on, my dear,' he said soothingly, reaching out to squeeze his wife's hand. 'Let's hear what the colonel has driven all this way to tell us.'

Conscious that he was treading on delicate ground, yet not fully understanding why, Harrison cleared his throat. 'What', he said, looking from one to the other, 'would either of you say if I told you that, under the original terms of the Bright Trust, you have a legal entitlement to the cottage?'

'Legal entitlement?' repeated the verger, his blue eyes opening wide. 'Sorry, sir, I don't quite get you.'

'It simply means this, George,' answered Harrison; 'you and Mavis have a claim to the tenancy under common law. Once I've passed you this formal notice to quit,' he said, drawing out the envelope sent round from Cave-Brown and Kent the previous day, 'as longtime residents of the parish, and you being church verger, you've every right to be rehoused in that cottage whatever Dr Cawthorne may say.' Pausing to allow Frome time to digest this information, he turned back to the man's wife. 'Well, Mavis?' he asked gently. 'If the cottage could be legally obtained, would you like to live there?'

Obviously troubled, the woman lowered her head. 'To tell truth, sir, I don't rightly know. It's a very nice cottage, pretty and all, but after what happened there between Jonathan and poor Rector, I don't reckon I could bide easy in the place.'

Though previously warned by Winnie to expect just this reaction, and irrational and unfair though he knew he was being, Harrison couldn't help feeling disappointed by the response. He was risking reputation and position—to say nothing of hearth and home—to help them, and, both in location and design, the old spite house would make the couple an ideal home. Receiving a warning frown from Winnie, he suppressed his irritation, however, and turned once more to Frome. 'And what about you, George? What's your view?'

The verger didn't immediately respond, but sat thoughtfully frowning. 'Well,' he said finally, his West Country accent more pronounced and his speech even slower and more deliberate than usual, 'what Mavis says is right, Colonel. It would be hard for us to go and live where that terrible thing happened. But there again,' he went on, turning to his wife, 'I reckon we ain't got much choice, my dear; not if you wants to stay close to your Sal and the kids.'

Not answering, Mavis remained looking down at the table with what Harrison regarded as obstinate unhappiness. The uncomfortable silence continued a few seconds before Winnie intruded. 'I don't know, Mavis,' she said gently, 'if this would help, but I understand from my husband that the room where the terrible events actually occurred is a poor-quality addition to the original structure. Also, it's apparently riddled with woodworm. If you and George were to take up the tenancy, I'm sure Colonel Harrison could persuade the Church to have the extension demolished—or, perhaps better still, have it rebuilt as a modern kitchen and utility block.'

'Good Lord!' exclaimed Frome, glancing wide-eyed at Harrison. 'That would cost a pretty penny, wouldn't it, sir?'

'It would be expensive, certainly,' murmured Harrison, as dazed as the verger by Winnie's suggestion. 'Nevertheless,' he continued with as much conviction as he was able to muster, 'if the diocesan architect considers the work necessary, I suppose the funds could always be found.'

'So, Mavis,' coaxed Winnie, 'what do you say now? Would the cottage suit if the mission hall was either demolished or rebuilt?'

'Well,' answered the other woman reluctantly, 'in that case, I suppose yes. After all,' she added, brightening, 'it is what Rector wanted: he always said George and me was to have the cottage after old Reverend Holloway passed on.'

Light burst upon Harrison at her words. Now at last he understood why the subject of the cottage was so painful to Mavis, and also why her late employer had so uncharacteristically demurred when he'd informed him of the archdeacon's wishes regarding its future: Lambkin had promised the tenancy to the Fromes, and what he'd done by obeying Cawthorne's instructions had been to deny the wretched man his sole means of repaying the couple's years of faithful service.

'And you reckon we could still have it, do you, Colonel?'

Frome's question broke into his thoughts. Looking up, he nodded emphatically. 'I do, George. Yes,' he answered, 'though, I'm afraid, there are at present one or two impediments that stand in your way.' Seeing the looks of dismay on the couple's faces, he gave a reassuring smile. 'Minor impediments, I hasten to add, and certainly nothing that can't be surmounted if you're willing to be guided by me.'

'Lawyers! Oh, I don't know about that!'

Ignoring this predictable outburst, Harrison went on calmly outlining the procedure of appealing against the Charity Commissioners' interim decision. The look of horror and fear that the first mention of the word 'solicitor' had inspired in his hostess's face only grew, however, as he continued. With a sinking heart, he ploughed resolutely on, concluding by saying, 'Of course, in the end, the decision can only be yours.'

'Well, if it's mine,' burst out Mavis, 'I know what it is: I don't want anything to do with lawyers, courts and the like!' She looked round at her husband for support. 'What do you say, George?'

Frome remained frowning down at the table, his normally cheerful countenance as troubled now as his wife's. 'It's what Rector would have said, that's what I'm thinking,' he said, eventually looking up at his visitors. 'He wouldn't have liked us going against the Church.'

'That's right, George!' chimed in Mavis. 'Nor he wouldn't! It's like what he said to us after your visit, Colonel: loyalty to the Church must come before everything else.'

Colouring slightly at this, Harrison nodded. 'That's a very commendable attitude,' he said. 'Nevertheless, the fact remains that in two months' time, unless you're prepared to fight for your rights, you could well find yourselves without a roof over your heads.'

'Well, if it comes to that, I'm sure my Sal would let us stay along with her,' cried Mavis defiantly. 'Her Bob wouldn't see us put on the street. He's always been very good to us, has that lad.'

At her words, Harrison automatically glanced towards the photographs on the television set: including the infant, he counted four curly-haired children among the portraits. Though Mavis's son-in-law might, he thought, be the most accommodating of men, it seemed hardly likely he'd wholeheartedly welcome the addition of two adults to a doubtless already grossly overcrowded farm labourer's cottage, especially with having to take in a man who was only his wife's stepfather, and not even a blood relation at all. The same consideration obviously struck Frome, for he now coughed and cleared his throat. 'So you reckon, sir,' he said, slightly sheepishly, 'if Mavis and I did as you suggests and took ourselves off to a lawyer, we'd get this legal aid thing?'

'Certainly you'd qualify.' Relieved that one at least of the pair was finally seeing sense, Harrison smiled. 'Unless, that is, either of you have private means of your own.'

To his relief, Frome laughed. 'Only private means I've got is the bit of pension I get from the navy for this gammy leg of mine!'

'Quite so. Therefore, if you wish to pursue your claim, the question of personal expense should present no impediment.'

'Well,' said Frome, scratching his chin, 'that sounds all right, Colonel, but still, Mavis and I will have to put our heads together before we decide. This would be a big step for us, taking the Church to law—somehow it seems all unnatural like.'

'That's right, George,' agreed Mavis, nodding. 'I can't see any good coming of going against the Church; it's like going against God.'

Though, selfishly, Harrison couldn't help feeling a large

measure of relief at the couple's unwillingness to go to law, nor fully suppress the hope they'd not pursue their claim on the cottage, he nevertheless felt, in fairness to them, it was his duty to press the matter as far as he could. 'Anyway,' he resumed, 'whatever you eventually decide, there's no harm in giving a few moments' thought as to who might legally represent you if you decide to go ahead with the claim.'

Giving them no chance to object, he drew two folded sheets from his inside pocket. 'In case you hadn't anyone particular in mind, I have taken the liberty of jotting down the names and addresses of one or two local solicitors I can personally vouch for. I have also penned a draft letter you may care to copy if you wish to proceed. Nevertheless, I must ask you to remember that the advice and information I've given is unofficial and completely off the record. You must not on any account mention to anyone the nature of my visit this morning.'

'No, sir, of course not,' answered Frome immediately. 'I'll put these papers safely out of sight straight away.'

Now that he'd done all that duty demanded as far as the Fromes were concerned, Harrison felt free to turn his attention to the mystery surrounding their late employer's death. As the verger rose from the table and went over to put the papers into one of the dresser drawers, he was strongly tempted to allude directly to the subject of the anonymous notes and ask outright whether George or Mavis had any idea who might have sent them. Remembering Winnie's advice, however, he said nothing at present, merely reiterating the importance of keeping the nature of his visit confidential.

'Don't you worry, Colonel,' said Frome, returning to his chair. 'Neither myself nor Mavis will mention a word of this to anyone.'

'That's right, sir, not a word,' echoed his wife. 'Whether George and I go ahead with the claim on the cottage or not, we'll always be very grateful for all the trouble you've taken.'

'Not at all.' Harrison smiled, his earlier irritation with the woman almost forgotten. 'Now,' he resumed briskly, rising to his feet, 'there's one little thing you could do for me. While I'm here, I feel I ought to take a quick look at the general state of the rectory. So I wonder, Mavis, if you'd kindly allow my wife to remain with you here whilst George accompanies me on a short tour of inspection?'

CHAPTER ELEVEN

Though the rain had at last stopped, the trees continued to drip heavily as Harrison toiled up the drive, his stocky companion limping at his side. Neither spoke and, what with the iron grey overcast above, the cawing of the rooks and the musty smell of damp vegetation, the atmosphere of forlorn emptiness and decay bore almost physically down as the two men crunched over the sodden gravel towards the shuttered house.

The mood of desolation and melancholy outside pervaded the rectory interior. Though still carpeted and furnished, there was a chilly, dead feel to the unheated building, and, following his guide into the hall, Harrison couldn't help contrasting the silent gloom of his surroundings with the snug, cheerful scene he'd left behind in the Fromes' parlour, with Winnie sitting talking to the verger's wife beside a glowing fire, the cat purring noisily on her lap and Lord Nelson chirping merrily away in one corner.

'Shall we start here, sir?'

Frome had stopped before the door on their immediate left. With Harrison's agreement, he bent and unlocked it. Then, opening it, he switched on the light and stood back for the other to enter.

Though tidied and partly cleared, Lambkin's study was still much as Harrison remembered it: a square, high-ceilinged room, normally lit by the now shuttered large window overlooking the drive. Though its walls remained lined with bookshelves and filing cabinets, there was a gap next to the safe where a photocopier had once stood. Apart from an already slightly dusty telephone and a pile of old parish bulletins, the once cluttered surface of the centrally positioned desk was now bare. Also missing was the stark, impressionistic picture, done in chalk and crayon, that had hung over the fireplace, its long occupancy clearly visible on the dusty, cream-painted wall. A pair of straight-backed, cane-seated chairs had been drawn back into one corner, and with an inward shudder, Harrison remembered sitting on one of them, strenuously arguing Cawthorne's case for the winding up of the Bright Trust, while Lambkin sat bowed at the desk before him with a look of hopeless misery on his face.

Glancing around, he felt not the slightest impulse to touch or examine anything: there was a neat tidiness that he had no wish nor felt any right to disturb. Anyway, as he knew, the police would have gone through the room with a fine-tooth comb. Instead, turning to the window, he drew open the shutters and looked down the drive towards the roof of the stables, wondering how Winnie was getting on, and how successful she was being at pumping Mavis for the details of Lambkin's private life.

'Tell me, George,' he said, glancing round, 'what's your view about those anonymous notes? Strictly in confidence, have you any theory as to who wrote them?'

'No, sir, I haven't.' As if constrained by some deep-seated sense of decorum, Frome had not actually entered his late master's study, but remained on the threshold, looking in. 'Like I told the police,' he continued, 'there was no reason why anyone should have wished Rector harm. In all my years with him, I never knew him quarrel or raise his voice to anyone.' The speaker broke off with a grimace, then burst out passionately, 'He was as quiet and Christian a gentleman as any there be!'

'Oh, quite,' murmured Harrison hurriedly, embarrassed by the deep feelings his question had evoked. Deciding to approach the delicate matter of Lambkin's personal relationships circum-spectly, he paused to allow Frome time to recover before asking, 'What about Mrs Gittings, then? The notes also attempted to blacken her name. Has she any enemies in the parish?'

'Enemies?' Scepticism combined with more than a trace of irritation in the other's tone. 'How she could have? Mrs Gittings is a kind soul, no harm to anyone. There was no more reason for anyone to want to hurt her than poor Rector.' Frome's face again contorted. 'Before all this happened, Fordington was a happy place.'

Harrison gave an inward sigh: loyal, hard-working and invaluable though doubtless he'd been to his employer, Frome, nevertheless, seemed extraordinarily obtuse—either that, or he was being extremely guarded for reasons of his own. 'Well,' he persisted, 'what about Mrs Gittings seeking ordination? Could someone have been trying to prevent that?'

Clearly neither the police nor anyone else had raised such a possibility, for Frome stared incredulously at him before vigor-ously shaking his head. 'No, I can't believe that! There's plenty here, like the wing commander, who ain't greatly keen on women wearing a collar back to front, but I can't see how that could be a reason for anyone making up cruel lies about her or Rector.'

Turning away, Harrison looked down the drive, devoutly hoping that Winnie was digging in slightly more fruitful soil. He remained watching the thin plume of smoke rising from the sta-ble chimney for a few seconds before reluctantly turning back to Frome.

'Now, George,' he said, with what he hoped was a companionable smile, 'strictly between ourselves, man to man, am I to take it there was not the slightest grain of truth in the allegations made in the notes: that, to the best of your knowledge, there never was, nor had ever been, any sort of sexual liaison between the Reverend Lambkin and Mrs Gittings, either before his wife's death or after?'

'No, sir.' The emphatic answer rang through the room.

'Or with any other woman?'

Frome shook his head violently, indignation writ large in his reddening face. 'No, Colonel! Rector was the last man on earth to go around chasing after other women, especially when dear, good Mrs Lambkin was alive!'

Harrison nodded and turned back to the window. 'I'm sorry, George, to upset you by asking such questions.'

Despite the disappointing lack of information in the other's answers, the short conversation had at least confirmed Harrison's opinion of Frome: he was clearly a deeply conservative man, whose view of Lambkin was naturally coloured by sentiment. Equally apparent was that, whatever gratitude he might feel for the information and advice he'd been given regarding the cottage tenancy, simple loyalty would almost certainly prevent him uttering a word that might in any way damage his late master's reputation. Realizing he was therefore unlikely to learn anything useful from him, Harrison could only feel profoundly thankful that he'd taken Winnie's advice to separate the couple, so as to give her the chance of questioning Mavis alone.

'Right,' he said briskly, turning back to his guide, 'let's move on then, shall we? I've already seen the drawing-room. Perhaps you could now show me the rest of the ground floor.'

'Very good, sir.'

Uncomfortably conscious of a new coldness in Frome, Harrison waited as the door was relocked, and then followed down the hall. Briefly they glanced in at the dining-room, then continued on into a wide kitchen area with an old-fashioned coal-range and a row of wire-tugged room-bells. The yellowed ceiling was studded over with rusting iron hooks, from which salted portions of generations of rectory pigs had doubtless hung. An inner room contained a small modern kitchen with fitted sink-unit, cupboards and electric stove—all, including the damp stains and cracked plasterwork, as depressingly predictable to Harrison as Frome's replies to his questions had been.

'Would you care to see out in the back, Colonel?'

'Thank you, George—that would be most useful.' Together they passed through a scullery out into a red-brick, high-walled yard. Opening off this was an Edwardian wash-house, complete with brick-based copper and a large cobweb-strewn mangle, but also with a modern washing machine and spin-drier plumbed in against the end wall. Making a mental note to advise Helen Middlebrook against a close inspection of the outbuildings when making her evaluation survey, Harrison turned to leave. As he did so, he noticed a child's bicycle with a collection of miniature garden implements propped in the corner behind it.

Going over, he picked out a tiny rusty rake.

'Jonathan's?' he said, holding it up.

It was more statement than question, and as he spoke a grimace of pain flashed across Frome's face. 'Aye,' he answered. 'I made them tools up for him when he was a tiddler. He used to like to come along with me to help in the garden.'

Guessing how close man and child had been, and how difficult Frome must be finding his tour of the house, Harrison replaced the implement with the rest. 'All right, George,' he said. 'I've seen enough out here. Let's get back inside. 'Then you can give me the keys so I can go up and take a quick look upstairs.'

'You don't want me to come up with you, sir?'

Harrison shook his head. 'No, there's no need for that. You stay below. I'll be all right poking around on my own.'

Strangely enough, the feeling of empty desolation faded as Harrison mounted the stairs. Indeed, on reaching the first-floor landing, he paused, hand on banister, glancing round the closed doors, almost expecting one of them to open and a member of the Lambkin family to appear and ask him what he was doing, venturing up here in the most private area of their home.

Far from sure what he hoped to achieve, beyond allowing Winnie time to complete her questioning, he followed the landing round to the final door on his left. Unlocking it, he turned on the light and peered into a blue-painted room dominated by a large old-fashioned double bed. From the complete lack of personal possessions, he guessed it had been used for guests. Ordinarily, with its pair of south-facing windows, it would have been sunny and bright. Now, with the shutters closed and the drab furnishings illuminated in the weak glare of a bulb, there was a melancholy bleakness to the bedroom that old Miss Lambkin had presumably used on both her sad stays.

Retracing his steps, he glanced in at an equally spartan bathroom, before reaching the door opposite the head of the stairs. Unlocking it, he switched on the light. This had clearly been the master bedroom, for though far from luxurious, it was more lavishly furnished than the first. A crucifix hung above the bed, and among the hairbrushes and combs arranged on the dressing-table stood two silver-mounted wedding photographs, one of Maurice and Bridget Lambkin posing together outside a church porch on their wedding day, and another, a group picture, showing them standing among their guests.

Thankful he'd spared Frome what he'd have doubtless felt as gross intrusion, Harrison entered the bedroom, himself feeling uncomfortably like some sort of voyeur. Crossing to the dressing-table, he picked up the portrait of the newlyweds. Holding it to the light, he peered at it curiously. There was no surprise about the appearance of the bride, for between the pretty young girl in the picture and the gravely sick, thin-cheeked woman in the drawing-room photograph ran a simple continuum. Between, however, the confidently smiling bridegroom at her side and the careworn Maurice Lambkin he remembered, had occurred a change so profound that Harrison could hardly credit the transformation.

Ingrams's attachment to Lambkin had always been a puzzle to him, and he'd often wondered how such a genial, clubbable man as the dean could ever have had anything in common with such a drab, dispiriting individual as Lambkin. Now, examining the features of the young bridegroom, he could see exactly what had originally drawn Ingrams to him. Not exactly handsome, there was, nevertheless, something strangely compelling about the curiously Janus-like face, with its broad, high forehead, prominent nose and wide-spaced dark eyes set against delicate, almost effeminate, lips and chin; it was the face of a highly strung, intelligent young man, suited in Harrison's view for a university chaplaincy, perhaps, or a fashionable London curacy—certainly not for the rough and tumble of inner-city parish work, let alone the running of hostels for a crowd of vagabond drunkards and wastrels.

Knowing what lay ahead of them, there seemed an almost painful poignancy about the couple themselves: Bridget Lambkin in her flowing white dress, her husband in his quaintly archaic clerical frock coat, both so young and obviously happy—and each so utterly unprepared and unfitted for the harsh and often sordid realities of the life that Lambkin so disastrously inflicted upon them.

Replacing the first photograph, Harrison picked up the second. Apart from the bride and groom, the only person among the wedding party that he recognized was Ingrams, looking every bit as chubby-faced and amiable as he still did. What was surprising, however, was how tiny the wedding party was, and that all the guests appeared as youthful as the newlyweds themselves.

Restoring the photograph to its place, Harrison retreated, softly closing the door. He then glanced at his watch. It was now almost noon, and he was beginning to feel distinctly hungry. Wondering how Winnie was getting on, and where they might stop for a bite to eat on their way home, he continued round the landing towards the one remaining unvisited room.

Selecting the correct key, he unlocked and pushed open the door. Instead of entering immediately, he paused on the threshold and, like Frome outside the study earlier, stood looking in as if reluctant to intrude into a world to which he didn't belong. Though it contained two single beds, the room he was gazing into was not merely another bedroom, but a miniature world— one where childhood, adolescence and young manhood lapped over each other and combined. In a corner beside an old bureau were propped a pair of red-scarred and bandaged cricket bats; plastic and balsa-wood model aircraft dangled on threads from the ceiling; dog-eared books were arranged higgledy-piggledy in over-filled shelves. On the walls were displayed a variety of posters: Louis Armstrong playing his trumpet; a pouting Marilyn Monroe; and, most prominent of all, an aerial view of Canterbury Cathedral precincts with a broad red arrow heavily crayoned upon it, pointing down like the finger of Zeus at one of the top-storey dormitory windows of the King's School.

Despite Ingrams's surprising revelations about his private affairs, since leaving the deanery the previous evening, Harrison had discounted the possibility of Jonathan having been the target of the poison-pen letters, for as Winnie had pointed out, if the allegations about Maurice Lambkin's supposed behaviour had been made only to hurt his son, what reason could the sender have had for sending the archdeacon a copy? Nevertheless, since picking up the tiny rake in the wash-house, thoughts of Jonathan had lingered in his mind, and as he now entered what had clearly been his room, Harrison looked about, hoping to find a clue to the young man's oddly ambiguous life in London.

Crossing straight to a window, he opened the shutters to find himself looking out across lawn and sunken orchard towards the churchyard. Bare wisteria stems were plaited thick about the frame, and, as he gazed out towards where the small family lay buried, he could only too easily imagine how, as a child, Jonathan must often have woken on summer mornings to a room thick with the musty sweetness of its perfume and amurmur with the sound of bees busy among the blossom.

Turning away, Harrison went to the bureau and opened its four main drawers in turn, finding them packed with clothing. He then drew up a chair and sat before it, and, pulling down the lid, began going through the tiny internal drawers. Their contents were varied: dried tubes of model-aircraft glue, mathematical instruments, penknives, badges and the rest of the usual grubby paraphernalia of young boyhood. Only when reaching the middle drawer of the lower tier did he pause, for lying scattered within was a loose collection of photographs, and as he bent and drew out the one that met his eye, he realized something that should have been immediately obvious from the pair of cricket bats propped beside him: that the room hadn't been the private sanctuary of a solitary individual as he'd imagined, but the shared world of two friends. In the small black-and-white photograph in his hand was the freckle-faced young man he'd talked to beneath the trees in the deanery orchard a decade before: Stephen Hardwick, the boy who'd stayed at the rectory during the holidays while his parents were overseas, and whose early death had, according to Ingrams, so tragically blighted Jonathan's subsequent life.

Removing the tiny drawer, he began going through the rest of the photographs. There were a number of Jonathan and his parents, together with more of young Hardwick, showing him variously as a boy sitting astride a bicycle beneath the mulberry tree outside, as an officer cadet standing in front of the familiar facade of the Royal Military College, and finally as a second lieutenant, wearing the dress uniform and insignia of the Enniskillen Fusiliers.

Having replaced the drawer, Harrison closed the bureau, then sat and thought. Clearly, with the photographs of his family and dead friend still in the desk, Jonathan had continued to count this room as his own. Surely, therefore, somewhere within it should be his private papers—birth and school certificates, and other such personal documents. He looked around, but seeing no suitable container, turned again to the bureau. Opening the top drawer, he began sifting through the clothes. In a moment he found what he was looking for: a large manila envelope and, next to it, a short cardboard tube, bearing the Cambridge University coat of arms—presumably containing Jonathan's degree certificate. Lifting the envelope out, he felt the unexpected weight of some solid object at the bottom. Withdrawing a sheaf of documents from the packet, he dipped in and drew out what appeared at first to be a necklace of coal black beads with a small gold cross and medallion attached. Holding it up, he dangled the object from his fingers, frowning as he recognized what it was.

A rosary was about the last thing expected to be found in an Anglican rectory, and for a few moments Harrison remained gazing at the strangely alien object in perplexed fascination. He then examined the attached medallion, finding on one side the conventional image of Virgin and Child, and on the other a name and date: *Bridget Fiona O'Brian—24.2.1955.*

Still not understanding, he stared at it. Then, remembering the curious sadness in old Miss Lambkin's voice on the evening of the funeral when she'd spoken of prejudice and narrow-mindedness, he understood suddenly both the reason why the old woman had not visited her nephew until the burial of his wife, and also why the wedding party in the photograph had been so small and so universally youthful: Maurice Lambkin, brought up in a strictly Protestant home in Northern Ireland, had met and fallen in love with a Roman Catholic, and had married her against the wishes of his two maiden aunts.

Moving the beads between finger and thumb, Harrison sat, his mind whirling on. Clearly the religious intolerance had not been on one side alone: there had never been any talk of Bridget Lambkin's family, and, as the photograph had shown, neither of her parents had attended her wedding. Like her husband, she'd obviously been disowned. As for the rosary, he guessed that had been presented to her at her confirmation by her parents, and, though forsaken by them, she'd continued to treasure it as a keepsake, finally passing it on to her son.

Back at the beginning of the seventies, at the start of the so-called 'Troubles', Harrison had done a tour of duty in Northern Ireland, running a small intelligence operation from the top floor of a temperance hotel overlooking Belfast Lough. With horror, he'd witnessed the degrees of hatred and suspicion that besmirched that beautiful land, with two opposed political aspirations struggling for mastery across the religious divide. Now, gazing at the coil of beads in his hand, Harrison thought with a shudder of how the centuries of bigotry and intolerance had stretched out to affect the happiness of the young couple in the wedding photograph, leaving them to face a hard and unsuitable life among London's poor and destitute as semi-exiled outcasts themselves.

'Colonel? Are you all right up there?'

At the sound of Frome's voice from the hall, Harrison got up and went out on to the landing, the rosary still dangling from his hand. 'I'm on my way down, George,' he called over the banisters. 'I just want to check the condition of one or two more of these windows. I'll be with you shortly.'

'Right, sir.'

Returning to the bedroom, he opened and slammed down the window a couple of times, then turned back to the papers left on the bureau. His first impulse was to thrust them and the rosary back in the envelope, then return them to the drawer. Remembering, however, that Ingrams was sorting the family documents, he decided to take them back with him to Canterbury. Accordingly, he repacked the envelope, then took the degree certificate from the bureau. Having done so, he glanced around the room for a last time before going out and carefully relocking the door behind him.

CHAPTER TWELVE

'Of course I knew Bridget was brought up a Catholic!' Winnie sipped her gin and tonic. 'Margaret told me years ago. Apparently there was terrible opposition from both families when she and Maurice married—but anyway, I thought you knew all that.'

'Well, I didn't,' answered her husband shortly. He raised his beer glass and drank, then, leaning back against the settle, peered towards the bar. 'Damn that blasted girl!' he murmured. 'I'm sure she's completely forgotten our order!'

It had been Winnie's idea to stop off for lunch at the Ferryman. Ordinarily, Harrison would have liked the unpretentious old tavern, with its nicotine-yellow ceilings and walls, crude high-backed settles and succession of dowdy little alcoves and snugs. Now, however, he'd started to worry once more about the possible consequences if the Fromes, despite their reluctance, finally decided to contest the cottage sale, fearing that Cawthorne's wrath (and grief) over the matter was likely to equal anything experienced by Maurice and Bridget Lambkin in their erstwhile roles of latter-day Irish Romeo and Juliet. Added to that, he felt as far as ever from tracking down the source of the anonymous notes, and now, with the search of the rectory completed, and having spoken to George Frome, he hadn't the faintest idea what further line of inquiry to pursue. With such thoughts oppressing him, and his stomach rumbling from lack of food, he was therefore in no mood for aesthetics, and quite unable to feel anything for the quaintly old-fashioned hostelry beyond a mounting frustration with its slatternly barmaid—who, at that moment, was leaning forward, grinning at whatever was being whispered to her by the disreputable-looking geriatric perched opposite her on a bar-stool.

Turning away from the giggling girl and her ancient swain, he looked out through the window. Rain had begun spotting again, and as he gazed across the road towards the rusting white gates and the shuttered house behind, he felt a sudden sympathy, not just for Lambkin, but for the still-living army of country parsons, eking out lonely lives in similar uncouth backwaters as the semi-impoverished ambassadors and plenipotentiaries of a distant, fading power.

'Well, don't you want to know what I've discovered?'

Harrison turned in surprise. From Winnie's expression when he'd collected her, he'd gained the impression that Mavis had made no startling revelations, and, as she'd mentioned nothing until now, he'd naturally assumed that her conversation with the verger's wife had been as unproductive as his own with the verger.

'Dear old Mavis is rather sweet, but she's no Einstein, I'm afraid,' resumed Winnie. 'All the same, she had a few interesting things to say. For example, did George tell you about the row between Maurice and Edith Gillmore back in the early autumn?'

'The schoolmistress?' Harrison shook his head. 'No,' he said, 'he never mentioned a thing. According to him, everything in the garden was rosy during Lambkin's time.'

'Hardly that, it would seem,' responded Winnie with a wry smile. 'Apparently a number of newcomers to the village have been unhappy about the standard of teaching at the local school. As Maurice was chairman of governors, Tony Brandon and the rest of the parish council pressed him to rectify matters. It ended up with him having to call in Edith to express the general dissatisfaction.'

Remembering the severe-looking, hatchet-faced woman from the funeral reception, and his rather awkward discussion with her on the state of the village hall, Harrison frowned. 'Which she didn't take very kindly, I imagine?'

'Apparently not: it seems she stormed out of the rectory in high dudgeon. Afterwards, she and Maurice hardly ever spoke— which, according to Mavis, was very sad as Miss Gillmore had been a close friend of the Lambkins, and had spent a great deal of time with them both when Bridget was alive.'

Incredulous, Harrison stared at the speaker, then, reddening, leaned across the table. 'God Almighty, woman!' he exclaimed, struggling to keep his voice low. 'Why didn't you tell me this straight away, instead of after we've been sitting here in this rat-hole nearly half an hour! Don't you realize it's the very sort of thing I've been hoping and expecting to find!'

'Exactly, and that's why I was rather reluctant to tell you at all. I knew the conclusion you'd jump to.'

Checked by the coolness of the reply, Harrison paused in momentary bewilderment, then all the strains of the morning seemed to whelm up together to stoke his fury. 'God dammit!' he burst out. 'What conclusion am I expected to come to? At last we've found someone with an obvious grudge against Lambkin: a humiliated spinster resenting a man she'd once trusted and liked; a woman spinning devil-knows-what fantasies about him and Stella Gittings. And not only that, but someone close enough to the family to know about Jonathan's attachment to his mother.'

'Yes,' came the answer, 'and also a person with a very soft

heart—someone too gentle and sensitive perhaps to make an ideal headmistress.'

'Who says so?'

'Almost everyone.' Winnie shook her head. 'No, Richard,' she continued, her tone becoming earnest, 'I had a long conversation with Edith after the funeral on Thursday, and I quite agree with Mavis's assessment: it's impossible to believe that she could ever have composed those cruel notes.'

Harrison made to protest, but then, remembering the expression on the headmistress's face when he'd seen her at the reception gazing forlornly out of the French windows, he instead merely sighed. 'You may be right,' he murmured, turning to look out across the road. A sense of futility weighed him down. Even if he could discover the identity of the poison-pen writer, he thought, how would it help? Maurice and Jonathan Lambkin were dead and buried, the flowers already rotting on their grave; and, far from being the Machiavellian contriver of his imaginings, whoever had prompted their deaths would likely turn out to be merely some pathetic, tormented, lonely soul.

As he stared out, a mud-splattered tractor came rumbling past, hauling an equally filthy muck-spreader through the now drizzling rain. He watched as machine and trailer headed away down the street, an inevitable column of cars crawling nose-to-tail in their wake. The sight perfectly matched his mood. 'Dung and death!' he thought miserably to himself as the cortege disappeared from sight. 'Nothing but dung, and death, stretching out eternally before and behind!'

'Anyway,' said Winnie brightly, 'wouldn't you like to hear about these other troubles Maurice is supposed to have had? There seem to have been quite a few, one way or another, including a little matter of a mechanical shovel and some empty graves.'

Harrison sighed. 'All right,' he said resignedly, 'go on then, tell me: what is this nonsense about a mechanical shovel and empty graves?'

For the moment, however, he was not to find out, for even as he spoke, lunch finally arrived—two steaming plates of home-made steak-and-kidney pudding borne by a cheerful young woman who profusely apologized for the delay. Between them, the civility of the waitress and the appearance of the food had a miraculously restorative effect on his soul. With some of the delicious hot food inside him, and a little more of the beer, he felt altogether happier. 'So,' he asked, clearing his mouth and sitting back, 'what was all this about empty graves?'

Winnie lowered her fork. 'You remember that it's been impossible to find anyone willing to take over the old sexton's duties? Well, as an interim measure, the parochial church council apparently contracted a local farmer to bring in his JCB tractor to dig a new grave. When the machine arrived, to save costs, Maurice took it upon himself to have a couple of additional ones scooped out at the same time and then loosely filled in.'

'Sounds good sense,' grunted Harrison, bending back to his plate. 'So what was wrong with that?'

'Only people's reactions—you know how superstitious these rural places can be. Some of the older villagers took it into their heads that Maurice had prior knowledge that two among them were soon to expire. That was bad enough, but then, tragically enough, a pair of local boys were killed on a motorcycle.'

'And Lambkin got the blame, I suppose?'

'Of course. Apparently the families involved were extremely bitter. It ended up with Stella Gittings having to take the funeral. Maurice was very upset.'

'I can imagine,' murmured Harrison, returning to his pie. Despite what Frome had said about the period of Lambkin's incumbency, what he'd just heard had come as no surprise. Both the story of Miss Gillmore's upset and that of the graves merely confirmed what years of diocesan administration had taught: that controversy, quarrels and rancour hovered about ecclesiastical life as inevitable as gulls round a fishing boat.

'What are you smiling to yourself about suddenly?'

He gave a rueful laugh. 'Just that, a few minutes ago, I couldn't see any reason on earth why someone like Lambkin would have made enemies. Now I realize, being a clergyman, the poor fellow couldn't help doing so: offending people comes with the job!'

'What's so funny about that?'

'Nothing really. It merely occurred to me that—given the various ways in which Lambkin might have inadvertently upset his parishioners over the years, and, consequently, the number of people with some real or imagined grudge against the poor chap—if I'm ever going to discover who sent those notes, I need a guide, someone perhaps to whisk me about the parish like that chap Faustus had in the play.' Laughing, he took a deep draught of his beer. 'What I should perhaps do is to try conjuring up a Mephistophilis of my own.'

Even as he spoke the words, there came a respectful low cough at his elbow, and a voice said, 'A little bird's just been along, saying you was likely interested in having a word with me.'

Harrison swung round and looked up in astonished indignation at the apparition at his side.

It was the elderly man who had been sitting until now, back turned towards him, engaged in conversation with the barmaid, and as he stared at his lean, wizened visage, he found himself struggling to remember where he'd recently seen that face before. As he did so, the intruder grinned, exposing a few unpleasantly yellowish, fang-like teeth. 'Young Molly from the kitchen overheard you talking about them graves that Rector had dug out with the JCB.'

The mention of graves triggered his memory. 'Good God!' he blurted out. 'I remember now! Aren't you the fellow who was skulking among the tombstones after the funeral?'

The stranger's grin vanished, and his dark leathery countenance took on the same expression of saturnine malevolence it had worn on that previous occasion. 'What you mean, "skulking"?' he demanded. 'I was only waiting for you and that other bugger to shove off so I could get on with my work!'

'Ah, of course!' intervened Winnie brightly. 'So you must be the sexton then! You were there, I imagine, to fill in the grave.'

'That's right,' answered the septuagenarian, partly mollified. 'The name's Charlie Hawthorn. I've been bell-ringer and grave-digger at St Philip's nigh on forty year.'

'Really! Forty years!' Winnie beamed at the speaker. 'How interesting! Oh, do sit and join us, won't you?' She turned to her husband. 'Richard, darling, why don't you go and get Mr Hawthorn a drink?'

Resentful at having to leave his half-eaten lunch, Harrison rose to his feet, and, taking with him the battered pewter mug the old man thrust into his hand, went off to the bar. There he waited as the barmaid continued a long, bantering conversation with yet another of her mainly geriatric clientele. Nor was his mood improved by the sight in the mirror in front of him of Hawthorn ensconced beside Winnie, she nodding and smiling at what he was saying exactly as if she were back in the close, entertaining a gathering of the cathedral clergy and their wives to afternoon tea.

'Ah, there you are at last, darling!' Winnie smiled up as he returned with the now-brimming tankard. 'Charlie here has been telling me the most fascinating things. Do you know, for example, how long a coffin will remain intact in the earth?'

'No, I don't,' he answered, carefully passing over the mug.

'At least fifteen years, apparently,' she said, flashing him a mischievous smile as he seated himself before the congealing remnants of his steak-and-kidney pie.

'Of course,' interposed Hawthorn, wiping froth from his mouth, 'it depends as to the wood that's used. Oak is best. Given dryish ground, she'll last you a good half-century.'

Fearing that he was now to be afflicted with a parody of the scene in Elsinore graveyard, Harrison determinedly resumed his interrupted meal. This wasn't easy, however, for though Hawthorn refrained from airing any more grisly details of his trade, he nevertheless remained like some memento mori on the other side of the table, eyeing him with what seemed like sardonic amusement.

Feigning not to notice, and suppressing a mounting irritation at this unsought guest, Harrison continued to eat, thinking that there was something so ominously unpleasant about the sexton's appearance that, given a scythe and an hour-glass, he'd make a perfect model for the traditional weather vane—either that, or swathed in black on the inn sign outside as a latter-day Charon, ferrying the souls of the departed across the Stour to the so-called 'Isle of the Dead'.

Hawthorn suddenly laughed. 'I knows why you're here,' he said winking conspiratorially. 'You've been over the road with old Hopalong and his missus, haven't you? Saw him earlier, letting you in.'

Frowning, Harrison lay down his knife and fork. 'Yes,' he replied, 'as it happens, I did have certain private business with Mr and Mrs Frome.'

As unabashed by the coolness of the tone as Cawthorne had been the day before, the sexton grinned. 'Aye,' he said, nodding with evident satisfaction. 'I told him that someone would be along to hook him out of his place just as soon as Rector was buried.' The grin widened. 'That's it, isn't it? You're from the Church? You've come to give Hopalong his notice to quit.'

At this point, Winnie intervened. 'I imagine, Charlie,' she said, 'you must know the Fromes very well?'

'Aye,' answered the other, nodding. 'I've known Mavis since she was a babe; old Hopalong since Rector first took him on.'

'Such a nice couple.'

The sexton gave a contemptuous snort. 'A pair of bloody fools more like! Working for next to nothing all them years! And what do they get for it? It's out on their ears for them, isn't it, and not any bugger to care!'

Barely suppressing his anger, Harrison looked down at his plate. Winnie, however, remained smiling as pleasantly as before. 'I think,' she said, 'that both George and Mavis were greatly attached to the Lambkin family.'

'Oh, aye! They was attached all right!' With a look of disdain, Hawthorn glanced out through the window towards the back of the stables. 'The more bloody fools them, I say!'

'And what about you, Charlie? What was your own opinion of the Lambkins?'

Pausing to consider, Hawthorn meditatively studied the depleted contents of his mug. 'Mrs Lambkin was fair enough, I suppose,' he murmured, 'though she was a sick woman most of the time. As for Rector, trouble with him was he couldn't stand up for himself: between 'em, the wing commander and Brandon and his wife regular pushed him around.'

'And their son—Jonathan? Did you know him?'

'Course I did—knew him when he was still a nipper, didn't I? He often used to come out to the churchyard when I was working, along with that other lad who used to stay up at the rectory.' The speaker paused reflectively. 'Aye,' he continued, 'young Jonathan was always a quiet one—butter wouldn't melt in his mouth! You'd never have guessed he'd grow to be wandering round the place like a blooming gipsy, nor end up blasting himself and his old man with a shotgun.'

The silence that followed was broken by Winnie. 'And the notes, Charlie? The ones that prompted the tragedy. I suppose you haven't any idea who might have sent them or why?'

Hawthorn shook his head and took another swig of his beer.

Husband and wife exchanged glances, and then, as the mug was lowered, Harrison cleared his throat. 'Regarding those extra graves Mr Lambkin had dug; I understand they gave rise to a degree of bad feeling locally. You don't think the notes that were sent could have had any connection with that matter?'

The sexton laughed and shook his head. 'No, all that about

them graves was nothing but summer thunder—a lot of noise soon past and no real damage done.'

'So you don't know of anyone in the village who had any particular grudge against Mr Lambkin, then?' asked Winnie.

'With him, no!' answered Hawthorn. 'There wasn't that in him to get angry about, if you knows what I mean. With his boy, of course, that was different.'

'With Jonathan!' exclaimed Harrison. 'But I thought he had little to do with the village: he was away at school, then, after university, he lived in London.'

'That's right,' responded the other, nodding, 'but then he started coming back to stay more regular with his old man, didn't he?'

'After his mother died, you mean?' Harrison frowned. 'I imagine he was trying to give his bereaved father some support.'

Hawthorn gave a contemptuous laugh. 'Trying to get off with a bit of skirt, more like!'

Again Harrison frowned. 'I don't understand. The Fromes never mentioned anything about Jonathan having a girlfriend here.'

'Mavis wouldn't know!' scoffed Hawthorn. 'That woman never had sense to see the truth of anything, not if it was stuck right under her nose. As for old Hopalong, he wouldn't tell you if he knew: listening to him, you'd think Rector and his family were blooming royalty, the way he goes on!'

'And this girl, Charlie?' interposed Winnie. 'Who was she?'

'Young Daphne Sparrow, wing commander's daughter.' The speaker grinned. 'They were careful, both of them, but I seen 'em together couple of times. One evening they were in the churchyard, holding hands beside Mrs Lambkin's grave.'

Thinking back to the tall, rather pale girl he'd noticed weeping at the funeral, Harrison considered for a moment. 'And do you think Wing Commander Sparrow knew of this relationship?'

'Course he knew—whatever he is, he ain't a bloody fool!'

'And he didn't exactly approve, I take it?'

'What? Of his beloved daughter being sweet on an idle scruff like Jonathan?' Laughingly, Hawthorn shook his head. 'No, he didn't! Not bloody likely! He couldn't stomach the lad.'

Remembering the look of indignation he'd spotted on the churchwarden's face as he'd straightened from dropping his token of earth into the grave, and then of his disparaging remarks about Jonathan at the reception, Harrison wasn't surprised at the old sexton's answer, and glanced significantly across at Winnie.

'Not that I blame him,' continued Hawthorn. 'It's as they say—no good ever come of a parson's son.'

The words came as a sudden intrusion on Harrison's now racing thoughts. Momentarily caught off-balance, he blinked at the speaker. 'Come now,' he said, irritated at what he took as an oblique attack on the Church, 'that's a rather tall statement, isn't it? After all,' he added, forcing a smile, "Lord Nelson was a country parson's son.'

Why this particular illustration should have leapt into his mind wasn't difficult to guess, having so recently been introduced to the Fromes' budgerigar. Instead of shaming him, however, the mention of the national hero's name only caused Hawthorn to laugh the more. 'There you are!' he said, chuckling. 'Point proved! Isn't he meant to have gone cavorting off with that fancy woman of his, leaving his wife back home to look after his old dad.' Raising his mug, the sexton quaffed what little remained of his beer, then wiped his mouth with the back of his hand. 'No,' he added with gleeful satisfaction, 'it's right what the old 'un's always said: son of the cloth is devil's spawn!'

CHAPTER THIRTEEN

Retracing the same route that he and Helen Middlebrook had originally taken, Harrison swung the Volvo off the main road just past the lych gate and, skirting the churchyard wall, began heading out of the village in the direction of Wetmarsh Marden. On that previous occasion, the leaves had still hung thick on the trees, and the morning sun, piercing the mist, had bathed the autumn countryside in a glory of russet and gold. Now, as Winnie and he splashed their way along the heavily puddled lane, all that magical loveliness had long since disappeared: bare branches rose starkly against a grey canopy of cloud, fine drizzle blew slantways before a rising east wind gusting in from the sea, while the surrounding landscape had about it all the bleak barrenness of winter, with only the flocks of gulls sheltering on the ploughed fields relieving the drab monotony of the scene.

Never, in truth, a great lover of the countryside at the best of times, he thought nostalgically of his comfortable chair in front of the sitting-room fire. Normally on a Saturday afternoon he'd be slumped in it now, glass in hand, reading a book or watching a rugby match on television. Nevertheless, much as he'd have preferred to be heading homeward that moment, he felt he had no choice but to be following the route he was taking. After the sexton had finally stumbled off to rejoin his cronies, Harrison had reluctantly agreed with Winnie that, before leaving the parish, he should make what efforts he could to track down the various unlikely hares that, between them, the verger's wife and the disagreeable old sexton had set running.

Winnie's voice broke into his thoughts. 'Did Stella Gittings mind you disturbing her Saturday afternoon?'

'God knows!' he grunted as the car splashed through a larger than usual puddle. 'The woman's so damned polite and cheerful, it's impossible to tell what she's thinking. All the same,' he added, frowning, 'that husband of hers sounded none too pleased when I asked if I might speak to her on a matter of Church business.'

Ahead, the marshes and river lay spread under a slate grey sky, with the flat expanse of Thanet stretching into the distance beyond. Nearer at hand, the familiar concave-roofed barns and high chimneys of Sanctuary Farm rose above wind-bent hedges. Slowing as he approached the final bend, Harrison swung the Volvo past the now deserted cowyard. As he did so, once more before him stood the high-gabled, whitewashed cottage—the setting of so many of his nightmares over the past weeks, and subject, especially of late, of an equally disproportionate amount of his waking thoughts.

'There you are!' he announced, swerving to a stop outside the front gate. 'Hannah Bright's cottage in all its glory!'

Whether because of its associations, or because of the dreariness of the day, Harrison felt none of his original admiration for the house. There was a drab, almost squalid, look about the building, and the blackish-green lichen stains that had recently appeared on its exterior surfaces made it seem more than ever like a whited sepulchre in his eyes—one whose inner corruption and foulness appeared to be seeping out through the thin brickwork of its cheapjack, jerry-built walls.

'Well, I suppose it's quite sweet in its way,' said Winnie, craning past, 'but quite impractical, of course; much too far from any shops, and, being so close to the river, it must get exceedingly damp at this time of year.'

Deeming it wiser not to disclose his own initial reactions to the cottage, Harrison merely grunted assent and began driving on towards the hamlet ahead. Doing so, however, he found himself wondering what on earth had possessed Lambkin to journey all this way over to the deserted cottage that night—and why, when there was the rectory available, had even the deranged Jonathan chosen a place without either heat or light for that terrible final confrontation with his father?

Wetmarsh Marden turned out to be not much more than a few cottages huddled beside an oozy riverbank. There was not even one shop, and, apart from a Victorian postbox, the only public utility appeared to be a gull-streaked telephone kiosk stranded on a muddy triangle of grass.

Stella Gittings had assured him that 'Owlets', as her home was called, couldn't possibly be missed. Standing well back from the road, separated from its humbler neighbours by a well-cultivated garden, it was a spacious modern bungalow with a broad front lawn, adorned at its centre with a miniature version of the traditional village well. Though usually he disliked such garden ornamentation, here Harrison found it oddly cheering: on this bleak winter's day, set between the muddy river and marshy, flat fields, the trim little structure, with its varnished yellow hoist, red-slated roof and matching brickwork surround, seemed a solitary gleam of civilization. It was, therefore, the more jarring to notice that one of the pair of more than adult-sized terracotta owls that guarded the drive entrance was almost completely minus its head, and squatted on the gate-pillar, a mere jagged torso of a bird.

Crunching through thick gravel, the car drew to a halt at the foot of a short flight of steps leading up to a paved terrace. Hardly had the engine been switched off before the front door opened and the dumpy form of Stella Gittings emerged, wearing a long gaberdine raincoat and a headscarf tightly knotted against the wind.

'Ah, good! So you managed to find the way!' she cried, hurrying across the terrace to greet the new arrivals. Reaching the car, she turned and looked back towards where a second figure had appeared. 'Donald, darling,' she called, 'do come and give the colonel a hand with Mrs Harrison's chair.'

Donald Gittings was a balding, lanky man in his mid or late fifties, somewhat nervy and shy. He had a curiously flattish, round face, and what little hair he had was swept back and hung in lank, grey strands down over his shirt collar. He moved slowly and stiffly, and as he helped unfold the wheelchair and bring it round to the passenger door, there seemed a melancholy lassitude about him that was in striking contrast to the bustling, purposeful energy of his much younger wife.

Unlike the ease with which it had been manoeuvred into the Fromes' parlour, getting Winnie's wheelchair indoors turned out to be a laborious business. With the wind gusting about them and the rain spitting in their faces, the two men struggled in vain to drag it up the steps, and the task was accomplished only after Gittings had contrived a ramp from planks collected from his garage. As a result, considerable time had passed before the chair was finally wheeled along a highly polished, uncarpeted hallway into a spacious lounge, one entire wall of which appeared to be composed of glass, with large sliding doors giving out on to a wood-slatted veranda overhanging the river.

'Oh, what a wonderful view!' exclaimed Winnie, thrusting her chair forward so as to enjoy the wide panorama.

'Yes, it's rather good, isn't it?' agreed Stella Gittings, going over to stand at her side. 'We love it here, don't we, darling?' she said, turning to smile back at her husband who, after his exertions outside, had relapsed into his former dumb passivity. 'We feel so close to Mother Nature here—one can easily imagine Mole, Ratty and the rest of the riverbank folk from *Wind in the Willows* paddling past.'

Whatever Gittings's response to this was, Harrison missed it. Having experienced quite sufficient contact with the raw creation for the time being, he was only too glad to be safe indoors, and stood looking about him appreciatively. Clearly, he thought, a great deal of money had been lavished on the decor and furnishings of the bungalow, and standing inches deep in what seemed like the fur of a gigantic Persian cat, he couldn't help comparing the pristine luxury of his present environment with Fordington Rectory, with its thread-bare carpets, drab walls and shoddy saleroom furniture.

'Now, shall we sit down and make ourselves comfortable,' announced Stella Gittings, leading to where armchairs and sofas were arranged round a low, glass-topped table. Having seen her visitors settled, she turned to her husband. 'Now, darling, I know you don't want to be sitting listening to a lot of boring old Church chat. Why don't you go and fetch in the tea things?'

Like some moody adolescent, Gittings silently left the room, avoiding all eyes as he went and moving with his curiously stiff-legged gait. With a pained smile, his wife watched him go, then apologetically turned to her guests. 'I'm afraid,' she said, taking the seat opposite Winnie, 'Donald is a little depressed at present. His business is causing him worry, and, though he doesn't say much, I know his legs give him a lot of pain during damp weather—but anyway,' she continued, 'you didn't drive all this way to hear our little problems. To what do I owe the pleasure of this visit? You said something on the phone, Colonel, about having visited the Fromes.'

'I'm afraid,' answered Harrison, 'I had the unpleasant duty of serving them two months' notice to quit.'

Stella Gittings's smile disappeared. 'Oh, the poor dears!' she murmured sadly. 'They've been expecting it, I know. Nevertheless, it must have been very upsetting for them, coming on top of everything else.'

'Yes, indeed.'

'Well, it was very thoughtful of you to come and inform me, Colonel. I appreciate it enormously, and you may be sure that I shall make it my business to visit them as soon as possible.' The speaker paused. 'I haven't, of course, forgotten your very kind promise to find them suitable alternative accommodation, but I'm afraid that won't be easy. Still,' she continued, readopting her characteristic brisk brightness of tone, 'I have one or two ideas of my own in that regard, and I certainly intend getting the locals to rally round in their support, however unpopular that may make me in certain quarters.'

'How kind!' murmured Harrison, wondering exactly what she meant, and at the same time feeling a trifle uneasy at the thought of her visiting the Fromes, fearing that they might be tempted to divulge to her the advice he'd given them. A look from Winnie interrupted these thoughts, reminding him of the real purpose of their visit. Self-consciously, he cleared his throat. 'Besides the matter of the Fromes, Mrs Gittings, I had another reason for requesting this meeting.'

'Really?'

Ever since leaving the Ferryman he'd been dreading this moment. Given the allegations in the anonymous notes, any reference to them was bound to be upsetting to his hostess. Nevertheless, if any headway was to be made in his investigations, painful or not, the subject had to be broached. Glancing to Winnie for support, he began, 'Whilst in the village, my wife and I heard one or two things that might possibly have a bearing on the identity of the sender of those dreadful communiqués that precipitated the recent tragedy. As the only representative of the Church in the parish now, and as someone with an intimate knowledge of the personalities concerned, we thought we should speak to you.'

Rather wishing he'd avoided the phrase 'intimate knowledge', he broke off, noticing that, just as expected, his interlocutor's face had paled and that she'd lowered her eyes.

'What exactly have you heard, Colonel?'

'It was something that Mavis said to me, actually,' intervened Winnie. 'She mentioned there'd been a slight tiff between Edith Gillmore and Maurice over the running of the school. Of course,' she added quickly, 'it's patently absurd to think that someone like Edith could be connected with those notes. Nevertheless, we wondered if you happened to know of that particular incident.'

As she spoke, the other woman's tension visibly lessened. 'Yes,' she answered, nodding, 'I did know about it. In fact, Edith and Maurice both mentioned the matter to me separately, and were equally sorry it ever happened. The truth, I fear, is that Maurice rather mishandled the situation and wasn't nearly as tactful as he should have been. But really,' she continued, looking earnestly from one to the other, 'I wouldn't like either of you to think that Edith bore Maurice any ill-will. She was very fond of him, and well aware that at that particular time he was distressed over a certain matter that had just cropped up.'

Imagining that whatever had been perturbing Lambkin was likely to have involved Jonathan, Harrison saw an opportunity of moving on to the subject of the young man's involvement with the wing commander's daughter. 'This thing that had upset him,' he said, leaning forward, 'would I be correct in assuming that it had something to do with his unfortunate son?'

Stella Gittings coloured at this. 'No,' she answered hurriedly, evading his eyes, 'it had nothing at all to do with him.'

Surprised by her obvious embarrassment, Harrison hesitated,

but then, ignoring Winnie's warning frown, he pressed the matter. 'I regret having to ask,' he said, 'but might we be told who or what exactly was the cause of this particular upset?'

Raising her head, his hostess faced him squarely. 'I regret saying this, Colonel, but I'm afraid the cause was you—by that, of course, I mean your visit to convey the archdeacon's wishes regarding the future of the Bright Trust.' She paused briefly before adding, 'I don't know if you're aware that Maurice had promised the cottage to the Fromes.'

Stunned by this reply, and himself suddenly quite pink in the face, it was Harrison who now looked down. 'Yes,' he said heavily. 'That is something I only happened to learn of today.'

Thankfully the impasse that followed was cut short by the rattle of crockery and trundle of wheels. With relief, all three looked round as Donald Gittings appeared in the doorway, wheeling in a laden tea trolley.

'Now how about you, Colonel?' Stella Gittings turned from serving Winnie and smiled across the low table at her male guest. 'You've hardly eaten a thing. Can't I tempt you with a little of the fruitcake or perhaps some of my lemon sponge?'

'Thank you, but no,' came the answer. 'I've already had quite sufficient.'

By now the last dregs of daylight were fast draining away, and already a standard lamp had been turned on in the sitting-room. The curtains, however, remained undrawn, and, through the rain-smeared panes, blurred clusters of light shone out from the villages of Monkton and Minster across the river, while further away, along the north-eastern horizon, the street lamps of the coastal towns of Margate, Broadstairs and Ramsgate cast a sickly orange glow on the low-lying blanket of cloud.

Partly from physical weariness, partly from the reminder of

his own part in forcing Lambkin to relinquish the cottage patronage, Harrison was suffering a similar depression of spirits to that
he'd experienced at the Ferryman earlier. As the two women
talked, he'd sat sipping his tea, ruminating on the often painful
consequences of Cawthorne's rationalization schemes as well as
the ambiguity of his own position regarding their implementation. Nor, sitting in the gathering dusk, was his mood greatly
lightened by the sight of his host, who sat listlessly slumped in
the armchair opposite, his flat, round face appearing in the dusk
like some pale, melancholy moon.

'Are you sure you won't have anything, Colonel? Not even
one teeny-weeny slice?'

'Thank you, no. I've really had more than enough.'

Her offer rebuffed, Stella Gittings lay down her knife and
regarded him with concern. 'You know,' she said, 'if it's the matter of the cottage that's on your mind, Colonel, I really wouldn't
let it concern you. After all, you were merely carrying out diocesan policy. Anyway,' she added, 'whatever promises he'd made the
Fromes, Maurice's reaction to the proposed sale was, in my opinion, completely out of all proportion, and only too typical of him
during the final weeks of his life.'

Her words were as balm to Harrison: his hostess was clearly
a perceptive and intelligent woman, and he was able now to
appreciate Winnie's wisdom in persuading him to visit her. Eager
suddenly to discover what more she could tell him of Lambkin's
state of mind, he leaned forward to question her. Before he had a
chance to speak, however, Donald Gittings intervened. 'Cottage?'
he said, looking round. 'Are we talking here of the old spite house
down the lane?'

'Oh, darling, I'm so sorry!' burst out his wife. 'I should have
explained. Colonel Harrison is secretary of the Diocesan
Dilapidations Board, and, as such, is directly responsible for the
future of Bright Cottage.'

'Really?' Turning to face Harrison, Gittings gave a thin

smile. 'How very interesting! So you are one of the movers and shakers of our little world then?'

There was more than a hint of mocking irony in the tone, and, feeling he was being laughed at, Harrison flushed. Before, however, he had chance to stumble out any sort of reply, Stella Gittings hastily intervened. 'As I was saying,' she said, 'Maurice was far from his normal self during those final weeks. In my opinion, he never recovered from his wife's death. Although he coped well enough at the actual funeral, there was a change in him afterwards. He'd always been such a gentle, unassuming man; but gradually his personality seemed to alter for the worse, and he began acting quite irrationally, even dictatorially at times, taking the most extraordinarily tactless decisions without informing or consulting anyone.'

'Like having those spare graves dug?'

'Ah, so you heard about that!' The speaker gave Winnie a smile. 'Yes, but I'm afraid things didn't stop there. In the end he seemed to be upsetting everyone—even dear, faithful Mavis, I noticed, came in for the sharp side of his tongue on occasions.' Pausing, Stella Gittings sipped her tea, then turned back to Harrison. 'Just how odd and irrational he'd become was finally revealed to me shortly after your visit, Colonel. I don't know if you remember the painting that used to hang in his study?'

'The one above the fireplace?'

'That's right. It had hung there, I believe, ever since he and his wife first moved in, and I knew he valued it highly. That's why I found it so surprising when he suddenly took it into his head to destroy it.'

'Destroy it?' echoed Winnie incredulously. 'The picture, you mean?'

'Apparently so. One day I met George carrying it out of the front door. When I asked what he was doing, he told me that Maurice had instructed him to throw it on the garden bonfire.'

'And he was willing to do it?'

'You obviously don't know George very well, Mrs Harrison,' answered Stella Gittings with a smile. 'Like Mavis, he was devoted to Maurice, and would have done anything he asked—even though, on that occasion, I could see that the poor man was obviously upset.'

'But you surely didn't allow him to burn the picture?'

The other woman laughed. 'Of course not! I insisted he hand it over to me, then I took it back into the house and confronted Maurice with it.'

'And what did he say?'

'Not much—only that he was tired of it, and that if I wished to preserve it, I should keep it for myself.'

'And did you?'

'Yes, it's in Donald's workshop now. Somehow its glass had got cracked, and my dear husband here,' said Stella Gittings, smiling round at the man at her side, 'promises to repair it when he gets the chance—don't you, my darling?'

Gittings, who, after his brief interruption earlier, had slipped back into brooding silence, gave a perfunctory smile but said nothing.

'I originally had the idea', resumed his wife, 'of hanging it here in the bungalow. Now I think it ought to be displayed in the Reading Room. It is, after all, a most powerful piece of work.' A sudden flush of joy rose in her face and she beamed with pleasure. 'But I was forgetting—you're an artist yourself, Mrs Harrison! I'd love to have your opinion of it.' Before Winnie could speak, she turned back to her husband. 'Donald, darling, be a pet and fetch the picture for Mrs Harrison to see.'

'Certainly I'd heard the odd whisper, but I was surprised to see her so obviously upset at the funeral.' Stella Gittings paused briefly. 'Daphne doesn't actually live in the parish any longer.

She's working in London for the British Library as some sort of archivist, though she still often comes back to the village to visit her parents.'

'And they, I take it,' said Winnie, 'would not exactly have welcomed the prospect of having Jonathan as their future son-in-law?'

'Most decidedly not. The wing commander, I'm afraid, tends to take a rather narrow view of things. I well remember his somewhat uncharitable comment the last time that Jonathan got himself...' Breaking off, Stella Gittings looked round as her husband re-entered the room, bearing a framed picture beneath his arm. 'Ah, you've found it!' she exclaimed, rising to greet him. 'Show it to Mrs Harrison. I'm longing to hear what she thinks.'

Gittings came forward and passed the picture to Winnie. As he did so, his wife cried out delightedly, 'But you've already replaced the glass! What a clever old thing you are!' Seizing his arm, she smiled up at him before turning to peer over Winnie's shoulder. 'Well, Mrs Harrison, what do you think? It's quite a remarkable piece of work, isn't it?'

'Yes, indeed—very powerful and original in its way.'

Partly from interest, but more perhaps from politeness, Harrison reluctantly dragged himself to his feet. Joining the couple behind Winnie's chair, he regarded the picture she held out at arm's length in front of her.

Looking at it now, he was able to appreciate it as he hadn't had the chance to during the interview with Lambkin. Done in chalk and pastels, it depicted the resurrected Lazarus, emerging from a tunnel of skeletons and bones, hands raised as if to shelter his eyes from the sunlight or from whatever unearthly glory was drawing him forth. Being close to it, he noticed that in the bottom right-hand corner, above the word TIM and the date 1972, was written the word *Redemption*—and with this as a guide, he was able to appreciate that the half-swaddled figure in the grave clothes was not so much stepping forth from literal death as emerging from a metaphorical dark tunnel of sin and corruption.

'Yes,' murmured Winnie again, 'it's certainly striking—a fine example of amateur work.'

'Amateur?' repeated Stella Gittings with more than a trace of disappointment in her voice.

'Oh, certainly,' answered Winnie. 'A gifted amateur, but an amateur none the less.' She pointed a finger. 'You notice that lack of perspective there and the crudity with which the figure itself is drawn.'

'Well,' said her hostess after a moment, 'amateur or not, whoever did it obviously worked from the heart. I'd dearly love to know who this Tim was who painted it, and why the picture meant so much to Maurice—and what insane impulse prompted him to order poor George to take it out and destroy it.'

'All right! Penny for them then!'

The wind had eased, and the rain that had been inter-mittently falling all day had finally ceased as the Volvo swung on to the A257 and accelerated westwards under a rapidly clearing sky. Lulled by the sound of the engine and the warmth from the heater, both occupants had fallen into a drowsy torpor since leaving Wetmarsh Marden and conversation had lapsed altogether. Now, however, roused by his wife's voice, the driver glanced inquiringly round. 'Sorry, dear? What was that you said?'

'I wondered what you were thinking about, that's all.'

'Oh, nothing much,' grunted Harrison; 'just about that pair of terracotta owls back there.'

'Owls!' exclaimed Winnie. 'The ones at the top of the bun-galow drive, you mean? What about them for goodness sake?'

'Merely how one of them came to get broken, that's all.' Harrison paused as a succession of heavy lorries thundered past, their slipstream rocking the car. 'I find it odd,' he resumed. 'Everything's so neat and tidy about the Gittings' place, then they go and leave that god-awful monstrosity perched up there with most of its head missing!'

Winnie turned to stare at the bright ribbon of Catseyes flashing out of the darkness ahead. It was only too easy to guess what memories the shattered statuette had stirred, and what hideous images were now churning in her husband's mind. 'You know,' she said with apparent lightness, 'what struck me about those owls was how like the Gittings they are: Stella so complete in herself, efficiently running the parish and looking forward to ordination; Donald, on the other hand, such a forlorn sort of creature, with his business in trouble, and obviously resenting the demands church work makes on his wife's time. As far as I could see,' she went on, 'the only thing that roused his interest the entire time we were there was learning that you're responsible for the disposal of Bright Cottage.'

'Yes, indeed,' murmured Harrison. 'Extraordinary how that blasted cottage keeps cropping up. It's almost as if that wretched Hannah Bright laid the primordial curse on the place!' He relapsed into silence for a moment, then burst out, 'Damn it, Winnie! I can't help thinking that if only that confounded meddling imp hadn't stirred everything up in the first place with his insistence on its sale, none of this need have happened, and Lambkin and his boy would still be alive today!'

'You mean Dr Cawthorne? Oh, really, Richard! How on earth can you blame the archdeacon for what happened between Maurice and Jonathan?'

'Easily!' Harrison slammed down a gear as they went into a bend. 'If nothing else, this expedition today has made one thing abundantly clear: whatever changes in his character there were following his wife's death, it was only after I'd pressurized him over the cottage sale that Lambkin really flipped his lid and began upsetting everyone in sight—including, I imagine, the writer of those anonymous notes!'

'Oh, come on!' said Winnie. 'It can't have been only the cottage that was upsetting Maurice, however much he might have wished the Fromes to have it. There must have been something else.'

'You'd think so, wouldn't you?' replied Harrison heavily. 'But rack my brain as I might, I can't think what it could have been—not unless, of course, our friend the wing commander had started kicking up the dust about Jonathan carrying on with his daughter.'

Conversation again lapsed. Soon Wingham and a number of smaller villages were well behind, and the lights of Canterbury could be seen glowing against the sky ahead. Then, as they rounded a bend beyond Littlebourne, the illuminated shape of the cathedral appeared in the distance, its triple towers gleaming white above the city. At the sight, Harrison groaned aloud. 'There you are!' he exclaimed. 'Almost back, and what in hell's name have we achieved? A whole day gone, and we're no nearer knowing who compiled those notes than when we left home this morning.'

'Well, we might be,' answered Winnie evenly. 'For example, we now know that Jonathan and Daphne Sparrow had some sort of relationship going. You could go and talk to her: it's possible that Jonathan may have confided to her what this thing was that was troubling his father.'

'What?' burst out Harrison. 'Go back to Fordington, you mean? Go and question a girl I've never met, with her father marching up and down in the background, snorting his disapproval? No, thank you very much! I've had more than enough of wild-goose chases for the present without inflicting myself with that dubious pleasure!'

Impatiently, Winnie turned away and, folding her arms, stared ahead. She said nothing more until they had reached the city outskirts, when, glancing round, she noticed the rapt frown on the driver's face. 'Come on, Richard,' she urged. 'What is it that's really bothering you? You've been like the proverbial bear with a sore head all day. If it's the Fromes and their claim on the cottage that's worrying you, I'm sure there's no need: old-fash-ioned people like them will never take the Church to law.'

'It isn't the Fromes.'

'Then what is it?'

Harrison gave a deep sigh. 'I don't know,' he answered heav-ily, 'it's just that I've got this feeling that, amongst all I've seen and learnt, I've managed to miss something absolutely obvious—some inconsistency which, if I could only put my finger on it, would explain the whole thing: the change in Lambkin and the oddity of his behaviour during his last weeks, the reason the notes were sent, and why he and Jonathan chose to drive all that way through the fog that night to an empty cottage. And why, when they were there, Jonathan should have gone so completely berserk as to end up emptying both barrels of a shotgun point-blank into his father's face!'

PART THREE

CHAPTER FOURTEEN

O come, O come, Emmanuel,
And ransom captive Israel
That mourns in lonely exile here,
Until the Son of God appear.
Rejoice! Rejoice! Emmanuel
Shall come to thee, O Israel.

The high-soaring nave resounded with the triumphant pro-
cessional hymn as a double file of red-robed choirboys and adult
male choristers, headed by a golden cross, began slowly pacing the
central aisle. Behind, led by a gowned sidesman, came the clergy,
followed in turn by the portly form of Simcocks, bearing his
ornate vesturer's staff and moving with ponderous solemnity as he
conducted a thoughtful-looking dean towards where, ahead of the
advancing column, a sombre-clad altar gleamed with festive light.

The unusually large numbers attending matins that morning
were partly a result of the weather, the clouds and rain of the pre-
ceding twenty-four hours having given way to blue skies and
bright sunshine. Nevertheless, the size of the congregation was,
in the main, due to factors beyond the merely meteorological, the

first Sunday in Advent being traditionally marked by the attendance at the cathedral of all the masters and pupils of the King's School. As a result, some eight hundred grey-suited youngsters stood in packed rows immediately facing the pulpit, their juvenile voices adding a slightly shrill note to the singing of those gathered to celebrate the official start of the new Christian year.

Advent Sunday or not, Harrison had been sorely tempted to skip matins altogether. Lack of sleep and the exertions of the day before had left him exhausted. If he hadn't remembered that he and Winnie were expected at the deanery for lunch, he'd have happily postponed his devotions until evensong, and remained where he had been when the bells rang out across the precincts: slumped in the sitting-room armchair, sipping freshly ground best Jamaican coffee whilst drowsily wading through the *Sunday Telegraph*.

The notion, however, of appearing at Ingrams's table without having previously attended divine service was not to be countenanced, representing, as it would, the grossest discourtesy, not only to his old friend and host, but also to a fellow guest, it being the dean's practice to invite the morning preacher to share the Ingrams' Sunday roast. Therefore, spurning a second cup of the delicious Blue Mountain, he'd dragged himself up at the very first peal of the bells, and, leaving an irredeemably heathen wife to enjoy his share of the paper in peace, had set out for the cathedral, yawning and still decidedly bleary-eyed.

> *O come, thou Rod of Jesse, free*
> *Thine own from Satan's tyranny*
> *From depths of hell thy people save,*
> *And give them victory o'er the grave.*

Now that he was actually there, standing in his usual place on the right of the aisle, with the voices of the choir growing louder behind, he was glad he'd made the effort to attend. The familiar tune and well-remembered words had a restorative effect on his jaded soul. Equally reassuring was the sight of so many he knew around him; the faces of Barton-Chadwick, Dr Quirk, Alan Tubman, Major Coles and the rest giving him the comforting sense of being safely back, as it were, in barracks again after the dispiriting, and ultimately frustrating, forays of the previous day.

Curiously enough, this sense of wellbeing was reinforced by the appearance of Simon Barnes and another boy of similar age processing past behind the leading cross. Both were dressed in the plain cassocks of probationary choristers and walked with angelically rapt faces bowed over pressed-together palms. So great was the disparity between the meekness of Barnes's present demeanour and his preposterous wild antics on the night of the Faustus dress rehearsal that Harrison smiled. Indeed, watching Barnes bow before the altar and turn away to the choir stalls, he had difficulty restraining himself from actually laughing aloud at the remembrance of the absurdly large toasting-fork and the child's manic jig round the ghostly, blank-faced figure of Mephistophilis.

Just as on that foggy evening, his enjoyment of the recollection was of short duration. This time, however, his pleasure was not curtailed by any unexpected loud knockings or other such ghostly intervention, but by the very ordinary and totally predictable appearance of Archdeacon Cawthorne passing by at the tail-end of the crocodile of clergy. The sight of the familiar freckled face and gingery hair brought rushing back all his conflicting guilts and worries regarding the Bright Trust. As choir and clergy filed to their designated places, and the dean was ceremoniously bowed into his stall, once again he found himself wondering what the Fromes would eventually decide, and whether they'd overcome their scruples about taking the Church to law.

In truth, he very much doubted it, inclining to Winnie's view that innate conservatism, combined with a very sensible fear of lawyers, would prevent them. All the same, as the hymn ended and the service proper began, he was uncomfortably aware that the possibility remained that, in a matter of days, the verger and his wife could be covering up the budgerigar cage and locking their front door, prior to setting out for Canterbury to assert a legal and moral claim on the cottage tenancy.

In many ways it was an affecting picture: outraged humility seeking redress against entrenched power and privilege. Nevertheless, as a member of the executive himself, Harrison couldn't help inwardly shuddering at the thought of it: not only would the precedent be disastrous to the Church if the claim was upheld, but on a purely personal level, he dreaded the quite justifiable wrath, not only of Cawthorne, but of the entire ecclesiastical hierarchy if it ever should come to light that he, a senior diocesan official, had instigated and encouraged this potentially disastrous act of rebellion.

> 'Dearly beloved brethren, the Scripture moveth us in sundry places to acknowledge and confess our manifold sins and wickedness; and that we should not dissemble nor cloke them, but confess them with an humble, lowly, penitent and obedient heart...'

Gentle and sonorous, the finely crafted phrases of Cranmer and Ridley echoed like a soothing incantation through the nave. Almost as unconsciously as he heard them, Harrison automatically joined in reciting the words of the general confession. During his many discussions on the subject with Winnie, one of his defences of the ancient *Prayer Book* form of service was that it allowed the initiated participant to pursue his devotions whatever his state of mind. Once set in motion, he argued, even the most distraught and unhappy of individuals could take part in divine worship while hardly aware perhaps of actually being in church at all. Similarly now, though his lips continued to utter the ancient responses, and his body to shift between seat, hassock and feet, his thoughts ran freely on, inevitably turning from the problem of the Fromes' accommodation to the identity of the poison-pen writer and the events leading up to that final terrible confrontation between Maurice Lambkin and his son.

Even after getting home the previous evening to find Ingrams's invitation to Sunday lunch awaiting him, he'd been unable to shake off the conviction that somehow, among all that he'd learnt and seen, he'd either not noticed something obvious, or else failed to make some simple connection that might have solved the mystery once and for all. As a result, he'd sat up into the early hours, grasping for an answer that seemed to hang tantalizingly just beyond his reach. Finally, sick to his soul of the whole wretched business, he'd stumbled off to bed, determined to pass what little he'd learnt to Chief Inspector Dowley and to wash his hands of the entire affair. Nevertheless, as matins rolled magnificently on, with the nave resounding with the canticle '*Benedicite, Omnia Opera*', helplessly, hopelessly, drawn like a dog to its vomit, he returned to going over all that he'd observed and heard during the long, frustrating day at Fordington and Wetmarsh Marden.

Beginning with his useless attempts to coax from Frome any revealing or useful confidences regarding his late employer, he trawled through all that he'd gleaned at the rectory. The exercise, however, proved as futile as it had in the early hours: apart from the rosary and the rather pathetic dearth of guests in the wedding photograph, everything had been depressingly predictable. His thoughts moved on to what he'd learnt later of the change in Lambkin after his wife's death, culminating in his uncharacteristic behaviour during his final weeks: his increasing irritability, the insensitivity he'd displayed in the handling of Edith Gillmore as well as over the matter of the empty graves—and the apparent insanity of consigning to the bonfire the much-prized picture from his study.

Just as in the car the evening before, he remained convinced that Lambkin had suffered some sort of breakdown brought on by the pressure he'd been put under to relinquish the cottage patronage. Now as he stood mouthing a hymn, he was suddenly struck by the possibility that the unhappy man might have actually composed the anonymous notes himself. Was that, he wondered, what had actually happened? Alone and isolated in that rambling great rectory, alienated from everyone, including his own son, had the wretched man's mind finally snapped, and impelled by heaven knows what guilt over long-suppressed sexual fantasies involving his female assistant, had he posted off those accusatory notes against himself, one to the archdeacon and one to his son, knowingly and willingly contriving the means of his own destruction by goading the unstable Jonathan to bring ruin literally down upon his head?

For a moment or two, the possibility seemed only too real, but then, recalling the raw, torn flesh of the wrists, he dismissed the idea: however unhappy his six-month widowhood, and whatever strange torments had afflicted him towards the close of his life, Maurice Lambkin had obviously perished struggling frantically to escape the horrific fate that had overtaken him that foggy night in the cottage.

He was just thinking this when he became aware that the singing had ended and the congregation were taking their seats. Hurriedly he did the same, then, realizing that the sermon was about to begin, he looked across the sea of schoolboy heads to see Cawthorne standing in the pulpit, for all the world like some ginger-haired jack-in-the-box. A second or so passed before the full implication hit him. As it did so, he turned towards the dean, who, oblivious of the expression of indignant surprise being directed at him, sat leaning back in his stall, palms placed together, looking up at the preacher with a complacent half-smile.

'Winnie?'

Obtaining no response, Harrison hung up his coat, then

went down the hall to the sitting-room, expecting to find his wife where he'd left her. The room was empty, however, though signs of her recent occupation were evident in the empty coffee mug and the copy of the *Sunday Telegraph* lying in scattered disorder on the sofa. Irritation mounting, he went over and gathered up the newspaper, just as it seemed he'd done every day since astonishing his brother officers by marrying what, to the majority, seemed a dangerously bohemian young art student. Lastly he picked up the mug and carried it out to the kitchen, pausing to call loudly, 'Winnie? Where have you got to? I'm home.'

'I'm in here—and you needn't shout!'

The muffled voice came faintly from the tiny room at the far end of the passage that he used as a study. His displeasure at having to tidy the sitting-room compounded now by what felt like intrusion into his personal space, he went into the kitchen to rinse out the mug. Having done so, he strode back along the hall and entered the study to find his wife sitting, back towards him, at the large desk that occupied most of the facing wall.

She glanced round as he came through the door. 'And how was the service, dear?'

'All right, I suppose,' he answered reluctantly, 'but you'll never guess who the preacher was.'

'I thought it was to be Michael Cawthorne,' said Winnie. 'Margaret mentioned something about Matthew having specially requested him to give the Advent Sunday sermon.'

'You knew!' exploded Harrison. 'Damn it! You might at least have warned me!'

'I thought you'd have known…Anyway,' said Winnie, turning back to the desk, 'what was so wrong with his sermon? He's meant to be a very effective preacher.'

'That isn't the point!' cried Harrison. 'Don't you understand? It means we've got to go and share a meal with the fellow!' Receiving no reply, he turned to the window and despondently looked out to where the organist's cat from next door sat washing herself on the cobbles. 'God knows,' he said, rapping on the glass to catch the animal's attention, 'what I'm meant to say if he asks how things went with the Fromes yesterday!'

'Just say that you handed them the notice to quit,' murmured Winnie, rustling through the papers before her. She suddenly laughed. 'Really, I don't know what you're so worried about. Dr Cawthorne is hardly likely to subject you to the third-degree over the roast potatoes and Brussels sprouts!'

Despite this quite reasonable assumption, Harrison remained glumly gazing out at the cat, who, having raised her head, stared unblinkingly back at him before recommencing her ablutions. He tapped again on the window, but receiving no further acknowledgement of his presence from the creature, he turned away and, crossing to the desk, looked down over his wife's shoulder to see spread out before her the contents of the envelope he'd collected from Jonathan's room the day before.

'For God's sake!' he cried out. 'What are you playing at, Winnie? It's bad enough having to tidy the entire house when I get home, without you coming in here, scattering the things I'd left ready to take over to the deanery!'

'I'm not scattering them! I was just looking through them, that's all.'

As his wife began angrily thrusting the documents back into the envelope, Harrison stood glowering over her shoulder. 'What's that?' he suddenly said, pointing at a photocopied page of a newspaper that lay beneath the coiled up rosary.

'It was among the various certificates in the envelope. Someone's ringed the report on it about a fatal accident involving one of Bridget Lambkin's family.'

Harrison frowned. 'But I thought there was no contact with them. Didn't you say that Bridget was completely disowned when she married Lambkin?'

'That's the impression Margaret gave me,' answered Winnie, sliding the photocopied sheet from beneath the rosary, 'but from the surname and the fact that Jonathan kept the report among his personal papers, I assume the victim must have been a relative.'

'Let's have a look.'

Taking the photocopied page, Harrison went to the window and held it to the light. It was from a five-year-old copy of the *Belfast Telegraph*, and the marked article referred to a coroner's case concerning the death of a twenty-two-year-old man named Brendan O'Brian, who'd apparently been killed in a road accident in the New Lodge area of the city. According to eyewitnesses, it appeared that he'd swerved to avoid a child who'd dashed out into the path of the van he was driving, causing him to collide with a parked vehicle.

'I imagine one of the family sent the photocopy to Bridget,' said Winnie, looking across. 'Brendan O'Brian may have been one of her nephews.'

'It's possible, I suppose,' murmured Harrison, 'but then why would Jonathan bother to keep an account of the death of a cousin he'd presumably never met?' Lowering the sheet, he looked round. 'You know,' he said, 'during Cawthorne's sermon, I kept thinking about Jonathan. Knowing he must have sat in that cathedral on so many occasions and that he'd grown up in its shadow somehow seemed to make that wastrel, useless life of his even odder and more inexplicable.' Pausing, he shook his head. 'What the devil was he doing in London all that time, and where did the money in his bank account come from? Ingrams refuses to believe it, but I'd stake my life he was up to something nefarious—drug dealing or something of the sort.'

Winnie gave a sigh. 'Really, I wish you'd take my advice and go and speak to Daphne Sparrow. You needn't see her at her parents' home: you could always get in touch with her through the British Library, and arrange to slip up and visit her in London— I'm sure she wouldn't mind.'

'Slip up to London?' repeated Harrison. 'For God's sake! What chance have I of finding the time to go gallivanting around the place with all the work that Cawthorne keeps heaping upon my desk?'

His mention of the archdeacon made him check his watch. 'I suppose we ought to be making a move,' he murmured, but instead of making any signs of leaving, he glanced once more at the newspaper report in his hand, then looked up through the window at the cathedral towers and gave a sigh. 'I just don't understand,' he murmured, 'what the fellow thought he was playing at.'

Winnie frowned. 'Jonathan, you mean? His keeping that article among his personal papers?'

'No, not him!' came the irritated response. 'I was thinking of Ingrams and this last-minute invitation of his. He knows that Cawthorne and I aren't exactly best of friends, so what in God's name possessed him to oblige me to share Sunday lunch with the man!'

'*Pig—let me speak his praise,*' declaimed the carver, pausing to smile round the table, '*the strong man may batten on him, and the weakling refuseth not his mild juices.*'

'Oh, Daddy! Do you have to?' protested one of the twins, raising her face to the ceiling with an expression of exquisite pain. 'You say that every Sunday!'

'No, he doesn't—only when we have pork!' snapped her sister, glaring across at her. 'Anyway, don't be so nasty! Daddy has a perfect right to say it if he likes to.'

'That's enough now!' intervened Margaret Ingrams, frowning at her daughters, who sat either side of her at the far end of the table. 'Instead of being silly, look after your guests. Jane, you can pass the apple sauce to Mrs Cawthorne, and you, Judith, help the colonel to some of the roast potatoes.'

Apparently oblivious to the outbreak of domestic discord he'd provoked, the dean resumed slicing the depleted remains of the joint, smiling as if at some private joke of his own. Having cut and served himself two thick slices, he stood against the bright light of the wide latticed window, looking round at the plates of his family and guests. 'Now, let me see—has everyone received sufficient?'

Despite the murmurs of appreciative assent, he continued his survey, his gaze moving from Winnie's plate on his left round the long table until it fell on the one immediately to his right. 'Archdeacon, I've rather skimped you, I fear! Allow me to cut you another slice.'

'No, really, Dean! It's most kind, but you've already been more than generous.'

'Nonsense, my dear fellow! After your exertions this morning, we must feed you up. If nothing else, let me at least pass you a little more of this delicious crackling.'

Disregarding Cawthorne's protests, Ingrams made a sizeable addition to the portion already bestowed, then beamed at his wife. 'Really, I must congratulate you, my dear—you've excelled yourself with this truly magnificent feast.' Reaching for his wineglass, he held it up. 'I propose a toast to our cook and her two able helpers, and also,' he added, turning back again to Cawthorne, 'to our good friend, the archdeacon here, on the triumph of his sermon.'

In many ways, Sunday lunch was the crowning event of the dean's week. After the tedious round of committee meetings and administrative work that occupied the greater part of his life, it was an occasion when he could relax and revel in the dual role of paterfamilias and munificent host.

With three services already over, and gowned and surpliced portraits of four of his illustrious predecessors gazing gravely down at him from the dark, walnut-panelled walls, as well as with the fruit of his skill as a gardener spread before him in the tangible form of roast potatoes, Brussels sprouts and buttered parsnips, he was at his happiest and most relaxed. Smilingly, he now drank his toast, fortified by the knowledge that later, after his guests had gone, he'd have the chance to slip away to his study for a well-deserved nap before venturing forth to round off the week by attending choral evensong, and then finally taking his part in the solemn, calm beauties of compline.

For Harrison, no such easy content or peace of mind was possible. Having arrived with Winnie in time for pre-lunch sherry, he'd entered the drawing-room to find the company already assembled, with Alan Tubman as well as the archdeacon and his wife present. Although the atmosphere had been one of relaxed cordiality, he'd remained apprehensive, certain that Cawthorne would find an opportunity to question him on the outcome of his visit the previous day. Predictably, the half-whispered inquiry had come after they'd all been summoned to eat, and he and Cawthorne were following the others out into the hall. Being prepared for it, he'd assured him that the notice to quit had been duly served and that, in addition, he'd appraised Stella Gittings of the situation. Clearly relieved, his superior had been all smiles and compliments, and entered the dinning-room as apparently relaxed and friendly towards him as during the short honeymoon period of their first acquaintanceship. Nevertheless, now sitting diagonally across the table from him, conscious of the information and advice he'd given the Fromes, Harrison couldn't help feeling a Judas-like unease in his presence, and, as he lowered his glass, he found himself hoping profoundly that no further reference would be made to Fordington or its inhabitants during the course of the meal.

'I thought Jews didn't eat pork.'

This unexpected remark, breaking into the momentary silence that followed the toast, caused all eyes to turn. Shy and quiet as ever, Janet Cawthorne had hardly said a word until this moment. Now, suddenly finding herself the centre of attention, she gave an embarrassed laugh. 'It's just that I found it odd,' she said, blushing as she looked towards the dean, 'hearing that bit from the Bible you quoted.'

Ingrams blinked at her, but before he could get out a word, Alan Tubman intervened. 'No, no, dear lady,' he said, turning to her, 'the dean's quotation was neither from the Song of Solomon nor one of the psalms, as it may have seemed from the light-hearted parody of biblical style. It was, if I'm not mistaken,' he continued, smiling at his host, 'an extract from one of the *Essays of Elia*—doubtless the famous "Dissertation upon Roast Pig".' He suddenly chortled and rubbed his hands. 'A lamb, you might say, frolicking in praise of swine!'

Clearly confused, Janet Cawthorne blushingly bent to her plate. Equally at a loss, Harrison bent to his own, thinking of the generations of boys the old schoolmaster must have similarly mystified. Luckily, Winnie came to the rescue, her voice breaking through the awkward silence that had fallen. 'Oh yes, speaking of agricultural animals reminds me,' she said, turning to the dean, 'while Richard and I were over at Fordington yesterday, we came across some of Jonathan's personal papers. We've left them for you on the hall table.'

'Indeed? How very kind.' Ingrams beamed. 'I'll put them with the other documents I've gathered together.'

'Glancing through them,' continued Winnie, 'there was one item that intrigued us: a five-year-old report from a Belfast news-paper concerning a road accident in which a young man called Brendan O'Brian was killed. We wondered if either you or Margaret knew who he was.'

'Brendan O'Brian?' Ingrams shook his head. 'No, I've never heard the name.' He looked down the table at his wife. 'Did Bridget ever mention a Brendan O'Brian to you, Margaret?'

'No, not a word.' The hostess turned to the schoolmaster. 'What about you, Mr Tubman? As his housemaster, you must have known Jonathan as well as any of us. Did he ever mention anything about his cousins or any of his mother's family to you?'

Tubman dabbed at his lips with a napkin. 'No, I don't think so.' He looked across at Winnie. 'This young man was killed in a road accident, you say, Mrs Harrison? How did it happen exactly?'

'Apparently a child ran out into the path of the laundry van he was driving. He crashed, swerving to avoid hitting the child.'

'Laundry van?' Frowning, Tubman paused. 'And this accident, it happened five years ago, you say?'

'Yes.'

'Most curious!'

Tubman said nothing more and in a few moments general conversation resumed. Harrison was inquiring of the twin on his left as to the Christmas festivities planned at Miss Hawkins' school when suddenly Ingrams's concerned tones cut through the hum of voices. 'Mr Tubman, is everything all right? I notice you're not eating.'

Sound died abruptly and heads turned to where Tubman sat, staring fixedly down at his plate. Emerging from his trance-like state, he looked up to meet the speaker's anxious look. 'Forgive me, Dean—the reference just now to that unfortunate street accident set off a certain train of thought in my mind. I was thinking about laundry services, and was lamenting the fact that these days one doesn't see the same number of those familiar white delivery vans about as one used to.'

Despite a muffled gulp of laughter from one of the twins, Tubman seemed blissfully unaware of any incongruity or oddity in his choice of subject. 'Yes,' he added musingly, taking a sip of his wine, 'one regrets the passing of the old-fashioned laundry collection service.'

'Well,' intervened Janet Cawthorne brightly, 'I suppose now that most people have their own washing machines, or at least can go to a launderette, there isn't quite the same need as there once was.'

'Oh, quite,' murmured Tubman, nodding sagely. 'Yet how valuable the regular laundry collection service was.' Turning, he looked across at Harrison. 'What would you say, Colonel?

Wouldn't you think it a valuable service, a weekly visit from a man dressed in an anonymous white coat, collecting all that soiled linen—those sheets, those pillow cases, those duvet covers as well, of course, as more personal items, such as shirts, socks...'

Before he could go further, his hostess broke in, darting a frown round as she did so to quiet her now giggling daughters. 'Yes,' she said brightly, 'I completely agree—a good laundry service is indispensable. In fact,' she added, smiling round at her guests, 'only a little while back my husband here was threatening to start one of his own.'

Incredulous laughter swept the table and all eyes turned towards the dean, who beamed happily back. 'Quite right,' he answered. 'I said that if school bills continued to rise, we might be forced to take in washing here at the deanery.'

All tension evaporated, conversation moved on to the more usual, and safer, subject of school bills and education in general. Harrison, however, made no contribution. Instead, he remained thinking of Tubman's extraordinary remarks, and, taking a sly glance at the old schoolmaster's face, he couldn't help wondering if retirement and comparative isolation wasn't having a detrimental effect on his psychological balance. His speculations were suddenly cut short by Ingrams's voice.

'Returning for a moment to the subject of my unfortunate godson, Archdeacon, I wonder if I might prevail on you to do me a great favour. With your permission, I'd like to borrow Richard here for one day this week.'

'Borrow him?'

'If I may. A little bird', he added with a guileless smile, 'informs me that you were kind enough to suggest he help me with any practical problems I might encounter as executor to the Lambkin estate.'

Cawthorne, his face as pink suddenly as his wife's had been earlier, forced a sickly smile. 'Of course, Dean, naturally—but might we be told what exactly you need the colonel for?'

'To help me—that's if you are willing, Richard—' answered Ingrams, looking towards Harrison, 'with the clearance of Jonathan's London flat. It's a task I can hardly bear the thought of attempting alone.'

'A pleasure, Dean,' answered Harrison, surprised by the request. 'I'd be delighted to give what help I can.'

'Excellent! Then if there are no impediments, perhaps we might travel up on Wednesday together in that very useful large car of yours.'

'Certainly.' A sudden grip on his wrist made Harrison look round, and understanding the words Winnie mouthed at him, he turned again to his host. 'But on second thoughts, I'd prefer to drive up alone early in the day, then meet you at the address later. That would be more convenient,' he added, avoiding Cawthorne's eyes, 'as it would give me the opportunity to deal with a rather urgent administrative matter requiring my personal attention.'

CHAPTER FIFTEEN

'Ah yes! Hampstead's breezy heath!'

The speaker paused as he topped the rise, and with the south-easterly gale blowing full in his face, stood looking out over the gorse- and shrub-covered slope of Parliament Hill. Before him, under an azure sky, stretched the silvery grey haze of the City of London, no longer the soot-blackened sprawl of his memory, with the delicate spires of Wren churches rising among the blitzed ruins and rubble-strewn bomb sites, but an amorphous mass of skyscrapers and modern office buildings, with only the familiar grey dome of St Paul's protruding as one instantly recognizable survivor of a world long-since submerged beneath a billowing sea of concrete and tinted glass.

'Talk about a peak in Darien!' he exclaimed again, clutching his collar against the wind as he turned to address the dark-haired, pale-faced young woman at his side. 'I don't know if our local poet had this particular eminence in mind, but one certainly needs to be something of a stout Cortez to be up here at all in this weather!'

'Oh, I'm so sorry, Colonel!' exclaimed Daphne Sparrow, observing his rather purplish cheeks with concern. 'You're obviously freezing cold!'

'No, really,' answered Harrison, smiling, 'that was just my little joke. Actually,' he said, turning back to gaze out across the shrubland, 'I'm only too glad to stretch my legs after all that time in the car, and this breeze should serve to blow a few cobwebs from the brain.' He paused, adding, 'And also perhaps to help chase away a few rather unhappy ghosts.'

The ghosts he spoke of had begun manifesting themselves soon after he'd taken the right fork at Chalk Farm underground station and begun the long climb up Haverstock Hill. So surprisingly familiar and unchanged was the territory, and so poignantly painful the memories it evoked, that by the time he'd found Willow Road South and managed to park, he'd been only too thankful to exchange the well-remembered streets for the spookless anonymity of Daphne Sparrow's little basement flat. Her almost immediate invitation to accompany her on a walk across the heath had, therefore, come as an unwelcome shock, which only politeness and the awareness of her tension and desire to escape the intimate confines of the apartment had prevented him from refusing.

During the first summer of his marriage, when Harrison was newly back from Germany and attached to Brigadier Greville's department at the old War Office, and Winnie was teaching at the Chelsea College of Art, the two of them had often escaped the stuffy heat of central London by driving up to Hampstead to spend weekends with a group of Winnie's friends who'd rented a house overlooking what he later was to regard as the ironically named Vale of Health. It had been a blissfully happy time for them both: tennis parties, walks on the heath, taking tea at Kenwood House, dropping in for drinks at the Spaniards and Jack Straw's Castle, visiting local places of interest, including the house where Keats had heard the famous nightingale sing. Then, on the very same night when that glorious long season of heat ended abruptly with a terrific thunderstorm, Winnie had been struck down with acute anterior poliomyelitis, after having apparently picked up the water-borne virus during a swimming-expedition to the so-called 'ponds'. Ever afterwards, the very name Hampstead had rung like a knell, and fifteen minutes before, when accompanying the wing commander's daughter along the narrow spur between the gale-ruffled pools, he'd been hardly able to look towards the spot on the grassy bank where, nearly forty years before, that youthful, light-hearted bathing party had frolicked under a blazing sun.

'Colonel, are you all right?' His companion's anxious voice intruded on his thoughts. 'You really don't look at all well. Wouldn't you care to sit down for a few moments' rest?'

Harrison nodded. 'Yes, I think I will if you don't mind. My early start this morning has rather fatigued me, I fear.'

He went over and sat on the public bench overlooking the view. Daphne Sparrow did the same, and for a while the two sat together, gazing at the panorama spread at their feet.

'But tell me,' said Harrison finally, 'what made you choose this area to live in? Don't you find it rather tiresome, having to travel in on a crowded underground train all the way to Bloomsbury?'

'Bloomsbury?'

'That's where the British Library is, isn't it?' He laughed. 'I may be wrong but I thought it was still based at the British Museum, awaiting the move to the New Jerusalem they're spending eternity building next to St Pancras Station.'

Unsmiling, the girl shook her head. 'Oh, I don't actually work at the main library itself, Colonel. I'm based in Colindale— that's only four stations north.'

'Colindale?' repeated Harrison with a frown, having a vague memory of a rather anonymous northern suburb to which he and Winnie had once journeyed to buy the second-hand Standard

Eight that had seen them through the first four years of their marriage. 'Good lord!' he exclaimed. 'What's the British Library doing with an outpost there—trying to educate the natives?'

To his enormous relief, this time his companion actually laughed. 'No,' she answered. 'Colindale is where the national newspaper archives are stored.' Her smile suddenly fading, she turned and looked away. 'In fact, it was at Colindale that Jonathan and I met.'

Although, in his letter, Harrison had said that he wished to discuss certain matters concerning Jonathan, he'd so far avoided any mention of his name. However, now that she'd mentioned it herself, he felt his constraint removed. 'Really?' he said, adopting as light a tone as he could. 'So you met here in London, then? I'd rather taken it for granted the pair of you had chummed up back in the village.'

'No, Jonathan came to research something in the archives, and happened to recognize me.' Pausing, Daphne shook her head sadly. 'Quite honestly, I don't think we'd ever have got to know each other back home. Dad disapproved of Jonathan, and Mum's opinion of him wasn't much better. Anyway, as I said to the police, Jonathan had always seemed rather aloof back in Fordington and never really mixed with anyone.'

'Did I hear you right just then? You say the police have interviewed you?'

'Oh yes, they arrived just after that horrible thing happened. I don't know how they knew about me, but anyway, they asked a lot of questions about Jonathan's relationship with his father, and if I'd known of any special strain between them.'

'What did you say?'

The speaker shook her head miserably. 'There was really nothing I could tell them. I knew that something was troubling Jonathan, and that whatever it was involved his father because he'd always go quiet whenever I mentioned him, but I couldn't work out what it was.'

She broke off and, dropping her gaze, sat looking down at her lap. Harrison didn't speak. It was only too easy to guess what she was feeling: a sense of inadequacy at having failed to foresee the tragedy; perhaps also guilt and remorse at not having prevented it by probing the cause of whatever had been oppressing the young man she'd obviously been very much in love with.

'The fact is,' she resumed at last, 'although we were close emotionally, Jonathan never allowed me to know much about him. He never said how he spent his time and he didn't introduce me to any of his friends. He would always come here to Hampstead to visit me, and never once invited me back to where he lived.' She paused, gnawing her lower lip. 'I couldn't even ring him,' she resumed, 'as it seems there was no telephone in this squat where he stayed; and the post office didn't deliver there, so I couldn't even write—I had to wait until he contacted me.'

'And you accepted this?'

Daphne shrugged. 'I had no choice. I don't know why, but I knew it had to be that way. Anyway,' she added bitterly, 'it wasn't as if we knew each other very long—a few months, that's all.'

There was a slight break in her voice as she finished, and, giving her time to recover, Harrison sat digesting what he heard. To learn that the police had already questioned her had come as a blow, for if she'd had information that might throw some light on the happenings in Bright Cottage, she would almost certainly have given it to them. Equally disappointing was that Jonathan hadn't trusted her with any information at all, either as to the manner of his life or on the state of his relations with his father; even misleading her, as he'd done everyone else, regarding the details of his accommodation.

Instead of leading a hunt, it felt as if the chase had long swept past, and that he was left merely following across broken ground in search of a scent long gone cold. Gloomily, he stared out over the city, certain that the trip to the capital was going to turn out as frustrating as the one to Fordington had been, and that the true nature of Jonathan's life was destined to remain closed to him for ever. With the wind ruffling his hair, he sat with knitted brows, arms crossed, until a question occurred to him. 'These researches that Jonathan conducted at Colindale—you wouldn't know if they were connected to a fatal road accident involving a laundry van in north Belfast?'

Obviously mystified, the girl shook her head. 'No, they weren't to do with anything like that. As far as I can make out, he was interested in the details of a raid on a bank security van that took place at Heathrow Airport back in the sixties.'

Disconcerted at this unexpected answer, Harrison stared at her, then, realizing what he'd just heard, he said, 'You used the present tense—do I take it you have access to his research material?'

'Oh yes, he made photocopies of pages from various newspapers which he asked me to keep for him. If you like,' she said, rising to her feet, 'when we get back you can look through them for yourself while I'm making us both a hot drink.'

'Was it too milky for you?'

Raising his head, Harrison blinked inquiringly over his reading spectacles at the questioner who stood observing him from the doorway separating the tiny kitchen from the equally minuscule dinette he was seated in.

'The coffee,' said Daphne, eyeing the still-brimming mug on the table beside him. 'You obviously didn't like it.'

'No! no!' protested her guest. 'It's fine—absolutely delicious, I assure you!' As if to prove the point, he hurriedly took a sip of the now decidedly tepid liquid, over which a thick skin had formed during the quarter of an hour that it had remained untasted and forgotten at his elbow. 'There,' he said, wiping his lips, then beaming up at his hostess, 'just the way I like it.'

With a sceptical smile, Daphne's gaze moved to the mass of

photocopied sheets laid before him on the formica surface. 'Well?' she said. 'I was right, wasn't I? It is that raid on the Heathrow security van that links them?'

Taking a second dutiful sip of his drink, Harrison nodded. 'Yes, indeed,' he murmured, again scanning the papers. 'What these contain is a very thorough and wide-ranging collection of press reports on that unpleasant little saga.'

The 1962 Heathrow Airport robbery had made huge headlines at the time, due to the violence employed in the carrying out of the crime, the value of the bank notes stolen, and the desperate resistance the cornered robbers later put up attempting to evade arrest. So shocking had it all seemed back in those comparatively gentle days, that, until superseded by the Great Train Robbery ten months later, the crime became a symbol of the lawless direction in which society appeared to be heading, and, as such, the subject of countless sermons and press articles. As soon as Harrison had begun skimming the contemporary news reports, the entire sequence of events had come back to him: the use of chloroform to overcome the van guards; the savage pistol-whipping of the member of the public who attempted to intervene; the Chicago-style shoot-out with the police after the gang was surrounded in their West London hideaway twenty-four hours later—a shoot-out during which two of the four gangsters had been shot dead, another severely wounded, while the last had badly injured himself whilst attempting to escape from an upstairs window—and finally, the uproar in the press when the trial judge, taking into account the grievous extent of the injuries both surviving gang members had sustained, sentenced them to what had seemed a shockingly lenient sentence of eighteen years apiece.

'But what about these?' said Daphne, pointing to the few photocopied sheets that had been placed apart from the rest. 'They're the ones taken from slightly more recent newspapers, aren't they? What's their link to the rest?'

'Ah, yes,' murmured Harrison, picking them up. 'That was a little more difficult to spot, but again they all turn out to contain something concerning the Heathrow robbery. For example, this one', he said, holding up the top sheet, 'is from the London *Evening Standard* of the eleventh of August, 1973. If you look at this,' he said, indicating a short item near the bottom of the page, 'you'll see it's a report of a coroner's inquest into the death of Thomas Ian Marshal, one of two surviving gangsters, who apparently died in the infirmary of Wormwood Scrubs Prison as an indirect result of the gunshot wound he'd sustained at the time of his arrest.'

'And the other two sheets?'

'Again, they both contain reports of a coroner's inquest, this time on the death of the final gang member—a man named James Franklin. His body was dragged out of the Thames a few weeks after his release from prison, two years after Marshal's death. Though the partly dismembered corpse was badly mutilated and already in an advanced state of decomposition, it was identified through the physical injuries he'd originally received when attempting to evade arrest and partly through the prison-issue underclothes he was wearing.' Pausing, Harrison glanced between the photocopied sheets in his hands. 'It would seem that he'd been shot through the base of the neck in an execution-style killing prior to being dumped in the river. There was also evidence that he'd been tortured prior to his murder, presumably by some criminal associate attempting to extract the whereabouts of the substantial residue of cash still unrecovered from the total amount stolen during the robbery.'

As he broke off, from overhead there came the clatter of footsteps and the sound of high-pitched voices and laughter from a file of schoolchildren passing along the pavement outside. 'What I don't understand,' said Daphne as the sounds faded, 'is what possible interest all this could have had for Jonathan. After all, he wasn't even born until six years after the robbery happened.'

Oppressed by the very same thought, Harrison gazed down at the papers for a few moments more before again looking up at the girl. 'I don't suppose,' he said, 'that you happen to know how long Jonathan took to compile this material?'

'No, not exactly, but he wasn't at Colindale more than one day.' The speaker frowned. 'But why do you ask, Colonel?'

Harrison shrugged. 'Only because that tells us that Jonathan obviously knew what he was looking for. To have covered all the years from the time of the robbery itself through to the deaths of Marshal and Franklin in a single day means he must already have had a good idea of the dates concerned.' Breaking off, he thought for a moment. 'There's no chance, I take it, that Jonathan left anything else here with you?'

'No,' said Daphne, 'nothing apart from some clothes.'

'May I see them?'

'Yes, of course—I'll get them. They're in the bedroom.'

As the girl went out, Harrison began replacing the photocopies in their folder. Far from illuminating the mystery, if anything they had only darkened the general gloom encircling the terrible events that night in the cottage. Why on earth should anyone bother to research the details of a thirty-year-old robbery, and what possible interest could the late rector's son have had in that now comparatively ancient crime? One possible explanation occurred to him: whilst living his disreputable life on the edge of the law and moving among the vast underclass of London, Jonathan had possibly stumbled across some lead on the missing money, and his trip to Colindale had been part of some sordid treasure-hunting expedition. Almost as quickly as the idea came, however, he dismissed it. Even if the man, Franklin, had remained silent under torture, and had taken the secret of where the missing money was hidden to his watery grave, between the time of the original robbery and now, the stolen bank notes would have long ceased to be legal tender, and as worthless, therefore, as Jonathan's own life had apparently been.

Placing the refilled folder in front of him, he looked round the tidy little room. It was curious, he thought, the degree of affection that the young man had managed to inspire, not only among warm-hearted, generously inclined souls like Ingrams and Tubman, but even in such a severe and formidable character as his father's aunt. Now once again, as during their walk across the heath, he found himself wondering what possible attraction an unemployed failure like Jonathan could have had for such an obviously intelligent, likeable and attractive girl as Daphne Sparrow. This speculation brought back to his mind the remembrance of the strangely taciturn, passive Donald Gittings, and, thinking of his bustling, purposeful wife, Harrison found himself marvelling at the capacity of the feminine heart to lose itself to the apparently most unprepossessing of men.

'Right, this is all of it, then,' announced Daphne, reentering the room with a bundle of clothes. 'As I told the police, I really haven't known what to do with them,' she said, laying on the cleared table a folded charcoal grey suit and dark overcoat, together with some clean shirts, a couple of silk ties and a pair of formal black shoes.

Harrison's surprise at the quiet good taste and obvious quality of the items was momentarily overlaid by the mention of the police, and by the depressing reminder that he was merely following in the wake of a long-abandoned hunt. 'I presume,' he murmured, fingering one sleeve of the suit, 'that the police have already gone through the pockets?'

'Yes, but they were all empty.'

Despondently, Harrison contemplated the pile of clothing, then looked up. 'Tell me,' he asked, 'why did Jonathan leave these things in your flat?'

Daphne shook her head. 'I don't know, just that he'd always arrive in some awful pair of torn jeans and that grubby old leather jacket he wore, then want to change into these things before we went out anywhere.'

'What sort of places did you go to together?'

'Oh, I don't know—just normal sort of places. Sometimes we'd go to a restaurant, sometimes we went to the theatre or a concert or the opera.'

'Opera?' repeated Harrison incredulously, remembering the sight of that scruffily dressed, blood-sodden corpse with its long ponytail and the gold ring in its ear. 'And Jonathan actually liked doing such things?'

'Oh yes,' she answered emphatically. 'He loved going out, especially to the theatre. We went up in my car to Stratford-on-Avon a couple of times, once to see *Hamlet* at the Memorial Theatre, another time to see a modern play.' She wrinkled her brow. 'I forget what it was called, but it was about the life of Kit Marlowe and the events leading to his death. We had a terrible time getting there,' she continued rather wistfully, 'with icy roads and really thick mist, but Jonathan insisted on going. He seemed to have quite a thing about Marlowe—partly, I suppose, because they'd been at the same school.'

Harrison hardly heard her: the clothes on the table in front of him and all that Daphne had said about the young man's tastes and interests were at such variance with his image of the rector's son that it might have been a completely different person she was speaking of—that other Jonathan who'd so impressed Christabel Lambkin on the day of his mother's funeral; the young man who'd died with a respectable bank balance and with an eminent firm of solicitors looking after his affairs.

'What about these clothes, Colonel? What should I do with them? Is there anyone to whom they should be sent?'

Harrison shook his head. 'No, not really. What I suggest is that you take them along to your local branch of Oxfam. As for these photocopied sheets, however,' he said, picking up the folder, 'I'd like to take them away with me, if I may—they might possibly be of some use.'

Daphne frowned. 'Use for what, Colonel?' she asked, a sudden sharpness in her tone. 'In your letter, you said that you wanted to talk about Jonathan, but you still haven't really explained why.'

'Haven't I?' Harrison smiled. 'It was nothing really important, just that my friend, Dean Ingrams, is chief executor to the Lambkin estate. All I'm doing is helping him tidy a few loose ends.' Seeing her perplexity deepen, he hurriedly glanced at his watch. 'And that reminds me,' he said, rising, 'I really must be going. As I said earlier, I've a rather important meeting with him this afternoon in what he informs me is one of the more historic and interesting areas of our capital.'

'Oh, no! You can't go yet,' burst out his hostess. 'I've a lasagne cooking in the oven, and your appointment isn't for another two hours.'

Either the appeal in her eyes or the thought of hot food made Harrison hesitate. Noticing, Daphne smiled winningly. 'Come on,' she coaxed, 'do stay—I promise I won't ask any more questions.' Even as she spoke, her smile vanished and she winced. 'Those,' she said sorrowfully, tears suddenly misting her eyes, 'were the very words I remember saying once to Jonathan—and now here I am again, promising you exactly the same thing.'

CHAPTER SIXTEEN

'**Y**ou can't miss it, squire—just follow the Stowage on to the end.' Withdrawing his florid face from the side window, the pedestrian straightened and, swaying slightly, pointed down the narrow lane. 'St Nicholas is on the right of the junction ahead. You'll find plenty of room to park alongside the green.'

The cheery confidence with which this information was imparted did something to restore the recipient's flagging spirits. Thanking his informant, but leaving his side window wound down to dispel the beer fumes now permeating the car, Harrison began driving on, glancing in the mirror to see the shabby figure turn to resume a weaving perambulation along the dusty cobbles behind.

Just as he'd feared, the so-called 'historic Deptford' of the dean's description was turning out to be a mere chimera of that cleric's somewhat rose-tinted imagination. Indeed, from the moment he'd emerged from the Rotherhithe Tunnel into the dreary wastes of south-east London, he'd been reminded of nothing so much as the time when, during a stopover at Tunis Airport, he'd made a hurried expedition to view the site of ancient Carthage. On that occasion, borne through the blazing North African heat in the back of a battered Peugeot taxi, he'd waited in vain for sight of the columns and walls of the city of Hannibal and Dido. Arriving finally in a nondescript suburban street, he'd been ushered into what seemed like someone's back garden, there to have a guide wave a hand over a few small lozenge-like tombstones and some broken segments of masonry, gleefully proclaiming, '*Voilà, Monsieur, c'est ça, Carthage!*' Similarly disillusioned, he now drove on between rusting cliffs of corrugated-iron and grimy redbrick walls, finding the once-bustling Elizabethan naval base so apparently blighted by inner-city neglect and decay that even the normally ubiquitous yellow lines were lacking from the roadsides, making it seem as if the birthplace of *Swiftsure, Peppercorn, Scourge of Malice* and all the other proud vessels that had sailed out to harry the Armada and plunder fortunes of gold on the Spanish Main had latterly sunk so low in national esteem as to be beyond even the reach of parking regulations.

If the mention of 'the green' and the evocatively named 'Stowage' had revived any lingering hopes of stumbling upon some quaintly preserved segment of sixteenth-century Deptford, Harrison was to be rapidly disabused. Reaching the junction, he looked across the road to see that the central square of grass had been completely built over, and where Howard, Hawkins, Raleigh and Drake might have trod the sward on summer evenings four centuries before, playing bowls and smoking long pipes, there now rose a massive complex of council flats, its tiers of windows and grey granite walls every bit as implacable and heart-quelling as the yawning gundecks and towering stern-castles of the erstwhile great galleons and carracks of Spain.

Swinging across the road, he drew the car to a stop below

the flats. As he turned off the engine, his ears were assailed by a miscellany of noise: cries of children from the open landings of the tenement block opposite; hoots of a tug manoeuvring out on the Thames; hammering and grinding of metal from a breaker's yard—and over and above it all, borne on the wind as from the nethermost regions of hell, the mournful, hoarse bawlings of what might have been the lost souls of generations of Deptford sailors.

Surprised by a sound so appropriate to a country rectory, yet so incongruous and unexpected in this dismal urban setting, Harrison looked up through the open window to see that the dean had not been entirely wrong after all, and that one remnant at least survived of the original riverside community. Protruding above the high wall beside the junction, and clustered about with lofty, swaying elms, rose an ancient, weather-beaten church tower, over which a colony of rooks wheeled and soared, making loud and continuous protest.

Although twenty minutes remained before the arranged meeting time, he went round to the back of the car and took out a pile of empty cardboard boxes. These he carried across to the churchyard entrance, noticing as he approached that, in the manner of the guardian owls at the top of the Gittings drive, its tall, ivy-covered gate-pillars were surmounted with a pair of huge stone skulls, each crowned with laurel and resting on a nest of ele-phantine-proportioned crossbones. Momentarily, he stood gazing up at these gruesome adornments before turning to peer in through the gate.

Within, the scene was the antithesis of the world without— a country churchyard, seemingly magically spirited across time and space from some primordial landscape of lowing herds and tinkling sheepfolds. Even in winter, the enclosed area appeared rich and verdant, with neatly trimmed lawns and with saplings and bushes overhanging well-tended graves. Reinforcing his favourable impression of the care and maintenance given this retired spot, Harrison noticed a burly figure moving head-bent among the tombstones in the distant corner.

Turning away, he placed his boxes on the pavement, then stood looking about, wondering from which direction Ingrams would arrive. He checked his watch, hoping that his old friend had not encountered any difficulty in persuading one of the notoriously reluctant London cabbies to venture south of the river. He was thinking this when, above the incessant cawing of the rooks, he heard his name called, and, swinging round, was astonished to see the very person he was thinking of hurrying across the churchyard towards him, carrying a large plastic bag.

'Ah, Richard! There you are! I saw you at the gate. I trust you haven't been waiting long.'

That he'd failed to recognize Ingrams immediately, and had mistaken him for some sort of sexton or groundsman, was quite understandable. Dressed as he was in a shapeless tweed jacket, corduroy trousers, red shirt and green tie, the gentle, scholarly Dean of Canterbury might well at that moment have passed as a local street trader or the owner of the nearby breaker's yard.

Catching the other's expression, Ingrams smiled self-consciously as he came through the gate. 'Forgive my appearing in mufti,' he said, 'but, given the locality, I thought it better to arrive incognito.'

'Quite—very wise, I'm sure,' murmured Harrison, feeling suddenly rather overdressed in his formal dark overcoat and pin-stripe suit.

'Having arrived early, I took the opportunity for a browse round St Nicholas,' resumed Ingrams, turning to look back at the church. 'As you see, the main structure has been largely rebuilt since being fire-bombed during the last war. Nevertheless, the building remains an absolute gem. The tower is original fourteenth century, and still much the same, I imagine, as on that summer's day when young Marlowe's body was carried over from Mrs Bull's tavern and laid to rest somewhere close to its foot.'

'The fellow's actually buried here?'

'Oh, yes indeed—the entry is still to be seen in the burial register: *Christopher Marlowe, slaine by Francis Frizer, the 1st of June 1593.*' The speaker unexpectedly laughed. 'Typical, as with so much else regarding that young man, that even in such few words, the late Reverend Thomas Macander should have managed to get one detail wrong—the killer's name was Ingram, not Francis Frizer—a sort of near namesake of mine,' he added with a small chuckle. Still,' he said, his smile disappearing, and finally turning away from the gate with a deep sigh, 'this perhaps isn't the moment for history lessons, fascinating as the Marlowe story is. As arranged, I went to Gray's Inn earlier and collected the keys from Littlebone & Gibb. According to them, Jonathan's flat is in the tenement block ahead of us here, adjoining the churchyard wall.'

Picking up the boxes, Harrison began following his companion along the deserted pavement. After a few steps, Ingrams paused to look up again at the tower. 'Well,' he sighed, 'whatever the reason my unhappy godson chose to follow his great predecessor to this somewhat unlikely spot, and however similarly irregular his existence here, at least—in a purely physical sense—he didn't stray far from Mother Church. Nor, it seems,' he added, craning back to view the wheeling dark birds overhead, 'did he ever manage to escape the sound of these same baleful harbingers of doom that everlastingly echoed about his childhood home.'

Though far smaller and less immediately forbidding than the massive, more modern complex opposite, Church Close was, nevertheless, a decidedly dreary, barrack-like warren of flats. Neither the liberal application of bright paint, nor the recent installation of varnished pinewood security doors and a modern entry-phone system at the foot of its semi-exposed staircases, could disguise or soften its stark austerity. As the two visitors approached across a tarmac yard, a host of small children scampered about the communal landings overhead, their high-pitched shrieks and yells resounding and echoing among the labyrinth of bare stone corridors and passageways.

Having reconnoitred in advance, Ingrams guided Harrison under a cat's cradle of washing-lines to lead the way up a flight of draughty steps to a second-floor landing. Bearing his load of cardboard boxes, Harrison followed along a narrow, windswept walkway overlooking the river, sensing already that the flat would have little to tell him of its late occupant's existence, yet at the same time unable fully to suppress the hope that here at last, in this bleak, unprepossessing environment, he might yet discover some clue as to whatever it was about his life that the rector's son had been so anxious to hide from his girlfriend and everyone else.

Reaching the last in the row of yellow-painted front doors, Ingrams paused and inserted a key. Instead of immediately entering, however, he turned away to gaze out across the Thames towards the Isle of Dogs—that outcrop of marshy ground in the bend of the river that, in the time of Deptford's greatness, had been little more than a stinking repository for London's middens and the despised refuge of an army of fugitives and criminals, but which latterly had become a burgeoning Manhattan of skyscrapers, office blocks and luxury waterside apartments.

'Well, Dean?' inquired Harrison gently, pausing at his shoulder. 'Do we venture in, then?'

'I suppose we must,' sighed the other, reluctantly turning again to the door. 'Though now that we're actually here, I must admit to finding myself more apprehensive than ever of what we are likely to encounter inside.'

Exactly what he was expecting—discarded needles and bloodied tufts of cotton wool, or merely the squalid evidence of incapacitating depression—the dean didn't say, but whatever it was, as it turned out, his forebodings proved completely unfounded. In fact, what immediately struck both men as they entered was the stark, almost clinically clean orderliness of the small, one-bedroomed flat. Its distempered white walls were bare of all pictures or posters, and, apart from a particularly fine example of a mounted ship-in-a-bottle propping up books on the lounge mantelpiece, no ornamentation or personal touches of any sort were apparent anywhere. What little furniture it contained was all blandly utilitarian, while the rooms and hallway were uniformly carpeted in a dark grey durable pile. Such, indeed, was its functional anonymity, that as Harrison followed Ingrams round the apartment, peering into cupboards and drawers, he was reminded of nothing so much as the rather dreary succession of married quarters in which he and Winnie had been forced to spend the greater part of their early married lives.

'I really must apologize, Richard,' said Ingrams finally as they re-entered the lounge. 'I'm afraid I've dragged you away from your labours unnecessarily. Apart from that useful little microwave oven in the kitchen and these paperback books in here, there's really nothing for us to collect or sort out beyond some bed linen and a few sorry oddments of clothes.'

Harrison went over to a wall and sniffed the plasterwork. 'This entire place,' he said, 'has been recently redecorated. No one at Littlebone & Gibb, I suppose, happened to mention who might have done it?'

'No,' said the other, shaking his head, 'nothing was said to me on the matter. I can only imagine that the local borough council, being the landlord, is responsible.'

Frowning, Harrison said nothing, and, going over to the window, gazed thoughtfully out across the rolling grey river towards where the massive, Babel-like, light-flashing monstrosity of the Canary Wharf Tower loomed up among the buildings on the opposite bank, completely dominating the skyline.

'I just don't understand it!' burst out Ingrams, looking about him unhappily. 'What on earth was Jonathan doing here these last five years, and why should he have given his father the impression that he was sharing a derelict building with a crowd of his fellow dropouts, when he was actually living here in this quite respectable, if somewhat depressing, little flat?'

'My guess', answered Harrison, still staring across the river, 'is that he simply didn't wish to be immediately contactable—illegally occupied empty buildings don't have phones, nor are they the sort of places that encourage surprise visits, either from parents or close family friends.'

'He simply went to ground, you mean—crawled away here to lick his wounds after young Stephen Hardwick's death?' The dean frowned. 'That's possible, I suppose, but somehow, for me, the notion of him seeking his quietus in this unlikely hermitage doesn't exactly square with the numerous scrapes he got himself into, nor, indeed, with being bound over by the magistrates to keep the peace.'

Harrison made no reply. Since his meeting with Daphne Sparrow, neither the condition of the flat nor the sight of its wall-mounted telephone had greatly surprised him. For whatever reason, there had clearly been an almost pathological secretiveness about Jonathan Lambkin as well as something oddly schizophrenic in his make-up—an inverted Jekyll-and-Hyde element. Behind the public face of the scruffy, lawless, bohemian parasite was hidden another personality altogether: that of the young man with the respectable bank balance and a discreet little firm of city solicitors to manage his affairs; someone who stole away at weekends with the wing commander's daughter to attend the theatre, concerts and operas, wearing well-cut dark suits and tasteful silk ties.

'Ah, well,' sighed Ingrams, 'who but God can fathom the torturous labyrinths of the human mind? What Jonathan was at heart and what was motivating him, I suppose we'll never know.'

So saying, he took up the bag that he'd brought with him and drew out a wodge of plastic bin-liners. 'Perhaps if you'd be kind enough to start gathering up the books in here, I'll go and make a start at clearing the bedroom.'

'One moment, Dean,' said Harrison suddenly as the other turned for the door. 'You wouldn't by any chance happen to know why your godson might have had a particular interest in the Heathrow Airport robbery back in the sixties?'

The question took Ingrams completely by surprise, and he blinked in startled astonishment at his friend. 'The Heathrow Airport robbery!' he repeated incredulously. 'Good lord! Why ever do you ask?'

'Only because it appears that he recently researched the subject at the national newspaper archives.'

'Really! You amaze me.' Ingrams wrinkled his brow. 'No,' he said, shaking his head, 'I really can't think why Jonathan might have had any interest in that dreadful incident—not unless, of course,' he added, his face suddenly brightening, 'he was planning to write an article or even a book on the subject.' The joy inspired in the good-natured scholar by this happy thought rapidly faded, however, as he turned and again surveyed the bare room. 'Though if he'd been seriously thinking of taking up a literary or journalistic career, one would have expected to have come across some sort of writing engine here in the flat—a word processor, perhaps, or an old-fashioned manual typewriter at the very least.'

Having once more drawn a blank, Harrison remained gazing through the window after his perplexed-looking companion had left the room. Out on the river, a tug was towing a rubbish barge downstream against wind and tide, and as he watched the little procession splashing its way through the choppy water, with gulls circling above the heavily laden lighter, he was reminded of the sight of the tractor and dung-spreader passing the Ferryman Inn through the drizzling rain—and just as then, he was momentarily overcome by a sense of almost cosmic futility and waste. Back to his mind came the remembrance of the empty, shuttered rectory, of Daphne Sparrow's wan, sad face when they'd parted, and finally of the young man's body lying sprawled across the toppled chair among the untidy lumber of the mission hall, with the rusty shotgun lying beside his outstretched, yellow-gloved hand.

Oppressed by the vision, he continued to stare after the slowly departing vessels, racking his brain for some explanation for Jonathan's strangely ambiguous existence, and why he should have left the photocopied reports on the Heathrow Airport robbery with his girlfriend, rather than bringing them back to this oddly barren little flat.

There was something about the apartment that rang a faint bell for him—but what it was, he couldn't quite put his finger on. Again he went over and sniffed at the walls, wishing he could have seen them before they were repainted, and wondering what, if anything, had been hung on them when Jonathan had been alive.

Still occupied by these thoughts, and feeling not just that he was bringing up the rear of a hunt that had long passed on, but that the very tracks he was attempting to follow had been deliberately obscured or erased, he carried one of the empty boxes to the mantelpiece. Carefully, he lifted down the ship-in-a-bottle that was propping up the row of paperback books, noticing as he did so that the model inside was of the *Cutty Sark*, the famous old tea-clipper now permanently moored in dry dock just a mile or so down river at Greenwich. Holding the bottle up against the light, he peered at the tiny vessel, observing with pleasure the intricate detail of the hull and its fitting as well as of the billowing sails and cobweb-thin rigging.

'You're awfully quiet.' Ingrams's muffled voice came from the bedroom. 'Are you all right in there?'

'Fine, thank you, Dean,' he called out. 'I was just taking a look at this very splendid ship-in-a-bottle.'

'Ah, yes! Beautiful, isn't it! George Frome made it for Jonathan. Frome and he were very close when he was a small boy.'

Remembering the child-sized garden implements that had been propped in the corner of the rectory wash-house, Harrison gently placed the model ship inside the box. Having done so, he began removing the books and wedging them in place around it. The box was soon full, and, as he went to close it, his attention was caught by the cover illustration of one of the books on the top layer. Drawing on his reading spectacles, he took it out and examined it curiously.

Gazing back up at him with a look of self-assurance bordering on arrogance was a striking-looking young man in his early twenties. The figure depicted stood arms folded, the wide collar of his shirt lying casually drawn back from the throat. The dark velveteen doublet he was wearing was heavily padded in the shoulders and sleeves, decorated with rows of large gold buttons and slashed all over in Tudor court style so as to display the costly peachy-orange lining beneath. Rich and ostentatious though the costume was, it was not that which held the viewer's attention, but the almost oval face of its wearer, with its broad, high forehead, wide-spaced dark eyes, the prominent nose and surprisingly delicate, almost girlish, lips and chin.

Even without the book's title, Harrison could hardly have failed to recognize the identity of the youth depicted. Living in Canterbury, especially during this anniversary year, he'd seen those features countless times, looking up at him from the circular portrait set in the pavement outside the city theatre, or gazing out from numerous posters and other advertising material about the town. Never until now, however, had he examined the face closely, nor had he ever previously seen a coloured reproduction of the Corpus Christi portrait on which the familiar profile was based, and he remained staring down intently at the supposed face of Canterbury's famous son for a few moments longer before carrying the book out across the narrow hallway to the bedroom.

'Ah, what's that you've found?' Ingrams was seated on the bed, attempting to stuff an obstinate duvet into one of his plastic bin-liners, and as Harrison entered the room, he squinted up at the book cover being held out for his inspection. 'A. L. Rowse's excellent biography of Christopher Marlowe!' The speaker beamed, clearly delighted at the other's interest. 'Of course, it's quite an old work now, but if you are looking for an introduction to the subject, I certainly can recommend it as a concise and perceptive account of...'

'No, Dean, forgive me, it's not the content that interests me,' burst out Harrison, interrupting him, 'but the portrait on the cover. Here, take a look.' Sitting down on the bed next to Ingrams, he placed a hand over the subject's great bush of swept-back brown hair, then glanced up to meet his companion's puzzled frown. 'Look at those wide-spaced eyes,' he said, 'at that high, broad forehead and the somewhat disappointingly weak lips and chin. Whose face does it remind you of?'

Intrigued, Ingrams bent forward and looked down at the cover illustration. 'I really don't know...' He paused. 'Unless you mean...' His voice faded away.

'Exactly so! Your old college friend, Maurice Lambkin, just as he used to look. Exchange that doublet there for an old-fashioned clerical frock coat, that open-necked shirt for a dog collar, remove that hint of a moustache and the faint trace of beard along the jawline, and what you have is almost the exact double of the man standing arm-in-arm with Bridget O'Brian outside the church porch on the day they were married.'

'Good Lord! You're absolutely right!' exclaimed Ingrams. 'Do you know, I never noticed!' Taking the book, he peered at it closely for a moment, then smiled wanly, nodding his head. 'And we used to all think it was Jonathan, with that great mop of hair of his, who looked like Marlowe—but now you point it out, it was really his father who most closely resembled him.'

With one already filled black sack at his feet, and piles of linen and towels heaped round him on the bed, Ingrams sat hunched over the book, all remembrance of the task in which he was engaged clearly quite vanished from his mind. 'Ah, dear, poor Maurice,' he murmured sadly, continuing to look down at the portrait. 'What high hopes', he resumed, 'we all had of him at his ordination, with his intellectual gifts and that enormous enthusiasm to serve the poor and outcast! And Jonathan also, all those years later, with his own bright promise similarly cut short like this confident-looking young dandy here in the picture—that is, of course,' he added, glancing round at Harrison with a smile, 'if we accept that the portrait hanging in Corpus Christi Hall is really of Christopher Marlowe at all, and that this gaudy young peacock depicted here was indeed the same student on whose behalf Queen Elizabeth's Privy Council interceded over the award of a master's degree.'

'The Privy Council?' repeated Harrison in surprise, then laughed. 'I don't understand,' he said, 'what possible interest was the educational progress of an obscure undergraduate to the Government of England? And, talking of students,' he added, glancing with a frown once more at the book cover, 'how could a poor scholarship boy, the son of a Canterbury cobbler, possibly afford those exceedingly fine clothes? Where on earth did the money come from for such obvious and ostentatious luxury?'

The dean turned and stared at him incredulously. 'My dear fellow, don't you know? I thought everyone did! Marlowe may have been from a modest background, but he was mightily connected. One of his closest friends at the King's School, Nicholas Faunt, became secretary to Francis Walsingham, who was, of course, Queen Elizabeth's spymaster, and who founded and ran the sixteenth-century equivalent of MI5 and MI6 combined—and the reason the university authorities were so reluctant to grant his degree was that he'd been absent from Cambridge so long, ostensively studying for the priesthood at Dr Allen's English seminary at Rheims.'

'What—Rheims in Catholic France?'

'Just so.' The dean smiled, all his former melancholy quite disappeared now as he talked on a subject so near to his heart. 'Forgive the rather melodramatic term, but our flashy young friend here was what today we call an undercover agent, or, to use the popular term, a mole. As the preparations for the Armada were gathering momentum in Spain, and the dockyards here in Deptford and elsewhere were hammering out the ships to repel them and save liberty of conscience and the protestant faith, Marlowe was busy collecting the names of his fellow students in the seminary in Rheims who were to be sent secretly back into England to stir up sedition against the monarchy—that's why the Privy Council wrote a stiff note to the university authorities when they were sniffy about awarding Marlowe his degree, saying it was not Her Majesty's pleasure that anyone employed, as he had been, in matters touching the benefit of his country should be defamed by those that are ignorant in the affairs he went about.'

'Good Lord!' muttered Harrison, getting to his feet. 'That I didn't know.' He paused, then burst out in protest, 'But damn it, Dean, young Marlowe was meant to be completely unreliable—a drunken reveller, a boaster and a brawler, a chap who got himself into all sorts of trouble—the very last sort of person I'd expect to be employed as...'

His voice died, and suddenly he was gazing round the bleak, bare-walled little bedroom, a look of understanding dawning on his face.

'Exactly so!' said the dean with a complacent smile. 'It is what I believe is known in the trade as cover. Continuing to work here in this country after coming down from university as a government agent, Marlowe could hardly be expected to pick up much in the way of sedition and treason if he'd confined himself to sipping the odd glass of madeira in the Elizabethan equivalent of a vicarage tea party. No, to be useful to his masters, he had to win the confidence of subversives; therefore, whether from natural inclination or not, he was forced to play the role of the blustering, blaspheming, sexually questionable *enfant terrible* of the English stage.'

Harrison didn't hear him. He was back in Fordington churchyard, seeing again the elegantly dressed official placing the wreath at the graveside and then standing, head bowed in tribute. From there, his thoughts raced on, moving to the little medallion on Bridget Lambkin's rosary, and then to the reception at the deanery the night of the play, and Alan Tubman gazing mournfully down into his wineglass as he'd made that inexplicable remark about Jonathan's background being perfect preparation for his playing the part of the horse-dealer in the earlier school production of *Doctor Faustus.*

'My dear fellow, are you all right? You suddenly look as if you've seen a ghost.'

'I'm sorry, Dean, I was just thinking of something someone once said to me.' Harrison managed to muster a smile. 'So, Marlowe lived the secret undercover existence of an Elizabethan spy, you say—and that presumably was the subject of the play that Jonathan and his girlfriend went up to see at Stratford.'

'Oh, undoubtedly,' replied Ingrams. 'With the knowledge we now have of Marlowe's involvement in Walsingham's spyring, many modern writers have speculated on the deep machinations that may well have led to the terrible events in Mrs Bull's tavern on that warm Wednesday evening in May when Marlowe was supposedly accidentally stabbed during a quarrel over the drinks bill.'

'Supposedly?'

Ingrams blushed slightly. 'Much as I hate sounding like

another of these conspiracy theorists, there is evidence to suggest, despite the coroner's verdict at the time, that the fight was an entirely staged affair—that Ingram Frizer and his companions were nothing but a bunch of hired assassins, and that young Kit Marlowe was, in the time-hallowed words of the law, "knowingly and cold-bloodedly, with malice aforethought, deliberately done to death.'"

CHAPTER SEVENTEEN

'Talk about hooking and drawing Leviathan up by the nose!' Pausing in his restless pacing, the speaker looked round at the bended figure seated in the lamplight at the sitting-room bureau. 'I tell you, Winnie, the only person who's been led by that particular appendage has been me, thanks to that confounded man!'

'Really, Richard! I wish you'd calm down,' said Winnie wearily, raising her head from the pile of Christmas cards she was inscribing. 'You'll end up giving yourself a cerebral haemorrhage the way you're carrying on! Anyway,' she added, turning back to her cards, 'I don't understand what you're so angry at Chief Inspector Dowley for—he may not have known anything about it.'

'Of course he knew!' exploded Harrison, glaring at her bended head. 'Why else do you think he came out so pat with the idea that the Home Office wreath was sent because of Lambkin's work running hostels for ex-offenders and the like? If Dowley hadn't said anything, I might have guessed then and there who the wreath was really for, and what Jonathan had actually been up to these last five years!'

Winnie laid down her pen. 'Come on now, darling!' she said appealingly, rotating her wheelchair to face hire. 'You don't know any of this for certain; it's only your theory.'

'Theory?' repeated the other, his voice rising. 'God almighty, woman! It's glaringly obvious! The truth's been staring me in the face for weeks, only I hadn't the sense to see it!' Breaking off, he sank wearily into an armchair. 'First, the chief constable sees fit to bring in a small army of metropolitan detectives to investigate a seemingly straightforward case of domestic slaying; then there was that very respectable sum of money in Jonathan's bank account, together with the fact that his affairs were managed by a discreet little firm of well thought of lawyers. Added to that was the huge discrepancy between Jonathan's disreputable appearance and lifestyle, and the very favourable impression he made on various people, including that formidable old aunt of his father's. And finally there was what Tubman said about the boy's background making him ideally suited to play the role of the horse-dealer in the school production of *Faustus*.'

'Horse-dealer? What about it, for goodness sake?'

'Oh, come on, Winnie! Comic horse-dealer! What do people immediately think of when anyone mentions horse sales?'

'I don't know,' answered Winnie mystified. 'Newmarket? Epsom Downs? Tattersall's auctions?'

'No! No!' cried the other impatiently. 'Irishmen, of course! In the popular mind, horse-dealers, trainers and breakers are always Irishmen: it's as if the entire population of the Emerald Isle had a peculiar affinity with that particular species of quadruped! That's why', he continued, 'Jonathan was so suited for the role: having an Irish mother and being a born actor, he could easily produce the accent.'

'Well, it's certainly true that Bridget always retained that lovely soft brogue of hers,' said Winnie thoughtfully. 'So what you're suggesting', she said, 'is that Jonathan's whole way of life was an act from start to finish, played on behalf of MI5 or whatever intelligence agency employed him; that he acted out the role of an embittered malcontent who'd rejected his father's culture and background in favour of his mother's so as to infiltrate those very small portions of the Irish community in this country sympathetic to the nationalist cause and willing to aid the IRA's terrorist campaigns—in other words, that he was an undercover agent worming his way into possible subversive groups, just as Matthew thinks Christopher Marlowe was doing in his own day?'

'Exactly,' answered Harrison. 'That explains his choosing to live in such an unlikely run-down area of London and the reason for him playing such a prominent part in various political demonstrations. It's also why that flat today should have had that semi-official feel about its furnishings, and why it had been tidied up and redecorated after, presumably, all the nationalist posters and the rest of the stage props had been quickly removed. It's also the reason why Jonathan was so careful to keep Daphne Sparrow and everyone else away.'

'But if you're right,' said Winnie, 'why did none of this come out at the inquest? Why should the authorities leave the world to think Jonathan had been nothing but a disaffected outcast even after he was dead?'

'Because they had no choice, I imagine,' replied Harrison. 'Surveillance must continue as long as the terrorist cells operate amongst us. The last thing MI5 would have wanted was for any of the groups he'd infiltrated to know what he'd been up to, and thus learn that their security was compromised. Presumably, it was as vital for Jonathan's cover to be maintained after his death as it had been that everybody should believe that the young van driver killed in north Belfast was a civilian named Brendan O'Brian, and not a second lieutenant of the Enniskillen Fusiliers.'

Winnie stared at her husband incredulously. 'You're not now saying that Jonathan's friend, Stephen Hardwick, was that driver?'

'Of course he was! It was young Hardwick's death, I imagine, that first took Jonathan into Intelligence work. I imagine it was while he was at Cambridge that he was encouraged to take up the baton dropped by his childhood friend.'

'But the newspaper cutting said that this man, Brendan O'Brian, was driving a laundry van when he crashed. If you're right, what on earth was an army officer doing going round houses, collecting dirty clothes?'

'Just that—helping to run a laundry,' came the immediate answer. 'Locally raised regiments such as the Enniskillen Fusiliers don't serve in Northern Ireland, for obvious reasons. Therefore, ever since the outbreak of the Troubles twenty years ago, some of their officers and NCOs have been free to work in the province on just the sort of undercover operations young Hardwick was engaged in.'

Harrison got up from the chair and went over to the window and looked out across the moonlit yard towards the single window of the cottage opposite from which a light shone. 'Tubman guessed the truth over lunch on Sunday,' he said. 'As I should have done, he noticed that the accident in Belfast happened five years ago, at the very same time that young Hardwick was supposed to have been killed on a training exercise on Salisbury Plain. Putting that together with the fact that Jonathan kept the newspaper cutting among his personal papers, and that the driver's chosen alias was the maiden name of his best friend's mother, it wasn't hard for him to deduce who this so-called Brendan O'Brian actually was and what he'd been up to, especially when he learnt that he'd been driving a laundry van.'

'I still don't understand!' protested Winnie. 'What on earth has a laundry service to do with undercover work?'

With an impatient sigh, Harrison turned to face her. 'It's

obvious! In fact, Tubman as good as spelt it out. Remember him listing the various items that a laundry collection service gathers: sheets, pillow cases, towels and all the rest of it? Don't you see, those things indicate how many people are living in a particular house, and if anyone has come and stayed a night or two. Who knows, a spot of blood or any bodily fluid, even the odd hair, might tell the forensic boys who the house guest was. Providing a good reliable laundry service for a street, you might say, is almost as good as planting a hidden camera or listening device in every house.'

Winnie wrinkled her nose. 'I think it's disgusting.'

'Yes,' answered Harrison coldly, returning to his chair, 'but not quite as disgusting perhaps as blowing kids' knees off with a pistol, or thugs using baseball bats to impose their rule—not quite as disgusting as what a bullet from an Armalite rifle does to the human head or what a few pounds of Semtex explosive can do to a crowd of peaceful Saturday-morning shoppers or customers in a pub enjoying a quiet drink!'

The clock in the hall began chiming, and then came the heavy booms of the cathedral bell. As the sounds died, and silence fell again over the precincts, Winnie spoke. 'Of course,' she said slowly, 'if you're right about all this, and Jonathan's lifestyle was merely a front, then it makes what happened between him and his father all the more difficult to accept.'

'Quite so,' murmured Harrison, nodding, 'and that's the reason why the police took all the trouble they did, and why Dowley bothered to recruit me as an additional pair of eyes and ears—though why I couldn't have been trusted with the full information I fail to understand! It's meant I've wasted half my time struggling to make sense of things I should have been told at the start!'

'Richard,' intervened Winnie, 'are you still absolutely sure that Jonathan killed his father? Isn't it possible that Christabel Lambkin could have been right, and that someone apart from Maurice and Jonathan was in the cottage that night?'

'No,' answered Harrison, shaking his head, 'absolutely not. As I told the police and repeated at the inquest, the place was locked and bolted from the inside, and the only set of keys apart from mine was lying in the mission hall. There was no possible way that anyone could have got out unless they were able to walk through brick walls or pop out of the furniture like our little friends in the play. And yet,' he added, shaking his head and screwing up his face as if in pain, 'impossible, as it is, one part of me fears that, instead of Jonathan going berserk and killing his father and then himself, the whole set-up was indeed an elaborately staged contrivance to mask cold-blooded murder—just as a drunken brawl over a drinks bill might have been used to disguise the assassination of Christopher Marlowe.'

One after another, like eyelids closing, the few remaining lit windows in the close became dark while, overhead, the full moon continued its creeping elevation. Finally its great, round, melancholy face hung directly over the central tower of the cathedral, bathing it and the surrounding cloisters and lawns in a ghostly, silvery light. Instead of diminishing the long shadows cast by brickwork and stone, however, the moonlight served only to deepen and lengthen them further, so that, although the cobbles of Bread Yard glistened like water, the frontage of the cottages opposite and the archway entrance lay entirely shrouded in cavernous black, as the yawning, dressing-gown-clad figure stood, arms folded, at the kitchen window, waiting for the milk on the stove to boil.

For Harrison, the checkerboard effect of moonlight and shadow only reinforced the impression created by the revelations of the day: that one solitary illumination necessarily plunged into gloom much that had previously appeared clear, and that the more spectacular and dazzling that light, the more impenetrable the surrounding darkness. It had been one thing to believe that a neurotic, unbalanced and alienated young man had been goaded to butchery by the absurd allegations in the anonymous note; quite another to accept that someone capable and emotionally strong enough to pursue the lonely work of an undercover agent would have reacted the same way. Nevertheless, all the known facts suggested that was what had indeed happened. Judging from the gun-oil marks on the clothing in his bag, Jonathan had travelled down on the train already armed and fuming with murderous rage. The eye-witness account of him shouting at his father and beating his fists on the car roof further indicated that he was already emotionally pent-up when he reached the station. That Lambkin had brought both the paraffin-lamp and the cottage keys with him proved that the venue for the horrific events had already been selected; while the fact that, along with the gun and cartridges in the bag, there must also have been the length of washing-line cord and the incongruous yellow rubber gloves, suggested that, like the story of Abraham and Isaac in reverse, the son had prepared in advance his brutally cold-blooded act of parricide.

The hiss of boiling milk behind him broke into Harrison's meditations. Hurriedly turning to snatch the pan from the heat, he began carefully pouring the just-saved contents into the pair of prepared mugs.

'Oh, this is nice!' Lowering her book, Winnie smiled over her reading-glasses as her husband entered the bedroom bearing a loaded tray. 'Cocoa and biscuits in bed!' she said, heaving herself a little further up against the pillows. 'What a wonderful treat!'

'Well, just make sure you don't go scattering crumbs,' grunted Harrison, pushing the door to with his foot. 'From bitter experience, I promise you that buttered fragments of cream crackers don't exactly help in knitting up the ravelled sleeve of care.'

Despite these reservations, this almost unprecedented indulgence of having their evening nightcap in bed had been entirely Harrison's own idea. Bone-weary after his London trip, he'd proposed it as the speediest means of achieving the recumbent position his body ached for. Having handed Winnie her cocoa and biscuits, and taken his own round to the other side of the bed, he now clambered in between the sheets with a feeling of profound relief. The long day was finally over, and whatever new questions it had raised, of one thing at least he could be entirely confident: that he'd slip into the welcoming embrace of Morpheus that night without the slightest need of an encouraging shove from Brother Bacchus.

'And how has everything been today?' he asked, leaning back against the pillows and sipping his cocoa. 'No messages from the office, I hope?'

'No, nothing,' answered his wife. 'Margaret drove me to the library after lunch, then we did a little more Christmas shopping. Apart from that, the only people I've seen were Simon and three of his friends who called by. I hope you don't mind, but I invited them over for high tea on Saturday. School will be finished for the holidays, and the poor little choristers will be stuck here all on their own.'

'No, that will be fine—let the little devils come.' Harrison yawned luxuriously. Revelling in the softness of mattress and pillows, and secure in the knowledge that sleep was at his command and now only a few moments away, he felt a peaceful benevolence towards all the other inhabitants of his own small stone-girdled world. 'Well, I don't know about you,' he said, yawning, 'but I'm shoving off for the land of Nod.'

Even after both the bedside lights had been turned off, the room remained strangely bright with the moonlight streaming between the curtains. Eyes closed, Harrison allowed his mind to wander back over the events of the day: walking with Daphne Sparrow on Hampstead Heath; the questioning sadness in her face back in her flat as he'd glanced up from reading the photo-copied reports of the Heathrow robbery; the dean's chubby face, wreathed in smiles, as he'd hurried across St Nicholas's church-yard towards him; and then later his look of wondering incredulity at the discovery of his companion's complete igno-rance of the secret life of Kit Marlowe.

'Richard?'

'What is it?'

'I keep thinking about Jonathan and what happened in that cottage,' murmured Winnie drowsily. 'I can't get it out of my mind.' She paused, then continued. 'Darling, are you absolutely sure there was nothing there to indicate that things happened in any way differently than they seemed?'

'I've told you, yes,' grunted Harrison. 'Now let me sleep!'

There was silence again in the room, and then, as he was slipping into unconsciousness, his wife's voice suddenly spoke again at his ear. 'There couldn't have been anyone hiding inside, could there? Someone who might have slipped out when you and Helen Middlebrook were looking round?'

The words caught him just as he was on the soft downward roll into sleep, jerking him immediately back into full con-sciousness. 'For God's sake!' he burst out angrily, tossing over on to his back. 'What is this? The blasted Spanish Inquisition? How many times have I said that I checked the whole place carefully after Helen had gone off to the farm to phone the police. As for anyone having got past us unnoticed when we were looking around the ground floor, he or she would have needed to be invis-ible and as small as a mouse! Now, for pity's sake, let me sleep!'

So saying, he rolled back on to his side and determinedly reclosed his eyes. He was now wide awake, however, and further from sleep than he'd been for the last half-hour. Something of this must have shown in his breathing and the rigidity of his body, for Winnie suddenly remarked, as naturally as if they were sitting together at the breakfast table, 'Richard, don't you think it might be useful to go over the whole thing again now in detail, saying exactly what you did and what you saw from the moment you and Helen arrived outside the cottage that morning?'

Harrison felt too exhausted to protest, and, anyway, it was easier to assent than argue. He merely sighed heavily and began recounting the sequence of events in a weary, mechanical tone. 'Helen and I sat in the car outside the gate for five minutes while I told her the story of the house. Whilst sitting there, I noticed a car apparently abandoned beside the lane a little way ahead. I then went with her to see her safely inside. We tried to open the front door, but it was bolted, so we walked round to the back. As we found the back door chained, we went off separately to check the windows, but none could be opened from outside. I, therefore, decided to try and break the chain. I ran at the door the first time, but with no result. I then took a really hard run at it and managed to tear the chain from the door frame and half fell into the passage inside. Then I turned back and invited Helen in, and we started going through the cottage together, ending, of course, when Helen unlocked the mission-hall door.'

'You haven't missed anything out?'

'No, I don't think so.' Harrison paused and thought back. Lying there, eyes closed, body relaxed, his position was rather like that of René Descartes curled up snug inside his warm baker's oven, with winter and war safely beyond the other side of the closed iron door, and, much like the philosopher, with his mind cut off from all external sights and sensations, he was free to focus completely on the object of his thought.

Thus, all these weeks later, he was now able to relive the whole sequence of events at the cottage in greater detail than he'd managed under cross-examination, either at the police station or in front of the court. 'Oh yes,' he murmured, 'there was just one other little thing. Before I invited Helen inside, I went into the kitchen.'

'Why?'

'Oh, just to check there weren't any spiders in the sink. I

didn't want the girl frightened out of her wits right at the very start of proceedings.'

'There was nothing at all strange or unusual in the kitchen, I take it?'

'No, nothing—apart from a slight smell of paraffin.'

'Paraffin?'

'Yes.' Pausing, Harrison yawned. 'Clearly either Lambkin himself or Jonathan must have filled the hurricane lantern over the sink, and a little of the liquid got spilt.'

Winnie eased herself up a little on the pillow. 'Did you tell the police this?'

Harrison considered. 'No, I don't think so. Amongst everything else, I had quite forgotten that little detail. Anyway,' he continued, yawning again, 'it isn't important. When they went through the place afterwards, the police would surely have smelt the paraffin for themselves and worked out that the lamp had been filled in the kitchen.' He lapsed into silence for a second or two, then added thoughtfully, 'But, come to think of it, they couldn't have, as I must have washed the paraffin away.'

'Washed it away!' Winnie suddenly pulled herself up on to one arm. 'How did you come to do that?'

'It was after Helen and I had seen the bodies,' he answered. 'Helen had vomited, so I went into the kitchen to get her a drink. I found an old plastic beaker and thoroughly washed it under the tap before filling it with water and taking it outside. Doing that, I imagine I must have washed away any last trace of the paraffin.'

Winnie reached over and switched on her bedside light. 'Richard,' she said, leaning over and looking down at him, 'think carefully now: were there any spent matches on the draining-board or in the sink?'

'Matches?' Blinking against the light, Harrison turned over and looked up at his wife's anxious face. 'Yes,' he said, 'there was one used match lying in the sink, but I imagine that also got washed down the plughole.'

'Oh, Richard! Why in heaven's name didn't you tell the police all this?'

Bewildered by the questions and alarmed by the gravity of her voice, Harrison shook his head. 'I told you, until now I had completely forgotten going into the kitchen at all. Anyway, what does it matter if the lamp was filled in the cottage or before Lambkin set out to collect Jonathan from the station?'

Winnie shook her head sorrowfully. 'Oh, my poor darling, don't you see? It changes everything. That paraffin in the sink means there was somebody else in the cottage besides Jonathan and Maurice that night, and when you rinsed out that beaker for Helen, you washed away the one piece of evidence that would have proved it.'

'What?' said Harrison, staring flabbergasted up at her face. 'Good God!' he exploded, sitting up. 'How in hell's name do you make that out?'

'It's simple,' answered Winnie quietly. 'At what time did Jonathan and Maurice arrive at the cottage?'

'I don't know: if Lambkin met the boy off the train around eleven, by the time they reached Bright Cottage, I suppose it must have been at least quarter to twelve.'

'In other words, after dark.'

'Yes, of course after dark! So what?'

'Then just ask yourself how anyone could have managed to fill the paraffin lamp in the kitchen. The electricity supply to the cottage had been disconnected, and there was only one dead match in the sink—the one that presumably was used to light the lamp. As there were no torches or candles found in the cottage, how could anyone see to fill the lamp in the dark?'

'I don't know!' burst Harrison in a frenzy of irritation, sitting up on his elbow and looking round the room. 'The same as the owl and the blasted pussycat in the nursery rhyme, I imagine: by the light of the moon.'

Winnie shook her head. 'No, that was impossible,' she said,

'even had there been a moon that night, it wouldn't have helped—the cottage would have remained pitch-black. Surely you remember: there was thick fog that night, and so without some artificial means of lighting, no one could have possibly been able to see to fill that lamp.'

Harrison turned and stared aghast at the speaker's face, unable for a moment to speak. 'My God! You're right!' he breathed, then cried out in anguish, 'Christ, and I was the one to convince the jury to bring in the verdicts they did, and also, as you say, I destroyed the one piece of evidence that proved somebody else had been in that house—someone who was almost certainly involved in the deaths of poor old Lambkin and his son!'

Winnie gently touched his arm. 'Richard, you've got to go and tell all this to Chief Inspector Dowley tomorrow.'

'Tell Dowley! Tell the fellow who didn't trust me with the truth about what Jonathan had been up to? Admit to him I've been a bloody fool and destroyed vital evidence? No!' he cried bitterly, scrambling from bed and reaching for his dressing-gown. 'Never!'

'But, darling, you must!' pleaded Winnie. 'After all, what else can you do?'

'What else?' Harrison turned and looked at the pale face looking up at him from the bed. 'I'll tell you what else!' he said, his eyes blazing. 'If it really was double murder that was committed inside that locked room, I'm going to find out for myself how it was done and what damnable trick was played to take me in!'

CHAPTER EIGHTEEN

'Good morning, Colonel.'

Mary Simpson looked up and smiled brightly as Harrison came through the door, her expression instantly changing to one of concern as she noticed the signs of tiredness and strain in his face. 'Did everything go all right in London yesterday?'

'Yes, thank you, Mary; tolerably well. And what about here?' Breathing in the pleasant aroma of freshly made coffee, Harrison glanced round the office. 'Nothing untoward cropped up in my absence, I trust?'

'No, nothing, except there was a call from a Mr Tony Brandon.' She glanced at her message-pad. 'He left a telephone number; he said he'd like you to ring him as soon as possible in connection with a certain house purchase you and he have apparently discussed.'

'Yes, I'm sure he would,' answered the other coldly. 'Now, more important than the devices and desires of Mr Brandon's heart, what have you got pencilled in for me today?'

'Well, to start with,' said Mary, somewhat taken aback by the unusual curtness of his tone, 'you've the postponed meeting with Mr Jamerson at ten. After that, Miss Middlebrook is due to call in to go over the plans for the new roof supports at St Mary's at Westwell.'

Harrison shook his head. 'I'm sorry, but I'm afraid you'll have to cancel both those appointments. Once I've had a glance through today's and yesterday's mail, I'm going straight out. I have no idea when I'll be back.'

Already shaken by his manner, his secretary stared up at him in dismay. 'Going out?' she repeated. 'But, Colonel, you can't possibly! The meeting with the auditor has already been put off once, and he's particularly anxious that...'

'I'm sorry,' cut in Harrison, 'but you'll have to give Jamerson my apologies. Tell him', he said, turning away, 'that something has cropped up requiring my complete attention. Until that's satisfactorily settled, everything else will, I'm afraid, just have to go hang for the moment!'

Shocked, Mary stared after him as he disappeared into his office. Everything about him—his testiness, his weary, haggard face and highly wrought state—only confirmed her fears. Ever since that terrible day back in the autumn when he and the new young diocesan architect had stumbled upon the bodies of the Reverend Lambkin and his son, he'd not seemed himself at all. In her estimation, he'd brooded on the matter to a dangerous degree, and, knowing only too well the burden the archdeacon's rationalization schemes placed upon him, as well as his distaste for implementing the cutbacks they entailed, she'd convinced herself that he might announce his retirement at any time—either that, or suffer some form of breakdown. Far from restoring his spirits as she'd fondly hoped, his day out in London seemed only to have made matters worse. Tender-hearted as she was, she felt profoundly upset; she'd cultivated a great deal of affection for the normally reticent, rather shy and awkward man she worked for.

Apart from that, she was used to his ways, and dreaded the thought of his replacement by one of Dr Cawthorne's appointees.

Sadly, she rose and began laying the tray for his morning coffee. Her gloomy ruminations were interrupted as she suddenly remembered the package that had been sent round from the deanery a quarter of an hour before. A flicker of hope returning, she picked up the brown paper-covered bottle-shaped object and placed it carefully on the tray beside the customary plate of Garibaldi biscuits.

Ensconced in the inner room, Harrison's thoughts and emotions were no happier than those of his secretary outside. He'd closed the door of his sanctuary with an uncomfortable feeling of guilt, for not only was he conscious of having been unnecessarily brusque, but the sight of the huge pile of post reminded him of his previous intention of arriving early to clear his desk. However, after the night he'd just endured, it had been as much as he could manage to arrive at all. Indeed, so exhausted and on edge did he feel that as he opened and started to read through a letter from the recently appointed incumbent of St Margaret's at Cliffe, he found himself unable to concentrate on the detailed and depressing account of the effect of subsidence on Norman archways and tower foundations.

To learn that he'd been misled by the scene in the mission hall had been terrible enough, God knows, but to realize that, in addition, he'd inadvertently erased the only evidence to prove the presence of a third party in the cottage on the night of the killings had been simply appalling—especially as he was now convinced that the tableau effect of the dead man bound to the chair and his son lying sprawled beside the gun had been nothing but a stage-managed contrivance to disguise a carefully planned double murder. What with that, and the realization that Chief Inspector

Dowley had kept the facts about Jonathan's real life from him, he had to face the unpalatable truth that he'd been duped and used by police and murderer alike.

Back in the night, after the first full shock of the revelations had worn off, he'd been left seething with impotent rage and unable to bear the thought of returning to bed. Much against Winnie's advice, and despite her repeated pleas, he'd insisted on making himself a mug of black coffee and taking it off with him to his study. There he'd sat up in the bitter chill of that freezing cold night, drawing ground-plans of the cottage and generally struggling to work out how the victims' bodies had been left behind a double set of internally locked doors. Unable to come up with an answer, he'd returned to collapse into bed in the early hours, sure only that, despite Jonathan's anti-terrorist activities, the killings in the cottage had no political dimension, but had been a purely local, domestic affair. Both the involvement of his father and the obscure but clever choice of venue, with only the deaf old woman's bedroom overlooking the cottage, pointed directly to intimate knowledge of the area. Determined to return to the scene of the crime the next day in the forlorn hope of finding some clue as to how the trick had been pulled off, he'd finally fallen into a restless, dream-haunted sleep. Now, tired out and depressed by his inability to solve the riddle of the Wetmarsh Marden killings, he sat at his desk, staring miserably down at the carefully worded epistle, hardly able to take in a word of what the clearly concerned cleric was saying.

The moment was thankfully cut short by a tap on the door and the appearance of Mary bearing the coffee tray. Grateful for the interruption, and determined to make amends for his earlier surliness, he managed to drag up a smile. 'Ah, yes, Mary! Do come in,' he said, pushing aside the post. 'I must say, that coffee smells absolutely delicious—just what I need. To tell the truth,' he added shamefacedly as the girl came forward, 'I'm feeling a trifle jaded this morning.'

Relieved at his sudden display of friendliness, Mary smiled in return. 'I forgot to tell you,' she said, placing the tray before him, 'that this package was sent round to you by the dean. I think it's a bottle of something nice.'

'Really? From the dean, you say? How typically kind.'

Slightly surprised at its lightness, Harrison began tearing the wrapping paper from the package. In a moment, he'd uncovered what Ingrams had sent: the ship-in-the-bottle he'd so much admired at Jonathan's flat, together with a note from Ingrams thanking him again for all his help the previous day.

'Oh, how lovely!' exclaimed Mary, leaning forward to look, her enthusiasm partly real and partly itself a contrivance. 'It's wonderful, really sweet—a little ship like that with all those delicate sails, ropes and things! But what I've never understood', she went on, 'is how they get them to fit through the neck of the bottle?'

Harrison smiled. 'Well, most of the ones you see in the shops these days are fakes: all they do is saw off the base of the bottle, slip the model inside, and then weld up the glass. But this one,' he said, holding up the bottle for her inspection, 'as you see, has no weld at the base.'

'Yes, but then how was the ship got in?'

'It's easy: the model-maker first builds the hull, then assembles the mast and rigging separately. Having done so, he glues the masts to the deck but leaves them lying down, and slips the boat through the neck. Finally he pulls up the masts before the glue has dried.'

'How? He can't get his fingers inside.'

'Oh, he uses a length of thread he's left looped round the front mast. He operates, as it were, from a distance, rather like a puppet-master operating a marionette. He just gives his thread a gentle pull until…' Harrison's voice faded and suddenly he was sitting, gazing intently at the bottle clutched between his hands.

'Colonel, are you all right?'

Not answering, Harrison rose to his feet and, taking the bottle with him, went to the window and stared down through the grimy panes at the passage below. 'Yes,' he repeated aloud, 'like a puppet-master operating his strings!' For a moment longer he stood there, gazing down, then suddenly he swung round, his face contorting. 'God almighty, Mary!' he exclaimed. 'What a complete damned fool I've been! Only one bolt pulled to, and the bolt lever not closed down! Talk about being blind—we've all of us, police and everyone else, been like newborn kittens!'

Startled, Mary began to say something, but at that moment her thoughts were distracted by the phone starting to ring in the outer office. Turning away, she left the room and hurried towards the source of the sound, her mind still occupied by Harrison's excited outburst.

Dimly conscious of the ringing stopping and the sound of Mary's voice speaking on the phone next door, Harrison stood staring down a moment or two longer at the bottle in his hand, then, quickly returning to his desk, he gulped down his coffee. This done, he turned and grabbed his coat and, pulling it on, went through to the outer office just as his secretary was replacing the receiver.

'Sorry, Mary, but I've changed my mind: I'm leaving at once—I'll deal with the post later. Oh, yes,' he added, pausing at the door, 'will you please ring Mr George Frome at Fordington immediately—you'll find his number in the rectory file. Tell him that I'm on my way over to see him on a matter of the greatest importance.'

He went to open the door, but before he could do so, Mary had interposed herself between him and it. 'No, Colonel, you can't possibly go!' she cried. 'That was Dr Cawthorne. He wants you to go over to the archdeaconry at once.'

'Now? At this time in the morning?' Harrison paused, then shook his head. 'I'm sorry,' he said, 'but you'll just have to ring him back and say I've been urgently called away.'

'No, sir,' answered the girl, remaining resolutely positioned in front of the door. 'I've already told him you'd be coming straight away. He's in a terrible state—I'm not quite sure why. It's all to do with the sale of one of the charity cottages.'

Harrison's blood seemed to run cold at her words. 'Charity cottage?' he repeated, staring aghast at her. 'For God's sake, Mary, what charity cottage?'

'He didn't say—just that some meddler has been stirring certain people up to dispute the diocese's right to sell it off.' She paused, staring up at the other's now stricken face, then added, 'Oh, Colonel, you'll have to go and see him—I've never heard Dr Cawthorne quite so upset.'

It was still comparatively early, and few people were about in the precincts on that bitterly cold morning as Harrison emerged from the Selling Archway into Green Court. Immediately turning left, he began following the wide, frosty path along the southern edge of the lawn towards the archdeaconry. After the events of the previous day and the disquieting revelations of the night, the problem of the Fromes' accommodation had completely slipped his mind, and all his former worries as to whether or not the verger and his wife would pursue their legal claim on the cottage had been utterly forgotten in his struggles to unravel the mystery surrounding the deaths of Maurice and Jonathan Lambkin. Thus to learn that they seemingly had decided to follow his advice after all had come as a devastating shock—the more so, as the news had broken at the very moment when it appeared he was finally on the verge of solving at least part of the riddle. So suddenly and unexpectedly had the tidings arrived, and so grave the implications, that even now his mind remained curiously numb as he strode on towards Cawthorne's garden gate as if in some nightmarish dream, with only the unusually rapid beating of his heart and, despite the cold, a slightly sweaty feel about his face and hands as physical proofs of the very real and imminent peril in which he stood.

Of course, it was quite possible, even likely, he reasoned, that despite this abrupt summons, the Fromes had kept their promise of confidentiality, and that Cawthorne had no idea who the instigator of this act of rebellion actually was—but whether he knew or not, in the end it didn't matter; the identity of the so-called 'meddler' would soon be common knowledge, he decided, and both honour and dignity demanded he should make a clean breast of the whole affair and then tender his resignation.

Wondering how best to break the news to Winnie, he arrived at the archdeaconry gate. Letting himself in, he began heading along beneath the ancient, wooden-roofed passageway, or pentise as it was known, that ran between the lawns and shrubberies to the front door. Before he reached it, however, it opened and Janet Cawthorne appeared, her normally placid face animated in an expression that struggled between anxiety and relief.

'Oh, Colonel, thank you for coming over so promptly!' she called, stepping forward to meet him. 'As I told Michael, if anyone knows a way of settling this awful business quietly, it's certainly you.'

Embarrassed by this unwarranted display of confidence, as well as being rather bewildered by her obvious distress, Harrison flushed. 'As always, Mrs Cawthorne,' he murmured uncomfortably, 'I shall be pleased to help the archdeacon in any way I can.'

'Oh, I knew you would! I only wish,' she said, looking away across the garden, 'that Michael didn't push ahead with his schemes in quite the headlong way he does—I knew he was upsetting people with his various schemes, and that it was bound to lead to trouble in the end.' Recovering herself, she turned back to the visitor. 'Michael's in his office,' she said. 'If you'd like to follow me, Colonel, I'll take you to him.'

'Thank you.'

Strangely enough, perhaps as a reaction to his untenable position and uncertain future, or merely as a result of the effects of lack of sleep and general exhaustion, even at this moment, when facing disgrace and possible homelessness, Harrison couldn't help but feel profoundly irritated that Cawthorne should call his study an office—somehow the Americanism seemed to summon up everything he disliked and feared about his superior's regime as well as the general direction in which the Church itself was heading. Grim-faced, like some recalcitrant schoolboy, he followed the archdeacon's wife into the house, determining to brazen matters out and to defend to the last his decision to inform the Fromes of their lawful rights.

'Darling, the colonel's arrived,' announced Janet Cawthorne, ushering him into the room in question. 'I'll leave you two together to sort everything out.'

The setting where Harrison expected to play out his last act as a church representative was just as he'd envisaged: a newly painted, virtually bookless chamber, spartanly furbished in the style of Seminar House with matching light oak desk, table and chairs—all of it as unecclesiastical in his eyes as the pale blue sweater Cawthorne was wearing as he sat, perched on the desk in front of him, telephone clamped to one ear. What he hadn't anticipated, however, was the expression of evident pleasure and relief at which his entrance was greeted, nor the friendly eagerness with which the archdeacon beckoned towards a chair as he went on talking into the phone.

'I'm sorry,' he said, 'but I really have to break off now. Colonel Harrison has just this moment arrived. After I've consulted him, I shall get back to you.'

Cawthorne replaced the receiver and rose to greet his visitor, who, despite the energetic handsignals, remained obstinately upright. 'Richard,' he said, 'I'm sorry to call you over like this, but the matter's urgent.' He paused, and then, to the other's surprise, an embarrassed half-flush rose in his face. 'I'm well aware', he continued, his colour deepening, 'that you and I have not always seen eye to eye on certain matters, and that you've had reservations regarding some aspects of our rationalization programme. Nevertheless,' he went on, 'I've always believed that you basically appreciate the necessity of the changes and cutbacks we've implemented together, and that, in times of crisis, I could always depend on your support.'

Feeling decidedly uncomfortable, Harrison hardly knew what to reply. From the original warmth with which he'd been greeted, it was obvious that Cawthorne still had no idea as to the part he'd played in encouraging the Fromes to lodge an appeal against the winding up of the Bright Trust. What, however, was not clear was why this normally confident man was so shaken by the Fromes' recourse to law, and why so determined and headstrong a person as Cawthorne should be taking so seriously what was, after all, only the latest of many attempts to subvert or water down his plans.

Deciding it best to say as little as possible for the moment, Harrison coughed and murmured awkwardly, 'Your confidence is most gratifying, Archdeacon. As I said to your wife, I'm always only too pleased to be of any help I can.'

'Yes, I know, and it's much appreciated.' Cawthorne went and sat down behind his desk. 'What I need now is your good judgement. So, please, my dear Richard, take a seat while I explain the position.'

Dreading the moment when he must inevitably reveal his own role in the affair, Harrison reluctantly drew up a chair and sat facing his superior across the polished width of wood.

'You understand', began Cawthorne, 'that this is all to do with the proposed sale of Bright Cottage?' Pausing, he frowned. 'Obviously you had no inkling of any trouble when you went over to Fordington to see the Fromes, or you would surely have mentioned it when we met over lunch last Sunday. It would, therefore, seem that it was after your visit that the wretched woman took it into her head to start going around the parish collecting names.'

'Collecting names?' Harrison blinked at the speaker. 'I'm sorry, Archdeacon, I don't quite follow: you're surely not saying that Mavis Frome has started up some sort of petition?'

It was Cawthorne who now looked surprised. 'Mavis Frome?' he repeated and shook his head. 'Good Lord, no! Of course not! I'm talking about Stella Gittings.'

Flabbergasted, Harrison struggled to digest this piece of information as Cawthorne continued to speak. 'What particularly hurts is that, as you know, I've always been a strong advocate of women's ordination. Indeed, I joined my voice with that of her local rural dean in recommending Mrs Gittings's candidature. And how does she repay me? By going around stirring up controversy. She's demanding that the proposed sale of the cottage he stopped and the tenancy given to the Fromes.' With an exasperated sigh, he shook his head. 'From what I gather, she's already managed to collect over two hundred names in support of her petition—including, believe it or not, that of one of the churchwardens!'

As Cawthorne sat venting his indignation, Harrison experienced an overwhelming joy. His assumption had been completely wrong: Frome and his wife had not, after all, gone to law, and he was therefore free to continue life as a respected and honoured diocesan official, enjoying the use of the Bread Yard cottage. For that he had Stella Gittings to thank, and it was with a profound sense of gratitude that he thought back to his conversation with her, remembering what she'd said about rallying people to the Fromes' support and making herself unpopular in certain quarters. Equally, he now understood her husband's reaction on learning that he was responsible for the future of the cottage. No wonder, he thought wryly, there'd been that ironic amusement in the fellow's voice when he'd referred to him as one of 'the shakers and movers', knowing the little earthquake being prepared beneath all their feet by his strong-willed and obviously highly-principled wife.

'It's clear', resumed Cawthorne bitterly, 'that the woman felt not the slightest compunction in going behind our backs against the interests of the diocese.'

Harrison cleared his throat. 'Pardon my saying so, Archdeacon, but setting aside any feelings of personal betrayal either of us might feel, I don't quite understand why you're so taxed by this matter.' He smiled encouragingly. 'We have faced down a number of such petitions in the past.'

'Yes, I know,' responded Cawthorne, 'but this petition is only the beginning of something far worse!'

'Worse?'

'The person I was speaking to on the phone when you came in was the archbishop's press secretary calling from Lambeth Palace. Someone seems to have tipped off one of the more sensational of our tabloid newspapers. After the salacious interest roused by the tragic happenings in Fordington, it seems the press is only too eager to create a *cause célèbre* out of the Church's supposed mistreatment of Lambkin's servants—especially as it involves what certain newspapers will still insist on calling "The Cottage of Death".' Breaking off with a grimace, Cawthorne leaned forward, his hands to his forehead. 'Heaven knows', he murmured, 'what another scandal will do to the diocese's reputation, to say nothing of the embarrassment the affair will cause the archbishop personally!'

There was in Cawthorne's attitude of hopeless misery something that strongly reminded Harrison of the time when he'd originally sat in Maurice Lambkin's study, breaking the news to him of the decision regarding the Bright Trust. Remembering it, he felt a sudden impatience at having to remain listening to Cawthorne talking of reputations and embarrassments when he longed to be away, testing his theories as to how that scene in the mission hall had been stage-managed so as to bamboozle everyone.

'Of course,' resumed Cawthorne, suddenly raising his head with something of his old defiance in his face, 'whatever slant may or may not be put on our actions from a moral point of view, at least, with the Charity Commissioners having provisionally accepted our deposition for the winding up of the trust, I imagine our legal position is impregnable—wouldn't you agree?'

Knowing he'd now been handed the very weapon he needed, Harrison took a deep breath. 'I fear,' he said, 'I'm not quite so sanguine as yourself regarding the legal aspects of the matter.'

Cawthorne stared at him. 'I don't understand—what do you mean?'

'Simply that a clever lawyer might argue that George Frome, as church verger, has a perfect right to the cottage under the original terms of the trust in question. If it should ever come to the courts, we might not only lose the case, but be forced to house the Fromes in the cottage at the originally stipulated twenty guineas a year.' He paused, relishing the moment before finally administering the *coup de grâce*. 'And,' he went on, 'if we were to lose, a precedent would have been established that would almost certainly mean having to scrap the greater part, if not all, of our rationalization plans.'

'You think so!' Cawthorne looked aghast. 'Good Lord, Richard! What should be done?'

Harrison smiled. 'Well,' he said, 'speaking as an ex-military man, I'd say the answer's obvious: the situation requires immediate strategic retreat. We must, as it were, defuse the situation before matters get completely out of hand.'

'But how?'

'By withdrawing our deposition to the Charity Commissioners and giving the Fromes the tenancy of the cottage. We might also add—as a little sweetener to their hurt feelings and to make us appear in as good a light as possible to our friends in the press—that we're prepared to undertake the complete demolition of the mission hall and build in its place a modern kitchen and utility block.' Before Cawthorne could protest, he hurried on. 'That would necessitate a large financial outlay on our part, but the diocese will doubtless more than recoup the money when the cottage is eventually sold.'

A look of enormous relief had risen in the listener's face. 'Richard, do you really think that would work? Would the Fromes be prepared to take such an offer?'

Harrison smiled. 'I have every reason to believe that they will, but we must work fast. With your permission, Archdeacon,' he said, getting to his feet, 'I shall drive straight over to Fordington this very moment and put our offer to them in person. Doing that, I think I can confidently guarantee we'll have them both eating out of our hands.'

CHAPTER NINETEEN

'**W**ell, Colonel, we're both of us very obliged to you, I'm sure—Mavis here and I will always remember and be grateful for your kindness and the trouble you've taken on our behalf.'

'Not at all, George. I'm only too glad to have been of some assistance.' Pausing, Harrison smiled at his hosts. 'And, in truth,' he went on, 'I'm as thankful as you two must be that the matter has finally been settled so satisfactorily for us all.'

'That's right,' chimed in the verger's wife, nodding emphatically, 'and settled with no need of lawyers, courts or the like. All I now hopes', she added, addressing her guest with a beaming smile, 'is that you and Mrs Harrison will do us the honour of dropping by for a cup of tea when we're settled in.'

'Of course—we'd both be delighted.'

Apart from the fact that the conversation was not being conducted against a background of drumming heavy rain, and that this time the participants were all seated on one level round the table, with bright winter sunlight streaming in through the window beside them, the scene in the Fromes's cosy little parlour was remarkably similar to that during Harrison's original visit: a fire burning brightly in the grate, the sleeping cat stretched before the hearth, the budgerigar singing its heart out in the corner cage. Despite, however, the superficial similarities, the whole feeling and atmosphere in the room was completely different from that first, somewhat fraught and awkward occasion. Instead of having to cajole and persuade, this time the visitor could relax, secure in the knowledge of his own and the diocese's narrow escape from disaster; and, enjoying the taste of success, he was more than happy to sit a few moments longer, discussing the details of how the Bright Cottage tenancy had actually been obtained.

'Mrs Gittings didn't say a word about any petition when she called in last Sunday—just said something about drumming up support for us in the parish.' Mavis broke off to sip her tea, then shook her head wonderingly. 'Who would have thought it!' she exclaimed. 'Her going to all that trouble, and even the wing commander putting his name to her list!'

'Ah! So it was Wing Commander Sparrow, was it? I heard that one of the churchwardens had put their name to the petition but, somehow, I had the idea that it would have been Mrs Brandon.'

'Oh, no, Colonel! It was the wing commander, all right,' insisted Mavis. 'I always said, didn't I, George,' she said, addressing her husband, 'that he was a good 'un, for all that he do come it a bit high and mighty at times.'

'Aye,' answered Frome, nodding, 'so you did, my dear.'

Feeling oddly pleased that Sparrow had turned up trumps after all, and that his original assessment of the senior churchwarden had proved so unfounded, Harrison glanced up at the picture above the fireplace of the aircraft carrier passing through the Straits of Gibraltar. 'Well,' he said, turning back to the verger with a smile, 'in that case, it would appear that all three of the armed services have been involved in our little victory: the air force through the wing commander, myself as ex-army, and you, George, representing the senior service.'

'That's right, sir,' said Frome, grinning, 'a sort of joint exercise, as you might say.'

'Anyway, with that happy thought in mind,' resumed Harrison, as the laughter faded, 'allow me to congratulate you again on obtaining the tenancy, and to say, on behalf of both myself and Archdeacon Cawthorne, how very pleased we are that this whole matter has been so amicably settled. And now,' he said, pushing back his chair, 'I must be thinking about returning to Canterbury.' He rose to his feet, but then, apparently struck by a sudden idea, he paused and again addressed the verger. 'But before I leave the parish, George, perhaps it would be a good idea if you and I were to slip over and have a quick glance round the cottage, just so I can get some impression of the amount of work necessary before you and Mavis actually move in.'

'Right, sir,' answered Frome enthusiastically. 'I'll go straight up to the rectory and fetch down the keys.'

'Oh, I'd like to come too, if I may, Colonel,' chimed in Mavis. 'I've never actually been inside the place.'

Harrison shook his head. 'No, not today, Mavis, if you don't mind,' he said. 'I only need George's help in checking the condition of the roof and external walls. But I'm sure', he added quickly, 'Mrs Gittings or someone else would be only too happy to drive you over at another time—remember, you've always got one set of keys here at the rectory and Wing Commander Sparrow has the other.'

'Yes, that's right I suppose, sir,' answered Mavis, reluctantly and with more than a trace of her former surliness in her voice. 'And anyway, if no one else will, my Sal would always be willing to take me over if I ask.'

'Oh, yes, and that reminds me,' said Harrison, hurriedly turning back to her husband, 'before we leave, George, perhaps we might stop off at one of the village shops. I wish to purchase a stout length of fishing-line. With the river so close, I imagine that will present no great problem.'

'Fishing-line?' repeated the verger, incredulity in his blue eyes. 'You're never thinking of going fishing, are you, Colonel? Not right in the middle of December?'

'No, no,' answered Harrison, laughing. 'I'm not intending to try and catch any fish today—or, at least,' he added as an after-thought, 'not any of the finny kind.'

'Well, what do you think, George? With the river behind and the little garden in front, and those rose bushes growing round the porch, it'll make quite an idyllic retreat for you both.'

For the third time in his life, Harrison had brought the car to a stop outside the garden gate and sat thoughtfully studying the exterior of Bright Cottage, that now, in the sunshine, despite the horrors of its recent past and the discolouring of the white-wash, actually seemed to be living up to its name. Frome sat beside him, craning for a better view. During the drive over, he'd said very little apart from agreeing that he and his wife would need some means of transport of their own after they'd moved, and stating that he intended putting the few hundred pounds they'd been left by the Reverend Lambkin towards the cost of a second-hand car. Now, as he gazed up the path towards his future home, he merely muttered, 'Yes, I reckon it'll do just fine, Colonel.'

'Right, let's go and see how things are inside.'

Harrison clambered from the car and, with Frome limping behind, proceeded up the stone-flagged path to the front porch. This time there was not the slightest problem about getting in: the key yielded smoothly in the lock, and the heavy-studded por-tal swung back unimpeded. Stepping into the vestibule behind, Harrison opened the glass-panelled inner door and entered the gloomy, narrow hallway. As he did so, his glance went straight to the spot beside the staircase banisters where Helen Middlebrook had vomited after recoiling in horror from the sight in the mission hall. No mark now showed on the bare flooring, and a brief look around showed the house had been thoroughly cleaned after the police and the various forensic experts had finished their investigations. Despite this, the long shut-up cottage was still pervaded by the same musty smell of damp and mould as it had been back in the autumn.

'Yes, well, obviously something will have to be done about installing a dampcourse,' said Harrison, glancing round as the verger entered behind him. 'But don't worry, George,' he added reassuringly as Frome began sniffing the air, 'I'll make sure all the work is completed before you and Mavis move in.'

'Thank you, sir.'

Whether it was the smell of the damp, or a quite understandable reaction to entering the building where his late master had met his terrible fate, all Frome's former delight and enthusiasm at obtaining the cottage tenancy appeared to have completely evaporated. With a troubled expression, he stood looking about him, then turned to watch as Harrison bent and began trying various keys in the lock of the mission-hall door. Making no comment nor asking any question, he waited in silence until the correct one had been found, then gravely followed the other through the doorway to confront the actual scene of the tragedy.

The curtains of both sets of facing windows were open, and the first impression Harrison had on entering was of light streaming in dust-moted beams through the south-facing panes into an amazingly transformed room. The great collection of chairs, old hassocks, parts of the demolished altar, decaying hymnals and all the rest of the jumble that had originally occupied the majority of the floor space had been moved back and neatly stacked against the further wall. As a result, most of the parquet flooring now lay bare and empty, with an extensive whitened area absolute conviction—that at least one other person was present here in this cottage on that occasion, and that, instead of Jonathan killing his father as it appeared, both of them were murdered by whoever it was, and the scene which confronted Miss Middlebrook and myself the following morning was a mere masquerade, a cunningly contrived piece of mummery, devised to fool us and everybody else.'

Blue eyes open wide, Frome stared at Harrison, horror and incredulity struggling in his face. 'Dear God!' he gasped. 'Young Jonathan and Rector murdered, you reckon?' Colour rushing to his cheeks, he grimaced, and as he stooped forward, his mouth working, for one terrible moment Harrison thought the obviously stricken man was actually going to be sick.

'I'm sorry to have given you this shock, George,' he said gently as the other recovered himself. 'Don't you worry, though—with your help, I'll make sure that, whoever the killer was, he or she will pay to the uttermost farthing.'

Frome shook his head in dazed disbelief, then, coming forward, gazed fixedly down at the faint chalk-marks beside Harrison's feet. 'But what I don't understand', he said, eventually looking up with a sudden doubt in his eyes, 'is how what you say could be true, sir. According to what you yourself said at the inquest, Colonel, the door of this room was locked, and the keys was found lying well inside—and didn't you have charge of the only spare set?'

'That's right, George, and now together we'll work out how the trick was played: how the door was first locked from outside, and then the keys got back here inside the room.'

Making no answer, Frome turned and looked towards the door, then shook his head. 'I don't see how they rightly could—there's not more than a half-inch gap between the bottom of the door and the floor to stuff anything under.'

'And yet,' answered Harrison, 'given that all the windows were latched, and that none of them had been opened for years,

towards the nearer end where the congealed blood had be
scrubbed and scraped away. Gone were the flies and the abattoi
like smell—and, apart from the discoloured expanse of interloc
ing wooden blocks and a slight tang of disinfectant in the air, t
only sign remaining that anything terrible had happened in t
room was a faint, almost indiscernible chalked outline wh
Jonathan's body had lain.

For Harrison, the metamorphosis came as both a huge rel
and a heart-numbing, sickening shock; the former because t
present airy lightness and cleanness was so utterly different fr
the twilit, stinking scene of mayhem that had met his eyes wl
he'd last entered the room; the latter, because it seemed that
process of cleansing and tidying had removed any chance he l
of discovering the truth of what lay behind the sight that l
originally confronted. Momentarily disorientated, he walked
where Jonathan had been found, and, looking down, used w
little could still be made out of the chalked outline to ascer
the exact position in which the young man's body had been ly
when he'd examined it. Having done so, he turned and loo
back to where Frome stood in the doorway, regarding him wi
perplexed frown.

'I'm afraid, George,' said Harrison gently, 'that I brought
here with me under somewhat false pretences. Today, des
what I said earlier, I'm not primarily concerned with the struc
and condition of the building: that can wait until l
Middlebrook has a chance to make her inspection. The real
son you're here is that I need your practical skills and experti
helping me work out what really happened in this room that
rible night.'

At the words, a tortured, anguished expression rose in
verger's face. Visibly paling, he stared at the speaker. 'What r
happened!' he repeated almost tonelessly, and shook his hea
bewilderment. 'Colonel, I don't understand what you mean.'

'Simply this,' continued the other, 'it's my belief—in fac

somehow the keys must have passed under.' He paused, surveying the uneven length of floor between himself and the door, and
as he did so, an explanation came. 'Of course!' he cried. 'Look at
the way the damp has caused those parquet blocks to rise in
places. My guess is that quite a few of them are loose and could
quite easily be prised up.' He turned to the man at his side. 'As an
ex-sailor and a practical man, George, I imagine you always keep
a sharp knife about you—if you'll lend it to me for a moment,
we'll see what a stout blade can achieve on those blocks around
the base of the door.'

'I've got a knife, sir,' answered Frome, drawing a large horn-
handled jackknife from a pocket. 'If you let me have a go, sir, I'll
soon find out if them blocks can be lifted or not.'

'Right—off you go then, my dear chap.'

Going to the doorway, Frome knelt, and, with Harrison
watching closely, drove the knife-blade between two of the loos-
est-looking of the blocks. With a few deft moments of his wrist,
he quickly levered one up and extracted it. It was clear that the
adhesive that had originally glued the wooden slabs to the concrete surface beneath had long ceased to be effective. It proved,
therefore, a simple matter to raise and remove a number of the
surrounding jigsaw of pieces.

'Aye, Colonel,' said Frome, eventually pulling himself
upright, 'it looks as if you might be right—there's certainly space
enough now to slip them keys easily under the door, and it
wouldn't be no trouble neither, slotting the blocks back into place
from here in the passage. But what I don't see', he continued,
turning to look in again at the mission hall, 'is, even if you could
push 'em under the door, how could you get them keys to lie all
the way out there where them chalk-marks are?'

Smiling, Harrison drew from his pocket the length of fishing-line he'd obtained in the village. 'For the answer to that,
George, I have to thank you personally.'

'Me, sir?'

'Yes—I believe you once made a very fine ship-in-the-bottle for Jonathan when he was a boy. I'm now going to try the same technique to get the keys out on the floor as you used to draw up the masts of your model of the *Cutty Sark*. But to achieve it,' he added, crossing back to the chalk-marks, 'I need a fixed point—something to use as a pulley, or a block, as I believe you sailors term it.' He paused, meditatively gazing down at the faint outline at his feet, then suddenly slapped a hand to his forehead. 'God, yes! It's glaringly obvious! How stupid of me! The fixed point was the chair that Jonathan was slumped across: the line would run around the armrest supports or simply one of the legs.'

As he'd talked, his gaze had turned to the stacked furniture at the end of the room, and now, walking forward, he ran his eyes across the heaped chairs, picking out from among them those of the high-backed type to which the dead rector had been bound and also over which the sprawled body of his son had been lying.

'Right, George,' he called, turning round, 'there are just four of the sort I'm looking for here. If you'll kindly help lift them down, I think I might be able to show how those keys were moved across the floor to lie close beside one of Jonathan's hands, and thereby prove, if we're lucky, that my theory is correct.'

With Frome's help, the four chairs were soon lifted down. None of them bore any obvious signs of blood, and it was clear that the cleaning-up operation in the mission hall had been at least as thorough as the one in the Deptford flat. Upturning them, Harrison crouched down and, putting on his reading-spectacles, moved from one to the other, examining each of them minutely. He'd reached the last of the small collection, and was beginning to fear that the traces he was looking for had been washed off, when he saw what he was hoping to see: a thin, brown semicircle just discernible against the varnished wood, running round the inner half of one of the three ornamental grooves near the lower end of one leg.

Triumphantly, he pointed to his find. 'There, you see! Just as

I expected—a trace of dried blood from the line that carried the keys across the floor, done of course when the blood on the floor was still liquid and wouldn't afterwards show that an object had been drawn through it.' Straightening, he smiled grimly. 'There's our proof of double murder, George—that some unknown person was literally pulling the strings that night when your late rector and his son were butchered in cold blood.'

Frome remained staring down at the tiny semicircle of dried blood for a moment, then turned away. 'My God!' he murmured, speaking with difficulty. 'You were right, then!' Breathing heavily, he shook his head. 'Let me just come up with that foxy damned bastard who did for them, and I'll give him a taste of both barrels of my own bloody shotgun!'

'Him or her, we'll discover who did it, never fear,' answered Harrison soothingly. 'But we still have to work out how exactly the keys were deposited beside the upturned chair—and to do that, I think the best thing would be to see if we can carry out the very same trick ourselves.'

First putting aside the chair that bore the marks of dry blood, Harrison carried one of the others across and lay it down beside the chalk-marks in the same toppled position as the other had been when Jonathan's body had lain half-stretched across it. He then weighed it down with a heap of the old hassocks before taking his fishing-line and looping it round one of the grooves on the nearer of the pair of legs resting on the floor. This done, he carried both ends back to the doorway, keeping them taut; then attaching the key-ring to the shorter, he hauled in, dragging the keys across the floor until they jammed fast in the narrow gap between the floor and the acute angle of the chair leg.

The difficulty was, however, to work out a method of releasing the keys without actually breaking the line, and so leaving an obvious clue as to how they'd been moved. After fruitless attempts with various types of slip knot, and having obtained no good result, Harrison left Frome to experiment while he went over to one of the windows overlooking the lane and stared at the farmhouse opposite. Once again, as when Tubman and old Miss Lambkin had questioned him, he forced himself to go back over the details of everything he'd seen when he'd made his examination of the room and bodies: the crumpled ball of paper beneath Lambkin's chair; the two spent cartridges and the mass of feathers and clean white matches floating in the concealed blood close to the keys. Bowing his head, he concentrated, and then from it all, he recalled the one tiny, rather odd little detail of the snapped-off match floating among the rest. As he remembered, he saw the explanation—the simple, ingenious way that the killer had contrived to deposit the keys beside Jonathan's outstretched hand.

'I've got it, George!' Excited, he turned to Frome, who was trying yet another type of knot on the key-ring. 'The killer used a match as a sacrificial-bar.'

'Sacrificial-bar? I don't understand, sir.'

'It's easy—I'll show you. Have you any matches on you?'

'Aye, Colonel, I've got a box in my pocket.'

'Right, in that case, if you give me one, we'll see whether my idea is right.'

Taking the match he was handed, he knotted the end of the fishing-line tightly round the middle, then slipped it through the ring at the top of one of the large, old-fashioned keys. This done, he looped the line round the chair leg as before and carried the two ends back out through the doorway into the passage outside. Then crouching down, and with Frome standing beside him, he closed the door and began hauling in the line with one hand, while using the other to ease the bunch of keys beneath the gap left where the parquet blocks had been removed. The keys vanished from sight, and he kept steadily pulling in on the line, hearing them dragging across the floor until he felt them jam under the chair leg.

Pausing, Harrison glanced up at Frome. 'Right,' he said with a confident smile, 'now we'll see if can hook our Leviathan up!'

So saying, he gave the line a hard tug. Immediately he felt it come free, and he continued to pull in the green nylon cord until the knotted end was once more back in his hand.

'Good,' he said, scrambling unsteadily to his feet. 'Let's go in and see how we've done.'

Opening the door, he went directly across to the chair and looked down with grim satisfaction: as expected, the bundle of keys lay half beneath the toppled chair, with the match lying close beside them in the same snapped back V-shape as the one he'd originally seen floating in the blood beside Jonathan's body.

'So far, so good,' he murmured. 'The next thing is to see how that front door was bolted from outside.'

'How did you know that would be there?'

Standing in the bright sunshine outside the cottage porch, Frome stared down at the multi-holed ventilation brick revealed low down on the wall behind the thick foliage of rose-stems to the left of the front door. Releasing the stems, Harrison straightened and looked round. 'How did I know? Simply because it had to be there: our ingenious puppet-master needed some way of getting his string through to the porch to draw the lower bolt into place. Anyway,' he added, taking the fishing-line from his pocket once more, 'knowing from experience the care and thoroughness of our Victorian forebears, as opposed to the rather slap-dash builders of the eighteenth century who erected the cottage, I guessed they'd given the porch some way to breathe. All I need to do now is to thread this loop through one of the holes in the brick, then go inside and slip it over the draw-knob—after that, I'll close the front door and pull the bolt into position from here.'

Like the finding of the match, what he proposed doing proved far easier to say than achieve. Though poking the line with a pencil through the brick was quickly accomplished, three times the looped fishing-line slipped off the protruding draw-knob as the front door was closed, and twice the line snapped with the bolt not moved. Finally kneeling with damp knees on the uncut grass, Harrison gave the line a heavy jerk and felt the bolt slide into place.

'Got it!' he grunted, and, releasing one end of the loop, he pulled the line out of the wall before staggering to his feet. Only then, as he stumbled upright with the line still dangling from his hand, did he notice that he and the verger were no longer alone. A small but attentive audience were regarding him with puzzled looks from across the garden wall.

As he'd knelt at the base of the porch, attempting to jerk the bolt into place, he'd been dimly aware of the sound of a tractor starting up over at the farm, then of the machine moving out into the lane. So absorbed had he been, that he'd taken no notice, and only now did he realize that the tractor had halted just outside the gate, and that the young man who was driving as well as the older man standing immediately behind him in the cab were peering curiously towards him.

As their eyes met, the driver turned away and, hurriedly engaging a gear, began heading along the lane towards Wetmarsh Marden. His companion, unabashed, remained staring back at the cottage through the twin glass-panelled doors at the rear of the cab.

Together, Frome and Harrison stood gazing after the departing tractor in silence. Only when it had eventually vanished from sight did the verger speak. 'Well, sir,' he said slowly, turning to Harrison with a troubled look, 'one thing we can depend on now is that the news of our pokings around here will be all over the parish before night. With the gossip that goes in the Ferryman, you can depend that whoever killed Rector and Jonathan will soon know that we've found out how his trick was carried out.'

Harrison nodded, cursing his carelessness in allowing himself to have been seen, and at the same time, hardly able to contain his irritation with Frome for failing to warn him of the tractor's approach.

'You understand what this could mean, Colonel?' continued his companion gloomily. 'Once he's been alerted, the killer could well come after us—and we've still no idea as to who the clever bastard is, nor do we know what he's likely to do!'

During their time in the cottage, a high bank of cloud had been steadily building on the northern horizon and starting to stretch across the sky. Now, just as the verger spoke the words, for the first time that morning the sun was temporarily shrouded, and a shadow ran across the fields and marshes suddenly to darken the little garden in which the two men stood.

CHAPTER TWENTY

A great billow of smoke wafted up from the deanery garden and sluggishly rolled over the top of the high redbrick wall to spill like the vaporous effusion of some alchemist's flask down into the north-eastern corner of Green Court. There it hung, diffusing gradually into thin-layered veils that spread out, coiling and twisting, over the central lawn to cling as a translucent halo among the frost-tinted branches of the quadrangle's few rather spindly trees. The unnatural quiet of the deserted school buildings, together with the graceful, slow convolutions of the drifting smoke and the all-pervading bittersweet tang of burning vegetation, combined to underline the tranquillity of the bright, if chilly, Saturday afternoon.

In contrast, the scene within the walled garden was one of purposeful activity. The Ingrams twins, both wearing jeans and heavy sweaters, and armed with long-handled rakes and brooms, were engaged in aiding their father in his annual pre-Christmas tidying of the grounds, this consisting in the main of sweeping from the paths and lawn the dead leaves left from the autumn, then carting them by the barrow-load to the smouldering bonfire at the far end of the orchard. Despite their initial reluctance to partake in the task, and the combination of cajolery and bribery employed to persuade them outdoors, both girls were now clearly enjoying themselves, occasionally breaking off from their labours to chase after and pelt each other with clumps of the more mushy and rotted of their gatherings—this to the accompaniment of high-pitched shrieks and squeals.

All the while, their father, wearing the same old tweed jacket and corduroy trousers he'd worn at Deptford, but with the addition of short-sided Wellington boots, was employed in feeding the slow-burning fire. Having already uprooted and transported a small forest of decayed cabbage and Brussels sprout stumps to the belching source of the smoke, he now wheeled a load of miscellaneous papers away from the house—this at the instigation of his wife, who, prompted by a long-suffering cleaner, had insisted on using the opportunity for a complete clear-out of his study. Like all hardened hoarders, he'd protested vigorously at first, but, forced to comply, it was with a sense of psychological release and wellbeing that he now trundled his quivering load towards the waiting flames—only pausing as he reached the lawn to deliver the most gentle of fatherly admonishments to his pair of boisterous daughters.

From one of the windows of the now-denuded study, Harrison gazed out at the scene with an expression of brooding perplexity. Two days had passed since the Bright Cottage experiments, two days in which he'd resisted Winnie's fervent appeals to inform Chief Inspector Dowley of his absolute conviction that Maurice Lambkin and his son had died at the hands of an unknown assassin. Lack of firm proof as well as a continuing resentment against Dowley for failing to confide the true nature of Jonathan's life, had so far prevented him doing so, and, not wishing to reveal he'd been responsible for inadvertently washing away the evidence of third-party involvement, he was strongly inclined to continue keeping authority at bay until he'd penetrated the heart of the mystery. Therefore, standing at the window, awaiting Margaret Ingrams's return from the kitchen, he found himself searching his mind yet again for some clue as to the identity of the murderer and a possible reason for the apparently motiveless crime.

Though he'd originally believed that the sender of the anonymous notes had been a woman, he now felt sure that the crude act of double butchery could only have been carried out by one of his own gender—a subtle, clever, essentially brutal individual, whose abnormality of mind was proved as much by the bizarrely composed note sent to Cawthorne as by the cold-blooded savagery of the killings themselves. Aware that such a person couldn't be trusted to react in any sane or rational manner, he'd taken Frome's warning of danger seriously from the first, advising him to stay as much as possible within the rectory grounds for the present. In the meantime, conscious of the potential danger overhanging Frome and himself, and remembering that the original note impugning Lambkin's behaviour had been sent directly to the archdeacon as the Church officer immediately responsible for clergy misdemeanours, he'd been in touch with a number of useful diocesan contacts, including the incumbents of both adjoining parishes, inquiring into the backgrounds and reputations of all those in the Fordington area having any official or semi-official involvement with the Church, or likely, through close personal contact or in any other way, to have knowledge of its disciplinary structures.

Unsurprisingly, the names of those he'd been given had all attended the rectory reception—apart, that is, from Donald Gittings. He, like the majority of the more well-to-do local inhabitants, was an interloper, having only moved into the district after transferring his computer software company from London to an industrial estate in Ramsgate. Regarding those business worries his wife had mentioned, it seemed that he'd borrowed heavily to finance the move; then, forced to cut back through the effects of recession, he'd been left with a heavy debt as well as unnecessarily large premises to maintain. Equally well known, at least in Church circles, was the fact that his wife's commitment to her parish duties and her desire for ordination rankled deeply with him, and that, because of this, a degree of animosity had existed between himself and the late rector.

Tony and Gwendolen Brandon were also originally Londoners, and, like Gittings, very much part of the so-called 'new enterprise culture'. Despite all their easy charm and apparent sophistication, they'd risen from comparatively lowly backgrounds, having reached their present level of prosperity through astute business acumen coupled with a certain ruthlessness. After establishing a successful double-glazing company, they'd turned to property speculation, prospering so mightily that they'd recently bought and extensively renovated the local manor house, and now enjoyed a life of horses, swimming-pools and foreign holidays, whilst at the same time attempting to wrap themselves in a cloak of respectability by playing prominent roles in church life and local affairs generally.

As an ex-serviceman, Wing Commander Sparrow's career was a matter of public record. Using one of his few remaining contacts in the Ministry of Defence, Harrison had obtained a detailed account of the churchwarden's period in the air force. Having joined on a short service commission, he'd been transferred to the general list after two tours of flying duty, being regarded as a conscientious and efficient officer, if somewhat of a martinet at times.

Harrison had also checked on the verger's service record, again finding that it accorded with what he'd imagined. Orphaned when young, Frome had been brought up in a Barnardo Home and joined the Royal Navy as a boy entrant.

Though not exactly dull, he'd certainly not shone during initial training, being considered by his instructors to lack initiative and independence of mind. Nevertheless, proving reliable and trustworthy, he had gone on to do moderately well, rising to junior petty officer rank before being invalided out.

Though his researches had uncovered no obvious local suspect, Harrison still felt certain that the choice of the cottage as the stage for the double murder, and the obvious intimate knowledge of its construction and interior, ruled out any involvement from those groups Jonathan had been infiltrating in London. As he stared despondently out into the garden, the sight of Ingrams emptying the contents of his wheelbarrow on to the bonfire brought to mind the curious tale of Lambkin ordering the burning of the Lazarus picture. Remembering that long, frustrating day when he'd learnt of the curious incident, he recalled his feeling at the time of having missed some very obvious anomaly amongst all that he'd seen or heard—something which, if only he'd been able to put his finger on it, might have led him directly to the solving of the crime.

Looking past the again romping girls towards their father's hazy outline, he began going over everything he'd observed or learnt from the time he and Frome had trudged up the rectory drive to begin the search of the house. In his mind's eye, he again moved along the ground floor from Lambkin's study to the back of the house, then up the stairs to the first floor. He'd just reached the moment when he'd entered the master-bedroom and was looking down at the photographs on the dressing-table when his thoughts were interrupted by the arrival of a rather flustered-looking Margaret Ingrams, bearing a large glass bowl wrapped in Cellophane.

'Oh, Richard, I'm sorry to have kept you waiting so long!' she exclaimed as she entered. 'After adding the cream, I had to search the cupboards for my packet of hundreds-and-thousands. I only hope', she said, passing the bowl into her visitor's hands, 'that Winnie will be pleased with my little efforts. It's been an absolute age, I'm afraid, since I made my last jelly-trifle.'

'Oh, I'm sure she will,' replied the recipient, peering down at the pudding through the transparent covering. 'It looks positively mouth-watering to me!'

'Well, just so long as your guests like it,' said the dean's wife, eyeing her handiwork doubtfully.

Harrison burst out laughing. 'My dear Margaret, of that there's not the slightest doubt, I assure you. If I know anything about these particular guests, they'll be gobbling it up like Gadarene swine!'

Despite his little joke and the polite enthusiasm with which he'd received Margaret Ingrams's generous donation, it was at a dilatory pace and with an abstracted, melancholy air that Harrison retraced his steps along the outside of the deanery wall. Until reminded over breakfast, he'd forgotten all about the tea party Winnie had arranged for young Simon Barnes and his friends. It had, therefore, come as an unpleasant shock to learn that, not only was he expected to trail round Sainsbury's as usual in the morning, but that the afternoon would inevitably go in making things ready—the blow the more painful in that he'd been looking forward to slumping in front of the television after lunch to watch England play the All Blacks at Twickenham.

For the past two days he'd gone about his duties as usual, attending meetings, answering correspondence and discussing various projects, including the renovation of Bright Cottage with Helen Middlebrook and a now embarrassingly grateful and quiescent archdeacon. Throughout it all, as if cocooned within an invisible envelope, he'd wrestled alone to solve the riddle of the Wetmarsh Marden slayings, and, oppressed by his inability to do so, the very last thing on earth he wanted was to have to play host to a gang of probationer choristers.

His feet faltered at the thought of it, and he paused on the smoke-veiled path, feeling a surge of angry resentment against Winnie for having issued the invitation in the first place, and also feeling annoyed with himself for ever having agreed to it. With the pudding-bowl clutched to his chest, he gazed forlornly across the long-shadowed lawn until roused from his thoughts by the striking of the cathedral clock—the four heavy booms echoing over the deserted close as audible reminders of the fast-approaching domestic festivities. Turning, he hurried on towards Bread Yard, wondering how preparations were going and feeling an uneasy, guilty anxiety about the time his small errand had taken him.

'Ah, good! You've got it!' exclaimed Winnie, smiling as he entered the kitchen bearing the trifle. 'Well done, darling! I was really starting to think you'd managed to drop it on the way.'

Relieved by the unexpected friendliness of his reception, Harrison placed the bowl on the table. After the chilly isolation of the darkening precincts, the pastry-scented warmth of the kitchen came as a welcome relief, and he stood blinking in the glare of the strip-lights as Winnie wheeled herself forward and began eagerly unwrapping the Cellophane covering.

'Oh, Richard, it's lovely! Hasn't Margaret done it well? It was so typically kind of her to insist on making it!' Delighted, Winnie looked up from admiring the gaudily decorated surface of the pudding. 'Come on,' she said, swinging her chair round, 'carry it through. I want you to see what I've achieved next door.'

Obediently, her husband followed her into the sitting-room, where, under protest, he'd earlier erected their folding oak dining-table—a wedding gift that had accompanied them through the varying fortunes of their married life, accommodating itself to a series of very differently sized spaces. Now, fully extended, it completely dominated the small room, the light of its candlelit épergne glinting on the glasses, cutlery and plates laid out around it.

Laying the trifle aside, Harrison went forward and surveyed the array of paper napkins, egg sandwiches, sausage rolls and Christmas crackers, then, turning back to his wife, he glimpsed the mixture of pride and anxiety in her face. Doing so, he was hit by the full realization of the importance of the occasion to the childless, crippled—so often painfully—woman he loved. Recalling the resentment he'd felt on the way back from the deanery, and his surliness at the supermarket earlier, he felt an enormous guilt, and now, as their eyes met in the candlelight, he suddenly saw his attempt to solve the Bright Cottage murders by himself for what it most likely was: nothing but an egotistical wish to prove himself to Dowley and a desire to revenge himself on the unknown killer who'd unknowingly recruited him as his unwilling accomplice.

'Well?' said Winnie. 'What do you think? Will it do?'

Harrison bent and kissed her forehead. 'It's lovely, my dear. You've done an absolutely splendid job.' Seeing her look of joyous relief, he gave her shoulder a squeeze. 'And incidentally,' he said, smiling down, 'you needn't worry about this wretched Wetmarsh Marden business any more. I've made up my mind to contact Dowley on Monday: I'll confess my stupid swilling away of the paraffin in the kitchen sink and tell him as well about the discoveries Frome and I have made at the cottage.'

'Oh, will you, Richard? Really? Do you promise?'

'Yes, of course: this thing can't be allowed to go on hanging over us throughout Christmas. Anyway,' he said with a rueful smile, 'it's obviously beyond my ability to fathom the thing; that I must leave to our friends of the Kent Constabulary. In the meantime,' he continued, briskly turning for the door, 'let's see what can be done about getting some drinks organized before these brats appear—and also, perhaps, preparing one or two little surprises of my own.'

As arranged, the visitors arrived punctually half an hour later, with scrupulously combed hair, their faces as pink and radiant with health as those of the Ingrams twins earlier, the four boys having dashed straight from evensong to wash and change before coming over. Whether from Harrison's presence or simply from the uniqueness of the occasion, they entered the cottage shyly, heads downcast, with even the normally forward and talkative young Barnes as suddenly tongue-tied, bashful and meek as any Victorian girl attending her first adult ball.

Any worries, however, that Winnie and Harrison might have had as to the success of their tea party were soon dispelled. With darkness fallen and curtains drawn, the sitting-room came alive with laughter and chatter as the warmth and cosiness of the domestic hearth worked its magic on children who spent the vast majority of their lives separated from parents and home, living in a spartan, purely masculine world of dormitories, refectories, common and choral-practice rooms. Lulled by the comfort of their surroundings and the delights of food, the youngsters' conversation rapidly moved from polite answer to inquiry, and on to a free-flowing lively babble of talk, the more expansive regaling their hosts with improbable anecdotes involving the cathedral clergy and staff as well as with a series of excruciating schoolboy jokes.

Meal over and table cleared, the party continued with the pleasant companionship of roasting chestnuts round the fire. It was now that Harrison came truly into his own, surprising and delighting his guests by performing those card tricks and sleights of hand he'd learnt when himself at school. Gauche, awkward and shy as a child, he'd found that the ability to make an egg vanish, to predict a card, draw a coin from behind an ear or, his *pièce de résistance*, to gulp up and produce from his mouth a succession of golf balls, a ready and easy way of ingratiating himself with his fellow scholars.

'Well,' said Winnie, after the golf balls had apparently been gulped up a third time and the resultant laughter had finally calmed, 'and what about Christmas, then? Will any of you have the chance of seeing your families on the actual day?'

'Oh, rather!' exclaimed Barnes. 'The dean has said there will be no choral evensong that afternoon. After matins, we're free to go home.'

'So you'll at least have some of the day with your parents.' With a wan, sorrowful look, Winnie surveyed the semicircle of faces in front of the fire. 'You're so brave, all of you! It's bad enough being sent away to school, as I know, but to be choristers must be doubly hard.'

'Ah, yes, but you see, Mrs Harrison,' replied the small, blond-haired boy who sat leaning against Harrison's armchair, 'if I weren't a chorister, I couldn't have private education. My father's a clergyman,' he continued, craning round to look up with great seriousness at the seated figure behind, 'and they, sir, hardly earn any money at all.'

'That's only too true, I'm afraid,' replied Harrison, smiling down at the earnest-faced child. 'Unfortunately the Church does not possess the same resources it once did, and men like your father must seek any way they can to obtain a suitable education for their offspring.' As he spoke, he recalled the recent scene in the deanery garden, and thought of all the physical labour that his old friend undertook to keep the twins at Miss Hawkins's school. 'As things stand,' he said, shaking his head sadly, 'the birth of children forces even the most unworldly and idealistic of clerics to make some sort of accommodation with the world.'

As he spoke, he found himself thinking of Fordington Rectory with its drab furnishings, its threadbare carpets and those terrible damp-stains on the walls. Then sitting there with the children at his feet and with a paper crown absurdly tilted on his head, he at last saw the thing that had been rankling at the back of his mind ever since that long day in Maurice

Lambkin's parish—the curious anomaly which he now realized had been literally staring him in the face from the group wedding photograph on the dressing-table in the late rector's bedroom.

'Darling, whatever's the matter? Aren't you feeling well?'

Winnie's voice seemed to come from a distance. For an instant longer, Harrison remained staring fixedly across the boys' heads, still seeing in his mind's eye the pathetically small group of young guests standing either side of the equally young newly-weds—then, blinking the vision away, he turned and smiled at his questioner. 'No, my dear, I'm perfectly all right. It's just that I suddenly remembered a little thing that, until this moment, had completely slipped my mind.'

Not wishing to disrupt proceedings further, Harrison determinedly resumed his role of avuncular host, recounting amusing anecdotes from army days, and even deigning, on popular request, to gulp up the golf balls again. Nevertheless, amidst all the jollity, one part of his mind remained preoccupied. Just as during the various meetings over the past two days, he couldn't always prevent his thoughts from straying from matters of immediate concern. By the time their guests came to leave, a burning desire had grown to share his revelation with Winnie and to ask her the various questions now occupying his mind. Resisting the impulse, however, he said nothing as he stood beside her at the front door, waving goodbye until the boys finally vanished beneath the yard archway. After they'd returned to the sitting-room, he still made no reference to the matter, allowing Winnie the chance to recount and remember all the small incidents and remarks that together had made up the undoubted success of the evening. Indeed, it wasn't until they had moved out to the kitchen and begun the washing-up that he brought up the subject that so dominated his thoughts—and even then, his question sounded deceptively casual.

'Winnie, that first evening when Ingrams came round to see

me about the anonymous note, didn't you mention something about Jonathan's education here at the school?'

'Did I?' answered the other absently, drying the glass she'd just been handed. 'What was it I said?'

'That it was paid for by a trust fund set up by Lavinia Lambkin in her will.'

'Yes, that's right. What about it?'

'Just that I don't believe it,' answered Harrison quietly, continuing to mop out the trifle bowl. 'As the wedding photographs show, neither of those sisters overcame their prejudices even to attend the Lambkins' wedding. Is it likely therefore that one of them would have subsequently arranged to fund the education of the fruit of a union they so strongly disapproved of?' Breaking off, he rinsed out the bowl under the tap, then carefully placed it on the draining-board. 'Anyway,' he resumed, turning away from the sink to address Winnie directly, 'remember what the old woman said to us at the end of the funeral reception about wishing that she and Lavinia had shown a modicum of charity towards Maurice and his family. She'd surely never have said such a thing if part of her sister's estate had gone towards paying Jonathan's school fees.'

'No, I suppose not.' Winnie looked up at him with a puzzled frown. 'But why then, if the money didn't come from Lavinia, did Maurice make everyone believe it did?'

'That,' answered Harrison, 'is the question I've been asking myself for the last hour or more. What was the point of giving the credit to his dead aunt if he'd scraped the money together himself? Then, of course,' he continued, 'there's another question that has to be asked: if not from Lavinia, then whence did the money actually come? How did such an impractical dreamer as Lambkin manage to get hold of sufficient cash to put his son first through prep school and then through King's?'

Winnie shook her head. 'I can't think. All I know is that before going to Fordington, he ran those university mission hostels in the East End of London, then went on to wear himself out working in various inner-city parishes. Apart from that, I know he did a spell as assistant chaplain at Wormwood Scrubs prison when Jonathan was still a small boy—but that, I imagine, wouldn't have paid very much.'

'Wormwood Scrubs prison, you say?'

'Yes, it was in a neighbouring parish.'

'Wormwood Scrubs prison?'

'Yes, dear, I told you.' Winnie suddenly laughed. 'Now, come on! You look as if you're in a dream. Are we going on with the washing-up or not? That water must be getting terribly cold by now.'

Not replying, Harrison stared vacantly at her for a moment longer before bursting out, 'Of course! Prisoners are offered extra-mural studies. People like yourself go in and teach basket-weaving, carpentry, Serbo-Croat and all the rest of it, including painting classes!'

'Richard, whatever are you talking about?'

'The picture, Winnie! The picture that Stella Gittings rescued from the bonfire—the one of Lazarus emerging from the grave.' Harrison's face contorted and, still clutching the dishmop, he took a step forward, then slammed a fist to his forehead. 'Oh, what a blind fool I've been! Damn it! The picture even had the date on it!'

'Yes,' said Winnie, frowning as she watched him begin pacing, head bent, about the kitchen, 'it had the date 1972 on it and also the artist's Christian name—Tim or Timothy, whoever he might have been.'

Pausing in his pacings, Harrison shook his head. 'No, not a name—those were initials. I'm certain they stand for Thomas Ian Marshal.'

'Thomas Ian Marshal? Who's he?'

'Who was he, you mean,' came the answer. 'He was one of the two surviving members of the Heathrow Airport gang who died in the infirmary of Wormwood Scrubs prison that same year.' Breaking off, he took a further step or two forward, then resumed, his voice rising, 'Someone who presumably repented his sins, and who gave his painting to the man who'd shown him the way to salvation—the same man who was very likely beside him when he died, and who doubtless would have given him absolution after he'd made his final confession!'

'Richard, do calm down and stop striding around for goodness sake! I still have no idea what you're talking about.'

Harrison spun round and faced her, eyes bright with excitement. 'About a compact with the devil, Winnie! About selling one's soul! Don't you see—Faustus may have sold his soul for power and prestige, but a good man, or at least a better than average man, might well risk his soul for the sake of his only child; and what does any parent think, especially a natural scholar like Lambkin, when he knows he's condemned that same child to the vagaries of some poor-quality inner-city primary school!'

'Please, darling! Calm down and explain yourself.'

'I will, my dear,' muttered Harrison, turning for the door, 'but not at this precise moment. I've got to go over to the deanery.'

'Now? But, Richard, you can't possibly, not on a Saturday evening!' called Winnie as he disappeared out into the hall. 'Matthew will be in the middle of writing his sermon.'

In many ways the scene was identical to that which had met Harrison's eyes when he'd called in on his old friend the evening prior to his first visit to the Fromes: Ingrams sitting sideways at his desk, pipe in mouth, the shutters closed and the double bar of the electric fire glowing brightly in the smoke-wafted dimness of the book-lined study. This time, however, the room was surprisingly neat and tidy, and the surface of the desk was bare apart from an open copy of Cruden's biblical concordance and a well-thumbed commentary on the Gospel of St John; and instead of having the wastepaper basket jammed between his knees, the dean sat nursing the family cat, stroking its head with one hand as he jotted down notes on a writing-pad with the other.

As the visitor entered, the sitter blinked up in mild surprise. 'Good Lord! Richard—whatever brings you out of a Saturday evening?' He frowned. 'Nothing wrong, I hope? Everything went well with your tea party?'

'Yes, thank you, Dean. Everything's fine. I'm sorry to crash in on you like this; it's just that something's cropped up that I need to check.'

'Ah!' His face clearing, Ingrams beamed. 'Something in your crossword, I imagine.' He waved towards his bookshelves. 'Please, my dear fellow, feel free to consult any volume you like.'

Harrison shook his head. 'No, it isn't a book I'm looking for—I need to glance through all the documents you collected from Fordington Rectory.'

'Maurice's papers?' A look of dismay rose in the dean's face. 'But I'm afraid you can't, Richard—you're a few hours too late.'

'Too late?' Taken aback, Harrison shook his head. 'I don't understand. I thought you were only sending the few necessary papers on to Lambkin's solicitor.'

'Yes, and I've done it, but the remainder, I'm afraid, went on the bonfire this afternoon.'

Stunned, Harrison stared horrified at the speaker. 'You burnt the whole lot?' he said numbly.

'I regret to say, yes. But why do you need them? Were they important?' Distressed, Ingrams looked round the room and shook his head. 'How many times have I told Margaret, it's terribly dangerous, these impetuous clear-outs of hers!'

'No, no, Dean,' murmured Harrison, recovering from his initial shock. 'It's not Margaret's fault. And anyway,' he continued, 'perhaps you can tell me what I need to know. When you checked through the papers, did you happen to notice anything involving the trust fund that was set up to pay for Jonathan's education?'

Ingrams frowned. 'There were some letters and statements from a bank regarding it, I recall. But, of course, they were years old and completely outdated, as the capital investment was fully used up by the time Jonathan left the King's School. It was on a county scholarship that he went up to Cambridge.'

'And this trust fund—was there anything among the papers to prove that Lavinia Lambkin originally set it up in her will?'

The dean thought for a moment, then shook his head. 'No, I don't think so. But why do you ask?'

'I just need to know if Lavinia Lambkin really did establish an educational trust fund for Jonathan in her will.'

Lowering his head, Ingrams frowned down at the cat on his lap, then looked up, smiling. 'But surely that presents no great difficulty: copies of all wills in Great Britain and Northern Ireland are freely available for public inspection. If you were to write to the Master of the Probate and Matrimonial Office at the Royal Courts of Justice in Belfast, you would be sent a copy of the will in exchange for a small fee.'

'Yes, quite! How foolish of me!' Slamming a fist into his open palm, Harrison began pacing the carpet, head bent. Perplexed, Ingrams eyed him with concern. 'My dear fellow, what's wrong? You're clearly agitated about something. May I ask what's on your mind?'

'On my mind?' Pausing, but still staring down at the carpet, Harrison answered slowly, 'I'm thinking of someone who might have consulted the office you speak of—someone who, at a certain funeral six months ago, could have heard something that made him doubt the long-accepted notion that Jonathan's education had been paid for by one of his father's maiden aunts.'

'Who do you mean?'

Harrison raised his head and looked across at the dean. 'I mean,' he said slowly, 'the real sponsor of that educational trust, Jonathan's unwittingly generous patron—someone whose mutilated corpse was fished out of the Thames by the river police many years ago.'

CHAPTER TWENTY-ONE

'I don't like it, Colonel—I don't like it at all!'

Arms folded, Chief Inspector Dowley stood at his office window, gazing down across the Old Dover Road, his face wearing much the same look of brooding perplexity as his visitor's had done when observing the scene in the deanery garden four days before. For a few moments more he remained watching the crowd of heavily burdened Christmas shoppers passing along the pavement in front of the glass-panelled doors of the fire station opposite before returning to his desk. Slumping down, he began again turning through the neatly ordered pile of papers in the folder lying on the surface, scanning them closely as if hoping to find among them some answer or way of escape from the matter troubling him. Finally, with a grimace, he flipped it closed and looked up to face the figure seated in front of him.

'I agree, Colonel, that according to these records, the ages and physical descriptions of the two men fit, and that the dates and places of residence also coincide. Added to that, the fact that an application was indeed made back in the spring of this year to the Probate and Matrimonial Office in Belfast to inspect Lavinia Lambkin's will, just as you'd guessed had been done, strongly supports your theory. What, however,' he continued dolefully, 'I'm not nearly so happy about is this proposal of yours for testing to see if your idea's right. Wouldn't it be a hell of a lot simpler and also safer if we were merely to bring our friend in for questioning in the usual way? Fingerprints will prove straight away if you're right, and then a few hours' close confinement with me and some of my lads here will soon have the full truth out of him.'

'Fingerprints will prove who he is,' answered Harrison, 'but not that he's the killer—he was far too careful to leave any prints in the cottage. As to him confessing under interrogation, my guess is you'd be more likely to get the cell walls to speak.' Harrison paused, then went on earnestly, 'No, Chief Inspector, with someone as clever and resourceful as this man obviously is, to prove my theory right, and to wring any sort of confession out of him, you'll have to allow me to play out my game. After all,' he added, 'I'm still far from sure what the thing was that actually prompted the killings, and without either an obvious motive or any forensic evidence, I'd say that there's little chance of us securing a conviction.'

Clearly troubled, Dowley sat back, thoughtfully scratching the back of his neck. 'And if,' he said finally, 'by some miracle, I did manage to get my superiors to agree to this harebrained scheme of yours, do you really think the fellow would accept your invitation? Wouldn't he just refuse to have any part of it?'

For the first time since the start of the interview, Harrison smiled. 'My dear Chief Inspector,' he said, 'he won't have any choice. To quote a character in a certain film enthusiastically recommended me by a small chorister friend of my wife's, I'll be making him an offer that he cannot refuse.'

An answering smile flickered momentarily across Dowley's mouth, but then he was once again gravely serious. 'Yes, but it could be damn risky, Colonel,' he answered. 'If you're right, the fellow's a cold-blooded killer, and very likely insane into the bargain. If anything happened to you, it would be my own head next on the chopping-block!' The speaker paused, and then unexpectedly grinned. 'And it wouldn't be just to the Chief Constable I'd have to answer to, either: if I were to allow the esteemed secretary of the Diocesan Dilapidations Board to end up as a mangled corpse, I'd likely find myself on my knees before the Archbishop of Canterbury!'

'I'm sure you'd find his Grace very merciful and understanding,' answered Harrison, laughing. 'But seriously, Chief Inspector,' he continued, 'please don't worry about me. I'll be perfectly all right, I assure you. And, anyway, it isn't as if I plan to confront the man absolutely alone.'

Dowley sat considering for a few moments before he again spoke. 'If I were to go ahead and recommend your scheme, Colonel, and my immediate superiors were to agree to it, how exactly do you plan to arrange matters?'

'Just as I outlined earlier: I shall arrive in time to make my various official calls and generally make my presence known around the village, so creating as much of a smokescreen as I'm able. After that, I propose taking supper at the local inn before proceeding...'

'No, no,' interrupted Dowley, 'I was thinking more of how you intend squaring things domestically. After all,' he added, 'I don't imagine your good lady wife would take kindly to the idea of you unnecessarily exposing yourself to risk. How then are you going to explain having suddenly to be away overnight?'

Harrison gave a faint smile. 'As you can imagine, Chief Inspector, I've already given that matter some careful thought. On this occasion I think I shall be forced to take advantage of the temporary good-standing that I presently enjoy in my own immediate superior's eyes.'

'I really don't understand Dr Cawthorne!' Winnie's voice rang down the hall as her husband was closing the lid of the battered leather suitcase in the bedroom. 'Whatever reason on earth could he have had for suddenly deciding to send you off to a three-day conference just before Christmas like this?'

Securing the binding strap, Harrison picked the loaded suitcase from the bed and carried it out into the passage. As he did so, his wife's voice again came from the kitchen. 'And anyway,' she called, 'what possible connection has a conference on "Expert Systems and the Practical Uses of Cyberspace in Business Management" got to do with your work? You've always hated computers,' she said, looking up over her coffee cup as he appeared in the doorway. 'I remember the fuss you made when Dr Cawthorne insisted that Mary Simpson exchange her typewriter for a word processor!'

Harrison gave a rueful smile. 'I'm afraid, my dear,' he said, laying down his case and going round to take his place at the breakfast table, 'that even the Church of England is not immune to the virus of modern technology, and to be absolutely fair to Cawthorne, information technology is obviously the stuff of the future, so perhaps it's only right that I should at least try to get abreast of it.'

Winnie gave him a sceptical look, then, lapsing into silence, began buttering her toast. 'And what about all your theories about the Wetmarsh Marden killings?' she resumed, looking across as he poured out his coffee. 'Since your last visit to see Chief Inspector Dowley, I notice you've been very quiet about it all.'

Harrison took a sip of the coffee, then shook his head. 'The matter's nothing to do with me any longer. It's all in Dowley's hands now. All you and I can do is wait and see what his investigations produce.'

Winnie made no reply, and, avoiding his eyes, began meditatively chewing her toast. Harrison drank a little more of his coffee, then caught sight of the familiar, thick paperback book that lay beside his wife's plate.

'What! Still not finished your reading of *Middlemarch*?' he remarked with false and rather forced jocularity. 'It must be nearly two months since you began the thing.'

'I've been enjoying it too much to hurry it,' came the cold answer. 'Anyway, with things as they've been, I haven't been able to concentrate. I've other things to think about.'

For a few minutes, breakfast continued in strained silence until Harrison, feeling increasingly uncomfortable, finally said in a tone of concern, 'My dear, what is it that's on your mind?'

Winnie shook her head but didn't answer.

'Come on,' he coaxed. 'Tell me, what is it that's upsetting you? You'll enjoy your stay at the deanery—I know that Margaret in particular is looking forward to it.' He paused and smiled encouragingly. 'I'll only be away two nights, so I can't understand quite why you're so upset.'

Winnie gave a tiny shrug. 'I suppose I just hate you going away at all,' she said miserably. 'You packing your case reminds me of all those times in the army when you used to vanish away suddenly for months on end, and I'd be left alone with no idea what you were doing or where you were—or, indeed, if I'd even see you again.'

Harrison laughed. 'My dear, that was all years ago—this is nothing like that. Tonight I shall merely be in Cambridge, enjoying what I hope is the convivial quietness of St John's College out of term time whilst preparing this rusty old brain of mine to encounter the mysteries of downloading, zip drives and bus masters and all the rest of the damned bunkum.'

'Are you sure?'

His wife's dark eyes were fixed on his face, and, under her searching gaze, Harrison felt himself flush. 'Sure of what?' he said. 'Whatever do you mean?'

Distressed, Winnie shook her head. 'I don't quite know, just that this last day or two you've been a bit too happy and tensely excited about something, almost as if you were going off to see some other woman: it's as you always were when you were about to go off on one of those clandestine operations I wasn't allowed to know anything about.'

Harrison took a deep breath. 'My dear, as I say, all that is long ago and absolutely finished with. Now I'm just a humble diocesan official about to go off and spend what will most likely turn out to be among the most boring hours of my life.' He suddenly laughed. 'The only danger I'm likely to encounter in the next day or two is through nodding off to sleep with the tedium of the whole thing and ending up breaking an arm by falling out of my chair.'

By mid-morning Harrison had left the cathedral precincts, and the Volvo was clear of the city traffic, bowling once more along the main Sandwich road. With a high-pressure weather system firmly established over the entire British Isles, in many ways the morning was a winter version of that autumn day when he'd set out to accompany Helen Middlebrook on her first diocesan assignment. Ground mist hung across the rolling landscape, veiling the leafless branches of the trees and hanging in great motionless swathes over the frost-rimmed countryside like the gunsmoke of some vast Napoleonic battlefield, while above, the shrouded sun shone through the haze like a blood red moon over a lifeless, frozen planet.

Despite the bitter cold outside, with the heater full on, Harrison felt snug and secure in the car, and what feelings of guilt still lingered from breakfast-time were rapidly dispelled as he sped along a virtually deserted A257. He was relishing the taste of freedom, and he found the sense of temporarily moving outside the narrow confines of his self-imposed existence as a diligent, plodding Church official exhilarating. So it was with a sense of mounting excitement and an intense impatience that he headed on eastwards.

At Ash-by-Sandwich he stopped off for an early lunch at the local pub, then took the opportunity of collecting the keys to the beautiful copper-spired church so he could take a look at the recent repairs to its famous chancel. Unusually pleased by the quality of the workmanship displayed, he wandered round the church, inspecting the various ancient monuments and brasses, charmed and moved in particular by a family tomb, with husband and wife reclining in Elizabethan glory above a procession of seven daughters, the five smaller of whom each carried in her hand a dainty little skull.

Refreshed by the break, he returned to his car, and, turning north, plunged on through the well-remembered labyrinth of lanes and by-roads until he reached Fordington. Following the serpentine route through the village, he turned off on the lane for Wetmarsh Marden. Twenty minutes or so later he was turning into the driveway of Owlets, his tyres crunching through the thick gravel towards the pair of green-painted garage doors.

'Well, Colonel, it was very kind of you to tell me of the archdeacon's decision, and I'm so pleased for the Fromes. I know they'll be enormously relieved.' Stella Gittings beamed as she showed her visitor out on to the front terrace. 'And I trust that the sketch map I've drawn will help you find the wing commander's bungalow easily. As for the manor house, as I say, it is just round the bend beyond St Philip's—you really can't miss it.'

'I'm sure I'll find both places easily enough,' answered Harrison, drawing on his gloves as he stepped out into the cold sunshine. 'Well, thank you so much again for arranging to see me, Mrs Gittings,' he said, turning back to face her, 'and may I say how much I admired and was grateful for your support of the couple.'

'It was the least I could do for the poor dears.' The speaker slightly blushed. 'I only hope that my little petition created no difficulties for you personally, Colonel.'

Harrison smiled. 'No, not all—the very contrary, I assure you.' He looked out across the lawn on to which the sun was shining from a now perfectly clear azure sky. 'Well, I'm only sorry to have missed your husband.'

'Ah, yes, poor Donald! He has to work so many hours—but anyway, I'll certainly pass your note on to him.'

'Thank you—it regards some rather attractive, economically priced industrial units in Canterbury that the Church holds the lease on. It merely occurred to me that one of them might be of possible interest to him.'

'How very thoughtful!'

'Not at all—only too pleased to be of any help.' Harrison turned away, but then paused, looking again across the lawn towards the top of the drive. 'Pardon me asking,' he said, 'but I'm intrigued to know how one of that charming pair of owl statuettes on your gateposts came to get damaged.'

With a frown, Stella Gittings stepped out on to the terrace beside him and looked towards the object in question. 'Yes,' she said, 'that was a strange, upsetting business. I was here on my own one night while Donald was away on business. I'd just fallen asleep when there was this sudden terrible loud bang outside. I got up and went to the window, thinking there had been a car crash, but there were no lights or any signs of life. Then in the morning the postman told me that somebody or other had shot off the head of one of the owls.'

'Extraordinary!' murmured Harrison and considered for a moment. 'I suppose you didn't happen to notice the exact time of night when this occurred?'

'Yes,' answered the other, 'as a matter of fact I did—while I was standing at the window trying to see what had happened, I distinctly heard the church clock of St Mary the Virgin at Minster striking midnight from across the river.'

'Really—midnight, you say? How very interesting.' Harrison paused, then asked, 'And would I be correct in assuming that this regrettable little incident happened between the time when I visited the Reverend Lambkin regarding the future of Bright Cottage and the terrible occurrence that took place in that same place a few weeks later?'

'Yes, that's right, Colonel,' replied the lady deacon with a look of surprise. 'In fact, it was a day or two after I'd managed to prevent Maurice from destroying the Lazarus painting—but however did you know?'

Smiling, Harrison shook his head. 'A mere guess, I assure you, Mrs Gittings. But now, if you'll excuse me, I'd better be off. After I've made my calls on the churchwardens to announce the archdeacon's revised intentions regarding Bright Cottage and also to discuss with them how the extensions and repairs to the parish reading room are now to be funded, I intend to drop in on the Fromes.'

It wasn't until late afternoon that the Volvo turned in through the rectory gates and drew to a stop in the stable yard. Almost immediately it did so, the door of the old saddle-room (now adorned with a small Christmas holly wreath) opened and Mavis Frome emerged with a mixture of pleasure and relief lighting her broad face.

'Ah, Colonel, I heard down at the shop that you were around

the village!' she called, brushing flour from her hands and apron as she bustled across the cobbles to meet her visitor as he clambered from the car. 'George will be right glad to see you. He's been going on for days now, saying he's been expecting to hear from you about something or other.'

'Ah yes,' said Harrison as he came round the back of the car to greet her, 'that will almost certainly be about the matter of the dampcourse at the cottage. Well,' he continued, smiling, 'I'm very pleased to be able to say that the news is good. The archdeacon has, in principle, generously approved the additional expenditure, and the diocesan architect will shortly be drawing up provisional plans for a complete renovation, including the rebuilding of the mission hall as a kitchen utility area, as agreed.'

The verger's wife flushed with joy at his words. 'Oh, Colonel,' she cried, 'that's wonderful! I don't know what to say! You and Mrs Gittings have both been so very kind to George and me.'

'Only too delighted.' Harrison looked about the yard with a sudden anxious frown. 'But talking of George, where is he? Not off the rectory grounds, I hope.'

'Oh no, sir, he's about here somewhere, pottering around the gardens, I expect. Earlier I heard him banging away again at them blooming rooks with his gun—the noise of 'em has been regular getting on his nerves of late.' Mavis's initial pleasure seemed now suddenly to fade. 'To tell you the truth, Colonel, he hasn't been himself at all these last days: something's been nagging him. He ain't been sleeping more than a couple of hours at night, and in the day he's as nervy as a cat. He don't even go over the road to the Ferryman for his usual drink in the evening!'

'I'm sorry to hear that,' murmured Harrison gravely. 'Let us hope the good news I bear from the archdeacon will ease his mind.'

'Oh, I hope so, sir! I do! As I said to my daughter only yesterday, George ain't barely liveable with as it is.' The speaker broke off. 'But now, sir, shall I go and find him and tell him you're here?'

Harrison shook his head. 'No, no, that really isn't necessary. I'll go and search him out for myself.'

Promising to return with her husband for tea and fresh-baked mince-pies, Harrison set off up the drive. As if indignant at the slaughter of their fellows earlier and fearful for their own survival, the shaken inhabitants of the rectory elms insistently cried their hoarse lamentations against an already red-tinted sky as he made his way up the steep drive. With their mournful caw-ing ringing in his ears, he paused in front of the house to glance along the crazy paving towards the churchyard entrance. Seeing no sign of Frome in that direction, he walked on under the mul-berry tree across the lawn and round to the rear of the rectory. Here he halted and looked out across the wide vegetable beds, past the slant-roofed old pumping-house, towards where the great orb of the sun was sinking over the distant horizon in the direction of Canterbury.

He didn't spot Frome at first glance, and thinking that he was not in this part of the grounds, Harrison was about to turn away when he noticed the verger standing motionless beside the empty corrugated-iron pigsties at the far end of the garden with a double-barrelled shotgun tucked under one arm. He was gazing away across the sold-off glebeland paddocks, obviously com-pletely lost in thought.

'George! George!' Harrison's voice rang out across the veg-etable beds. 'I'd appreciate a quick word.'

Frome swung round at once and, half-raising his gun, peered in the direction of the call. His initial look of fear vanished, how-ever, as he made out who the figure was beckoning from the cor-ner of the house, and he came limping quickly towards him between the vegetable beds with a look of anxious inquiry.

'Is everything all right, Colonel?' he shouted above the hoarse, incessant crying of the rooks.

'Yes, George—everything's fine.' Harrison waited until the panting man had reached him before resuming. 'As I had to be in the village, I thought I'd drop by to tell you how I'm getting on with my investigations.' He paused, and glanced either side before saying, 'I've made some inquiries and I'm now fairly positive I know the identity of the other person who was in the cottage that night.'

'You are?' Amazement lit the verger's face, and then he leant forward, eager earnestness in his eyes. 'Come on then, Colonel! Tell me, for God's sake! Who do you reckon he was?'

Harrison shook his head. 'No, I don't want to tell you that until I've got firm proof: it wouldn't be fair on the person concerned.'

Frome frowned. 'But I've got to know, sir! I don't feel safe at the moment. The whole thing's getting on my nerves! It hangs over me all the time.'

'It's all right, George,' answered Harrison soothingly. 'It isn't going to last much longer. Tonight I intend to confront the person in question.'

'You do?' Frome stared at him, then his face took on a look of wondering concern. 'Christ, you mean you're going to see him on your own? Won't that be dangerous?'

Harrison shook his head. 'No, I don't think so: I've got the whole thing planned in my head. Anyway,' he added with a smile, 'I don't intend going to meet him on my own unless I really have to. That's really the reason why I've come to see you now. I'd like to have you at my side when I come face to face with him.' He paused, his expression growing grave. 'Of course, I'm not saying there'll be no danger at all—it's always possible the fellow will react violently.'

The other looked perplexed and didn't answer for a moment. 'I'll come with you, if you want me,' he said at last. 'It's the least I can do. But what do you actually intend doing, Colonel? Going to his house or what?'

'No,' said Harrison. 'What I've done is left him a message, asking him to meet me at Bright Cottage tonight after his wife has gone to bed.'

Aghast, Frome stared at the speaker. 'What? Meet him over at the cottage, just like poor old Rector and Jonathan did?' he said, bewildered horror in his eyes. 'Good God! It's crazy! He'll never come!'

Harrison smiled. 'Oh, yes, he'll come. I've put him into a position in which he has no choice: he knows that going along with my wishes and meeting me in the cottage at midnight is the only chance he has of getting away with what he's done.'

Frome considered for a moment, then shook his head. 'It all sounds far too bloody dangerous to me by half. Why don't you just go to the police, Colonel, if you're so sure who he is?'

'Because I've no possible proof that could stand up in court.' Harrison shook his head. 'No, my dear George, I've got to confront him and try to squeeze the truth out of him, and to do that, I'd feel a great deal safer to have you at my side—someone I can depend on, and also someone he knows and who won't immediately frighten him away.'

Frome nodded slowly. 'All right, Colonel, of course I'll come.' He took a deep breath and turned away. 'God, I look forward to coming face to face with that murderous bastard who did for poor Rector and Jonathan!' He paused, turning back to face Harrison. 'But, Colonel, I ain't going over there to that cottage tonight without this old gun of mine in my hands!'

'Right,' said Harrison, 'bring it along with you by all means. It will be nice to have it should matters get out of hand.' He paused and considered for a moment. 'Yes,' he said, 'and we'll also need some sort of light to take with us as there's still no electricity connected.'

'Well,' said Frome, 'there's the hurricane lamp in the garage, same sort as Rector took with him that night.'

'Good, bring it along with you, then. And make sure you're

really wrapped up: from the look of the sky, it's sure to be as cold as the grave in that cottage tonight.' As he spoke, Harrison turned and gazed away to where in the distance the Stour could just be made out between the bare trees, glittering crimson and red in the fiery glow of the now fast setting sun.

CHAPTER TWENTY-TWO

The clear winter sky and the glorious sunset attendant to it had to be paid for. Within half an hour of the sun's final disappearance, the air temperature had dropped below its dewpoint, and radiation fog was smoking up along the muddy banks of the Stour. Beyond the river, the lights of Thanet gradually dwindled and vanished as the mist spread out over the surrounding marshes and fields towards the nearby coast. By the time Harrison had finished a solitary supper at the Ferryman and had rung the deanery to reassure Winnie that he had safely reached Cambridge and was comfortably installed in one of the college rooms, the entire Fordington area was completely enveloped by fog. Indeed, as he groped his way out to the pub car park shortly before closing time, the misty darkness seemed to him every bit as dense and impenetrable as it had that evening back in the autumn when Alan Tubman's cry had summoned him from his desk, and he'd peered down from the office window to see the ominous apparition emerge from the mouth of Dark Entry.

Cursing the adverse conditions and apprehensive as to their possible effect on forthcoming events, he clambered into the Volvo's chilly interior, then cautiously drove across the road to halt outside the rectory gates. There he found Frome already waiting, his heavily muffled form emerging out of the murk, shotgun in one hand, unlit hurricane-lamp in the other.

'Good, you're here! Jump in then—I'm afraid it's going to be the devil's own job finding our way through this infernal witches' brew!'

With the verger seated next to him, Harrison swung the Volvo back on to the road, then, turning off past the lych gate, began creeping the vehicle out of the village towards Wetmarsh Marden. Beyond a brief inquiry as to how Mavis had received the news that confidential parish business necessitated her husband's absence that night, hardly a word was spoken. Without the assistance of Catseyes, driving proved difficult, and Harrison's attention was almost wholly concentrated on what little he could make out through the swirling greyness ahead. For his part, Frome sat tense and silent, shotgun resting between his knees, hurricane-lamp gripped on his lap, only muttering the occasional warning as they approached an unusually sharp bend.

According to the dashboard clock, it was ten minutes past eleven before they eventually reached their destination. No light showed at the front of Sanctuary Farm, the old woman whose bedroom overlooked the lane having presumably long fallen asleep. The only illumination were shafts of light shining into the cattle-yard from the side of the farmhouse, as the Volvo, headlamps extinguished, coasted past in the darkness and swung across the road to stop in front of the cottage garage.

'Right, George, if you'd like to hop out and open the doors, we'll tuck the car out of sight.'

Gun clutched in his hands, Frome appeared in the glow of the sidelights. Glancing about nervously, he pulled the doors wide, allowing the vehicle to be eased into the oil-tainted interior.

After the engine was turned off, the silence was absolute, the darkness so complete that, apart from the misty bowl of light beyond the farmhouse, virtually nothing could be made out at all. With Harrison moving ahead carrying the unlit lamp, and Frome limping behind with the gun, the pair cautiously felt their way along the garden wall to the gate. Slipping it open, they carefully negotiated the now decidedly greasy path to the front porch and let themselves into the cottage.

Partly because of its associations, partly because of his apprehensions as to what lay ahead, the pitch-black interior seemed chillier and more unpleasantly clammy to Harrison than even the dank night outside. Groping for the banisters, he knelt at the foot of the stairs and struck a match, then, having lit the lamp, carried it back into the porch and relocked the front door.

'Now,' he said, turning back to Frome, 'next thing is to make sure we haven't been preceded—we don't want to find that our visitor has slipped in before us.'

There was a slight intake of breath from the verger at the words, and, for the first time, Harrison sensed the extent of his fear.

'I take it that shotgun of yours is loaded?'

'Aye, Colonel, he's loaded all right.'

'Better check it, though.'

Holding it close to the light, Frome broke open the gun, tilting the double barrel so that the twin brass detonator caps could be seen glinting in the dim beam of the lamp. Removing a glove, Harrison reached over and plucked out both cartridges and weighed them in his fist.

'These feel dampish to me, George—you think they're all right?'

'They're fine,' replied Frome with more than a hint of impatience. 'It's just that they've been hanging up on the garage wall, that's all. They worked well enough on them bloody rooks this afternoon; you can take my word they'll fire if they have to.'

'I only hope you're right,' murmured Harrison, sounding decidedly dubious. 'Our lives may depend on it. Here,' he said, stretching out his hand through the dimness, 'have them back. Reload and then we'll get on with checking the house.'

Frome reached for the cartridges, and, as Harrison drew his glove back on, there came a sharp click as Frome snapped the breech shut.

'Good! First, let's take a shufti at the back door. You follow me, George—but, for God's sake, keep that gun barrel low! Damp cartridges or not, I don't want to risk ending up tonight with half my own head blown away!'

With the shadows dancing on the walls around them, they made their way down the passage to the back door. As expected, it was locked, but finding the security chain had been screwed back into place, Harrison additionally slid the bolt, whispering, 'Just to make doubly sure.'

Frome remained close at his heels as he then proceeded to check the rest of the cottage, peering into all the upstairs and downstairs rooms in turn, exactly as he'd done two months before after Helen Middlebrook had gone over to the farm to phone the police. Having completed their inspection, the two of them descended the stairs and let themselves into the mission hall. Locking the door behind them, they pulled the curtains closed before searching among the furniture piled against the end wall. Both finally satisfied they were completely alone, Harrison turned again to Frome. 'There's still nearly half an hour before our caller's due. I, therefore, suggest we make ourselves as comfortable as possible.'

Taking two chairs, he carried them across and placed them immediately facing the door. He and Frome then took their seats and sat with the lamp at their feet, wick turned down so low that it gave the merest flickering, yellowish-orange glow.

Around the cottage the fog hung like a moist blanket, deadening what sounds broke the silence. Along the lane, a heavy motorcycle throbbed past, its single headlamp casting a diffuse halo into the mist. High overhead came the rumble of aircraft engines, and, as the noise faded, there echoed the eerie, blood-tingling scream of a fox; while always, from the far distance, there continued the melancholy wailing of the foghorn on the North Foreland lighthouse.

The temperature in the mission hall seemed to drop with each passing moment. Turning up his coat collar, Harrison squinted down at his watch. Beside him, Frome didn't move; the shadow of his gun barrel aimed unwaveringly at the base of the door. With only the groaning wail of the far away foghorn break-ing the silence, they continued to sit in the paraffin-scented dim-ness until finally, from across the river, came the muffled chimes of St Mary the Virgin at Minster striking the midnight hour.

'You still think he's going to come?'

Whether from the bitter chill or merely the tedium of wait-ing, a querulous note had crept into the questioner's voice, as well as an obvious degree of scepticism.

'Don't worry,' grunted Harrison, hugging his coat about him and shivering despite himself. 'As I told you this afternoon, I gave him no choice—he just has to be here.'

Again the silence fell, and the minutes crawled by until at last Frome gave an impatient snort. 'No!' he burst out. 'Nothing and nobody's coming! It's long gone midnight. At this rate, we'll be sitting freezing till dawn!' He turned in his chair to face the man at his side. 'Come on, Colonel! You've got to tell me now—who is it that's meant to be coming, this person you reckon killed Rector and young Jonathan?'

Not answering, Harrison craned his head, looking towards the crack in the curtains.

'No!' cried Frome in exasperation. 'There's nothing out there but fog, cow-muck and damp! This whole thing is right getting on my wick! I checked after you called in, and I heard you had been round the parish visiting the Gittings' place as well as seeing Brandon and Sparrow—which of them is it that you made this invitation of yours to?'

'Shush, man! Listen! Something's coming!'

Faint in the distance there could now just be made out the murmur of a car approaching from the direction of the village. Intent, both men listened, hearing the sound growing louder and diminishing by turns as the slow-moving vehicle negotiated the series of bends in the lane. After what seemed an eternity, its headlamps glowed along the roadway outside.

'It's going on past.'

'Wait!'

Like Frome, Harrison had risen to his feet and gone to the window. They stood peering between the curtains, watching the apparently departing tail-lights—then saw them suddenly gleam bright red as the vehicle braked to a halt just beyond the cottage. A moment later the lights were extinguished and the engine turned off.

'Right! It's him!' Harrison said urgently. 'Come on, let's take our seats and blow out the lamp. When he comes through this door, we'll be sitting ready to confront him.'

Seated once more, this time in complete darkness, the two men waited, hearing nothing until there came the click of the garden gate being unlatched, followed by the sound of someone making their way up the path. The steps grew nearer and torch-light momentarily shone across the window. Then, whoever it was paused outside the porch, and there came the noise of a key being inserted in a doorlock.

From beside him, Harrison could now hear Frome breathing fast. The key turned, the front door opened, and then light gleamed beneath the mission hall door as the intruder entered the room. The brilliance grew nearer, glinting now between lintel and

door edge—then abruptly disappeared as the torchbearer continued past down the passageway towards the kitchen area at the
rear.

'Where's he off to?' breathed Frome into Harrison's ear.

'Same as us, I imagine—going to check the back door.'

As he spoke, they heard another lock being turned, then the
click of a latch and the sound of a door being opened, followed
almost immediately by a harsh crunch as it came up hard against
the security chain. Next moment the door was being violently
shaken against the constraining links, the noise resounding
through the empty cottage like the rattling of the bars of a cage.

'What's he up to, Colonel? Is he off his bloody head?'

'Steady, man! We'll be all right. But quiet now! He's on his
way back.'

Along the passage could be heard the tread of returning feet,
and once again light gleamed around the edges of the door. A
faint jingle of metal was followed by the sound of a key being
inserted. It turned, and then, very slowly, almost imperceptibly at
first, the strip of light began to widen and stretch over the adjoining wall as the door was slowly pushed open.

The barrel of Frome's shotgun rose a fraction, and there was
the tiniest double click as the hammers were drawn back. At the
sound, Harrison leaned over and thrust down the barrel, hissing
urgently, 'For God's sake! Don't fire unless you have to!'

Feeling the gun trembling beneath his grasp, he continued
holding it down, whilst, in front of him, the gleam of light
widened a fraction more—then seemed to freeze with the door
still slightly less than half-open. There was utter silence for a second or two, with the two sitters hardly breathing, then abruptly,
without the slightest warning, the light was gone and there was
the sound of someone moving rapidly away. A moment later the
front door was thrown open and slammed shut, and whoever it
had been was moving rapidly away down the front path.

'Christ, Colonel!' burst out Frome, jumping to his feet and

limping rapidly over to the window. 'He heard you! Now the bastard's bolting!'

Not answering, Harrison reached down in the darkness and felt for the lamp, then began fumbling in his pocket for matches. From outside came the faint thud of a car door closing, the noise of an engine starting up, and next moment the vehicle was rapidly accelerating away.

With an exasperated sigh, Frome turned from peering out. 'Well, that's bloody well it then! He's scooted! We might as well pack up and go home.'

'Not so fast, George,' murmured Harrison, applying a match to the lamp-wick. 'Who knows? The killer could still be lurking around here somewhere.'

Frome stopped and stared at him incredulously. 'But he can't be! You heard him—he's gone! There's only the two of us here.'

'No, George,' answered Harrison, getting stiffly to his feet. 'I'm certain there's still someone else in the cottage.'

Frome took a step towards the partly opened door and listened intently.

'I can't hear nothing.'

'No, of course you can't,' replied Harrison, raising the lamp to eye-level. 'You couldn't possibly. After all,' he went on in the same quiet, steady voice, 'the other person in this cottage has been dead and in his grave nearly twenty years.' Pausing, he turned the wick up fully. 'I refer to the late James Franklin, last survivor of the infamous Heathrow Airport gang—the man who semi-crippled himself in a futile attempt to evade the police, and who, after spending more than ten years in prison, was discovered floating in the Pool of London with a bullet in the back of his head.'

Speechless, mouth fallen open, the verger gaped at the speaker, a film of moisture gathering on his skin as if, instead of the dank, chilly mission hall, he stood facing Harrison in the dim light of a Finnish sauna. And as the other's voice continued in the same quiet, unhurried, conversational tone as before, the sweat mounted on his brow and his breath began coming in shallow, rapid pants, as if again, instead of continuing to hold up the hurricane-lamp and look directly into his eyes, his tormentor had now bent and was tipping a scoopful of water over baking-hot granite stones to raise the stifling humidity further.

'But it was not actually Franklin himself who was dragged from the water, was it, George? Merely the body of someone wearing prison underclothes and carrying Franklin's papers. Whose then, we might ask, was that poor, mutilated corpse that the police fished from the Thames all those years ago?'

As if in expectation of an answer, Harrison paused, but, receiving none, he resumed, 'I suggest it was that of a certain ex-petty officer who'd been living a somewhat bleak existence in an East End hostel for the homeless after being invalided out of the Royal Navy: a rather lonely, not especially intelligent man, without family or any other close connections ashore, who, unluckily for him, happened to be approximately of the same age, height and build as one of his fellow inmates—a recently discharged convict who had suffered a remarkably similar injury to the knee of his left leg.'

'You're mad!'

'Am I, George?' A cold smile flitted across Harrison's lips. 'Or shouldn't I be calling you Franklin? For that, of course, is who you really are—the late, unlamented James Franklin, one-time inmate of a fair number of Her Majesty's prisons.' Again a fleeting, humourless smile swept the speaker's mouth. 'Oh yes, Mr Franklin, you carried out your change of identity with praiseworthy thoroughness, learning naval slang, getting your picture taken in uniform, having that anchor tattooed on the back of your hand—though the British sailors' tradition of decorating the skin in the Polynesian manner necessitated having to hack off Frome's arm so that the original tattoo wouldn't be found on what was meant to be your own body.'

'I don't know what you're on about.' The verger's voice had taken on a husky, half-strangulated sound, as if his throat were parched by the same heat that was causing his now ashen face to glisten with perspiration.

'And once you had your new identity,' continued Harrison, 'as well as a useful bit of naval pension to draw on, you were free to set about tracking down the person who had purloined the unrecovered proceeds of the Heathrow robbery. And who was this person you were certain had gone off with that portion of the loot that you and your three associates had managed to stash away before the arrival of the police? None other than the person who had been closest to the dying Thomas Ian Marshal during his final months in Wormwood Scrubs—the hardworking, zealous assistant prison chaplain whom he doubtless wrote to you about, the idealistic young clergyman who had befriended and brought about his conversion, the only person he was likely to have confessed the details of the robbery to, including where the missing banknotes had been hidden. In other words, your late employer, the Reverend Maurice Lambkin.'

'I tell you, you're off your head! You don't know what you're talking about!' shouted the other, finally emerging from his horrified, trancelike state. Face contorting, he took a step forward, brandishing his gun.

Apparently unperturbed, Harrison eyed him steadily, then calmly resumed his seat, carefully placing the hurricane-lamp on the floor before him—and, by doing so, drawing in the darkness, so that he and the standing figure seemed suddenly cloistered together within a dim cave of light.

'Being an Anglican clergyman,' recommenced Harrison, leaning back and folding his arms, 'Lambkin would have been easy enough to track down. Not only was his name well known around those hostels for the homeless you lived in after leaving prison, but any current edition of *Crockfords' Clerical Directory* would have told you that he'd moved out of London to a country living in the Canterbury diocese. After that, it was simply a matter of following him there and using your new identity as the homeless, invalided ex-serviceman to win his sympathy. But then—surprise, surprise—you discovered no sign of your missing money. No expensive car in the garage! No smart clothes! No holidays in the Bahamas! Instead, just a humble country parson, living modestly with his sick wife and small son in a rambling, great, draughty barn of a rectory!'

So calm and unhurried was the speaker's voice that Franklin appeared to relax, and, half-lowering the gun, he stood listening as if mesmerized.

'The doubts would have begun almost at once, and soon you must have completely discounted your theory that Lambkin had taken the money. But what could you do? You were semi-crippled and already getting on in age. Anyway, you hadn't a clue as to who else might have got their hands on your ill-gotten gains. Very sensibly, therefore, you decided to make the best of things: to marry a good-hearted, kind woman and settle for a similarly modest existence to that of your well-meaning benefactor.' Harrison paused. 'And that, of course, is exactly what you did, living the useful, respectable, pleasant enough life that Lambkin gave you until his wife finally died. And then, when old Miss Lambkin came to stay at the rectory for the first time, you learnt from her that her late sister hadn't in fact set up the educational trust for Jonathan as the Reverend Lambkin had led everyone to believe. Now, at last, you guessed where the money that had cost you your liberty had gone: all of it swallowed up paying for a child's very privileged schooling—squandered on a seemingly idle, self-indulgent young man, who'd apparently wasted those opportunities that you, for all your undoubted intelligence, had never had a chance of.'

All traces of his former baffled fury and fear had now disappeared from the other's face. Saying nothing, he limped forward to stand before Harrison, looming over him with the shadows cast by the lamplight veiling his eyes and giving his features a curiously mask-like appearance.

'Over the years, you must have built up a trust and liking for your employer,' resumed Harrison. 'The revelation, therefore, that he had indeed taken the money must have come as a terrible disillusionment. But once again, what could you do, apart from confronting him with your knowledge of his crime? The money was all spent, and he presumably had no way of repaying you. It was at this time that people began to notice a change in Lambkin's personality, and there began those uncharacteristic outbursts of irritability that he inflicted on Edith Gillmore and others—and this state of affairs continued until you, for whatever reason, decided on your horrific revenge, demanding that he should contact Jonathan, and that the three of you should secretly meet to discuss matters late at night in this cottage. Poor old Lambkin couldn't stand up to you. And Jonathan—who'd been told the truth by his father and who had taken the trouble of looking up the details of the original robbery from the newspapers of the time—understandably protested at this bizarre midnight excursion, but finally went along with it, neither he nor his father dreaming for a moment that they'd arrive here to find you armed and determined to kill them both.'

'Kill 'em?' Franklin's voice was suddenly quietly mocking. 'But I couldn't have killed them. You forget, I was at home, wasn't I? I have Mavis to back me up; I woke her at midnight and showed her the time.'

'Oh yes, of course you did—or, rather, you showed her what purported to be the time: a clock whose hands had been moved back to cover however long it had taken you to return to the village and let yourself back into the house.' Harrison smiled faintly. 'Mavis is a simple, gullible woman—a person who, as someone so appositely once put it to me, "wouldn't recognize the truth of any-thing, not if it was stuck right under her nose.'"

Franklin's mouth twisted into a cold smile. 'Even if you're right, none of this can be proved. It's all just notions in your head.'

Harrison nodded. 'Yes, Mr Franklin, I agree: as I told you this afternoon, none of this would stand up for a moment in a court of law. You've been far too clever for that. All I wanted was the chance of this quiet little meeting between the two of us in this isolated place just to tell you to your face that I know what and who you are, and also everything you've done, including how, shortly before the actual killings, you conducted a bizarre little dress-rehearsal. After you'd slipped Mavis some sort of sleeping draught and she'd gone off to bed, you left the house late at night and cycled over on that bicycle of yours to the Gittings' bunga-low. There you blasted away the head of one of the pair of orna-mental owls with the sawn-off shotgun—thus revenging yourself on Mrs Gittings for frustrating your efforts to destroy the Lazarus picture which you'd doubtless seized from Lambkin by force, cracking the glass in the process.'

Expressionless, Franklin made no reply.

Harrison sat back, looking up at the inscrutable face. 'There is just one more thing I'd like to know,' he continued. 'What was it that finally spurred you to kill Maurice and Jonathan Lambkin? In God's name, what possible motive had you, or what could you possibly hope to gain by butchering a pair of defenceless men?'

'Motive?' As if he'd been touched by a red-hot iron, all Franklin's impassivity disappeared on the instant. He leaned for-ward, his face becoming a twisted, snarling vision of rage. 'Motive?' he repeated, bawling the word directly into the sitter's face. 'Bloody Christ—you of all people ask me that!'

Shocked, Harrison stared up. 'I don't understand,' he fal-tered. 'What do you mean? What possible connection could I have with any motive of yours?'

'Because you gave it me, that's why! It was you and that damned archdeacon of yours who finally did for Lambkin and his son. The pair of you signed their death warrants. Mavis and I was going to have the cottage; it had been agreed on between Lambkin and me—it was to be my payback for the money I'd been robbed of and for all the work I had done for him over the years. When old Reverend Holloway died, it was all fixed up that I should have the tenancy, and then you—you pompous, self-righteous old bastard—arrive out of the blue one morning to tell Rector he couldn't pass the tenancy on because it had been decided that the Bright Trust was to be wound up and the cottage sold off.'

Harrison's composure vanished, and he winced, blinking up with horror at the contorted, gargoyle-like face above his. 'My God!' he breathed. 'Are you telling me you committed double murder simply out of spite, just because you couldn't have this house to live in?'

'No, you blind fool! So I could have it, of course! You really think that I needed you to come creeping round to tell me my rights! I was verger here, wasn't I? I knew the bloody terms of the Bright Trust, and that, if I could only make myself homeless before the sale went through, I'd have a strong legal claim on this cottage!'

Dazed, Harrison shook his head in disbelief. 'And you did all that—composed those notes to give Jonathan an apparent motive for murdering his father, carefully planned and carried out that horrendous, vile act of double butchery—all of it just for this damp little place?'

'Yes, and bloody well do it again if I had to! Mavis and I had nowhere to go to, no money, no nothing—not even a bloody old ex-stable we could call our own! This house was rightfully mine. God knows, I'd paid for it! I wasn't going to allow you, nor no bloody archdeacon or anyone else to...'

Franklin's words died away, and, turning suddenly, he looked towards the black mouth of the half open door behind him, all his original expression of horror and fear rushing to his face. He then swung back to face Harrison. 'Who was that fellow who came here just now—the one that was rattling the back door?' Again he looked round into the ink-black darkness beyond the door. 'My God, did you fix up that he should…'

'Yes, Mr Franklin, exactly that,' answered Harrison as the other broke off. 'I arranged that he should leave the back door unlocked under the cover of all that mad rattling of the chain.' Pausing, Harrison looked at the other man steadily. 'Just as you contrived to make it look as if only Lambkin and his son had been alone here in the cottage that night, so, with Wing Commander Sparrow's help, I contrived to make it appear that only you and I were here now, and that no one could possibly have been overhearing everything said. That is the reason why I invited you here—an invitation that you, as the apparently faithful servant of the late Reverend Lambkin, could hardly refuse.' He paused, then added with a pained smile, 'I'm afraid, Mr Franklin, midnight tolls for us all in the end, one way or another, and the time comes when we each of us has to pay for our misdeeds.' Turning towards the doorway, he called out loudly, 'All right, Chief Inspector. I believe you've heard all you need to. You and your men can now safely make your entrance.'

As he spoke, there was slight rustle of movement in the passage, then the door was suddenly kicked fully open and powerful torchbeams stabbed through the darkness. From behind them came Dowley's voice. 'Right, Franklin, drop the gun; you're under arrest.'

Dazzled by the lights, Franklin didn't move.

'We're armed and you're covered. Be sensible and let it drop now—we don't want any accidents here, do we?'

For a moment longer Franklin remained as if frozen, then, without warning, he spun round, aiming the shotgun point-blank into Harrison's face. 'Right,' he bellowed, 'you go follow your friends into hell!'

Before Harrison could get out a word or raise a hand, both gun hammers jerked forward and fell—and next moment, he was staring along the length of the twin barrels up into Franklin's incredulous, disbelieving face.

Shaken though he was, still Harrison somehow managed to contrive a sickly smile. 'I told you; damp cartridges,' he said.

He dipped a trembling hand into his pocket and drew out two cartridges and held them up. 'Or rather, damp sand, I should say. As arranged with the Chief Inspector and his colleagues, I performed a small sleight of hand back there in the hallway earlier and substituted a couple of duds for these.'

Franklin stared down at the objects in the outstretched hand for a moment, dazed disbelief on his face—then he swung the gun up like a sledge-hammer above his head.

'No!'

As the cry left Harrison's lips, there came a dazzling triple flash of fire from the doorway, and a simultaneous report rang through the room. Deafened and appalled, for an instant Harrison glimpsed Franklin's figure seeming to hang as if motionless above him in the beams of the torches, arms upraised, the gun still in his hands—and then with a stifled cry he was gone, fallen into the darkness beside him as abruptly as if a trap-door had sprung open beneath his feet. All that was left was the huge ringing in Harrison's ears, the swirl of gunsmoke in the torchbeams and the thick, cloying fumes of the cordite in his nostrils—and then, faint as if coming from a great distance, Dowley's concerned voice calling out to know if he was all right.

EPILOGUE

All along the pedestrian precincts, the crowds thronged and surged beneath a crisscross of overhanging coloured lights and tinsel stars, the clatter of feet and the sound of their voices almost drowning the strains of the carols being played by the Salvation Army band positioned at the intersection of St Margaret's Street and the Parade. For weeks before, the old Roman road that bisects the ancient heart of Canterbury had teemed with Christmas shoppers. Now, however, in the falling dusk of the festival eve, it was as if all the inhabitants of the surrounding countryside had flocked into the city to take part in a frenzied saturnalia of last-minute buying before the shutters finally rattled down and the bleeping electronic cash registers fell silent.

Seated opposite each other at a small table in the window of the cafe to which they'd retreated with their own belated purchases (in their case, an always useful extra pint of milk, a bottle of Bristol Cream Sherry and a box of embroidered handkerchiefs for the school bursar's wife), Harrison and Winnie sat listlessly gazing out into the street. The noise of the music and passers-by was muffled, and as husband and wife sipped frothy, chocolate-flecked cups of cappuccino, they watched the pedestrians flowing to and fro beyond the glass as if observing the inhabitants of some garishly illuminated aquatic tank.

'You know,' said Winnie, 'looking out at those people, I keep remembering George Eliot's *Middlemarch*—all those characters in that imaginary town of hers, either achieving happiness or destroying themselves through the choices they make.'

'You're thinking of Lambkin, I take it?' murmured Harrison, turning towards her.

'One can't help it,' answered Winnie. 'Kind and well-meaning though he was, Maurice certainly ruined his life with the disastrous decisions he took: first committing himself to such unsuitable work for one of his temperament in those inner-city parishes; then, faced with the prospect of having to send his young son to one of the poor-quality local schools, taking stolen money to pay for private education. But, of course,' she added, 'what's even more terrible is that, in doing so, he ended up also destroying the very person he'd originally tried to help.'

'Jonathan, you mean?'

'Yes, but it wasn't only Jonathan who had to suffer, was it? There's also Mavis, and Daphne Sparrow.' Winnie glanced out at the street. 'I wonder what sort of Christmas those two are going to have this year.'

'Yes, indeed.' Harrison stared gloomily down at his cup for a moment or two before again looking up. 'Still,' he said in a forced attempt at brightness, 'according to Ingrams, Mavis's daughter and son-in-law have taken her in. That means at least she'll have those grandchildren of hers around to cheer her up.'

'Cheer her up!' Winnie sighed. 'Oh, come on, Richard! That poor woman's life is absolutely shattered, and you know it! Her husband's dead, and she has to live with the knowledge that he cold-bloodedly murdered two people she was fond of. And, on top of all that, she has to face the fact that their marriage was nothing but a sham, and that right from the very beginning, she was lied to and misled.'

Harrison turned away. For a few seconds, Winnie sat observing the guilty, hunted expression on his half-averted face before crying out, 'Oh, Richard, why couldn't you have told me the truth? What was the need for all that deception? Because I'm bound to this wheelchair, do you think I have to be protected like a child!' She paused, then added sadly, 'If only you'd trusted me, and I'd known what you were planning, I'd never have let you go ahead with such a stupid, dangerous experiment!'

'It wasn't an experiment!' answered Harrison wearily. 'Contriving that situation was the only way I could see of catching Franklin off his guard. Just ask yourself, how else was I supposed to drag an admission out of him within the hearing of witnesses?'

Not replying, Winnie looked down, avoiding his eyes. Harrison gazed across at her lowered face, then leaned over the table towards her. 'Honestly, my dear,' he said earnestly, 'I didn't think for a moment that things would turn out the way they did: I simply didn't appreciate the amount of rage bottled up in Franklin, and had no idea he'd turn on me in quite the way he did.' Obtaining no response, he paused and then burst out passionately, 'For God's sake, Winnie! Whatever that man had done, and whatever he deserved, do you really think I wanted to see him shot down like a dog?'

Still looking down, Winnie shook her head miserably. 'No, of course not! It would have been the last thing you wanted. But then,' she asked, raising her head, 'why on earth did you take such a risk? You knew what that man had done, and what he was capable of—surely it was obvious that someone was likely to get killed! How could you have been so utterly reckless?'

Harrison winced. 'I don't know,' he answered unhappily. 'I suppose I simply allowed myself to get over-confident: I really thought I had the whole situation under control.' He sighed and rubbed his forehead. 'Anyway, whatever the reason, I clearly misjudged the situation, and now, damn it, I have to live with that wretched man's blood on my hands!'

He broke off and remained staring down in silence at his cup as the last of the other customers got up and left. Finally Winnie spoke. 'Come on,' she said gently, 'it's no good sitting here like this—it doesn't help anyone! Finish up your coffee and then we'll go.'

Although the press of the crowds had decreased, the pavement remained thronged as Harrison began wheeling Winnie through the rest of the homeward-heading shoppers. Invisible among the sea of heads, the Salvation Army band now struck up with a sprightly rendering of 'Jingle Bells'. Anxious to avoid the crush ahead, as well as any closer proximity with the band, Harrison immediately veered the chair diagonally across the flow of pedestrians, aiming to turn into the Friars and return to the precincts via the warren of medieval backways and alleys on the other side of the Stour.

Reaching the Oxfam bookshop, he thankfully swung the wheelchair off the main thoroughfare into the comparatively deserted side-street. Before them gleamed the brightly lit facade of the Marlowe Theatre, on which was displayed an illuminated hoarding advertising the current pantomime, *Puss in Boots*. Oppressed by his thoughts and barely aware of his surroundings, Harrison trundled his wife towards it, following the curving roadway round past St Peter's Church in the direction of the river. Head bent, he plodded steadily on through the gloom until he suddenly brought the chair to halt.

Roused from the reverie into which she'd fallen, Winnie looked up to see that they'd paused before the large, circular, portrait of Christopher Marlowe set in the paving outside the theatre entrance. Curious, she gazed at it for a moment before twisting round to look up at her husband questioningly. 'Well, what is it?' she asked. 'Why have we stopped?'

Harrison shrugged. 'I don't know. I was thinking of *Faustus*, I suppose. Isn't that what the play is about? How power goes to our heads and clouds our judgement, so we end up overreaching ourselves, and getting damned in the process!'

Winnie craned down to peer at the portrait at her feet. 'You know,' she said thoughtfully, 'what's so sad about Marlowe is that he died so young, before he had a chance to learn the full complexity of human emotions and actions. If he'd only lived longer, I'm sure he would have gone on to write something less harsh and narrow, where the hero might have found his way to some sort of personal redemption like Goethe's Faust.'

'Redemption!' retorted Harrison bitterly. 'What redemption was there for poor old Lambkin! Or Franklin for that matter! They died, both of them, reaping the consequences of their actions as surely as ever Faustus did! Isn't that what you were saying back there in the cafe: what happens to us is all a matter of cause and effect; we simply make our choices and suffer as a result!'

'Nonsense!' exclaimed Winnie. 'That's far too simplistic! In this world there's nearly always hope, forgiveness and the chance of change. Good Lord,' she added laughing, 'even George Eliot allows for the possibility of redemption through the power of love!' Smiling, she reached up and squeezed his hand. 'Come on,' she coaxed, 'this is Christmas Eve after all! Surely, on this night of all nights, you must believe that too!'

'Must I?' Harrison looked away across the narrow bridge ahead. Beyond it, the cathedral reared up against the evening sky, looming above a higgledy-piggledy mass of close-packed roofs. 'Well, who knows?' he sighed, gazing towards its massive floodlit towers. 'Perhaps you're right.'

'Of course I'm right! I thought that was supposed to be the whole message of Christmas!' Winnie readjusted the blanket over her knees. 'Now come on!' she urged. 'Push me home. I want time to wash and change if you wish me to accompany you to the midnight service.'

Harrison nodded and trundled the wheelchair towards the bridge. As he reached it and began crossing over, the Salvation Army band struck up again in the distance. Pausing at the sound, he turned his head and looked down over the stone parapet towards where, in the darkness below, the ink black waters of the Stour glided invisibly by beneath the lichened walls and overhanging gables of the Weavers. Winnie did the same, and, for a short time, husband and wife remained listening to the music being borne towards them on the silently running stream as it continued to wash along past the ancient pilgrims' hostel. Neither said a word, but then, as her husband resumed pushing the chair on, Winnie started humming the tune. A few moments later, she quietly began to sing, and as she did so, despite himself, Harrison found himself joining in.